She opened the door and began to step in, when he suddenly spun her around into his arms.

Without a word, he brutally closed his mouth over hers.

Too shocked to resist, Lisa stood motionless, her lips parting at the insistence of his tongue. He was angry, she could feel it in the bruising crush of his lips, and it fed her own anger.

Then it occurred to her that kissing was quite a useful and fascinating way to express anger, so she worked diligently at putting every bit of her irritation and displeasure into her response. She wrapped her arms around him and kissed him back so uninhibitedly that he stiffened abruptly, stepped back, and gazed at her with a startled expression.

Briefly, he looked pleased, then his eyes narrowed swiftly. "I doona like you, and I will *not* tolerate you complicating my life."

"Ditto," she clipped through swollen lips.

"Then we understand each other," he said.

"Mm-hmm," she said. "Perfectly."

"Good."

They stared at each other.

"Doona forget who's in control in this castle, lass," he snarled before stalking off down the hallway.

If that was how he asserted his control, she might just have to challenge his authority more often.

Books by Karen Marie Moning

THE
HIGHLANDER'S
TOUCH

KAREN MARIE
MONING

A DELL BOOK

THE HIGHLANDER'S TOUCH
A Dell Book

PUBLISHING HISTORY
Dell mass market edition published November 2000
Dell mass market reissue / June 2007

Published by Bantam Dell
A Division of Random House, Inc.
New York, New York

This is a work of fiction. Names, characters, places, and incidents
either are the product of the author's imagination or are used
fictitiously. Any resemblance to actual persons, living or dead,
events, or locales is entirely coincidental.

Dell is a registered trademark of Random House, Inc., and the
colophon is a trademark of Random House, Inc.

ISBN 978-0-440-23652-8

Printed in the United States of America

www.bantamdell.com

OPM 30 29 28 27 26 25 24 23 22

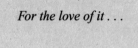

For the love of it . . .

I am that merry wanderer of the night
I jest to Oberon and make him smile . . .

—*A Midsummer Night's Dream*/Shakespeare

PROLOGUE

ADAM BLACK MATERIALIZED IN THE GREATHALL.

Silently, he observed the towering warrior who paced before the fire.

Circenn Brodie, laird and thane of Brodie, exuded the magnetism of a man born not merely to exist in his world, but to conquer it. *Power has never been so seductive,* Adam thought, *except, perhaps, in me.*

The object of his study turned from the fire, unruffled by Adam's silent presence.

"What do *you* want?" Circenn said.

Adam was not surprised by his tone. He'd learned long ago not to expect civility from this particular Highland laird. Adam Black, the deadly jester in the Fairy Queen's court, was an irritant Circenn suffered unwillingly. Kicking a chair close to the fire, Adam lounged in it backward, resting his arms over the slatted back. "Is that any way to greet me after months of absence?"

"You know I despise it when you appear without warning.

And as to your absence, I had been savoring my good fortune." Circenn turned back toward the fire.

"You would miss me if I were gone for long," Adam assured him, studying his profile. *Sinful that he looks such a powerful beast, yet comports himself with such decorum,* Adam thought. If Circenn Brodie was going to look like a savage Pict warrior, then by Dagda he should act like one.

"The same way I might miss a hole in my shield, a warthog in my bed, or a fire in my stables," Circenn said. "Turn around in your chair and sit like a proper person."

"Ah, but I am neither proper nor a person, so you needn't expect me to conform to your requirements. I shudder to think what you would do without all your rules for a 'normal' existence, Circenn." When Circenn stiffened, Adam grinned and extended a graceful hand to a maid who'd been lingering in the shadows at the perimeter of the Greathall. He tossed his head, casting silky dark hair over his shoulder. "Come."

The maid approached, her gaze darting between Circenn and Adam, as if uncertain which man posed the greater threat. Or which the greater lure.

"May I serve milords?" she said breathlessly.

"Nay, Gillendria," Circenn dismissed her. "Off to bed with you. It is well past the goblin's hour"—he shot a dark look at Adam—"and my guest has no needs I care to see filled."

"Aye, Gillendria," Adam purred. "There are many ways you may serve me this night. I will take pleasure in teaching you all of them. Off to your quarters while we men talk. I will join you there."

The young maid's eyes widened as she hastened to obey him.

"Leave my wenches alone," Circenn ordered.

"I don't get them pregnant." Adam flashed his most insolent grin.

"That is not my concern; it is the fact that they are all but witless once you have finished with them."

"Witless? Who was witless tonight?"

Circenn tensed but said nothing.

"Where are the hallows, Circenn?" A glint of mischief kindled in Adam's remote eyes.

Circenn turned his back fully to the fairy.

"You *did* protect them for us, did you not?" Adam asked. "Don't tell me you *lost* them?" he chided when Circenn failed to reply.

Circenn turned back to face him, legs wide, head cocked, arms folded; his usual position when quietly furious. "Why do you waste my time asking me questions when you already know the answers?"

Adam shrugged elegantly. "Because the droppers at the eaves will be unable to follow this splendid saga if we do not speak of it aloud."

"No one eavesdrops in my castle."

"I forgot," Adam purred, "no one misbehaves at Castle Brodie. Ever-spotless, ever-disciplined, perfect Castle Brodie. You bore me, Circenn. This paragon of restraint you pretend to be is a waste of the fine breeding that forged you."

"Let us have done with this conversation, shall we?"

Adam folded his arms across the back of the chair. "All right. What happened tonight? Templars were to meet you at Ballyhock. They were to entrust the hallows to your care. I heard they were ambushed."

"You heard correctly," Circenn replied evenly.

"Do you understand how important it is that the Templars be given sanctuary in Scotland, now that they've been disbanded?"

"Of course I understand," Circenn growled.

"And how imperative it is that the hallows do not fall into the wrong hands?"

Circenn waved Adam's question away with an impatient hand. "The four hallows have been secured. The moment we suspected the Templars were going to come under siege, the spear, the cauldron, the sword, and the stone were rushed back into Scotland, despite the war going on. Better they rest in a country torn than with the persecuted Templars, whose Order is being ripped asunder. The hallows are safe—"

"Except for the flask, Circenn," Adam said. "What of it? Where is it?"

"The flask is not a hallow," Circenn prevaricated.

"I know that," Adam said dryly. "But the flask is a sacred relic of our race, and we could all be in danger should it fall into the wrong hands. I repeat, where is the flask?"

Circenn plunged a hand into his hair, pushing it back from his face. Adam was struck by the sensual majesty of the man. Silky black hair was gripped between elegant fingers, revealing a face composed of strong planes, a chiseled jaw, and dark brows. He had the olive-toned skin, the intense eyes, and the aggressive, dominant temperament of his Brude ancestors.

"I doona know," Circenn finally said.

"You doona know?" Adam mimicked his brogue, aware that such an admission must have tasted foul on Circenn Brodie's tongue. Nothing was ever out of the laird of Brodie's control. Rules and more rules governed everything and everyone in Circenn's world. "A flask containing a sacred elixir, created by my race, disappears from your very grasp and you *doona know* where it is?"

"The situation is not so dire, Adam. It is not permanently lost. Think of it as . . . temporarily displaced, and soon to be regained."

Adam arched a brow. "You split hairs with a battle-ax. Skillful prevarication is a woman's art, Brodie. What happened?"

"Ian was carrying the chest that holds the flask. When the attack came, I was on the south side of the bridge waiting for Ian to cross over from the north. He took a blow to the head and was knocked off the bridge, into the river below. The chest was whisked away by the current—"

"And you say that is not so bad? Anyone could have it now. Would you like to see the English king get his hands on that flask? Do you understand the danger it presents?"

"Of course I do. It will not come to that, Adam," Circenn said. "I laid a geas upon the flask. It will not fall into another's hands, because the moment it is discovered it will be returned to me."

"A geas?" Adam snorted. "Puny magic. A proper fairy would have simply spelled it back out of the river."

"I am not fae. I am Brude-Scot and proud of it. Count yourself fortunate I cursed it at all. You know I have no fondness for the druid ways. Curses are unpredictable."

"What clever invocation did you choose, Circenn?" Adam asked silkily. "You *did* choose your words well, did you not?"

"Of course I did. Think you I have learned nothing from past mistakes? The moment the chest is opened and the flask is touched by a human hand it will be returned to me. I cursed it very specifically."

"Did you specify whether the flask would come by it-self?" Adam asked with sudden amusement.

"What?" Circenn regarded him blankly.

"The flask. Did you consider that the mortal who touches it might be transported with the flask, if you used a bind-ing spell?"

Circenn closed his eyes and rubbed his forehead.

"You used a binding spell." Adam sighed.

"I used a binding spell," Circenn admitted. "It was the only one I knew," he added defensively.

"And whose fault is that? How many times have you refused the honor of training among my people? And the answer is yes, Circenn, the man *will* be carried by the binding spell. Both man and flask will be delivered to you."

Circenn growled his frustration.

"What will you do with this man when he arrives?" Adam pressed.

"Question him, then return him to his home with all haste."

"You will kill him."

"I *knew* you would say that. Adam, he may not even understand what it is. What if an innocent man finds the chest washed up on the bank of the river somewhere?"

"You will kill the innocent man, then," Adam said easily.

"I will do no such thing."

Adam rose with the graceful surety of a snake uncoil-ing for the death strike. He crossed the space between them and paused an inch from Circenn. "But you will," he said softly. "Because you cursed it foolishly, with insuffi-cient thought as to the outcome. Whoever comes with the flask will arrive in the midst of a Templar sanctuary. Your curse will bring him, innocent or not, into a place where none but your fugitive warriors may trespass. You think you can simply send him away with a fare-thee-well and never-speak-of-this, stranger? And a by-the-bye, please don't mention that half the missing Templars linger within my walls, and don't be tempted by the price on their heads." Adam rolled his eyes. "So you *will* kill him, because you pledged your life to put Robert the Bruce firmly on the throne, and to take no unnecessary risks."

"I will not kill an innocent man."

"You will or I will. And you know I have a habit of playing with my prey."

"You would torture an innocent man to death." It was not a question.

"Ah, you understand me. Your choices are simple: either you do it, or I do it. Choose."

Circenn searched the fairy's eyes. *Don't seek compassion, I have none* was the message he read there. After a protracted moment, Circenn inclined his head. "I will take care of the bearer of the flask."

"You will kill the bearer of the flask," Adam insisted. "Or I will."

Circenn's voice was flat and furious. "I will kill the man who brings the flask. But it will be done my way. Painlessly and swiftly, and you will not interfere."

"Good enough." Adam took one step backward. "Swear it upon my race. Swear it upon the *Tuatha de Danaan*."

"On one condition. In exchange for the vow I now give you, you will not darken my door again without invitation, Adam Black."

"Are you certain that's what you want?" Adam's lips

thinned with displeasure. Circenn had reverted to his arms-folded, furious stance. *Such a glorious warrior, dark angel. You could have been my mightiest ally.*

"That's what I want."

Adam inclined his dark head, a mocking smile playing at the corners of his lips. "So be it as you asked it, Brodie, son of the Brude kings. Now swear."

To save a man from a painful death at the fairy's hands, Circenn Brodie sank to his knees and pledged upon the oldest race in Scotland, the *Tuatha de Danaan*, that he would honor his vow to kill the man who arrived with the flask. Then he sighed with relief as Adam Black, the *sin siriche du*, the blackest elf, disappeared, never to darken Circenn's door again because Circenn certainly wouldn't extend an invitation, even if he lived a thousand years.

FALLING . . .

Up and down, up and down,
I will lead them up and down
I am feared in field and town.
Goblin lead them up and down.

—*A Midsummer Night's Dream*/Shakespeare

CHAPTER 1

"HEY! WATCH WHERE YOU'RE GOING!" LISA CRIED, AS the Mercedes zipped around an idling taxi and passed dangerously near the curb where she stood, splashing sheets of dirty water up her jeans-clad legs.

"Well, get out of the street, you idiot!" the driver of the Mercedes yelled into his cell phone. Lisa was close enough to hear him say into the phone, "No, not you. It looked like some homeless person. You'd think as much as we pay in taxes . . ." His voice faded as he drove off.

"I wasn't in the street!" Lisa yelled after him, tugging her baseball cap lower on her head. Then his words sunk in. "Homeless?" *Dear God, is that what I look like?* She glanced down at her faded jeans, worn and frayed at the hems. Her white T-shirt, although clean, was soft and thin from hundreds of washings. Maybe her slicker had seen better days, a few years before she'd bought it at Secondhand Sadie's, but it was durable and kept her dry. Her boot had a hole, but he couldn't have seen that, it was in the sole. The chilly puddles from the recent rain seeped into her boot, soaking her sock. She wriggled uncomfortable toes and made a mental note to duct tape her boot again. But surely she didn't look homeless? She was spotlessly clean, or at least she had been before he'd come whizzing by.

"You don't look like a homeless person, Lisa." Ruby's indignant voice interrupted her thoughts. "He's a pompous ass who thinks anybody not driving a Mercedes doesn't deserve to live."

Lisa flashed Ruby a grateful smile. Ruby was Lisa's best friend. Every evening they chatted as they waited together for the express shuttle to the city, where Lisa went to her cleaning job and Ruby sang in a downtown club.

Lisa eyed Ruby's outfit longingly. Beneath a dove-gray raincoat with classic lines she wore a stunning black dress adorned with a string of pearls. Strappy, sexy shoes displayed French-manicured toenails; shoes that would feed Lisa and her mom for a month. Not a man alive would let his car splash Ruby Lanoue. Once, Lisa might have looked like that, too. But not now, when she was so deeply in debt that she couldn't fathom a way out.

"And I know he didn't get a good look at your face." Ruby wrinkled her nose, irritated with the long-gone driver. "If he had, he certainly would've stopped and apologized."

"Because I look so depressed?" Lisa asked wryly.

"Because you're so beautiful, honey."

"Yeah. Right," Lisa said, and if there was a trace of bitterness, Ruby tactfully ignored it. "It doesn't matter. It's not like I'm trying to impress anyone."

"But you could. You have no idea what you look like, Lisa. He must have been gay. That's the only reason a man could miss a woman as gorgeous as you."

Lisa smiled faintly. "You just never give up, do you, Ruby?"

"Lisa, you *are* beautiful. Let me doll you up and show

you off. Take off that cap and let your hair down. Why do you think God gave you such magnificent hair?"

"I like my cap." Lisa tugged at the faded bill of her Cincinnati Reds cap protectively, as if she feared Ruby might snatch it away. "Daddy bought it for me."

Ruby bit her lip hesitantly, then shrugged. "You can't hide beneath that hat forever. You know how much I care about you, and yes"—she waved away Lisa's protest before it even reached her lips—"I know your mother is dying, but that doesn't mean you are too, Lisa. You can't let it defeat you."

Lisa's expression grew shuttered. "What are you singing for your opening number tonight, Ruby?"

"Don't try to change the subject. I won't let you give up on life," Ruby said gently. "Lisa, there's so much ahead of you. You'll survive this, I promise."

Lisa averted her gaze. "But will I want to?" she muttered, kicking at the curb. Her mom, Catherine, had been diagnosed with cancer a few months ago. The diagnosis had come too late, and now little could be done with the exception of making her as comfortable as possible. *Six months, maybe a year,* the doctors had advised cautiously. *We can try experimental procedures, but . . .* The message was clear: Catherine would die anyway.

Her mom had refused, with unwavering determination, to be the target of experimental procedures. Spending the last months of her life in a hospital was not how either Lisa or Catherine wanted it to end. Lisa had arranged for home health care, and now money, which had always been tight for them, was even tighter.

Since the car accident five years ago that had crippled her mother and killed her father, Lisa had been working two jobs. Her life had changed overnight following her father's death. At eighteen, she'd been the cherished daughter of wealthy parents, living in Cincinnati's most elite, private community, with a brilliant, secure future ahead of her. Twenty-four hours later, on the night of her high-school graduation, her life had become a nightmare from which there'd been no awakening. Instead of going to college, Lisa had gone to work as a waitress, then picked up a night job. Lisa knew that after her mother was gone she would continue to work two jobs, trying to pay off the astronomical medical bills that had accumulated.

She winced, recalling her mother's recent instructions that she be cremated because it was less expensive than a burial. If she thought about that comment too long she might get sick right there at the bus stop. She understood that her mom was trying to be practical, seeking to minimize expenses so Lisa would have some small chance at life when she was gone, but frankly, the prospect of life alone, without her mother, held little appeal for her.

This week Catherine had taken an irrevocable turn for the worse, and Lisa had been slapped in the face with the inescapable fact that she could do nothing to ease her mother's pain. It would stop only with death. The gamut of emotions she experienced lately was bewildering to her. Some days she felt anger at the world in general; other days she would have offered her soul in exchange for her mom's health. But the worst days were the ones when she felt a twinge of resentment beneath her grief. Those days were the worst because with the resentment came a crushing load of guilt that made her aware of how ungrateful she was. Many people had not had the chance to love their mothers for as long as she had. Some people had far less than Lisa: *Half full, Lisa,* Catherine would remind.

As they boarded the shuttle, Ruby pulled Lisa into the seat next to her and maintained a stream of bright chatter intended to lift her spirits. It didn't work. Lisa tuned her out, trying not to think at all—and certainly not about "after." Now was bad enough.

How did it come to this? God—what has happened to my life? she wondered, massaging her temples. Beyond the glass and steel panes of the express shuttle to downtown Cincinnati, the chilly March rain began to fall again in uniform sheets of gray.

* * *

Lisa breathed deeply as she entered the museum. In its tomblike silence, she felt a cocoon of peace settle around her. Glass exhibit cases graced marble floors that were polished to a high sheen and reflected the low light from the recessed wall sconces. She paused to wipe her wet boots carefully on the mat before stepping into her sanctuary. No soggy footsteps would mar these hallowed floors.

Lisa's mind had been starved for stimulation since her last day of high school, five years ago, and she imagined that the museum spoke to her, whispering seductively of things she would never experience: lush, exotic climates, mystery, adventure. She looked forward to going to work each night, despite having spent an exhausting day waiting tables. She loved the domed ceilings with their brilliantly painted mosaics depicting famous sagas. She could describe in vivid detail the most minute nuances of the latest acquisitions. She could recite the placards by heart: each battle, each conquest, each larger-than-life hero or heroine.

When her boots were dry, Lisa hung her slicker by the door and strode briskly past the introductory exhibits, hurrying toward the medieval wing. She brushed her fingers over the plaque outside the entrance, tracing the contours of the gilded letters:

LET HISTORY BE YOUR MAGIC DOORWAY TO THE PAST
EXCITING NEW WORLDS AWAIT YOU

A wry smile curved her lips. She could use a magic doorway to a new world: a world in which she'd been able to attend college when all her high-school friends had scampered off with brand-new luggage to brand-new friends, leaving her behind in the dust of broken hopes and dreams. College? *Bang!* Parties, friends? *Bang, bang!* Parents who would live to see her grow up, perhaps marry? *Bang!*

She glanced at her watch and buried her misery in a burst of activity. Working quickly, she swept and mopped the wing until it was spotless. Dusting the presentations was a pleasure she savored, running her hands over treasures in a way no day guard would have permitted. As was her custom, she saved Director Steinmann's office for last. Not only was he the most meticulous, he often had interesting new acquisitions in his office to be cataloged prior to being placed on display. She could have spent hours wandering the silent museum, studying the weapons, the armor, the legends and battles, but Steinmann had a strict policy that she leave the museum by 5:00 A.M.

Lisa rolled her eyes as she returned books to their slots in the mahogany bookcases that lined his office. Steinmann was a pompous, condescending man. At the conclusion of her interview, she had risen and offered her hand, and Steinmann had stared at it with distaste. Then, his tone pinched with displeasure, he'd informed her that the only evidence he wanted of her nocturnal presence was impeccably clean offices. He'd gone on to remind her of the five o'clock "curfew" so strenuously that she'd felt like Cinderella, certain that Steinmann would turn her into something far worse than a pumpkin should she fail to leave the museum on time.

Despite his rude dismissal, she'd been so elated to get the job that she'd allowed her mom to talk her into going out with Ruby for a belated birthday dinner. Recalling that fiasco, Lisa closed her eyes and sighed. After dinner, Lisa had waited at the bar for change so she and Ruby could play a game of pool. A handsome, well-dressed man had approached her. He'd flirted with her and Lisa had felt special for a few moments. When he'd asked what she did for a living, she'd replied, proudly, that she worked at a museum. He'd pressed her, teasing: Director? Sales? Tour guide?

Night maid, she'd said. *And during the day I waitress at First Watch.*

He'd made his excuses a moment later and moved away. A flush of humiliation had stained her cheeks as she'd waited at the bar for Ruby to rescue her.

Remembering the slight, Lisa skimmed her dust cloth over the bookshelves and flicked it angrily across the large globe in the corner of the office, upset that the incident still bothered her. She had nothing to be ashamed of; she was a responsible, dedicated person, and she wasn't stupid. Her life had been curtailed by responsibilities that had been thrust on her, and in the final analysis, she felt she'd handled things pretty well.

Eventually her anger was doused by a wave of the ever-present exhaustion that nervous energy usually kept at bay. Dropping into a chair that faced Steinmann's desk, she caressed the buttery soft leather, relaxing into it. She noticed an exotic-looking chest on the corner of Steinmann's desk. She hadn't seen it before. It was about two feet long and ten

inches wide. Fashioned of African ebony buffed to a deep
luster, the edges carved with exquisitely detailed knot work,
it was obviously a new acquisition. Contrary to Steinmann's
customary vigilance, he had not locked it in the glass case
where he stored new treasures yet to be cataloged.

Why would he leave such a valuable relic on his desk?
Lisa wondered as she closed her eyes. She'd rest just for a
minute or two. As she did so, she treated herself to a moment of fantasy: She was a financially independent woman
in a beautiful home, and her mother was healthy. She had
lovely hand-carved furniture and comfortable chairs. Maybe
a boyfriend . . .

Imagining the perfect place for the lovely ebony chest
in her dream home, Lisa drifted off to sleep.

* * *

"You should have called me the moment it arrived,"
Professor Taylor rebuked.

Steinmann ushered the professor past the exhibits
toward his office. "It arrived yesterday, Taylor. It was
shipped to us immediately upon excavation. The man who
dug it up refused to touch it, he wouldn't even remove it
from the ground." Steinmann paused. "There's a curse engraved on the lid of the chest. Although it's in ancient
Gaelic, he understood enough of the language to discern
its intent. Did you bring gloves?"

Taylor nodded. "And tongs to handle the contents. You
haven't opened it?"

"I couldn't find the mechanism that releases the lid,"
Steinmann said dryly. "Initially, I wasn't certain it would
open. It appears to be fashioned of a single piece of
wood."

"We'll use the tongs to handle everything, until the lab

has a chance to examine it. Where did you say it was found?"

"Buried near a riverbank in the Highlands of Scotland. The farmer who unearthed it was dredging creek rock to build a wall."

"How on earth did you get it out of the country?" Taylor exclaimed.

"The farmer called the curator of a small antiquities firm in Edinburgh who coincidentally owed me a favor."

Taylor didn't press for more information. The transfer of priceless relics to private collections infuriated him, but it would serve no purpose to alienate Steinmann before he got his chance to study the chest. Taylor was obsessed with all things Celtic, and when Steinmann had called him to discuss the unusual medieval piece, Taylor had barely managed to conceal his interest. To reveal it would only give Steinmann power to manipulate him, and any power in the director's hands was a dangerous thing.

"Idiot maid," Steinmann muttered as they entered the wing. "Would you look at that? She left the lights on again." A thin beam of light showed beneath his office door.

* * *

Lisa awoke abruptly, uncertain of where she was or what had awakened her. Then she heard men's voices in the hallway outside the office.

Galvanized into action, Lisa leaped to her feet and shot a panicked glance at her watch. It was 5:20 A.M.—she would lose her job! Instinctively she dropped to the floor and took a nasty blow to her temple on the corner of the desk in the process. Wincing, she crawled under the desk as she heard a key in the lock, followed by Steinmann's

voice: "It's impossible to get decent help. Worthless maid
didn't even lock up. All she had to do was press the button.
Even a child could do it."

Lisa curled into a silent ball as the men entered the office. Although the footfalls were cushioned by thick
Berber carpet, she heard them approaching the desk.

"Here it is." Steinmann's spotlessly buffed shoes stopped
inches from her knees. Lisa drew a cautious, tiny breath
and eased her knees back. Steinmann's shoes were joined
by a pair of tasseled loafers encrusted with mud from the
recent rain. It took every ounce of her willpower not to
reach out and pluck the offending bits of sod from the
carpet.

"What amazing detail. It's beautiful." The second voice
was hushed.

"Isn't it?" Steinmann agreed.

"Wait a minute, Steinmann. Where did you say this
chest was found?"

"Beneath a crush of rock near a riverbank in Scotland."

"That doesn't make any sense. How did it remain untouched by the elements? Ebony is obdurate wood, but it
isn't impervious to decay. This chest is in mint condition.
Has it been dated yet?"

"No, but my source in Edinburgh swore by it. Can you
open it, Taylor?" Steinmann said.

There was a rustle of noise. A softly murmured "Let's
see . . . How do you work, you lovely little mystery?"

Beneath the desk, Lisa scarcely dared to breathe as a
prolonged silence ensued.

"Perhaps here?" Taylor said finally. "Maybe this little
raised square . . . Ah, I have it! I've seen this before. It's a
pressure latch." The chest made a faint popping noise. "It

was tightly sealed," he observed. "Look at this, Steinmann. This latching mechanism is brilliant, and do you see
the gummy resin that seals the inner channels of wood
where the grooves interlock? Don't you wonder how our
ancestors managed to create such clever devices? Some of
the things I've seen simply defy—"

"Move the fabric and let's see what's under it, Taylor,"
Steinmann cut him off impatiently.

"But the cloth may disintegrate when handled," Taylor
protested.

"We haven't come this far to leave without discovering
what's in the chest," Steinmann snapped. "Move the cloth."

Lisa battled an urge to pop out from under the desk, curiosity nearly overriding her common sense and instinct
for self-preservation.

There was a long pause. "Well? What is it?" Steinmann
asked.

"I have no idea," Taylor said slowly. "I've neither translated tales of it nor seen sketches in my research. It doesn't
look quite medieval, does it? It almost looks . . . why . . .
futuristic," he said uneasily. "Frankly, I'm baffled. The
chest is pristine, yet the fabric is ancient, and this"—he
gestured at the flask—"is damned odd."

"Perhaps you aren't as much of an expert as you would
have me believe, Taylor."

"No one knows more about the Gaels and Picts than I
do," he replied stiffly. "But some artifacts simply aren't
mentioned in any records. I assure you, I will find the answers."

"And you'll have it examined?" Steinmann said.

"I'll take it with me now—"

"No. I'll call you when we're ready to release it."

There was a pause, then: "You plan to invite someone else to examine it, don't you?" Taylor said. "You question my ability."

"I simply need to get it cataloged, photographed, and logged into our files."

"And logged into someone else's collection?" Taylor said tightly.

"Put it back, Taylor." Steinmann closed his fingers around Taylor's wrist, lowering the flask back to the cloth. He slipped the tongs from Taylor's hand, closed the chest, and placed the tongs beside it. "I brought you here. I'll tell you what I need from you and when. And I'd advise you to stay out of my business."

"Fine," Taylor snapped. "But when you discover no one else knows what it is, you'll be calling me. You can't move an artifact that can't be identified. I'm the only one who can track this thing down and you know it."

Steinmann laughed. "I'll see you out."

"I can find my own way."

"But I'll rest easier knowing I've escorted you," Steinmann said softly. "It wouldn't do to leave such a passionate antiquity worshiper as yourself wandering the museum on his own."

The shoes retreated with muffled steps across the carpet. The click of a key in the lock jarred Lisa into action. *Damn and double damn!* Normally when she left, she depressed the button latch on the door—no lowly maid was entrusted with keys. Steinmann had bypassed the button latch and actually used a key to lock the deadbolt. She jerked upright and banged her head against the underside of the desk. "Ow!" she exclaimed softly. As she clutched the edge and drew herself upright, she paused to look at the chest.

Fascinated, she touched the cool wood. Beautifully engraved, the black wood gleamed in the low light. Bold letters were seared into the top in angry, slanted strokes. What did the chest contain that had perplexed two sophisticated purveyors of antiquities? Despite the fact that she was locked in Steinmann's office and had no doubt that he would return in moments, she was consumed by curiosity. *Futuristic?* Gingerly, she ran her fingers over the chest, seeking the square pressure latch they'd mentioned, then paused. The strange letters on the lid seemed almost to . . . pulse. A shiver of foreboding raced up her spine.

Silly goose—open it! It can't hurt you. They *touched it*.

Resolved, she isolated the square and depressed it with her thumb. The lid swung upward with the faint popping sound she'd heard earlier. A flask lay inside, surrounded by dusty tatters of ancient fabric. The flask was fashioned of a silver metal and seemed to shimmer, as if the contents were energized. She cast a nervous glance at the door. She knew she had to get out of the office before Steinmann returned, yet she felt strangely transfixed by the flask. Her eyes drifted from door to flask and back again, but the flask beckoned. It said, *Touch me,* in the same tone all the artifacts in the museum spoke to Lisa. *Touch me while no guards are about, and I will tell you of my history and my legends. I am knowledge. . . .*

Lisa's fingertips curled around the flask.

The world shifted on its axis beneath her feet. She stumbled, and suddenly she . . .

Couldn't . . .

Stop . . .

Falling . . .

CHAPTER 2

WATER SPRAYED LISA'S JEANS-CLAD LEGS FOR THE SEC-
ond time that day as the man surged from the bath. He
towered over her, his lips drawn back from his teeth in a
snarl.

Lisa blinked incredulously. Once. Twice. And a third
time very slowly, giving the apparition time to evaporate.
It didn't. The nude giant remained, his fierce expression
unwavering, his eyes narrowed. *What on earth had happened to Steinmann's office? He wouldn't fire her if he
found her with a nude man—he'd have her arrested!*

Lisa closed her eyes and shifted her feet, cautiously as-
certaining that the world was solid beneath her boots again.
Only when she was firmly convinced that she stood in Steinmann's office clutching a medieval flask did she open them.

She was *not* in Steinmann's office.

She lost her breath in a great exhalation of astonishment as she looked—really looked—at the man. Droplets
of water glistened on his skin. Flames leaped in the hearth
behind him, bronzing and shadowing the slopes of his
muscles. He was the tallest man she'd ever seen, but his

size was not confined to his improbable height. His shoulders were massive, and his broad chest tapered to a lean, muscled abdomen, tight hips, and long, powerful legs.

And he was nude.

She expelled a sigh of protest. He could *not* be real. And because he couldn't be real, there was no harm in dropping her gaze for a quick tally of his perfection. A flawlessly proportioned man who didn't really exist was standing naked before her. Where would *any* healthy twenty-three-year-old woman look? She looked.

That sealed it. He couldn't be real. Cheeks flaming, she averted her gaze and faltered back a step.

He roared something at her in a language she didn't understand.

Stealing a glance at his face, she shrugged helplessly, unable to make sense of her situation.

He bellowed again, gesturing angrily. He spoke nonstop in a stream of words for several minutes, waving his arms and glowering.

She watched him, mouth agape, her confusion deepening. It didn't help that the man seemed oblivious to the disconcerting fact that he was gloriously nude. She found her tongue and, with some difficulty, coaxed it into action. "I'm sorry, but I don't understand you. I have no idea what you're saying."

He flinched as if she'd hit him; his dark eyes narrowed and he scowled. If she'd thought he was angry before, that was only because she hadn't yet seen him truly furious. "You are *English!*" he spat, swiftly switching to English, though with a thick, rolling brogue.

Lisa spread her hands as if to say *So what?* What was his point, and why was he so angry with her?

"Doona move!" he roared.

She remained motionless, cataloging him as if he were one of the museum's recent acquisitions, absorbing the incredible length and breadth of his body. The man dripped such intense sexuality that fantasies of a savage warrior, recognizing no law but his own, shivered through her ancestral memory. The danger rolling off him was frightening and seductive. *You're dreaming, remember? You fell asleep and only dreamed you woke up and Steinmann came. But you're still asleep and none of this is really happening.*

She scarcely noticed when the man reached for the weapon propped against the tub. Her mind registered dim amusement that her figment of fancy came replete with avenging sword. Until, with a graceful flick of his wrist, he pointed the deadly weapon at her.

It was her dream, she reminded herself. She could simply ignore the sword. Dreams were penalty-free zones. If she couldn't have a boyfriend in real life, at least she could savor this virtual experience. Smiling, she extended a hand to touch his flawlessly sculpted abdomen—certainly the stuff of dreams—and the tip of the sword grazed her jaw, forcing her eyes to meet his. A girl could get a kink in her neck from looking that high, she decided.

"Doona think to distract me from my cause," he growled.

"What cause?" she asked, feeling short of breath.

At that moment the door crashed open. A second man, dark haired and clad in a strange wrap of cloth, burst into the room.

"Whatever it is, I doona have time for it now, Galan!" said the man holding the blade to her neck.

The other man looked astounded at the sight of Lisa. "We heard you roar nigh down to the kitchen, Cin."

"Sin?" Lisa echoed disbelievingly. *Oh yes, he is definitely sin. Any man who looks like this must be pure sin.*

"Get out!" Circenn thundered.

Galan hesitated for a moment, then reluctantly retreated from the room and closed the door.

As Lisa's gaze returned to Sin, she looked down again at his improbable endowments.

"Stop *looking* there, woman!"

Her eyes swept up to his. "Nobody looks like you. And no one speaks like you, except maybe Sean Connery in *The Highlander*. See? Proof positive that I'm dreaming. You're a figment of my overtaxed, sleep-deprived, traumatized mind." She nodded firmly.

"I assure you, I am most certainly *not* a dream."

"Oh, please." She rolled her eyes. Closed them. Opened them. He was still there. "I was in the museum and now I'm in a bedroom with a nude man named Sin? How foolish do you think I am?"

"Circenn. Cir-*cin*," he repeated. "Those who are close to me call me Cin."

"You can't be real."

He had sleepy, hooded eyes so dark that they seemed rimmed by kohl. His nose was strong, arrogant. His teeth— and God knows she was getting a good look at them with all the scowling he was doing—were straight and white enough to make her dentist weep with envy. His forehead was high, and a mane of midnight hair fell to his shoulders. Although none of his features was current model material, except for his sensual lips, the overall effect was that of a savagely beautiful face. *Warrior-lord* was the word perched on her tongue.

The tip of the sword gently poked the soft underside of

her chin. When she felt a bead of moisture on her neck, she was amazed by the verisimilitude of her dream. She brushed her fingers over the spot, then gazed at the drop of blood in astonishment.

"Does one bleed in a dream? I've never bled in a dream before," she murmured.

He flicked the baseball cap off her head so quickly that it frightened her. She hadn't even glimpsed the movement of his hand. Her hair tumbled over her shoulders, and she lunged for the cap, only to draw up short on the point of the sword. The top of her head barely reached his chest.

"Give me my cap," she snapped. "Daddy gave it to me."

He regarded her in silence.

"It's all I have from him, and he's dead!" she said heatedly.

Was that a flicker of compassion in his dark eyes?

He extended the cap without a word.

"Thank you," she said stiffly, folding the bill and stuffing it into the back pocket of her jeans. Her gaze dropped to the floor as she pondered the sword at her throat. If it was a dream, she could will things to happen. Or unhappen. Squeezing her eyes shut, she willed the sword to disappear, then swallowed tightly as cold metal bit into her neck. Next, she tried willing the man to disappear; the tub and fire she graciously conceded to keep.

Opening her eyes, she found the man still towering over her.

"Give me the flask, lass."

Lisa's eyebrows rose. "The flask? This is part of the dream? You *see* this?"

"Of course I do! Blinding though your beauty is, I am not a fool!"

My beauty is blinding? Flabbergasted, she handed over the flask.

"Who are you?" he demanded.

Lisa sought refuge in formality; it had served her well in the past as a compass through unknown territory. This dream certainly qualified as unknown territory. Never before had she dreamed so lucidly yet been so out of control of the elements of her dream, nor had her subconscious ever before conjured up a man like this. She wanted to know from what prehistoric corner of her soul the leviathan had come.

"Would you mind dressing? Your . . . er . . . state of, uh . . . undress is not conducive to a serious discussion. If you put on some clothes and put down your sword, I'm certain we'll be able to sort things out." She hoped he would find the note of optimism in her voice persuasive.

He scowled as he looked down at his body. Lisa could have sworn that the color in his face deepened as he realized his state of arousal.

"What do you expect of me when you have clad yourself in such a fashion?" he demanded. "I am a man."

As if I've been suffering doubts on that score, she thought wryly. *A dream of a man, no less.*

Snatching a woven blanket of crimson and black, he tossed it over his shoulder so that it draped the front of his body. He grabbed a small pouch, stuffed the flask into it, and finally lowered his sword.

Lisa relaxed and took a few steps back, but as she did so, her hat fell out of her back pocket. She turned around and bent to retrieve it. Turning back to face him, she caught his gaze fixed in the vicinity where her behind, encased in tight jeans, had been only an instant ago. Dumbfounded

by the realization that the flawless apparition had been pe-
rusing her derriere, she glanced at the fabric he'd wrapped
around himself, then cautiously at his face. His dark eyes
smoldered. She had a sudden insight that wherever she
was, women didn't usually wear jeans. Perhaps not even
trousers.

His jaw tensed and his breathing quickened noticeably.
He looked every inch a predator, poised in the heightened
alertness that precedes the kill.

"They're all I have!" she said defensively.

He raised his hands in a conciliatory gesture. "I doona
wish to discuss it, lass. Not now. Perhaps never."

They looked at each other in measuring silence. Then,
for no reason she could define, drawn by a force beyond
her ability to resist, she found herself moving toward him.
It was *he* who stepped back this time. With one swift rip-
ple of gorgeous muscle, he was out of the room.

The instant the door swung shut, Lisa's legs buckled and
she collapsed to her knees, her heart pounding painfully in
her chest. The familiar sound of metal sliding across the
door told her she was once more locked in. Dear God, she
had to wake up.

But somewhere in her heart she had begun to suspect
that she was not dreaming.

CHAPTER 3

"SHALL WE REMOVE THE BODY, CIRCENN?" GALAN asked, when Circenn entered the kitchen.

Circenn drew a quick breath. "The body?" He rubbed his jaw, concealing a wince of anger behind his hand. Nothing was unfolding as he wished. He'd left his chambers, planning to find some cider wine in the kitchen, clear his head in private, and make some decisions—specifically, what to do with the lovely woman he was bound by honor to kill. But he was to be granted no such reprieve. Galan and Duncan Douglas, his trusted friends and advisers, occupied a small table in the kitchen of the keep, watching him intently.

Since either the English or the Scots kept burning down Dunnottar every time it changed hands, the hastily patched ruin of the keep was drafty, cold, and unfinished. They were stationed at Dunnottar only until the Bruce's men relieved them, which was expected any day now, so no further repairs would be made. The Greathall opened to the night sky where the roof should have been, so the kitchen was substituted for the dining hall. Tonight, unfortunately, it was a gathering place as well.

"The bearer of the flask," Galan prodded helpfully.

Circenn scowled. He had hidden the flask in his sporran, hoping for time to resign himself to fulfilling his oath. Several years ago, he'd informed the Douglas brothers of the binding curse he had placed on the chest and of the vow he had sworn to Adam Black. He had felt more comfortable knowing that when it did appear, if for some reason he was unable to fulfill his oath, this trusted pair would see it finished.

But what did one do when oaths were in direct opposition to each other? To Adam, he had sworn to kill the bearer of the flask. Long ago, at his mother's knee, he'd sworn never to harm a woman for any reason.

Galan merely shrugged at Circenn's scowl and said, "I told Duncan she had arrived. I saw the flask in her hand. We have been awaiting its return. Shall we remove the body?"

"That might be a bit awkward. 'The body' is still breathing," Circenn said irritably.

"Why?" Duncan frowned.

"Because I have not yet killed her."

Galan appraised him for a moment. "She *is* lovely, is she not?"

Circenn didn't miss the accusation. "Have I ever allowed loveliness to corrupt my honor?"

"Nay, and I am certain you will not now. You have never broken an oath." Galan's challenge was unmistakable.

Circenn sank into a chair.

At thirty, Galan was the second eldest of the five Douglas brothers. Tall and dark, he was a disciplined warrior who, like Circenn, believed in strict adherence to rules. His idea of a proper battle included months of careful preparation, intense study of the enemy, and a detailed strategy from which they would not waver once the attack was begun.

Duncan, the youngest in the family, held a more nonchalant attitude. Six feet tall, he was ruggedly handsome, always had a day's growth of beard so black that it made his jaw look blue, and his plaid was usually rumpled, hastily knotted, and looked like it was about to slip off. He drew lasses like flies to honey and wholeheartedly availed himself of the fairer sex's attraction to him. Duncan's idea of a proper battle was to wench right up to the last minute, fall out of bed, then dash off with a plaid and a sword and plunge into the melee, laughing all the while. Duncan was a bit unusual, but all the Douglases were forces to be reckoned with in one way or another. The eldest brother, James, was the Bruce's chief lieutenant and a brilliant strategist.

Galan and Duncan had been Circenn's trusted council for years. They'd warred together, implemented attacks and counterattacks under Robert the Bruce's standard, and trained vigorously for the final battle they prayed would soon liberate Scotland from the English.

"I am not certain I see what harm this woman might do to our cause," Circenn hedged, cautiously gauging their reaction to his words. Silently, he was gauging his own reaction as well. Usually his rules comforted him, gave him a sense of purpose and direction, but every ounce of his conscience rebelled at the thought of killing the woman abovestairs. He began to tally the possible repercussions of allowing her to live, besides destroying his honor.

Galan laced his fingers together and studied his calluses while speaking. "I scarce think that matters. You swore an oath to Adam Black that you would eliminate the bearer of the flask. While I can see that a woman might evoke sympathy, you have no knowledge of who she really is. She was dressed strangely. Could she be of Druid descent?"

"I think not. I sensed no magic in her."

"Is she English? I was surprised to hear her speak that tongue. We have been speaking English since the Templars arrived, but why does she?"

"Speaking English is not a crime," Circenn said dryly. It was true that since the Templars had arrived they'd been conversing more often in English than in any other tongue. The majority of Circenn's men did not speak French, and most of the Templars did not speak Gaelic, but nearly all of them had learned some English, due to England's far-reaching borders. Circenn found it frustrating that he was unable to use Gaelic—a language he felt was beautiful beyond compare—but he accepted that times were changing and that when men from many different countries came together, English was the most commonly known tongue. It galled him to speak the language of his enemy. "Most of our Templars do not speak Gaelic. That doesn't make them spies."

"She does not speak Gaelic at all?" Galan pressed.

Circenn sighed. "Nay," he said, "she did not understand our tongue, but that alone is insufficient to condemn her. Perhaps she was raised in England. You know many of our clans tread both sides of the border. Besides, it was unlike any English I have ever heard."

"More reason to be suspicious, more reason to dispose of her promptly," Galan said.

"As with any other potential threat, one must first study and assess the extent of the threat," Circenn equivocated.

"Your oath, Circenn, supersedes all else. Your mind

must be on holding Dunnottar and opening the Bruce's path to a secure throne and a liberated Scotland, not on some woman who should be dead even as we speak," Galan reminded him.

"Have I ever failed to live up to my duties in any way?" Circenn held Galan's gaze.

"Nay," Galan admitted. "Not yet," he added.

"Nay," Duncan said easily.

"Then why do you question me now? Have I not far more experience with people, wars, and choices than any of you?"

Galan nodded wryly. "But if you break your vow, how will you explain it to Adam?"

Circenn stiffened. The words *break your vow* lingered uncomfortably in his mind and wove a promise of failure, defeat, and potential for corruption. It was critical that he adhere to his rules. "Let me handle Adam, as I always have," he said coolly.

Galan shook his head. "The men will not like this, should they catch wind of it. You know the Templars are a fierce lot and are particularly wary of women—"

"Because they can't have any," Duncan interrupted. "They seek any reason to mistrust women in their effort to keep lustful thoughts at bay. A vow of celibacy is not natural for men; it makes them cold, irritable bastards. I, on the other hand, am always relaxed, even-tempered, and amiable." He flashed a pleasant smile at them both, as if to prove the validity of his theory.

Despite his problems, Circenn's mouth quirked. Duncan had a tendency to behave outrageously, and the more irreverent he was, the more irritated Galan became. Galan never seemed to realize that his younger brother did it on

purpose, and the entire time Duncan was acting like an irresponsible youth, his astute Douglas mind wasn't missing
a thing going on around him.

"Lack of discipline does not a warrior make, little
brother," Galan said stiffly. "You are one extreme and the
Templars are the other."

"Wenching does not diminish my battle prowess one
whit and you know it," Duncan said, sitting up straighter in
his chair, his eyes sparkling in anticipation of the argument to come.

"Enough," Circenn interrupted. "We were discussing
my oath and the fact that I am forsworn to kill an innocent
woman."

"You doona know she is innocent," Galan protested.

"I doona know she is *not*," Circenn said. "Until I have
some indication of guilt or innocence, I—" He broke off
and sighed heavily. He found it nearly impossible to say
the next words.

"You what?" Duncan asked, watching him with fascination. When Circenn didn't reply, he pushed, "Will you
refuse to kill her? Will you break a forsworn oath?" Duncan's incredulity was etched all over his handsome face.

"I didn't say that," Circenn snapped.

"You didn't *not* say it," Galan said warily. "I would appreciate it if you would clarify your intentions. Do you
plan to kill her or not?"

Circenn rubbed his jaw again. He cleared his throat,
trying to form the words his conscience demanded he say,
but the warrior in him resisted.

Duncan's eyes narrowed as he regarded Circenn thoughtfully. After a moment, he glanced at his brother. "We know
what Adam is like, Galan. His way has oft been swift, unnecessary destruction, and enough blameless lives have

been taken in the quest to secure the throne. I propose Circenn take the time to discover who the woman is and whence she comes prior to passing sentence. I cannot speak for you, Galan, but I doona wish the blood of another innocent on my hands, and if we urge him to kill her, the deed becomes ours as well. Besides, recall that although Circenn swore to kill the bearer of the flask, nothing in his oath addressed timeliness. He might wait twenty years to kill her without breaking his oath."

Circenn glanced up at Duncan's last words, surprised. He hadn't considered that possibility. In truth, his oath had not contained one word specifying how swiftly he must kill the bearer of the flask—hence it was neither amoral nor a violation of his oath to refrain for a short time in order to study the person. One might even argue that it was wise, he decided. *You split hairs with a battle-ax.* Adam's words, from six years ago, surfaced in Circenn's mind to mock him.

"But you had best be aware," Galan warned, "that if you doona kill her, and should any of the Templars discover who she is and the nature of the oath you swore, the knights will lose faith in your ability to lead. They will see a vow broken as an unforgivable weakness. The only reason they agreed to fight for our country is because of you. Sometimes I think they would follow you into hell. You know they are fanatic in their beliefs. To them, there is no justification for breaking an oath. Ever."

"Then we will not tell them who she is or what I swore, will we?" Circenn said softly, knowing the brothers would support his decision whether they agreed with it or not. The Douglases always stood behind the laird and thane of Brodie—an ancient blood oath had united the two clans long ago.

The brothers studied him, then nodded. "It will remain between us until you reach your decision."

* * *

Breathing deeply of the crisp, cool air, Circenn paced the courtyard while the woman waited in his chambers for mercy that was not his to grant. He struggled to harden himself against her. He had lived so long by the rules that he almost hadn't heard his conscience clamor when he'd raised his sword to her neck. While his warrior's training had insisted he honor the vow, a thing he had thought dead in him had undermined his resolution.

Compassion. Sympathy. And an insidious little voice that had softly, but relentlessly, questioned the sagacity of his rules. He had recognized that voice; it was doubt—a thing he hadn't suffered for an eternity.

I swear to kill the bearer of the flask, he had pledged years ago.

A warrior's oaths were his lifeblood, an unbreakable code by which he lived and died. Circenn Brodie's rules were the only thing standing between him and a swift descent into chaos and corruption. What was the solution?

She must die.

She.

By Dagda, how could it be a woman? Circenn liked women; he had adored his mother and treated all women with the same deference and courtesy. He felt women exhibited some of the best characteristics of humanity. Circenn was Brude, whose line of royal succession was matrilineal. Years ago, when Circenn had sworn his oath to Adam Black, he had not once considered that the flask might be found by a woman, and such a delightful one at that. When he'd torn the strange bonnet from her head, her thick hair had cascaded nearly to her waist in a fall of copper and gold highlights. Green eyes, uptilted at the outer corners, had widened with fear, then quickly narrowed with anger as she'd pronounced the bonnet a gift from her da. It was only fitting that he return the family heirloom, no matter how ugly it was.

Unusually tall for a woman, and lithe, her breasts were full and firm, and he had glimpsed the press of her nipples against the thin fabric of her strange garment. Her legs were generously long—long enough to wrap around his waist and permit her to comfortably cross her ankles while he buried himself between them. When she had bent to retrieve her bonnet he'd nearly snaked an arm around her waist, pulled her against him, and let his demanding nature take free reign. *And then slit her throat when your desire was sated?*

She. Had Adam suspected that the bearer of the flask might be a female? Might he have seen into the future with his fairy vision and even now be laughing at his dilemma? Yet, if he hadn't used a binding curse in the first place, the woman's life wouldn't be in danger now. It was his inept curse that had brought her here, and now he was supposed to kill the unsuspecting soul. Unless he found some proof of duplicity on her part, her death would be innocent blood on his hands that would haunt him for the rest of his life.

Circenn girded his will, conceding that the best solution was to kill her. He would fulfill his oath; then, come tomorrow, life would be normal again. He would secure the flask in the secret place with the other hallows and continue their war. He would return to his tidy regimen and find solace in knowing that he would never become the abomination he so feared he had the potential to be.

Circenn Brodie's primary goal was to see the Bruce securely on the throne of Scotland.

Upon the English king Longshanks' death, his son Edward II had continued his father's war, relentlessly chipping away at Scotland's heritage. Soon nothing of their unique culture would remain. They would be Britons: weak and obedient, taxed into starvation and submission. Their greatest hope against the ruthless king of England was the renegade Templars who had sought sanctuary at Castle Brodie.

Circenn blew out a breath of frustration. The persecution of the Templars grieved and infuriated him. He had once considered joining the renowned Order of warrior-monks, but some of their rules hadn't been quite to his taste. He'd settled instead for working closely with the religious knights, since both he and the Order protected hallowed artifacts of immense value and power. Circenn respected the Order's many causes, and knew its history as well as any Templar.

The Order had been founded in 1118 when a group of nine predominantly French knights had gone to Jerusalem and petitioned King Baudouin to allow them to live in the ancient ruin of the Temple of Solomon. In exchange, the nine knights had offered their services to protect pilgrims traveling to the Holy Land from robbers and murderers along the public highways leading into Jerusalem. In 1128, the Pope had given his official approval to the Order.

The knights had been handsomely paid for their services, and the Order had increased dramatically in numbers, wealth, and power through the twelfth and thirteenth centuries. By the fourteenth century, the Order owned over nine thousand manors and castles across Europe. Independent of royal or episcopal control, the Order's profits were free of taxation. The Order's many estates were farmed, producing revenues that served as the basis for the largest financing system in Europe. In the thirteenth and fourteenth centuries, the Parisian Order of the Templars virtually functioned as the French Royal Treasury, lending large sums to European royalty and individual nobles. However, as the Templars' wealth and power increased, so did the suspicion and jealousy among some members of the nobility.

Circenn hadn't been surprised when the Order's success became the very reason for its downfall. He'd anticipated it, yet been helpless to prevent it; the politics of Pope and king were too mighty for one man to influence.

Circenn recalled well how, nearly a dozen years past, the Templars' wealth had drawn the deadly attention of the French king, Philippe the Fair, who was desperate to line his coffers. In 1305, Philippe maligned the Order, convincing Pope Clement V that the Templars were not holy defenders of the Catholic faith, but rather seeking to destroy it.

Philippe campaigned exhaustively against the knights, and accused the Templars of heinous acts of heresy and sacrilege. In 1307, the Pope gave the king the order he'd been waiting for: the right to arrest all the Templars in France, to confiscate their properties, and to direct an inquisition. So the infamous, bloody, and biased trial of the Templars had begun.

Circenn ran a hand through his hair and scowled. Knights had been arrested, imprisoned, and forced through torture to confess to sins of Philippe's choosing. Even more had been burned at the stake. In trial, the knights had been permitted no defense advocates; they had not even been allowed to know the names of their accusers and witnesses against them. The so-called "trial" had been a witch-hunt, deviously orchestrated to strip the Templars of their fabulous riches.

Adding insult to injury, the Pope had issued a papal bull that suppressed the Order and denied it recognition. The few knights who managed to escape imprisonment or death had become outcasts, without country or home.

When Circenn had realized the knights' downfall was inevitable, he had hastened to meet with Robert the Bruce and, with Robert's approval, had sent word to the Order that they would be welcomed in Scotland. Robert had offered them sanctuary, and in return, the powerful warrior-monks had turned their fighting skills to the battle against England.

The Templars were formidable warriors, trained in weaponry and strategy, and they were essential to Scotland's cause. Over the past few years, Circenn had been stealthily slipping them into the Bruce's troops as commanders, with the Bruce's assent. Already the Scots were warring better, implementing cunning strategies, and winning minor battles.

Circenn knew that if he faltered now, if he began to break oaths or did anything that jeopardized the Templar's loyalty, he might as well throw away the past ten years of his life, along with his love for his motherland.

* * *

Lisa had no idea how much time had passed since she'd sat on the floor. But it was long enough for her to realize that time didn't pass in such a fashion for dreamers. If one sat still in a dream and did nothing, the dream either ended or moved on to some new and incredible adventure colored by shades of the absurd. *Absurd like the proportions of that man's body,* she thought irritably.

Pushing herself up from the floor with her hands, she paused in a crouch, observing the wide, flat stones beneath her palms. Cool. Hard. Dry, with a skimming of stone dust. *Entirely* too tangible. Rising to her feet, she began to examine her surroundings.

The chamber was large, lit by fat, soapy candles. The walls, fashioned of massive stone blocks, were hung with random tapestries. A huge bed occupied the center of the room, and several chests were scattered about with neatly folded fabrics piled atop them. The room was spartan, tidy. The fireplace was the only concession to atmosphere; there was not a single woman's touch in the room. Pausing near the bathtub, she dipped her hand in the water; tepid—another sensation too tangible to deny.

She moved to the fireplace and flinched at the confoundingly real sensation of warmth. She studied the flames a moment, marveling that the rest of the room was so chilly when the hearth was throwing off such a blaze. It was as if the fire were the sole source of heat, she thought. Struck by that notion, she briskly walked the perimeter of the room. Her suspicion was quickly confirmed: There was not one heating vent in the entire chamber. No radiators in the corners collecting dust. No little metal vents in the floors. No pipes or, for that matter, a single electrical outlet. No phone jack. No closets. The door was made of what looked like solid oak; no hollow-core veneer there.

She took a deep, calming breath and assured herself that she must have overlooked something, at least in terms of the heating. Circling the room a second time, she surveyed every nook and cranny as she trailed her hand along the wall—another way of testing the solidity of her prison. Her fingertips brushed a thick tapestry that yielded beneath them and felt far colder than the stones. The rough fabric shivered beneath her palm as if the wind were batting at it from the other side. Mystified, she tugged it aside.

She lost her breath in a sudden rush of air. The view from the window struck her as intensely as an unexpected blow to her stomach.

She gazed out upon a misty night from ancient history.

Fifty feet above the ground, she was in a stone castle that stood on an island promontory surrounded by a thundering sea. Waves hurled themselves at the rocky crags, breaking into foam and becoming one with the mist that swirled up from the black surface of the ocean. On a cobbled walkway, men carrying torches moved silently between the castle and small outbuildings. The distant cry of a wolf competed with faint strains of bagpipes. The night sky was blue-black, tinted purple where it met the water, dancing with thousands of stars and a thin scythe of a moon. She'd never seen so many constellations in Cincinnati; smog and the halo effect of the brilliantly lit city dimmed such beauty. The view from the window was breathtakingly stark, majestic. A bitter wind howled up from the sea and across the promontory, buffeting the tapestry in her hand.

She dropped it as if she'd been burned and it fell across the window, blessedly sealing out the inexplicable vista. Unfortunately, as her eyes focused on the tapestry, she discovered a new horror. It was brilliantly woven and far too detailed: a warrior riding a horse into battle while an army of men clad in bloodstained plaid cheered. At the bottom of the hanging, embroidered in crimson, were four numbers that chipped away at her sanity: 1314.

Lisa moved to the bed and sank limply onto it, her energy sapped by the successive shocks. She stared blankly at the bed for a moment, then her hand flashed out and poked frantically at the mattress as she tested another part of her environment. *Not your run-of-the-mill Serta Sleeper here, Lisa.* Filled with a growing sense of panic, she pulled back the tightly tucked blankets and was momentarily sidetracked by the fragrance that clung to the linens. *His* scent: spice, danger, and man.

Firmly ignoring a desire to bury her nose in the sheets, she tugged at the mattress, which was little more than thin pallets laid atop one another encased in bristly fabric. One crunched like dried brush, the next seemed stuffed with lumpy wooly stuff, and the top had the feel of limp feathers. For the next twenty minutes Lisa scrutinized her surroundings, driven by increasing desperation. The stones felt cool, the fire felt hot. The liquid in the cup near the bed tasted vile. She heard the bagpipes. Every sense she possessed was activated by her tests. Absently, she swiped at her neck with the back of her hand, and when she drew it away a single drop of blood lay crimson upon her skin.

She understood with sudden certainty that she should never have touched the flask. Although it defied rational explanation, she was neither in Cincinnati nor in the twenty-first century. She felt the last of her hope that she was dreaming slip from her tenuous grasp. Dreams she knew well. But this was too real to be a dream, detailed far beyond her mind's ability to fabricate.

Give me the flask, he'd demanded.

You see this? This is part of the dream? She'd been astonished.

But now, reflecting upon it, she realized that he'd seen it because it was *not* part of a dream. It was part of reality, his reality, a reality she now shared. That it was the flask she had touched just before she'd started to feel like she was falling, and the flask that he'd demanded, seemed too logical a connection to exist within a dream. Had the flask somehow carried her back to a man who had direct or indirect proprietary rights to it? And if so, was she truly in the fourteenth century?

With growing horror, she saw the frightening pattern: His odd manner of dress, his intent perusal of her clothing as if he'd never seen the like before, the primitive wooden tub situated before the fire, the strange language he'd spoken, the tapestry on the wall. All of it hinted at the impossible.

Stricken, she glanced around the room, reassessing it from a different perspective. She viewed it as her employment in the museum had led her to believe a medieval chamber would appear.

And all the oddities made perfect sense.

Logic insisted she was in a medieval stone castle, and according to the wall hanging, at some point in the fourteenth century, despite the improbability of it.

Lisa blew her breath out in a frantic attempt to calm down. She couldn't be somewhere else in time, because if this was medieval Scotland, Catherine was some seven hundred years in the future—alone. Her mother desperately needed her and had no one else to rely on. That was unacceptable. Being stuck in a strange dream was now relegated to the minor problem it would have been, had it been true. A dream would have been easy to manage; eventually she would have awakened, no matter how awful things had been in the dream. If she was actually *in* the past, which was what all her senses insisted, she *had* to get back home.

But how?

Would touching the flask do it again? As she pondered that possibility she heard footsteps in the corridor outside the chamber. She moved quickly to the door, debated cowering behind it, then pressed her ear to it instead. It would be wise to discover everything she could about her environment.

"Do you think he'll do it?" a voice echoed in the hall.

There was a long silence, then a sigh so loud that it carried through the thick wood. "I believe so. He does not take oaths lightly and knows the woman must die. Nothing can come in the way of our cause, Duncan. Dunnottar must be held, that bastard Edward must be defeated, and oaths sworn must be honored. He will kill her."

As the steps faded down the corridor, Lisa leaned limply against the door. There was no doubt in her mind exactly which woman they'd meant.

Dunnottar? Edward? Dear God! She hadn't merely traveled through time—she'd been dropped smack into the sequel to Braveheart!

CHAPTER 4

IT WAS LATE AT NIGHT WHEN CIRCENN QUIETLY EASED his chamber door open a few inches. Peering through the narrow aperture, he saw that the room was dark. Only a faint bar of moonlight fell from behind the tapestry. She must be sleeping, he decided, which would give him the advantage of surprise. He would get this over with, quickly.

He swung the door open, stepped into the room with swift conviction, and promptly lost his footing. As he hit the floor of his chamber, he cursed; it had been cunningly littered with sharp pieces of broken stoneware. He scarcely had time to register that he'd tripped over a taut and cleverly tied cord, when he was smashed on the back of his head with a stoneware basin. "By Dagda, lass!" he roared, rolling over on his side and clutching his head. "Are you trying to kill me?"

"Of course I am!" she hissed.

Circenn could discern nothing more than a blur of motion in the darkness when, much to his astonishment and pain, she kicked him in a most sensitive part of his body— a part most women touched reverently. When he doubled over, his hands grazed more of the jagged shards on the floor, and he winced. She leaped over his body like a frightened doe, bounding for the open doorway.

Deadening himself to the pain, he moved swiftly. His hand flashed out and fastened on her ankle. "Leave this room and you are dead," he said flatly. "My men will kill you the moment they see you."

"So what's the difference? You will too!" she cried. "Let go of me!" She kicked ineffectually at the hand clasped around her ankle.

He growled and banged the door shut with his foot. Then, pulling on her ankle, he caused her to lose her balance and brought her crashing down on top of him. He'd tried to roll her toward him as she fell to keep her from striking any of the stoneware she'd so deviously strewn about, but she bucked as she hit him and bounced over his side. A grapple ensued and she fought him with a surprising amount of courage and strength. Aware of his superior brawn, he focused his efforts on subduing her without hurting her or allowing her to harm herself. If anyone was going to be harming her, it was he.

They wrestled in silence, except for his grunts when she landed a particularly painful shot and her gasps when he finally captured her hands and held them above her head and stretched her on her back on the floor. His grasp nearly slipped when his hand closed around a band of metal on her wrist. As he forcefully restrained her arms, it slipped off and he closed his fist over it, then placed it in his sporran for later inspection—it might yield clues to her identity. He deliberately let the full weight of his body settle atop hers, knowing she would not be able to breathe. *Submit,* he willed silently as she bucked against him, trying to win her freedom. "I am stronger than you, lass. Cede this battle to me. Doona be foolish."

"And let you kill me? Never! I heard your men." She

panted, trying to draw air into her lungs while crushed beneath his weight.

Circenn scowled. So that was why she'd laid a trap for him. She must have overheard Galan and Duncan as they'd retired to their rooms; they'd obviously said something about his killing her. He'd have to speak with those two about discretion, perhaps encourage them to revert to Gaelic while within the walls of the keep. He suffered a momentary lapse in concentration while admiring her resourcefulness, and she exploited it by bashing her forehead into his chin, and it *hurt*. He shook her forcefully and was astonished when the woman didn't yield, but tried to head butt him again.

She showed no signs of giving up the fight, and he realized that she would beat at him until she passed out from lack of breath. Since the only part of their respective bodies they both had free were their heads, he did the only thing he could think of—he kissed her. It would be impossible for her to head butt him with her lips pressed against his, and he'd learned long ago that the best way to control a fight was to get as far into his enemy's space as possible. It took nerves of steel to handle six feet and seven inches of ruthless Brodie a breath away from one's heart.

While congratulating himself for the inventive strategy he'd employed to keep her from hitting him with the only part of her body she could move, he acknowledged his attempt at self-deceit. He had wanted to kiss her since the moment she'd materialized in front of his bath—yet another violation of his careful rules. He knew that physical intimacy with this woman might skew his impartiality. But their skirmish had brought him into contact with every inch of her body, her curves were pressed against his hard length as if they were naked together, and her fierce, intelligent ambush had aroused him even more than her beauty had.

He had the scent of her in his nostrils: fear and woman and fury. It made him rock hard.

He sought to subdue her with his kiss, to make her understand his complete dominance, but the crush of her breasts beneath his chest heated him, and he found himself plunging his tongue between her lips with the intention of seducing rather than conquering. He sensed the moment when his kisses stopped being his way of controlling her and became nothing but a savage desire to indulge his appetite for the woman. All he need do was push aside his plaid, peel off her strange trousers, and push himself inside her. The temptation was exquisite.

His breathing quickened, sounding harsh to his own ears. It had been too long since he'd been with a woman, and his body was tightly strung. He angled himself away, drawing back to stop the painful press of his arousal against the cradle of her hips.

When she went motionless beneath him, he girded his will. Loath to lose the fullness of her lower lip, he sucked it hard as he drew away. He gazed down at her; her eyes were closed, her lashes dark fans against her cheeks.

"Are you going to kill me now?" she whispered.

Circenn stared at her, conflicting directives warring within him. In their tussle, he'd freed his dirk, and now he laid it against her throat. One swift plunge and it would be over. Brief, merciful, simple. His oath would be fulfilled, and there would be naught to do but remove the lass with the torn neck and forever-silenced heart and return to his carefully orchestrated world. Her eyes widened in alarm as she felt the chill metal brush against her skin.

He made the mistake of gazing into them. He closed his eyes and clenched his jaw. *Cut,* he ordered himself, but his fingers didn't so much as tense around the handle of the short knife. *Cut!* he raged at himself. Perversely, his body hardened against her, and he felt a sudden wave of desire to drop the knife and kiss her again.

Kill her now! he commanded himself.

Not a finger flinched. The knife lay useless against her skin.

"I can't die now," she whispered. "I haven't even *lived* yet."

The muscles in his arm recognized defeat before his mind did. There were no other words she could have said that would have dismayed him more. *I haven't even* lived *yet.* An eloquent plea to taste what life had to offer, and, whether she realized it or not, quite revealing. It told him much about her.

His arm relaxed, and he removed the knife from her throat with far greater ease than he'd placed it there. He muttered a curse as he flung it across the room and it sank into the door with a satisfying sound.

"Nay, lass, I will not kill you." *Not tonight,* he appended silently. He would question her, study her, determine her involvement. Judge her: guilty or innocent. If he found evidence of subterfuge or a shallow and avaricious personality, his blade would easily find the mark, he assured himself. "I need to ask you some questions. If I let you up, will you sit quietly on the bed and answer me?"

"Yes. I can't breathe," she added. "Hurry."

Circenn shifted so his weight was not resting fully on her. He allowed her to regain her freedom in regulated stages so she understood that he was giving it to her. It was neither a freedom she had earned nor one she could ever hope to take. He granted her passage, permitted her range of motion. It was imperative she understand that his control over her was absolute.

Despite his uncomfortable state of arousal, he forced her to keep close contact as she slipped her body from beneath his. It was a purely male show of dominance. He scarcely gave her room enough to find her knees beneath her. He leaned back minutely so she was forced to falter to her feet by clutching his shoulders, which put her lips a mere breath away from his. He would be all over her, until she acquiesced to his dictates.

She kept her gaze defiantly averted, refusing to look at him while she used his body to pull herself up. *Had you met my gaze, lass, I would have pushed you farther,* he thought, for had she still possessed enough defiance to meet his eyes he would have provoked submission some other way. He rose in tandem with her so their bodies touched at many contact points, and didn't miss her swift intake of breath when he deliberately shifted so her breasts brushed against his abdomen. He backed her to the bed and, with one gentle push, seated her upon it.

Then he turned his back on her as if she were nothing, no threat, insignificant. Another lesson she must learn—he had nothing to fear from her. He could turn his back on her with impunity. His movement had the secondary boon of giving him time to quell his desire. He took several deep breaths, bolted the door from the inside, and whipped his dirk from the wood and slapped it into his boot. He lit tapers before turning back to face her. By then he was breathing evenly and his plaid was carefully bunched at the front. She didn't need to know what toll their enforced closeness had taken on him.

She had buried her face in her hands and her coppery

hair slipped in a glossy fall across her knees. He reminded himself not to look at her long legs in those revealing trousers. Scarcely concealed by the pale blue fabric, a man could follow the slim line of her ankles over muscled calves and up shapely thighs to the vee of her woman's privacy. Those trousers could seduce a Templar Grand Master.

"Who are you?" he began quietly. He would continue in a gentle voice until she demonstrated resistance. Then he might roar at her. With a small measure of amusement, he conceded the probability that this lass would roar back.

"My name is Lisa," she murmured into her palms.

A good start, obedient and swift. "Lisa, I am Circenn Brodie. Would that we had met under different circumstances, but we did not, and we must make the best of it. Where did you find my flask?"

"In the museum where I work," she said in a monotone.

"What is a museum?"

"A place that displays treasures and artifacts."

"My flask was on display? For people to see?" he asked indignantly. *Hadn't the curse worked?*

"No. It had just been found and was still in the chest. It hadn't been placed on display yet." She didn't raise her head from her hands.

"Ah, so the chest had not been opened. You were the first one to touch it."

"No, two men touched it before I did."

"You saw them touch it—truly touch the flask?"

She was silent for a long moment. "Oh my God, the tongs!" she exclaimed. Her head shot up and she stared at him with an expression of horror. "No. I didn't actually see them touch it. But there was a pair of tongs lying next to the chest. I'll bet Steinmann and his cohort never touched the chest or the flask at all! Is that what did this to me—touching the flask? I *knew* I shouldn't have pried into business that wasn't mine."

"This is very important, lass. You must answer me truthfully. Do you know what the flask contains?"

She gave him a look of utter innocence. She was either the consummate actress or was telling the truth. "No. What?"

Actress or innocent? He rubbed his jaw while he scrutinized her. "Where are you from, lass? England?"

"No. Cincinnati."

"Where is that?"

"In the United States."

"But you speak English."

"Our people fled from England several hundred years ago. Once, my countrymen were English. Now we call ourselves American."

Circenn regarded her blankly. A look of sudden revelation crossed her face, and he wondered at it.

"That was silly of me. Of course you couldn't possibly understand. The United States is far across the sea from Scotland," she said. "We didn't like England either, so I can empathize," she said reassuringly. "You've probably never heard of my land, but I'm from very far away and it's imperative that I get back. Soon."

When he shook his head, her jaw tightened, and Circenn felt a flash of admiration; the lass was a fighter to the last. He suspected that if he had attempted to kill her, there would have been no pleas from her lips but vows of vengeance to the bitter finale. "I am afraid I cannot send you back just now."

"But you *can* send me back at some point? You know how?" She held her breath, awaiting his reply.

"I am certain we can manage," he said noncommittally. If she was from a land across the sea, and if he could find a way to accept not killing her, he could surely find a ship to put her on, if it was decided that she could be released. The fact that she was from so far away might make it easier for him to free her, because it was doubtful her homeland had any interest in Scotland; and once she was gone, perhaps he could force himself to forget he'd broken a rule. Out of sight might well be out of mind. Her appearance in the keep could truly have been a vast mistake. But how had his chest gotten to a land so far away? "How did your museum obtain my chest?"

"They send people all over looking for unusual treasures—"

"Who are 'they'?" he asked quickly. Perhaps she was innocent, but perhaps the men she'd mentioned were not.

"My employers." Her gaze flickered to his, then away.

He narrowed his eyes and studied her thoughtfully. Why had she averted her gaze? She seemed to be making a genuine effort to communicate with him. Although he saw no sign of outright deception, he sensed strong emotions in her; there were things she was not saying. As he pondered the direction of his inquisition, she stunned him by saying "So how do you send me through time? Is it magic?"

Circenn released a soft whistle. *By Dagda, how far had this lass come?*

CHAPTER 5

LISA SAT ON THE BED ANXIOUSLY AWAITING HIS REPLY. She found it difficult to look at him, partly because he frightened her and partly because he was so damn beautiful. How was she supposed to think of him as the enemy when her body—without even briefly consulting her mind—had already decided to like him? She'd never felt such a visceral, instant attraction. Lying beneath his overwhelming body, she'd been flooded with a frantic sexual desire that she'd hastily attributed to fear of dying; she'd read somewhere that happened sometimes.

She forced herself to remain motionless so she would betray neither the panic she felt nor her unacceptable fascination with him. In the past few minutes she'd been transported from fear and rage that her life might end so inauspiciously, to astonishment when he'd kissed her. Now she settled into wary numbness.

She realized—the man had some seriously intimidating body language—that he was in complete control, and unless she could catch him unaware, she didn't have a chance of escaping. She had already blown her best opportunity to catch him off guard when she'd ambushed him at the door. He was well over six-and-a-half-feet tall, more massive

than any professional football player she'd ever seen, and
she wouldn't have been surprised if he weighed in at three-
hundred-plus pounds of solid muscle. This man didn't miss
a thing; he was a natural-born predator and warrior, scruti-
nizing her every move and expression. She fancied that he
could smell her emotions. Didn't animals attack when they
scented fear?

"I see I must approach this from a different angle, lass.
When are you from?"

She forced herself to look at him. He'd lowered himself
to the floor and was leaning back against the door, his
powerful bare legs outstretched in front of him. The jew-
eled handle of his knife protruded from his boots. There
was blood trickling down his temple and his lower lip was
swollen. When he wiped absently at it with the back of his
hand, tendons and muscles rippled in his forearm. "You're
bleeding." The inane comment slipped from her mouth.
And wearing a tartan, she marveled. An actual plaid, woven of crimson and black, draped about his body, care-
lessly revealing much more than it concealed.

The corner of his lip curved. "Imagine that," he mocked.
"I was ambushed by a spitting banshee and now I am bleeding. I was tripped, bashed in the head, rolled over broken
stoneware, head butted, *kicked* in the—"

"I'm sorry."

"You should be."

"You were trying to kill me," Lisa said defensively.
"How dare you get mad at me when I was mad at you first?
You started it."

He ran an impatient hand through his hair. "Aye, and
now I am ending it. I told you I have decided not to kill
you for the moment, but I require information from you. I
have fifty men outside this door"—he gestured over his

shoulder with a thumb—"who will need reasons to trust you and let you live. Although I am the laird here, I cannot keep you safe all the time if I doona give my men plausible reasons why you are not a threat."

"Why do any of you want to kill me in the first place?" Lisa asked. "What have I done?"

"I am in charge of this inquiry, lass." With deliberate leisure, he folded his arms across his chest.

Lisa had no doubt that he'd struck the pose to make a point. It made all the muscles in his arms bunch and reminded her how small she was compared to him, even at five feet ten inches. She'd just learned another lesson: He could be courteous, even demonstrate a droll sense of humor, but he was always deadly, always in command. "Right," she said tightly. "But it might help if I understood why you consider me a threat to begin with."

"Because of what is in the flask."

"What's in it?" she asked, then berated herself for her incessant curiosity. Unchecked curiosity had created this situation.

"If you doona know, your innocence will protect you. Doona ask me again."

Lisa blew out a nervous breath.

"When are you from?" he asked softly, circling back to his initial question.

"The twenty-first century."

He blinked and cocked his head. "You expect me to believe you are from a time seven hundred years from now?"

"You expect *me* to believe that I'm in the fourteenth century?" she said, unable to conceal a note of peevishness in her voice. *Why did he expect such madness to be any easier for her to deal with?*

A quick smile flashed across his face, and she breathed

more easily, but then the smile vanished and he was again the remote savage. "This conversation is not about you, lass, or what you think or what you believe. It is about me, and whether I can find a reason to trust you and let you live. Your being from the future and your feelings about being here mean nothing to me. It is irrelevant where or when you are from. The fact is that you are here now and you have become my problem. And I doona like problems."

"So send me home," she said in a small voice. "That should solve your problem." She flinched as his intense gaze fixed on her face. His dark eyes latched on to hers and for a space of time unmeasured, she couldn't look away.

"If you are from the future, who is Scotland's king?" he asked silkily.

She drew a cautious breath. "I'm afraid I don't know, I've never followed politics," she lied. She certainly wasn't about to tell a warrior who was fighting over kings and territories that seven hundred years from now Scotland *still* didn't have a recognized king. She might not have a college degree, but she wasn't a complete fool.

His eyes narrowed and she suffered the uncanny sensation that he was gauging far more than her facial expressions. Finally he said, "I accept that. Few women follow politics. But perhaps you know your history?" he encouraged softly.

"Do you know *yours* from seven hundred years ago?" Lisa evaded, quickly intuiting where he was headed. He would want to know who won what battle and who fought where and the next thing she knew she'd be all tangled up in screwing up the future. If she really was in the past, she was not going to participate in instigating world chaos.

"Much of it," he said arrogantly.

"Well, I don't. I'm just a woman," she said with as much guilelessness as she could muster.

He regarded her appraisingly and the corner of his lip lifted in a half-smile. "Ah, lass, you are decidedly not 'just' a woman. I suspect it would be a vast mistake to deem you *merely* anything. Have you a clan?"

"What?"

"To which clan do you belong?" When she didn't answer, he said, "Do you have clans in Cincinnati?"

"No," Lisa said succinctly. He certainly didn't have to worry about someone trying to rescue her; she hardly had a family anymore. Hers was a clan of two, and one was dying.

He made an impatient gesture with his hands. "Your clan name, lass. That is all I am after. Lisa what?"

"Oh, you want to know my last name! Stone. Lisa Stone."

His eyes widened incredulously. "Like rock? Or boulder?" No half-smile this time: A full grin curved his lips, and the impact was devastating.

Her fingers itched with the urge to smack it off. *Enemy,* she reminded herself. "No! Like Sharon Stone. The famous actress," she added at his blank look.

His eyes narrowed. "You descend from a line of actresses?" he demanded.

What on earth had she said wrong? "No." She sighed. "That was my attempt at a joke, but it wasn't funny because you don't know who I meant. My last name *is* Stone, though."

"How foolish do you think I am?" he echoed the exact words she'd said to him about his name only hours ago. "Lisa Rock? That will not do. I can hardly present you to

my men, should I decide to, as Lisa Stone. I may as well
tell them you are Lisa Mud or Lisa Straw. Why would your
people take the name of a stone?"

"It's a perfectly respectable name," she said stiffly. "I've
always thought it a strong name, like me: capable of enduring calamity, mighty and able. Stones have a certain majesty
and mystery. You should know that, being from Scotland.
Aren't your stones sacred?"

He mulled over her words a moment and nodded.
"There is that. I had not considered it as such, but aye, our
stones are beautiful and treasured monuments to our heritage. Lisa Stone it is. Did your museum say where they
found my chest?" he coolly resumed his inquisition.

Lisa reflected, trying to recall the discussion she'd overheard as she'd hidden beneath Steinmann's desk. "Buried
in some rocks near a riverbank in Scotland."

"Ah, it begins to make sense," he murmured. "It did not
occur to me when I cursed it that if my chest went undis-
covered for centuries, the person who touched it would
have to travel through both terrain and time." He shook his
head. "I have little patience for this cursing business."

"It would also seem you have little aptitude for it." The
words tumbled from her mouth before she could stop
them.

"It worked, did it not?" he said stiffly.

Shut up, Lisa, she warned herself, but her tongue paid
no heed. "Well, yes, but you can't judge something simply
by its outcome. The end does not necessarily justify the
means."

He smiled faintly. "My mother was inclined to say
that."

Mother.

Lisa closed her eyes. God, how she wished she could

keep them closed and maybe it would all go away. No matter how fascinating this was, how gorgeous he was, she had to get out of there. Even as they spoke, somewhere in the future the night nurse was being relieved by the day nurse, and her mother would have expected her home hours ago. Who would check her medicines to be certain the nurses had gotten the doses right? Who would hold her hand while she slept so if she slipped away she wouldn't die alone? Who would cook her favorite foods to tempt her appetite? "Curse me back," she pleaded.

He regarded her intently and she again suffered the sensation of being examined on a deeper level. His gaze was a nearly tangible pressure. After a long silence he said, "I cannot send you back, lass. I doona know how."

"What do you *mean* you don't know how?" she exclaimed. "Wouldn't touching the flask do it?"

He jerked his head in a sharp gesture of negation. "That is not the flask's power. Traveling through time—if indeed you did—was an incidental part of the curse. I doona know how to send you back home. When you said you were from across the sea, I thought I could put you on a ship and sail you home, but your home is seven hundred years from happening."

"So curse something *else* to send me back!" she cried.

"Lass, it does not work like that. Curses are wily little creatures and none can command time."

"So what are you going to do with me?" she asked faintly.

He rose to his feet, his face devoid of expression, and he was once again warrior-lord, icy and remote. "I will tell you when I have decided, lass."

She dropped her head in her hands and didn't need to look up to know he was leaving the room and locking her in again. It offended her that he was so much in control of her, and she felt an overwhelming need to have the last word, childish though the impulse was. She decided that making small demands early on might strengthen her position.

"Well, are you going to starve me?" she yelled at the closed door. She'd also learned years ago that mustering defiance could prevent tears from spilling. Sometimes anger was the only defense one had.

She wasn't certain if she heard a rumble of laughter or if she imagined it.

CHAPTER 6

LISA WOKE WITH SORE, KNOTTED MUSCLES AND A KINK in her neck from sleeping without a pillow—sensations so tangible they shouted, *Welcome to reality*. She was surprised she'd managed to fall asleep at all, but exhaustion had finally overcome her paranoia. She'd slept in her clothes and her jeans were stiff and uncomfortable. She was cold, her T-shirt was twisted around her neck, her bra had come unsnapped, and her lower back ached from the lumpy mattresses.

She sighed and rolled over onto her back, stretching gingerly. She had slept, dreamed anxious, eerie dreams, and awakened to the same stone chamber. That sealed it: This was no dream. Had she any residual doubts, they disintegrated in the pale light of dawn that lined the edges of the gently blowing tapestries. No nightmare could have conjured the nauseating food she'd choked down late last night, nor in any dream would she have subconsciously surrounded herself with such primitive amenities. Fertile though her imagination was, it was not sadistic.

Although, she reflected, Circenn Brodie was indisputably the stuff of dreams.

He'd kissed her. He'd lowered his mouth to hers and the

touch of his tongue had sent heat lancing through her body, despite her fear. She'd trembled, actually *shaken* from head to toe, when his lips had bruised hers. She'd read about things like that happening but never thought to experience it. Before she'd fallen asleep last night, she had filed every detail of the kiss away in her memory, a priceless artifact in the barren museum of her life.

Why had he kissed her? He was so intent and controlled, she had imagined that if he ever touched a woman it would have been with a disciplined caress, not such a kiss as he'd given her—one that had been wild, hot, and uninhibited. Bordering on savage, yet infinitely seductive. Made a woman want to toss her head back and whimper with pleasure while he ravished her. He was skilled, and she knew she was out of her league with Circenn Brodie.

It must have been a strategy, she decided; the man dripped strategies. Perhaps he'd thought to seduce her into compliance. Given his appearance coupled with the dark sexuality he exuded, he'd probably controlled women all his life in such a fashion.

"Somebody—anybody—please help me," she whispered softly. "I'm in *way* over my head."

Pushing the memory of his kiss far from her mind, she stretched her arms over her head, testing for bruises from their skirmish last night. When she heard a scrabbling at the door and the sound of the bolt being slid, she squeezed her eyes shut, pretending she was asleep. She was not ready to face him this morning.

"Well, come on with ye, lassie! Ye willna escape by being a lie-about in bed all day," said a mischievous voice.

Lisa's eyes flew open. A boy stood beside her, peering down. "Och, aren't ye the bonniest lassie!" he exclaimed. The lad had auburn hair, a gamin grin, and unusually dark eyes and skin. His chin was pointy, his cheekbones high. Quite a fey-looking child, she thought.

"Come! Follow me!" he cried. When he darted from the room, Lisa tossed back the covers and dashed out the door behind him without a second thought. *Heavens, the boy was quick!* She had to stretch her long legs to keep pace as he skimmed over the stones toward a door at the end of the dim corridor. "Here, quickly!" he cried, as he ducked through the doorway.

Had it been anyone but a child she would never have blindly followed, but waking up and being granted a chance to escape by an innocent child overrode her common sense, and she found herself trailing him into a small turret. As she ducked in, he closed the door swiftly. They stood in a circular stone room, with stairs winding both up and down. When he grabbed her hand and started to pull her down the stairs, Lisa's eyes narrowed suspiciously. Who was this child and why was he intent on helping her flee? She resisted his grip so suddenly that he stumbled backward.

"Wait a minute." She held him by the shoulders. "Who are you?"

The boy shrugged innocently, dislodging her grip. "Me? Just a wee lad who has the run of the keep. Dinna fash yerself, lassie, no one notices me. I've come to help ye escape."

"Why?"

The boy shrugged again, a hasty up-and-down of thin shoulders. "Does it matter to ye? Dinna ye wish to flee?"

"But where will I go?" Lisa drew several deep breaths, trying to wake up. She needed to think this through. What would escaping the keep accomplish?

"Away from here," he said, peeved by her obtuseness.

"And where to?" Lisa repeated, as her sleepy mind finally started functioning with a semblance of intelligence. "Become one of the Bruce's camp followers? Go talk to Longshank's son?" she said dryly.

"Are ye a spy?" he exclaimed indignantly.

"No! But where am I going to go? Escaping the keep is only the beginning of my problems."

"Dinna ye have a home, lassie?" he asked, perplexed.

"Not in this century," Lisa said, as she sank to the floor with a sigh. Adrenaline had flooded her body at the prospect of escape. Vanquished by logic, it now fled her veins as swiftly as it had arrived, and its sudden absence made her feel limp. Judging by the coldness of the wall behind her back and the chilly draft circling through the tower, it was cold outside. If she left, how would she eat? Where would she go? How could she escape when there was no place for her to escape *to*? She eyed the boy, who appeared crestfallen.

"I dinna ken what ye mean, but I thought only to help ye. I ken what these men do to the lassies. 'Tisna pleasant."

"Thanks for the reassurance," Lisa said dryly. She studied the lad for a moment. His gaze was bright and direct, his eyes were old for such a young face.

He sank to the floor beside her. "So, what can I do for ye, lassie," he asked dejectedly, "if ye haven't a home and I canna be freeing ye?"

There was one thing he could help her with, she realized, for she certainly wouldn't ask the illustrious Circenn Brodie this question. "I need to . . . um . . . I drank too much water," she informed him carefully.

A quicksilver grin flashed across his face. "Wait here with ye." He dashed off up the stairs. When he came back he was carrying a stoneware basin that looked identical to the one she had struck Circenn in the head with last night.

She regarded it uncertainly. "And then what?"

"Why, then ye dump it out a window," he said, as if she were daft.

Lisa winced. "There is no window in this tower."

"I'll dump it for ye," he said simply, and she realized that this was the way of things. He'd probably dumped hundreds of them in his short life. "Och, but I'll be giving ye some privacy for the now," he added, and dashed off again up the stairs.

True to his word, he returned in a few moments and dashed off a third time with the basin.

Lisa sat on the stairs, waiting for the lad to return. Her options were limited: She could foolishly escape the castle and likely die out there, or go back to her room and get as close to her enemy as possible in hopes of finding that flask—which she *had* to believe was a two-way ticket. It was either that or accept that she was condemned to the fourteenth century forever, and with her mother dying back home, she would sooner die herself than accept that fate.

"Tell me about Circenn Brodie," she said when the boy returned. He hunkered down on the step beside her.

"What do ye wish to ken?"

Does he kiss all the lassies? "Is he a fair man?"

"None fairer," the lad assured her.

"As in honorable, not attractive," Lisa clarified.

He grinned. "I ken what ye meant. The laird is a fair man, he doesna make hasty judgments."

"Then why were you trying to help me escape?"

Another shrug. "I heard his men speaking last night of killin' ye. I figured if ye was still breathing this morning

I'd be helping ye go free." His thin face stilled and his eyes grew distant. "Me mam was killed when I was five. I doona like to see a lassie suffer. Ye could be someone's mam." Guileless brown eyes sought hers.

Lisa's heart went out to the motherless boy. She understood all too well the pain of losing a mother. She hoped his "mam" had not suffered long, but had met with a swift and merciful death. She gently brushed his tangled hair back from his forehead. He leaned in to her caress as if he'd been starved for such a touch. "What's your name, boy?"

"Ye may call me Eirren, but in truth I'd answer to anything from ye," he said with a flirtatious grin.

She shook her head in mock reproach. "How old are you?"

He cocked an eyebrow and grinned. "Old enough to know yer a bonny lassie. I may not be a man yet, but one day I will, so I better be getting all the practice I can."

"Incorrigible," she murmured.

"Nay, just thirteen," he said easily. "The way I see it, a boy can get away with a lot a man can't, so I'd best do it all now. What else did ye wish to ken, lassie?"

"Is he married?" *What kind of wife could handle a man like him?* She could have kicked herself the moment she said it, but then she decided Eirren surely wouldn't understand her interest.

"Ye wish to tup him?" he asked curiously.

Tup him? Lisa puzzled over that for a moment. "Oh!" she said, as she realized what he meant. "Stop that!" she exclaimed. "You can't think like that! You're *too* young. Tup, indeed."

He grinned. "I grew up hearing it from the men, how could I not? I haven't had me a mam in a long time."

"Well, you need one," Lisa said softly. "No one should be without a mother."

"Did he kiss ye?"

"No!" she lied hastily. She ducked her head, bringing a fall of hair forward to hide her blush from the too-perceptive boy.

"Fool he is, then," Eirren said with his gamin grin. "Well, lassie, ye better be deciding what ye wish to do. If yer not going, yer staying, and if yer staying ye best go back to yer room afore he discovers ye missing. He doesna like rules bein' broken, and ye escaping yer room would fair give him a fit." He rose to his feet and dusted off his scabbed knees.

"You need a bath," she informed him, deciding that if she had anything to say about it while she was there, he'd have a mother of sorts.

"Aye, and there are some things I dinna miss about me mam being gone *at all*," Eirren said cheerfully. "Come on with ye. I see ye've decided to stay in the cave with the bear, which isna all bad; his growl is much worse than his bite, once ye get him to relax."

Lisa smiled as she followed him from the stairwell. Young Eirren saw far too much for her comfort, but he might prove a useful ally for that very reason. Scampering about like a busy mouse, the inquisitive lad probably knew every nook and cranny of the castle. She would do well to cultivate his company, surreptitiously of course. As if he'd read her thoughts, Eirren spoke, as he gently pushed her back in her room. "Doona be telling the laird about me, lassie. He willna like me speaking with ye. It must be a secret between only two. I ken ye wouldna wish to get me in trouble, would ye now?" He held her gaze.

"Our secret," Lisa agreed.

CHAPTER 7

CIRCENN SMACKED DUNCAN'S THIGH WITH THE FLAT OF his blade. "Pay attention, Douglas," he growled. "Distraction will kill a man in battle."

Duncan shook his head and frowned as he counted off five paces and faced Circenn. "Sorry, but I thought I saw a child dart into the bothy behind the keep."

"Most likely that young serving lass Floria, who scarce reaches my ribs," Circenn said. "You know no children are permitted at Dunnottar."

"If so, it was a bloody small lass." Duncan leveled his sword with a smooth flick of his muscled forearm. "And although you and Galan think I like 'em all, I doona like 'em *that* young."

Their swords met in a clash of steel that sent sparks cartwheeling into the mist as dawn broke over Dunnottar. Dimly visible beyond damp low-hanging clouds, the sun bobbed on the shimmering horizon of the ocean, and the mist that had blown in with the night tide began to steam off slowly.

"Come, Douglas, fight me," Circenn goaded. Duncan had trained with Circenn since youth and was one of the few men who could hold his own in battle against him, for a short time, at least; then Circenn's superior strength and endurance finished him.

Parry and thrust, feint and spin. The two performed an ancient warrior's dance around the courtyard until suddenly Duncan penetrated Circenn's protective stance, the tip of his blade resting at the laird's throat.

The circle of knights flinched collectively as Circenn froze, his gaze fixed not on Duncan's blade but high on the east face of the keep.

"She is walking calamity. The lass is absolutely without wits, I vow it," Circenn said. He released a string of curses that caused even Duncan to raise a brow.

All eyes turned to the east where a slender woman clung to the stone wall, fifty feet above the ground. Knotted linens flapped in the breeze, dangling a dozen feet beneath her. It was obvious what she was doing, dropping down the dozen feet to the window beneath hers, preparing to enter it.

"Why does she not simply use the door, milord?" one of the Templars asked.

"I locked it," Circenn muttered.

Duncan lowered his sword and cursed. "I should have known I didn't beat you fairly."

"Who is she?" another knight asked. "And what manner of dress is she wearing?· It is as if she has naught a stitch on. You can see the separate curves of her . . . er . . ."

"Yes, who is she, milord?" a half-dozen knights echoed.

Circenn's eyes never strayed from the slim figure descending the wall with no small degree of finesse. Clad in those strange trousers, one could indeed see every inch of her shapely derriere as her long legs stretched to find a toehold. He'd been holding his breath since the moment the flicker of linen had caught his eye. Now he expelled it in a gusty sigh. "I was not supposed to reveal her," he lied swiftly, meeting Duncan's gaze with a silent warning. He was momentarily appalled at how easily the lie had sprung to his lips. *See,* he berated himself, *break one rule and they all go to hell.* "She is cousin to the Bruce and I have been entrusted with her keeping. You will protect her as you would fight for Robert himself. Apparently she cares little for being secured. I suppose we may have to give her run of the keep." With those words, he thrust his sword into his scabbard and stalked off into the ruin.

At the door, Circenn glanced over his shoulder at Duncan with another warning look that threatened grave repercussions if Duncan didn't support his story and protect the lass. The look on Duncan's face made him feel two inches tall. His friend and trusted adviser was gazing at him with astonishment, as if a stranger had taken over the laird of Brodie's body. Duncan shook his head and his expression clearly said, *What the hell are you doing? Have you lost your mind?*

As Circenn entered the tower and took the stairs two at a time, he decided he very possibly had.

✳   ✳   ✳

Lisa kicked her feet and gently swung herself into the window, exhaling a sigh of relief. With her daddy's encouragement she'd taken extracurricular tumbling and rappelling through junior high and high school. Although this climb hadn't looked too difficult, it certainly had been unnerving dangling above the courtyard, praying her knots would hold. She'd hoped the mist would take longer to burn off, and when the sun had begun to steam away the thick clouds she'd hurried, aware that the fighters below would have a clear view at any moment—*if* they looked up.

But Lisa was counting on the fact that people rarely looked up; the vast majority kept their gaze fixed firmly on the ground or on some nonexistent point in the sea of people surging down the city sidewalks. Only Lisa and some of the homeless people scanned the sky, watching the clouds break and scuttle. *Dreamer,* her father had teased. *Only dreamers watch the sky. You're a romantic, Lisa. Are you waiting for a winged horse to break through the clouds carrying your prince on his back?*

After Eirren had left, she'd waited in her room for Circenn Brodie to come, and when he didn't appear she'd grown increasingly restless. She needed to find the flask, and with her door bolted from the outside, she didn't have many options. She'd looked out the window and discovered another one a dozen feet below it. She'd quickly decided to have a look around while it was possible.

And if he caught her? She didn't care. The lord of the castle needed to know that she was not the kind of woman who would sit about waiting for his decisions, abiding his control. She'd considered her situation thoroughly, and yes, it appeared that she was truly in the fourteenth century. And yes, she had a mother who was dying in the twenty-first. She couldn't escape the castle, but she needed to assert herself as an innocent woman who was due a modicum of respect, and whom Circenn should help return to her time. Doing nothing was simply not an option. The only way she'd ever been able to cope with the difficulties in her life had been to meet them head-on, eyes open, mind working to achieve resolution.

She shoved aside the tapestry and leaped down from the windowsill. Her boots hit the floor with a soft thud just as he burst through the door.

"What an idiotic, insensible, stupid thing to do!"

"It was *not* stupid," she snapped, harboring a special hatred for that word. "It was a perfectly calculated and well-thought-out risk. Don't even start. If you hadn't locked me in, I wouldn't have been forced to do it."

He crossed the room swiftly and grabbed her. "Do you realize you could have fallen?" he roared.

She drew herself up to her full height, her back ramrod straight. "Of course I do. That's why I knotted the linens together. For heaven's sake, it was only a dozen feet."

"And the wind could have snatched you off at any moment. While it may only be a dozen feet from window to window, it is a fifty-foot fall to the ground. Even my men wouldn't do something so stupid."

"It wasn't stupid," she repeated evenly. "It was an intelligent exercise of my skills. Where I come from I've done it before, and besides, I had no way of knowing whether you planned to feed me today or talk to me or listen to the fact that I desperately need to get back home. And while we're on the subject of idiocy—is lunging at each other with sharp swords any less stupid? I saw what you were doing down there."

"We train," he said, lowering his voice with obvious effort. "We prepare for war." If the man clenched his teeth any harder, his jaw would lock, she decided.

"And war is a particularly intelligent venture, is it not? I'm merely battling for my rights and trying to return home. I have a life, you know. I have responsibilities at home."

He opened his mouth, then snapped it shut and regarded her for a moment. "What exactly are those responsibilities?" he asked finally, very softly.

Very softly from this man made her nervous, as did his hands on her waist, as did his moving so near that his breath fanned her face as she stared up at him. She felt suddenly cowed. *Damn* the man for having such an impact. She was not going to cry her heart out to this wall of warrior.

She took a deep breath and willed herself to calm down. "I know this is not the best situation for you but it's not for me either. How would you feel if you were suddenly yanked from your time, thrown somewhere else, and held captive? Wouldn't you do everything in your power to get your life back? To return to your homeland and win your battle for freedom?"

His jaw relaxed as he pondered her words. "You behave like a warrior," he said grudgingly. "Aye, I would do everything in my power to return."

"Then you can't blame me for trying. Or for being here, or for complicating your life. I'm the one whose life has been messed up. At least you still understand where you are. You still have your friends and family. You still have security. All I know is that I must get back home."

He was quiet for what seemed an interminable time, looking into her eyes. She could feel tension emanating from his body as he studied her, and she realized that this fourteenth-century warrior was struggling as hard as she was to figure out what to do next.

"You frightened me, lass. I thought you would fall. Doona climb my walls again, eh? I will find a way to give you some small freedom within the keep. I trust you were not trying to escape the keep itself; you are obviously intelligent enough to see you have no place to go. But doona climb my walls," he repeated. Then he rubbed his jaw, looking suddenly weary. "I am unable to send you back home, lass, I told you the truth about that last night. There's something else you should know as well. The conversation you overheard before you attacked me last night was correct: I did swear an oath to kill whoever arrived with my flask."

Lisa swallowed, her mouth suddenly dry. He *had* come to kill her last night. Would he have slipped in stealthily and slit her throat if she hadn't been awake and ambushed him first?

He looked directly into her eyes. "But I have made the decision to temporarily refrain from fulfilling my oath. That is not an easy thing for a warrior to do. We hold our vows sacred."

"Oh, how gracious of you," she said dryly. "So you don't plan to kill me today, but you might just decide to tomorrow. Am I supposed to find that reassuring?"

"There are valid reasons why I swore my oath. And aye, you should be grateful that I am letting you live for the now."

She would take what she could get. It wasn't as if she had much to bargain with. "What possible threat could I be to you? Why would you swear an oath to kill a person you didn't even know?" But even as she asked, she knew the answer to her question—whatever was in the flask was immensely valuable. Perhaps it was a tool to travel through time; that would certainly explain why people were casting curses upon it and willing to kill for it. Hadn't he snatched it from her the moment she'd arrived?

"My reasons doona concern you."

"I think they do concern me, when your reasons determine whether *I* live or die." She knew that oaths were sacred to knights of yore. He had nothing to lose by killing her. She was a woman lost in time; no one would miss her. Keeping her alive created a liability for him, and what would prevent him from suddenly changing his mind and honoring his vow? She would not be able to stand living day to day, always wondering if this would be the day he killed her. She needed to gain insight into how this warrior thought so that she could plan a defense. "Why did you decide to break your oath?"

"Temporarily," he corrected stiffly. "I did not break the oath, I merely have not filled it. Yet."

"Temporarily," she conceded. A ruthless murderer would not have bothered to have this conversation with her, which meant he had reservations about killing her. Once she knew what they were, she would exploit them to her advantage. "So, why? Is it because I'm a woman?" If that was the case, she resolved, she would be as feminine as possible from this moment on. She would drip vulnerability, bat her eyelashes, and ooze helplessness while doing everything in her power to steal the flask back and regain the upper hand.

"That is what I thought at first, but nay, it is because I doona know if you are guilty of anything. I have no problem killing a traitor, but I have not yet taken an innocent life and I doona wish to start now. But, Lisa, should I discover you are guilty of *anything*, no matter how small the transgression . . ." He trailed off, but his point was perfectly clear.

Lisa closed her eyes. So, he intended to watch her, study her, before he decided whether he would kill her. But she didn't have time to be studied and watched. Her mother needed her now. Time was of the essence, and if she didn't find a way back soon, she might lose Catherine without getting to say good-bye, and there was much she needed to say to her mother still. She'd been so obsessed with earning enough money to make ends meet, and with maintaining a cheerful smile on her face to keep her mom's spirits up, that somehow they had quit talking. Both mother and daughter had retreated into cautious pleasantries because the reality was too painful. But Lisa had always thought there would be time, a few special hours, maybe a week, in which she stopped going to work, incurred more debt, and did what she most wanted—stayed at home with Catherine, holding her hand and talking until the very end.

She shook her head, bewildered and more than a little angry at what life had dealt her. How *dare* her life keep getting worse? She stiffened her spine and her eyes flew open. "I *must* get back home," she insisted.

"It is impossible, lass. Returning you is not in my power."

"Do you know anyone who can?" she pushed. "You must concede, it would be the best solution. All our problems would be solved if you simply sent me back."

"Nay. I know no one who has such power."

Did he hesitate briefly? Or did her desperate need to cling to hope conjure the illusion? "What about the flask?" she said quickly. "What if I touched—"

"Forget the flask," he shouted, straightening to his full height and glaring down at her. "It belongs to me, and I have already told you that it cannot return you to your time. The flask is *my* property. You would do well to forsake all thought of it and never mention it to me again."

"I refuse to believe there is no way for me to return."

"But that is the first fact you must accept. Until you acknowledge that you cannot return home, you will have no hope of surviving here. One of the first lessons a warrior is taught is that denial of one's circumstances only results in failure to recognize real danger. And I assure you, Lisa Stone, there is infinite danger in your present situation."

"You don't scare me," she said defiantly.

He stepped so close that his body brushed against hers,

but she refused to back up an inch. For all she cared, he could stand on top of her, but she would not yield ground; she had a feeling that lost ground was not something a person ever got back from Circenn Brodie. She returned his glare.

"You should be afraid of me, lass. You are a fool if you are not afraid of me."

"Then I'm a fool. If I went through time once, it can happen again."

"Would that it could, for it would certainly make my life easier. Then I would not be caught in this dilemma. But I doona know how to make it happen. Believe that much, at least."

Lisa found herself studying his face the way he'd searched her eyes moments ago, seeking some way to gauge if he was telling her the truth. But she was intelligent enough to recognize that she was in the defensive position—he being the massive and invincible offense. She would be wise not to push him too far.

"Temporary truce?" she offered at last, not meaning a word of it, resolved to find the flask at the earliest opportunity and fight him any way she could.

"You will abstain from climbing my walls?"

"You promise you won't try to kill me without first telling me, so I can have a bit of time to accept it? A few days would do," she countered, postponing the possibility of death any way she could.

"Will you pretend to be cousin to the Bruce, as I told my men?" he said gravely.

"Will you promise that if there is a way for me to get back home, you'll let me go? *Alive*," she added, stressing the word.

"Say 'aye' first, lass," he demanded.

Lisa held her breath for a moment, looking at him. She had little choice but to pledge this bizarre truce to him. If she tried to back out now, she suspected they'd be fighting again in a matter of moments. "Aye," she mimicked his accent.

He studied her, as if measuring the depth of her honesty and commitment to her words. "Then aye, lass. If a way can be found to return you, I will help you do it." The corner of his mouth twitched in a strangely bitter smile. "It will get you the hell out of my life and my compromised integrity," he added softly, more to himself than to her.

"Truce," she accepted. *Integrity,* she jotted in her mental file of significant facts about Circenn Brodie. It was important to him. She experienced a flash of hope: The precise knightly characteristics that might drive him to fulfill his oath—which included integrity, honor, protection of those weaker than he, and respect and chivalry toward women—could also be prevailed upon to *prevent* him from doing it. Killing a helpless woman would surely not be easy for him. She knew that sealing an agreement was no small matter to a knight, so she extended her hand for the seal of a handshake, not realizing how thoroughly modern-day the gesture was.

He eyed it for a moment, took it, then pressed it to his lips and kissed it.

Lisa snatched back her hand with a scowl. Heat tingled where his lips had brushed her skin.

"You offered it," he snapped.

"That wasn't what I—oh, forget it," Lisa floundered, then explained, "We don't kiss hands in my time—"

"But we are not in your time. You are in my time now, lass. I cannot stress enough how important it is for you to remember that, at all times." His voice was low, his words clipped as if he were irritated by her response. "And so there are no further misunderstandings between us, I will explain: Should you offer me a part of your body, lass, I will kiss it. That is what men in my century do." His smile was mocking, couching a none-too-subtle challenge.

Lisa folded her hands behind her back. "I understand," she said, casting her gaze to the floor in a deceptively submissive manner.

He waited for a moment as if not quite trusting her acquiescence, but when she didn't raise her eyes again, he turned toward the door. "Good. Now we need to find you decent clothing and teach you how to be a proper fourteenth-century lass. The better you blend in, the less risk you will face, and the less risky your presence will be for me."

"I will not empty chamber pots," she said firmly.

He looked at her as if she'd lost her mind.

* * *

Circenn returned Lisa to his chambers, had hot water sent up for her to wash with, then went off in search of clothing for her. Chamber pots, indeed. Did she think they were so barbaric that they did not have garderobes? Chamber pots were used only for nocturnal emergencies, primarily by children and the infirm, and in his opinion there was no reason why anyone could not manage to make it down the hallway, unless they were possessed of extreme laziness and lack of discipline.

He snorted, focusing his mind on the task at hand. He couldn't give her run of the keep until he'd managed to hide some of those curves and long legs beneath the ugliest gown he could find. His men needed no distractions. He gathered the maids and instructed them to procure a gown, all the while brooding over what to do with her.

When he'd questioned Lisa last night, he'd nearly begun to believe she was innocent. She had a disarming air about her, an attitude of sincerity. He'd relaxed a bit, even glimpsed a wry humor in their conversation. Then she'd admitted that she was from the future, and he'd realized that his curse had inadvertently carried her through time.

Although it had stunned him, it made sense: Her strange English, her odd clothing, her mention of countries of which he'd never heard, all were explained by her being from the future. He could certainly understand her people fleeing England, he thought wryly—who wouldn't want to? It didn't surprise him that in the future, England was still trying to control everyone.

He laughed softly, thinking that she didn't know how lucky she was that she'd been brought to him and not some other medieval lord. Circenn accepted time travel, but he was an extreme exception. Any other laird would have burned her for a witch. But then again, he thought dryly, no other laird would have had the power to curse the damned flask to begin with.

It was due to Adam Black that he was familiar with the art of sifting time. Adam did it frequently, had often spoken of other centuries, and he'd brought Circenn odd "gifts" in some of his attempts to buy the laird's loyalty and obedience. They were gifts Circenn had refused, but when Adam wouldn't take them back, he had locked them securely in a private room off his chambers, not trusting their powers. He knew that Adam was trying to tempt him, hoping to make him become like Adam—a thing Circenn would destroy himself before permitting that to happen.

The lass had been wearing one of those strange "gifts" fastened about her wrist, before Circenn had slipped it from her arm in their struggle last night. He'd inspected it later; it was what Adam had once called a "watch." Adam had found it endlessly amusing, saying it was how mortals counted their "pathetic span of life." Her watch seemed to confirm her story.

If he believed her version of events, his chest had washed down the river, surfacing in some remote area. It had not been found, and, over time, nature had buried it. Hundreds of years had passed before it had been dug up, and when she'd touched it, it had brought her back to him.

Was it possible that in the future, men still sought the hallows and the secret of the flask as avariciously as they did in his century? Was it possible she had come there to uncover the treasures of the *Tuatha de Danaan* and the Templars? He might have suspected Adam's involvement in this, but for two reasons: There was no point in Adam's bringing to him a woman he was forsworn to kill, and Adam didn't manipulate events unless there was a very specific thing he wanted to gain from his devious machinations. Circenn couldn't see one possible thing Adam might be after in this tangle. The flask and the hallows already belonged to Adam's race; Circenn was merely the guardian. Adam had already shaped Circenn as he wanted—there was nothing more he could possibly hope to "change" about the laird of Brodie. No, Circenn mused, there was nothing of Adam in this. But the lass might be in league with the "employers" she'd mentioned; she could well be from a treacherous future, after his secrets.

He would have to watch her, study her, keep her near. It would take time, and time was a luxury he could ill afford in the thick of an ongoing war. Besides, he brooded, any time spent in the lass's presence was a slow torture. Loath though he was to admit it, he was susceptible where she was concerned. Stunning, proud, sensual, and intelligent, the woman would be a formidable foe—or a valued ally. He hadn't met a woman like her in centuries.

Curse me home, she'd said. Circenn snorted, recalling her plea. The only person who could send her back home was the one person who would kill her instantly if he knew she was there: Adam. He certainly couldn't call on Adam and ask *him* to send the woman home, nor could he risk meeting with Adam to dig for clues as to whether he was somehow involved. The blackest elf was far too clever to be probed, even by Circenn.

He was acting against everything he had lived by, all his careful rules designed to keep him human; he was breaking an oath, defending a person who could be a spy, lying to his men. He was taking a huge risk by letting her live, and if he was wrong . . .

Sighing, he finished giving orders and headed off for the kitchen to prepare his men for the introduction of Lisa MacRobertson, cousin to Robert the Bruce.

* * *

Adam Black didn't bother to materialize. He remained invisible, a wisp of sultry air lightly scented with jasmine and sandalwood, dogging Circenn's footsteps, consumed by curiosity. That perfect paragon of a man—Circenn Brodie, who'd never broken a rule, never betrayed a weakness, not once wavered on rigid issues of morality—was breaking a sworn oath and willfully deceiving his men. *Fascinating,* Adam marveled. He'd long thought the laird of Brodie had no breaking point, and had nearly despaired of ever finding the proper catalyst.

He sensed that Circenn didn't believe Adam was involved in his present tangle, because he couldn't pinpoint anything Adam might want. Adam smiled faintly. Circenn hated being manipulated. It was best that the laird of Brodie remain blissfully unaware that Adam had carefully orchestrated every move in this game, and was playing for the highest stakes of all.

CHAPTER 8

LISA STEPPED INTO THE GOWN AND TURNED TO FACE
the polished metal propped against the wall. She'd been surprised when a mirror had been brought to her chamber. Sifting through her history studies, she recalled that mirrors
dated as far back as Egyptian times, perhaps earlier. She
knew the Romans had constructed sophisticated sewage
systems thousands of years ago, so why should a mere mirror surprise her? It was too bad she couldn't help them re-
discover plumbing, she mused. She rubbed at the soot on
the chipped metal until it revealed her shadowy reflection.

The soft dress clung to her hips, so full of static it
crackled. She struggled for a moment, trying to pull it up
over her shoulders, but the gown had been made for someone considerably smaller than she. Although she was slim,
she was tall and had full breasts; half of her wouldn't fit in
the dress. Sighing, she slipped the gown from her hips and
stepped out of it. She was moving toward the bed to retrieve her jeans when the door opened.

"I brought you—" The words terminated abruptly.

She whirled around to find Circenn frozen in the doorway, his gaze fixed on her, a cloak tossed over his arm. It
slipped to the floor, unheeded.

Then he stepped into the room and kicked the door shut behind him. "What manner of dress have you donned?" he thundered. His dark eyes glittered as they swept her body from head to toe. He sucked in a rough breath.

Lisa shivered. He *would* have to catch her standing there in the only frivolous thing she owned, a pair of lavender bikini panties and a matching lace push-up bra that Ruby had given her for her birthday. And skin. And a damp nervousness she attributed to fear.

He stalked to her side and slipped a finger beneath the delicate lace edging one cup of her bra. "What *is* this?"

"It . . . it . . . Oh!" She couldn't form a coherent sentence. His finger lay against her pale skin, and she was mesmerized by the contrast in colors and textures. He had large hands, callused and strong from swordplay, with elegant fingers, one of which now rested against the smooth swell of her breast. She closed her eyes. "Bra," she managed. Grasping at formality, she pretended she was giving a history lesson in reverse, teaching him what the future held: "It's a garment designed t-to protect a woman's, you know, and k-keeps them from, well, you know. . . ."

"Nay, I doona think I know at all," he said softly, his lips a few breaths from meeting hers. "Why doona you enlighten me, lass?"

Her breath caught in her throat with a small gasp—a consummately feminine sound, and she cursed herself silently for it. *Just pant, why don't you?* she berated herself. They were scant, dangerous inches from full body contact, his finger tugging gently at the edging of her bra. She was acutely aware of her near nudity, of her nipples beneath the thin fabric in perilous proximity to his hands, and the fact that he wore nothing more than a drape of easily discarded cloth. She felt electricity race through her body everywhere his gaze skimmed. If he ripped off his plaid and covered her body with his, would she have the strength to protest? Would she even want to? How could her body betray her to a man who was her enemy? "The gown was too small," she managed.

"I see. And you astutely concluded this would cover more of you?"

"I was just about to put my j-jeans back on," she informed his chest.

"I think not. Not until you tell me what this"—he tugged lightly at the strap—"keeps your 'you knows' from doing."

Was he teasing her? She forced herself to meet his gaze and instantly wished she hadn't. His dark eyes were intensely sexual, his lips parted in a faint smile.

"Drooping when you get older." The words escaped her in a rush of air.

He tossed his head back and laughed. When he lowered his head she saw the unnerving intensity in his eyes, and she realized he was aroused. *By her.* The knowledge astounded her. She'd decided that his kiss last night and his innuendos today had simply been part of his strategy, but now, looking at him, she understood that he had a fierce physical reaction to her, possibly as painful as her attraction to him. It was simultaneously a heady feeling and a frightening one. She had a sudden premonition that if she gave him the slightest indication of her interest, he would descend upon her with the gale force of a Saharan sirocco, every bit as hot and devastating. Hungry for it, aching with inexperience and curiosity, she wanted desperately to discover what a man like Circenn Brodie might do to a woman.

But she dared not explore that desire. She would be as a

lamb to the slaughter. She had never been romanced, and the laird of Brodie could seduce a saint, she thought. Although she'd wanted him to be aware of her as a woman, thinking it might make him more protective of her, she had a dreadful feeling that she would lose herself entirely if he kissed her again. He was just too overwhelming. She had to defuse the sexual chemistry between them, and the best way to do that was to get her clothing back on.

She dropped to her knees, lunging for the gown pooled at her feet, but he moved in flawless accord and she ended up kneeling nose to nose with him, and *he* was holding her dress.

They stared at each other while she counted her heartbeats; she'd reached twenty before he favored her with a slow smile. Tension crackled in the air between them.

"You are a beauty, lass." He cupped her cheek with his hand and swept a light kiss across her lips before she could protest. "Long legs, beautiful hair"—he slipped his hand into it, letting silky strands sweep through his fingers—"and fire in your eyes. I have seen many bonny lasses but I doona believe I have ever encountered one quite like you. You make me think I might discover parts of myself I doona know exist. What am I to do with you?" He waited, his lips mere inches from hers.

"Let me get dressed," she breathed.

He searched her face intently. She held her breath then, terrified that if she opened her mouth she would cry, *Yes! Touch me, feel me, love me, damn it, because I don't know what it feels like any more to forget that I hurt and that my mother is dying!*

Often, during her mother's illness, Lisa had found herself longing for a boyfriend, a lover: someone she could take her battered heart to and curl up with, even if only for an hour, for the illusion of security, warmth, and love. Now, half terrified, worried about her mother dying alone, she had a perverse impulse to seek shelter in the arms of the very man sworn to kill her.

Don't try to use a Band-Aid on your heart, Lisa, Catherine would have reminded her, had she been there. Any sense of security or intimacy with him would be nothing but an illusion. She needed to keep her mind clear, not filled with romantic fancy about some medieval Highland laird who might decide to kill her tomorrow.

He dropped his hand from her hair, skimming her collarbone and curving his fingers over the lacy scallop of her bra. He studied the sheer fabric with fascination, his gaze caressing the uplifted curves of her breasts, the deeper shadow of her cleavage. "Look at me, lass," he whispered. Lisa raised her eyes to his and wondered what he saw in them. Hesitation? Curiosity? Desire she couldn't hide?

Whatever it was he saw in her eyes, it wasn't a Yes, and this man was a proud one.

He traced a finger down the hollow between her breasts and the smile he gave her held a sadness she couldn't fathom.

"I will send someone to fetch you another gown, lass," he said. Then he left the room.

Lisa sank to the floor, clutching the gown. *Dear heavens,* she thought, *what am I going to do?*

*   *   *

Circenn stomped from her room, his mood worsening by the moment. His body ached from head to toe with the effort of being *gentle* with the lass. His face felt stiff from smiling *gently*; his fingers clenched and unclenched from touching the swell of her breasts *gently*. His body rebelled at his gracious, honorable, *gentle* retreat from her room, and the man within him that had been born into the world five hundred years ago roared that the woman was his, by Dagda! Gentleness be damned! In the ninth century a man had not asked—a man had taken! In the ninth century a woman had been amenable, grateful to find such a fierce protector and able provider.

Circenn laughed softly, bitterly. He'd been far too long without a woman to endure such torment. When he'd walked into the room, carrying the cloak that would have drowned her in its oversized folds, his mind had been focused solely upon covering as much of her as possible—only to find her clad in nothing but two lacy, gauzy pieces of fabric. With little bows! By Dagda, a tiny satin ribbon had perched jauntily between her breasts, and another at the front of the silky fabric that slipped between her legs. *Like a gift,* he thought. *Untie my bows and see what I have to give you. . . .*

He'd tried to look away. To spin on his heel and leave the room, refusing himself the pleasure of viewing her lovely body. He'd sternly reminded himself of rule number four—no physical intimacy. But it had done him no good. Rule number four seemed to have become quite friendly with rule number one—never break an oath—and was cozying up nicely to rule number two—do not lie. What a crowd they were becoming, his broken rules.

Seeing her clad in such a fashion had been worse than if he'd caught her in complete undress. Nude, his hungry eyes could have feasted upon every crevice and hollow of her body; but those pieces of fabric had been cunningly designed to torture a man with the promise of the private slopes and hollows, while granting none of them. Secrets lay beneath that fabric. Were her nipples round dusky coins or puckered coral buds? Was her hair golden and copper there, too? If he had dropped to the floor at her feet, closed his hands around her ankles, and kissed his way up her long, lovely legs, would she have moaned softly, or was she silent when she made love? Nay, he decided abruptly, Lisa Stone would sound like a lioness mating when he took her. *Good.* He liked that in a woman.

She'd made him feel like a hungry animal, caged by his own rules, and all the more dangerous for it. For a few moments, lust had risen so furiously that he'd feared he might drag her beneath his body, uncaring whether she wished it. Instead, he'd clenched his shaking hands behind his back, dropping the cloak to the floor and thinking of his mother, Morganna, who would have disowned him even for thinking about taking by force that which must be gifted. Never had he felt so nearly violent with desire. She had roused deep, primitive feelings in him: possessiveness, jealousy that another man might see her clad thus, a need to hear her say his name and gaze at him with approval and desire.

Circenn drew a deep breath, held it until his heart slowed, then released it. Now that he knew what was beneath her clothing—no matter what gown he made her wear—how would he be able to look at her again without seeing in his mind the endless expanse of silken skin? The gentle swells of her breasts, the tight nipples peaking the sheer gauze, the slight mound between her thighs.

Thwarted desire translated well into rage. He stomped down the stairs to the kitchen, determined to find Alesone or Floria and have one of them see to it that the lass was properly attired. Then he would send one of the Douglas brothers to teach her about their time, something he should have done himself, but he simply couldn't trust himself near her at the moment. He would go train with his men and release some of his frustration in the pure, clean joy of swinging a heavy sword, grunting and cursing. And he would *not* entertain one more erotic thought for the remainder of the day.

Shaking his head, he burst into the kitchen. It took him only an instant to realize that none of his plans for the day was going to go right. In fact, the day seemed to have taken on a devilish persona, determined to mock him.

He drew to an abrupt halt, hastily averting his gaze from the sight of the rounded and flushed bare bottom gripped in Duncan Douglas's hands.

Alesone had one long leg wrapped around Duncan's waist, her arms twined around his neck and her skirts tossed up to her shoulders. The foot that remained on the floor was arched upon the tips of her toes, as Duncan's hands guided her against him in a steady, intense rhythm. The low, sensual sounds of passion filled the room, soft intakes of air, husky murmurs of pleasure, and damned if Duncan wasn't emitting a deeply satisfied sound with each thrust.

"Oh, for Christ's sake!" Circenn roared, glancing at the ceiling, the walls, the floor—anywhere but at Alesone's shapely derriere. "Duncan! Alesone! Get out of the kitchen! Take it to the rooms upstairs! You know I have rules—"

"Ah, yes, the legendary Brodie rules," Duncan said dryly. He stopped rocking the maid against him with more leisure than Circenn appreciated. "Which include among them: When knights are in residence, no tupping in the kitchen."

Alesone made a soft sound of protest at being interrupted.

"I *eat* in here!" Circenn thundered, feeling entirely too put upon.

"So does Duncan," Alesone purred suggestively. She

slid her leg down from Duncan's waist slowly, giving Circenn a good, long look. With a coy smile, she dropped a lid onto the honey pot perched on the table near Duncan.

Circenn did *not* want to know what they'd been doing with the honey, and his expression must have clearly said as much, for Duncan burst into laughter.

"Excuse us, Cin." He grinned as he dropped Alesone's skirts with one hand, swung her up into his arms, and swept her from the kitchen.

Images of one-person-in-particular's bare, rounded bottom assaulted him.

Circenn kicked out a chair, dropped his head on the table, and reconsidered killing the lass just to put himself out of his misery.

CHAPTER 9

RUBY TOOK THE STAIRS TO THE STONES' APARTMENT two at a time, but slowed her stride when she reached the third floor and proceeded down the dimly lit corridor. A colorful welcome mat—one of Lisa's determinedly optimistic touches—brightened the appearance of the dismal door with its chips of peeling brown paint curling up from the underlying gray metal. APT. 3-G dangled at a lopsided slant from a single screw. Ruby raised her hand to knock but found herself straightening the sign instead, then dropped her fist to her side. She was dreading this visit. Twining a strand of hair around a nervous finger, she reminded herself that Lisa always faced things head-on; the least she could do was emulate her. When she raised her hand again, she knocked firmly. Elizabeth, the day nurse, opened it and ushered her in.

"Lisa? Is that you, darling?" Catherine called, a note of hope in her voice.

"No, Mrs. Stone. It's just me, Ruby," she replied as she crossed the small living room and turned down the narrow hallway to the bedroom. Entering the cozy room, she sank into a chair next to Catherine's bed and wondered where to begin. She plucked idly at the half-finished patchwork quilt resting on the arm of the chair. How was she going to break the latest news to Lisa's mom? Catherine was critically ill, her daughter had disappeared, and now Ruby had even worse news for her.

"What did the man at the museum say?" Catherine asked anxiously.

Ruby smoothed her hair and shifted in her seat. "Would you like some tea, honey?" she evaded.

Catherine's green eyes, uptilted and once as bright as her daughter's, met Ruby's with a cool reminder that she wasn't dead yet and wasn't stupid either. "What did you find out, Ruby? Don't try to distract me with tea. Has anyone seen my daughter?"

Ruby gently rubbed her eyes with her fingertips, careful not to smear her mascara. She'd been up most of the night and wondered for the tenth time how Lisa had managed to survive working two jobs for so long. She had been closing at the club when she received an urgent message from Mrs. Stone saying that Lisa had been missing since the night before last. She had immediately phoned the police, then gone to the museum to see if Lisa had arrived at work last night—which she hadn't—then gone directly to the police station after speaking with that horse's ass Steinmann.

The officer had dutifully filed a missing person's report, which had been amended in a matter of hours by a warrant for Lisa Stone's arrest.

"No one has seen her since night before last," Ruby informed Catherine. "The museum's security cameras have her on tape. The last recorded image of her is outside Steinmann's office."

"So at least we know that she made it to work the night

you saw her at the bus stop," Catherine said. "Do the cameras show her leaving that night?"

"No. That's what's so strange. Her slicker is still hanging by the door, and none of the cameras register her leaving. There are no cameras in Steinnman's office, but he was quick to point out that there's a window she might have used." And quicker to make heinous accusations that Ruby knew weren't true. But how was she to prove it, and where on earth was Lisa? She didn't mention to Catherine that she'd gone to the police a second time, then had called every hospital within a sixty-mile radius, praying there were no Jane Does; blessedly, there hadn't been.

"Isn't Steinmann's office on the third floor?" Catherine asked, perplexed.

"Yes. But he promptly pointed out that Lisa took rappelling when she was younger. I guess she listed that on her application as one of her hobbies. I know she was pretty proud of that skill." Ruby shifted in her chair and took a deep breath. "Mrs. Stone, there's an artifact missing from the museum, and . . ."

"They've accused my daughter of stealing," Catherine said tightly. "Is that what you're telling me?"

"Her . . . er . . . disappearance does make things look bad. According to Steinmann and his trusty tapes, he and a colleague entered his office several hours after Lisa had. The door wasn't locked and initially he thought she'd simply failed to lock up. Now he thinks she was hiding in the office, took the artifact after they left, and slipped out the window."

"What is this artifact?"

"They won't say. It seems they aren't completely certain what it was."

"My daughter is not a thief," Catherine said stiffly. "I will go speak with them."

"Catherine, let me handle this for you. You can't get up—"

"I have a wheelchair!" She gripped the sides of her hospital bed with thin hands and tried to push herself up.

"Catherine, honey," Ruby said, her heart breaking. "We'll find her. I promise. And we'll clear her name." She placed her hand over Catherine's, gently loosening her grip on the rails. "We both know Lisa would never do something like this. We'll find a way to prove it."

"My daughter would never steal and she certainly wouldn't leave me!" Catherine snapped. "She *should* leave me, but she wouldn't." The sudden burst of anger drained her, and she lay still for a moment. She drew a shuddering breath, then said faintly, "Steinnman pressed charges, didn't he? There's a . . . warrant . . . out for her, isn't there?"

Ruby flinched. "Yes."

Catherine inclined her head stiffly, then sank back against the pillows and closed her eyes. She was silent for so long that Ruby wondered if she'd fallen asleep. When she spoke again there was steel in her voice: "My daughter did not steal anything, and she's in great trouble. Lisa is too responsible not to come home unless something awful happened to her." Catherine opened her eyes. "Ruby, I hate to ask anything more of you, but for Lisa . . ."

Ruby didn't hesitate. "There's no need for apologies, honey, you know I love Lisa like a sister. Until she comes home—and she will be found and cleared—I'll be spending most of my time here. She may call or try to get a message to you, and someone who can move at the drop of a hat needs to be here in case she does."

"But you have your own life . . ." Catherine said gently.

Ruby's eyes filled with tears. Catherine's health had deteriorated rapidly since she'd last seen her, the night they had gone out to celebrate Lisa's birthday. She clasped Catherine's hand in hers and said firmly, "We're going to find her, Catherine, and I'm hanging around until we do. I won't hear any arguments about it. We'll *find* her."

If she's still alive, Ruby thought, with a silent prayer.

CHAPTER 10

DUNCAN WHISTLED A LIVELY TUNE AS HE MADE HIS WAY to Circenn's chambers. Things had become quite interesting since the lass from the future had arrived. Circenn had willfully broken an oath and lied, and that, in Duncan's mind, was nearly cause for celebration. Even Galan had conceded over breakfast this morning that it was something of a breakthrough. Although Galan had pushed Circenn to fulfill his vow last night, this morning he'd admitted to Duncan that he hadn't seen Circenn Brodie quite so off balance in years. Nor had he seen such a look of fascination on his face as he'd glimpsed when he'd burst into Circenn's chambers last night. Galan had agreed with Duncan that the lass might be the best thing that could have happened to Circenn, shaking up his rigid rules, forcing him to question himself.

Eighteen generations of Douglases had served the immortal laird of Brodie, and in the past few generations there had been much talk and deep concern about his increasing withdrawal. The Douglases were worried about him. In the not-so-distant past, the laird of Brodie had presided over the courts of his eleven manors. But he hadn't done so in over a century, leaving it to the various knights he'd appointed in his place to settle his people's disputes. It used to be that the laird of Brodie had actively ridden out to his villages, talked with and been well acquainted with his people. Now Duncan wasn't sure Circenn could identify one of his own villagers if he stood before him.

For the past hundred years, Circenn had spent most of his time traveling from country to country, fighting other people's wars, and never being touched by any of it. He had only returned to Scotland to join the fight for his motherland when Robert the Bruce had been crowned king by Isabel, Countess of Buchan, at Scone.

Duncan's Uncle Tomas argued that the laird of Brodie needed to wed, that it would draw him back into the joys of life. But Circenn refused to wed again, and they could hardly force him. Duncan's father had settled for trying to get him to be intimate with a woman, but it seemed that Circenn Brodie had taken another of his absurd oaths and sworn off intimacy.

Circenn's origins were lost in the mists of time, and the few times Duncan had questioned him about how he'd come to be immortal, the laird had grown taciturn, refusing to discuss it. But while sharing excessive quantities of whisky with Circenn one night, Duncan had come to understand a bit of why Circenn had decided not to become involved with another woman. Two hundred and twenty-eight years ago, Circenn's second wife had died at the age of forty-eight, and Circenn had admitted, in a whisky-induced confidence, that he simply refused to watch another wife die.

"So, just tup every now and then," Duncan had offered.

Circenn had sighed. "I cannot. I cannot seem to keep my heart from following where my body goes. If I am interested enough in a woman to take her to my bed, I want more of her. I want her out of my bed, too."

Duncan had been shaken by that comment. "So spend time with her until it wears off," he'd said easily.

Circenn had shot him a dark look. "Have you never met a woman with whom it did not wear off? A woman with whom you went to sleep at night, with the scent of her in your nostrils, and woke up in the morning wanting her as badly as you wanted to breathe?"

"Nay," Duncan had assured him. "Lasses are merely lasses. You attribute too much significance to it. It is simply tupping."

But it was not simply tupping to the laird of Brodie, and Duncan knew that. Lately, "simply tupping" wasn't scratching Duncan's endless itch, either. He wondered if it might be related to aging—that as a man grew older, indiscriminate intimacy began to chafe rather than to soothe.

Recently, Duncan had surprised himself by lingering with a wench past the duration of their physical intimacy, prolonging the afterglow, even asking questions besides "When is your husband expected back?"

Damned unnerving was what that was.

He shrugged, pushing the thought from his mind with a more pleasurable musing about Circenn. He had bet Galan his best horse that Circenn couldn't bring himself to kill the woman from the future, and it was a bet he planned to collect on. The laird of Brodie needed to come back to life, and perhaps the unusual lass was the one to help him do it.

* * *

Lisa sat in the window of her room in Circenn's chambers, gazing out at the afternoon. Behind a thick bank of clouds, the sun had passed midpoint and begun its slow descent toward the ocean. She instinctively glanced at her wrist to see what time it was and realized she didn't have her watch on. She tried to recall if she'd had it on at the museum but wasn't certain. She often took it off and put it in her coat pocket when she cleaned, so it wouldn't get wet or dirty. She imagined she must have done so two nights ago and, caught up in her current mess, simply hadn't thought about it since then.

She inhaled deeply, enjoying the crisp, salt air. *I'm at Dunnottar,* she thought, her amazement in no way diminished by twenty-four consecutive hours in the keep. She'd seen pictures of it, and one in particular had been etched into her memory, a black-and-white shot in which the enormous bluff towered up from the misty sea. It had looked a gothic, romantic place, and more than once Lisa had dreamed of someday going to Scotland to see it. She knew from the photo that the bluff was surrounded by ocean on three sides, connected to the mainland by a land bridge that she surmised was behind the keep. She knew also that Dunnottar had been taken by the English repeatedly, then reclaimed by the Scots, and that the Bruce had developed the habit of burning down every Scottish castle he reclaimed to prevent the English from taking it again.

Lisa had studied this period of history, snatching time to read on the shuttle bus, and had mourned the loss of so many glorious castles, but she conceded that the Bruce had been smart to do what he'd done. The Scots had built cleverly defensible castles; when the English took them, their men became nearly invincible. By destroying the stone keeps, the Bruce forced the battles led by Edward II to build their own fortresses, which were not nearly as defensible. While the English wasted an immense amount of time and resources building their own strongholds in Scotland, the Bruce gained time to replenish his forces and rouse the country.

This is 1314 Scotland! Lisa marveled. There would be a decisive battle at Bannockburn only a few months away, in which the Bruce resoundingly defeated England, finally turning the war in Scotland's favor.

A sharp knock on the door interrupted her thoughts. Rising quickly, she tripped over the hem of her gown. At least this one fit her, she thought, but it certainly was uncomfortable. She suspected that part of Circenn's desire to see her properly attired was because she wouldn't be able to climb walls in such clothing. "Coming," she said, snatching a wad of the fabric in her hand. She raised it from the floor, crossed the room, and opened the door.

A man clad in a plaid of gray and cobalt stood in the doorway. His muscular arms were brown and bare, and he had the highly developed musculature of a dancer. There wasn't one ounce of flesh on his body that wasn't necessary. His dark hair was loose around his face and brushed his shoulders. He wore a braid at each temple, and when he grinned he flashed straight white teeth, although his nose looked as if it had been broken a time or two. His alert, mischievous dark eyes studied her, and his sensual mouth curved appreciatively.

"I am Duncan Douglas, lass. Circenn asked me to teach you a bit about our time so you might fit in." His gaze traveled the length of her body. "I see they found a gown that fits you. You look lovely, lass."

"Come in," Lisa said, feeling a bit short of breath. While Duncan didn't compare to Circenn Brodie, she knew a dozen women in her time who would have gone absolutely nuts over him.

Duncan entered and glanced about the room. "By Dagda, it's as tidy as all his chambers." He snorted. "Doona you wish to mess things up in here a bit? Maybe nudge the tapestry so it hangs crooked? Invite spiders in, to weave great drooping cobwebs in the corners and collect dust? Assuming, of course, dust possessed the effrontery to gather in the laird of Brodie's chambers. At times I suspect even the elements dare not cross him." He walked to the perfectly covered bed with the neatly folded throws. Plunging his arms beneath the covers, he pushed them into a ball. "Wouldn't you like to just rumple the bed a bit and defy his sense of order?"

Lisa begrudged a smile. It was reassuring to hear someone poke fun at the disciplined laird of Brodie. The neatness of the room *had* annoyed her. The bed had been so tightly tucked that she'd had to peel the blankets down to sleep in it last night. She'd left them in a tangle, but when she'd returned from descending the wall, it had been perfectly remade, daring her to sleep so wantonly again. "Yes," she agreed.

"Aye," he corrected. "Aye and nay and tup and doona."

"I hardly think I will be using the word tup," she said, embarrassed.

He looked her up and down. "Well, you should. You are a lovely lass, and if ever I met a man who needed to tup, it is Circenn Brodie."

Lisa quickly masked her surprise. She'd perceived the laird as a man who would tup with great frequency. "It almost sounds as if you're encouraging me. Don't you wish to kill me too?"

Duncan snorted and, pushing the blankets into a comfortable pillow, dropped himself onto the bed. "Unlike Circenn and my brothers, I doona see everything in terms of plots and counterplots. Sometimes bad things happen to good people. I consider people innocent, unless proven guilty. Your appearance with the flask does not necessarily signify guilt. Besides, he said you handed the flask over to him when he asked for it." He eyed her thoughtfully. "He said you stumbled upon it in a place that displays artifacts. You must be quite shocked by all of this."

"Thank you," Lisa exclaimed. "You're the only person who has given any thought to how I must feel."

"I always consider how a woman feels," he replied smoothly.

Lisa had no doubt of that, but she sensed that entering a flirtatious conversation with Duncan Douglas might be a street with no U-turns permitted. So she guided the conversation back to Circenn. "He would realize I'm an innocent victim if he ever stopped growling at me and stomping about. All I want is to return home. I didn't choose to come here. I need to be back home."

"Why? Have you a lover there for whom your heart pines?"

"Hardly. But I have responsibilities—"

"Och!" Duncan interrupted, waving a hand. "Doona say that word to me. I loathe that word, I detest that word. It is a foul-tasting word."

"And a very important word," Lisa said. "There are things that I must take care of back in my time. Duncan, you must persuade him to send me back."

"Lass, Circenn cannot send you back. He cannot sift time. He may have some unusual qualities, but sending people through time is not counted among them."

"Would the flask send me back?" she asked quickly, studying Duncan carefully for his reaction. The man's face grew as shuttered as Circenn's had when she'd mentioned it to him.

"Nay," he said succinctly. "And I would not recommend bringing that up to Circenn. He is damned prickly about that flask and you will only succeed in inciting his suspicions should you inquire after it. A large part of what proclaims your innocence to him is that you relinquished it so easily."

Lisa sighed inwardly. Great; so when she went searching for it, if she was caught it would only make her look guilty. "You know of no way I can return home?" she pressed.

Duncan eyed her curiously. "Why do wish to go back so badly? Is it so distasteful here? When I saw you gazing out the window earlier, you were watching the sea with an expression of pleasure. It seemed you found this country beautiful. Was I wrong?"

"No, I mean nay, you weren't wrong, but that's not the point."

"If you will not tell me what it is you are so desperate to return to, I am afraid I cannot feel much sympathy for you," Duncan said.

Lisa expelled a breath and glanced away. She might cry if she started talking about Catherine. "Someone who loves me very much needs me right now, Duncan. I can't fail her."

"Her," he repeated, seeming pleased. "Who?"

Lisa glared at him. "Isn't that enough? Someone is depending on me. I can't let her down!"

Duncan studied her, measuring her. Finally he spread his hands in the air. "It grieves me, lass, but I cannot help you. I know of no way for you to return to your time. I suggest you confide whatever your plight is in Circenn—"

"But you said he couldn't return me," Lisa said quickly.

"Nay, but he is a fine listener."

"Ha! A turnip would listen better," she said and rolled her eyes.

"Judge not the man you see on the surface, lass. There are depths and there are depths to Circenn Brodie. Think you he will kill you?"

Lisa saw in his dark eyes the assurance that Circenn Brodie would not. "He can't bring himself to do it, can he?"

"What do you think?"

"I think he abhors the thought of it. Although he stomps and glowers, I think he's more angry at himself than me most of the time."

"Clever lass," Duncan said. "He is indeed angry because he's torn between oaths. I doona believe he truly thinks you are a spy, or guilty of something. If anything, he's angry at himself for swearing the oath in the first place. Circenn has never broken his word before, and it does not sit well with him. It will take him time to accept what he perceives as a failure. Once he does so, he will not hold any oath above your life, consequences be damned."

"Well, that's a relief," Lisa said. It occurred to her that perhaps Circenn and his friend were merely playing "good cop, bad cop" but she didn't think so. She regarded Duncan curiously. "Don't you have questions about what my time is like? I would if I were you."

Duncan's expression turned serious. "I am a man who is content with his lot in life, lass. I have no wish to know the future, no desire to meddle. A small slice of a small life is good enough for me. Such things are best left alone. The less I know about your time, the more we can work to help you adapt to my time. Speaking of your century would only keep it alive for you, and, lass, since I know of no way to return you, I would advise against clinging to any memories."

Lisa took a deep breath and exhaled it slowly. "Then teach me, Duncan," she said sadly. "But I will be honest with you: I have no intention of giving up. If there is a way home for me, I will find it."

* * *

Circenn paced the courtyard, kicking irritably at the loose stones. The terrace needed to be repaired, he noted, as did the keep itself. He was tired of living in half-burned-out castles, not because of the lack of amenities—that scarcely bothered him—but because the general chaos and disrepair of Dunnottar too accurately mirrored his own condition.

He eyed the cornerstone of the keep. During the last siege, the great stone that supported the tower had been pushed off center, causing the wall above it to list dangerously. And he felt just like that—his cornerstone was askew and his entire fortress dangerously weakened.

No more, he thought. He had uttered his last lie, broken his last rule.

He had given matters serious consideration and decided that Duncan's loophole indeed protected him from actually breaking his oath. He would accept that slight bending of his rules. Should Adam someday show up, he would simply point out to him that he hadn't killed her *yet*.

But lying about who she was, and entertaining the notion of becoming physically intimate with her . . . ah, those were unacceptable. He would not utter one more lie, nor would he permit himself to be tempted by her.

Sighing, he headed for the outer courtyard, resolved to

take one of the feistiest stallions out for a punishing ride. As he loped down the rocky slope, he noted a cloud of dust spiraling beyond the land bridge behind the keep, at the same moment as his guard cried a warning.

Narrowing his eyes, he studied the approaching dust cloud. His body tensed, eager for a battle. It would do good to fight right now, to conquer, to reaffirm his identity as a warrior. As the first riders crested the ridge, the adrenaline flooding his body altered swiftly to dismay, and then to something akin to desperation.

The banner of Robert the Bruce was splayed between his standard bearers, announcing his arrival to relieve Circenn's men and send them home to Brodie.

And as for his last lie having been told, he thought sardonically, *Hmph!* Here came the lass's "cousin" himself.

CHAPTER 11

CIRCENN RODE LIKE A MAN POSSESSED—OR PERHAPS, HE thought, aggrieved, more accurately *obsessed* with a long-legged, unpredictable woman—to intercept the Bruce before he could reach the keep. As he rode, he marveled over how his one wee decision not to kill her yet had created dozens of problems. Each time he tried to address one of those problems, he succeeded only in creating a new set of problems. Committed thus far, he could not turn back. He dared not stop perpetuating the lies he'd begun without exposing her to risk.

Robert raised his hand in greeting and quickly broke off from his troops, his personal guard falling back a few paces, but not leaving his side. Directing the bulk of his men toward the keep, he kicked his horse into a gallop.

Circenn's gaze swept over the king's guard. Instinctively, he dropped his chin, looking up from beneath his brows. No hint of a smile touched his face. In warrior's language, the look—head lowered, eyes unwaveringly fixed—was a challenge. Circenn assumed the posture subconsciously, his blood responding to the two men flanking his king. It was the simple and timeless instinct of a wolf when confronted by another mighty wolf stalking the same territory. Nothing personal, just a need to assert his masculinity and superiority, he thought with an inward grin.

When Circenn had last seen Robert, the king had not had these two men with him. Their presence meant that the deepest Highland clans were now fully in the forefront of the war. Circenn was pleased that his king merited two of the legendary warriors to protect him. They were massive men with eyes of preternatural blue marking them as what they were—Berserkers.

"Circenn." Robert greeted him with a smile. "It has been too long since last we met. I see Dunnottar is still the ruin I left last fall." His gaze played across the overgrown landscape, the piles of rocks, the blackened stones of the keep.

"Welcome, milord. I hope you have come to tell us it is time to join forces with your men," Circenn said pointedly. "Since Jacques de Molay was burned a fortnight past, my Templars are seething with the need to do battle. I doona know how much longer I can placate them with minor missions."

Robert shook his head, a wry smile curving his mouth. "You are as impatient as ever, Circenn. I'm certain you'll manage to rein in their tempers, as you always do. Your Templars serve me better in their stealthy, circumspect missions than on the front for the now. The dozen I've slipped into my troops have done remarkable things. I trust you will keep the rest ready for my command." He gestured to his guard. "I believe you know Niall and Lulach McIllioch."

Circenn inclined his head. As his gaze moved over the McIllioch brothers, he smiled with anticipation. One move from either of them and he would be off his mount and at their throats. Admittedly the brawl would end in laughter, but every time he saw these two men he reacted the same way. They were the strongest warriors he'd ever trained with, and fighting with them was as exhilarating as it was futile. He could no more take a Berserker than a Berserker could take him. Their fights ended in a draw every time. Of course, that was one on one. Circenn had no doubt that if ever both of them combined forces they would bring him down with little effort unless he used magic.

"Brodie," Lulach said with a nod.

"Perhaps we'll have time for swordplay before you ride to Brodie," Niall offered. "I think you could use another lesson," he provoked.

"And you think you can teach me one?" He'd love nothing more than to channel his frustration into a challenging fight, but his mind was consumed with the problem at hand. "Perhaps later." He dismissed them from his thoughts and turned to Robert. "May we speak in private, milord?"

The Bruce nodded to Niall and Lulach. "Go on with you. I am well guarded with Brodie. I will join you shortly."

Circenn kneed his horse around and he and Robert rode in silence to the edge of the cliff. Robert looked out to the sea, breathing deeply of the chill, salty air. The waves crashed against the rocks below, sending silver plumes of foam spraying up the cliffs.

"I love this place. It is wild and full of power. Each time I visit Dunnottar I feel it seeping into my veins and leave renewed."

"This bluff does have that effect," Circenn agreed.

"But perhaps what I sense is nothing more than the ghostly courage of the many men who have died defending this coveted rock." Robert was silent for a moment, and

Circenn knew he was brooding over the numbers of Scots-men who had fallen and would continue to fall before their country was free.

Circenn waited until Robert roused himself from his thoughts. "Yet it does not compare with Castle Brodie, does it? You must be eager to return."

"More eager to join the battle," Circenn said quickly. Weary of holding critical sites, tired of protecting and run-ning messages, he needed to bury his frustration in the all-consuming heat of battle.

"You know I need you in other places, Circenn. You also know the Templars are hunted for the price on their heads. Although I have given them sanctuary, parading them out in force would invite an attack before I'm ready. Mine have shaved their beards and doffed their tunics, masquerading as Scots. Do yours still cling to their ways?"

"Aye, they have a hard time breaking any of their rules. But I might be able to persuade them, if they thought they would be permitted to wage war. We could help take back some of the castles," Circenn pointed out irritably.

"You help me best precisely where I have you. I will summon your private forces to battle when I am ready and no sooner. But I doona wish to argue, Circenn. Tell me what is weighing upon your mind so heavily that you rode out to greet me with unusually grim countenance, even for you."

"I need to request a favor from you, milord."

Robert quirked a brow at him. "Formality between us in private, Circenn? With our past?"

Circenn smiled faintly. "Robert, I need ask of you a boon, and that you not question me, but simply grant it."

Robert angled his horse closer to Circenn's and placed a hand on his shoulder. "Do you mean trust you as you trusted me so many years ago when I'd fought for Long-shanks against my own motherland? Do you mean grant you my faith as unwaveringly as you granted me yours when you had no reason to believe I wouldn't cross the lines and go back to England again?" Robert's mouth curved in a bitter smile. "Circenn, not too long ago you gave me reason to believe in myself. When you came at my summons I knew naught of you but that you were ru-mored to be the fiercest warrior in all the lands. I believed that with you behind me, I could regain Scotland's free-dom. You came to me, and you gave me your fealty when I did not deserve it. You had no reason to trust me—yet you did, and in the strength of your faith I rediscovered my own. Since that day I have come to believe that I have earned a place in this land again. Ask. Ask me and it is yours."

Robert's words had the impact of a fist in Circenn's gut. His king gave him his faith and trust, and he was asking Circenn to help him break a vow and perpetuate a lie. What would Robert say if he knew the truth?

Circenn expelled a breath. "It is a woman," he said fi-nally. "I need you to claim her as your cousin, and when you meet her to pretend it is the renewal of an old acquain-tance. Cousin by blood—Lisa MacRobertson."

Robert laughed. His eyes sparkled and he whistled. "With pleasure. It is long past time you took a wife and had sons to continue your line. This land needs your blood to fight for our freedom."

"It is not that kind of—"

"Please!" Robert raised his hands. "I see in your eyes what kind of situation it is. I see passion I have seen only in battle. I also see discomfort, which tells me you have deep feelings about this matter. And since I haven't seen any feeling in you for far too long, I am pleased. It is done. I am eager to reacquaint myself with my 'cousin.' "

Deep feelings indeed, Circenn thought morosely. *Deep disgust with myself.* But if Robert needed to believe there was marriage interest in order to acknowledge her, so be it. The end result was what mattered. In a few hours, he, his men, and Lisa would be on their way to Brodie, and Robert would have no more involvement in the issue. She need never know he had secured the king's cooperation by leading him to believe he cared for her. Circenn remained silent, wallowing in his guilt, ashamed that his king trusted him so readily.

"Do you recall when we were in the caves in the valley of North Esk?" Robert asked, his gaze on the horizon.

"Aye."

"It was the blackest hour of my life. I had warred against my own motherland for wealth, land, and Longshanks' promise that he would spare my clan. Whether from sharing too much whisky with you, or inspired by a moment of divine clarity, I saw myself as I was—a traitor to my own people. Do you recall the spider?"

Circenn smiled. *Did he recall the spider?* He'd coaxed it in, compelled it to perform its feat before Robert's eyes as he lay healing from battle wounds, and in watching the spider try time and again to weave a web across a span of futility, Robert had remembered his own strength and determination. When the spider had succeeded on the seventh try, Robert the Bruce had dragged his battered body and soul from the damp soil of the cave and shaken his fist toward the sky, and the battle to liberate Scotland had begun in earnest.

Robert regarded him intently. "I have never seen a spider of that kind, before or since. One almost wonders if it was a natural occurrence. I do not question some things, Circenn. Now take me to your woman."

*   *   *

After Duncan left her chamber, Lisa waited three minutes, impatiently tapping her foot, then ventured into the hall, determined to track down the flask. She'd made it no more than halfway down the corridor when Duncan came storming back up the stairs.

"I thought you'd left," she exclaimed.

"I did. Then I looked out the window. We have a problem and I suggest you pack."

"Pack what? I don't have anything!"

"Circenn's things. Put them in the chests and the men will load them. We'll be riding out very soon. As soon as we can possibly manage. As soon as I can sneak you out of the castle," he muttered, glancing nervously about.

"To where?" she exclaimed. "What's wrong?"

Duncan stalked to her side, took her none-too-gently by the arm, and steered her back down the hall and into Circenn's chambers. "I am not going to ask what you were doing outside of your room. I feel better not knowing. But, lass, as I glanced out the window I saw your 'cousin' arriving to relieve our post at Dunnottar. Unless you wish to encounter him and reminisce over old times that never happened, I suggest you keep out of sight and do as I tell you. Would you please indulge me and exercise blind obedience now? It may keep you alive."

"Would someone really try to harm me if they knew I was from the future?"

Duncan's expression was glum. "The Templars doona trust women, they doona care for Druid magic, and they feel there is never a reason to break an oath. Should they

discover Circenn lied about you, they will lose faith in
him, and if they do that, he will not be in much of a position to protect you. Not to mention the fact that the Bruce
will also wonder who you are. Then it will come out that
you are from the future, and och—I doona even wish to
think about it. We must hide you."

"I'll pack," she offered hastily.

"Good lass." Duncan whirled around and raced back
down the corridor.

* * *

Lisa finished packing in fifteen minutes, having simply
thrown everything that wasn't too heavy to move into the
many chests scattered about the room. Afterward, she
paced between the door and the window for another ten
minutes, trying to convince herself that she must not, under any circumstances, leave the room.

It wasn't working. In the keep just below her room,
there were legends walking, talking, planning. Unable to
resist the lure of the voices of history, she slipped from the
chamber and followed the noise to the balcony that encircled the Greathall. With no roof, the hall was freezing but
the men didn't seem to notice, nor did any of them look
up, as they were far too engrossed in battle plans. She
lurked abovestairs, surreptitiously watching from behind
the balustrade, prepared to duck and cower at any moment. She knew Duncan would strangle her if he had an
inkling of the risk she was taking, but the lure was irresistible: How many twenty-first-century women could lay
claim to watching Robert the Bruce plan the ousting of
England, battle by battle?

Not that anyone would believe her, but there he was,

standing below her, pacing, bending over maps and gesturing angrily, orating, breathing, inspiring. His voice, rich and strong, was persuasive and full of passion. God in heaven, she was watching Robert the Bruce plan to vanquish England! Chills raced up her spine.

"Milady, would you like to reacquaint yourself with your cousin?" a man said behind her.

Lisa winced. She hadn't considered that someone might venture upstairs, or have *been* upstairs before she'd come out. She'd been so worried about someone beneath her looking up that she hadn't devoted any attention to the stairs. This man must have slipped up while her fascinated gaze had been focused on the king. Heart hammering, she turned slowly to see who had discovered her spying, hoping that whoever it was could be persuaded not to tell Duncan or anyone else.

It was one of the knights she'd glimpsed in the courtyard earlier as she'd watched them train. He sank swiftly to one knee. "Milady," he murmured, "I am Armand Berard, a knight in your protector's service. Shall I escort you belowstairs?"

The knight rose to his feet and she noted that although they were identical in height, his neck and shoulders were as thick as a football player's. His chestnut-brown hair was close cropped; his gray eyes were serious and intelligent. A thick beard covered his jaw, and she glimpsed the flash of a crimson cross beneath his multiple tunics.

"No . . . er . . . nay, I am fair certain he's too busy for me."

"Robert the Bruce is never too busy for clan," he said. "It is one of the many things I admire about him. Come." He extended his hand. "I will take you to him."

"Nay!" she exclaimed, then added more gently, "Circenn advised me to stay in my room and he'll be upset should he discover I've disobeyed. He said he would see to it I had time to speak with my cousin later."

"He will not be upset with you. Never fear, milady. Come. The Bruce will be eager to see you again, and smitten by the king's pleasure, the laird of Brodie will forgive your transgression. It is only natural you would be overjoyed to see your cousin again. Come."

He latched a hand around her wrist and leaned over the balustrade.

"Milord!" he called down to the Greathall. "I bring your cousin to you!"

Robert the Bruce looked up, a curious expression on his face.

CHAPTER 12

LISA FROZE. THIS WAS IT, SHE RUED. CIRCENN BRODIE might have permitted her to live, but her curiosity had just delivered the fatal blow. First, her curiosity had led her to try to get a job in a museum, so she could learn. Then her curiosity had compelled her to open the chest and touch the flask; and finally, her curiosity had led her from her room, into the middle of a deadly situation. She was doomed.

She flinched when Armand Berard took her hand and looped it through his elbow. Her shoulders slumped in defeat, her chin slipped a notch. *Never let anyone take your dignity, Lisa,* Catherine whispered in her mind. *Sometimes it is all one has.*

Her chin shot back up. If she was going to her death, by God, she would do it regally. During all her suffering her mother had never relinquished her dignity, and Lisa would do no less. Inclining her head, she smoothed her gown and straightened her spine.

It seemed to take forever to descend the few dozen stairs. The hall was jammed with Templars and the Bruce's travel-weary men, and nearly a hundred warriors gazed curiously up at her, including the furious glare of one warlord who definitely looked like he wanted her dead, and the inquisitive gaze of the king of Scotland.

She pasted a defiant smile on her lips. As they reached the bottom, the dark-haired king broke away from the crowd. He moved toward her, his arms extended.

"Lisa," he exclaimed. "How lovely to see you again. You have blossomed under Circenn's care, but I suspected you would."

He wrapped her in a fierce hug, and her face was buried in a thick beard that smelled of wood smoke from camping in the open country. She pressed close, concealing her stunned expression in his cheek. Circenn must have gotten to him first, she realized. He squeezed her so tightly, she nearly squeaked. When he fondly patted her rump, she did squeak, and tried to draw away. He was grinning at her.

Close to her ear, he whispered, "Doona fash yourself, lassie. Circenn told me all. I am pleased he has chosen a wife."

Wife? She squeaked again as her knees weakened. *Surely that oversized, scowling barbarian didn't think she would marry him just to stay alive?* She glanced over the Bruce's shoulder and saw Circenn standing five paces behind him, eyeing her with a glare that wordlessly instructed, *Obey. Behave.*

On second thought . . . "Did he tell you that? He promised me he wouldn't announce it yet," she lied glibly. If that was what Circenn had told him, and it would keep her alive, she'd go along with it for the moment. There would be ample time to amend things later.

"Nay, lass, he didn't say it. His eyes did."

Whose eyes has he been looking at? she wondered, because the only eyes she'd seen held murder in their depths.

The Bruce smiled broadly. "May you be as fertile as the

hare. We need dozens of his sons in this land." He laughed
and patted her abdomen.

Lisa blushed, concerned that he might pat her breasts
and inquire about her nursing abilities. She'd just been patted more familiarly by the king of Scotland than she'd
been touched by any man, save Circenn.

"Does your clan breed well?"

"Uh . . . aye," she said brightly, with another blush.

The Bruce hooked an arm behind him and drew Circenn
forward, hugging them together. For a moment, her cheekbone was smashed against Circenn's chest. After a few moments of the most uncomfortable group hug she'd ever been
subjected to, the Bruce flung back his head and yelled, "I
give you my cousin, Lisa MacRobertson!"

The Bruce stepped back, nudging them closer together.
He took Lisa's hand and curled her fingers into her palm,
making a fist. Ignoring her look of confusion, he placed
her balled fist in Circenn's large hand. Lisa's gaze flew to
Circenn's face and she saw the fury there, though the king
seemed oblivious to it.

"It is with great pleasure I give this lass, my beloved
cousin, hand-in-fist, to my favored laird and knight in our
blessed cause, Circenn Brodie, along with four additional
manors outlying his demesne. The wedding will be at
Brodie when we meet there in three months' time. *Hail the
future mistress of Brodie!*" Robert roared, smiling at them
both.

Circenn's hand clenched around her fist. As the hall
erupted into cheers, the look he turned on her was ven-
omous.

"Don't you dare look at me like that! I didn't tell him
that," she hissed. "*You're* the one who told him that."

Circenn took advantage of the momentary chaos and

pulled her into his arms. His mouth to her hair, he growled in a brogue thickened by anger, "I did *not* tell him that. The king decided, wholly independent of me, so, lass, if you truly can be leaving this century, I suggest you set your mind to determining how to do so, long before the third moon passes. Or you'll be finding yourself wed to me, and I promise, lass, you will not fare well for it."

"A kiss to seal it, Brodie!" the Bruce cried.

Only Lisa saw the fierce look on his face before he kissed her punishingly.

* * *

Galan found Duncan lying on the floor of the kitchen, clutching his sides. Every few seconds he drew a deep, wheezing breath, stuttered, then lost himself again in waves of laughter.

Galan watched him repeat the ridiculous sequence several times before nudging him with the toe of his boot. "Would you *stop* it," he said disgustedly.

Duncan gasped, pounding his chest with his fist, then collapsed again into guffaws. "D-did—*ah-hahaha*—did you see his f-face?" Duncan roared, holding his stomach.

Galan's lips twitched, and he bit the bottom one to remain serious. "This is a fankle, Duncan," Galan chastised. "Now he's nearly handfasted to the wench."

Duncan's only response was another roar of laughter. "N-nearly? H-he *is*!"

"I doona know what you think is so amusing about this. Circenn is going to be furious."

"But he's st-stuck!" Duncan gasped between near-sobs of laughter. Then he rose to his feet, took several great breaths, and finally managed to subdue his laughter for the moment, yet the corners of his mouth twitched furiously.

"Doona you see what must have happened, Galan? Circenn must have requested the Bruce acknowledge her, and the king—knowing Circenn is of Brude descent—assumed Circenn wished her to be of royal alliance so he might wed her. So, Robert took it a little further, kindly thinking he was clearing the way for the woman to be accepted as his wife. Thinking he was giving Circenn exactly what he wanted."

"Oh, really?" a cool voice said.

Duncan and Galan both sobered to immediate attention.

"Milord." They nodded respectfully.

"You underestimate me," Robert the Bruce said softly.

"Where's Circenn?" Galan asked, glancing warily behind the Bruce.

"I left Circenn in the Greathall, accepting congratulations with his new lady on his arm," Robert said smugly. "Think you I doona know the man has taken one of his ridiculous oaths not to wed?"

Duncan gazed at the king admiringly. "You clever bastard."

"Duncan!" Galan roared. "You doona address the king as such!"

Robert raised his hand and grinned. "Your brother has called me worse, as I have him, besotted with whisky and wenches. He and I understand each other well, Galan. In fact, it was while wenching with your brother at Edinburgh that we discussed this very concern. It is no longer a concern, is it? I fixed what most of your clan has not been able to fix for years." Robert looked enormously pleased with himself.

Galan glared at Duncan. "That's where you went when you said you were getting supplies? Wenching and drinking with the king? Have you no sense of responsibility?"

Duncan smiled innocently. "Robert needed to alleviate some tension, and I know of no better way. And while we were being entertained most grandly by a few lasses, we discussed the fact that Circenn was getting no closer to making sons for Scotland. As Robert pointed out—he has managed to fix what none of us could. I, for one, am grateful."

Galan shook his head. "Circenn would kill us all if he suspected this wasn't a vast misunderstanding."

"But he'll never know, will he?" Robert said calmly.

Duncan burst into laughter again, and after a brief, startled look, Galan joined him.

* * *

"I am *not* marrying you," Circenn rumbled behind a flawless smile.

"I didn't *ask* you to," Lisa hissed back, a smile of spun glass bowing her lips.

With brittle displays of teeth, they glared at each other, while accepting congratulations from the various men standing in the hall. Each time they had a moment of near privacy, or their mouths and ears were pressed close together, one of them hissed at the other. To the room at large, they looked like a happily whispering couple.

"Doona think this changes a thing," he snapped, lips tautly stretched over his teeth.

"I'm not the one who told him a lie," Lisa snapped back, certain she appeared to be snarling. She smiled with effort.

"Congratulations, milord." Armand Berard clapped Circenn's shoulder.

"Thank you," Circenn said, beaming as he forcefully pounded Armand on the shoulder.

Armand's brows dipped. "Why did you not tell us this morn, Circenn, when you told us who she was?"

Circenn didn't even pause before spilling another lie. Och, but they were coming fast and furious, with shocking ease. He managed a self-effacing smile. "I wasn't certain the king wished it announced, but it seems he was eager."

"Milady." Armand bowed low over her hand and kissed it. "We are pleased Circenn has chosen to settle down and begin a family. Although those of our order do not wed, we believe if a man is not going to take an oath of celibacy, he should take a wife. It keeps him humble and inclined toward sobriety."

Lisa smiled brightly at Armand. *Humble indeed,* she thought. There wasn't a humble bone in Circenn Brodie's body. Although, dislike him as she may, she wouldn't have minded searching for one.

"Where did he go?" Circenn growled, the moment Armand melted into the crowd.

"Armand?" Lisa asked blankly. "He's right there." She pointed to his retreating back.

"*Rrroberrrt!* That traitorous bastard." His burr was so thick on the name that that the *r*s were a growl with a weak *t* at the end.

"How should I know where the king went?" Lisa rolled her eyes. "I'm the last person who ever knows what's going on around here."

"This entire fiasco is your fault for leaving your chamber! Did I not tell you to remain in your chamber? How many times did I tell you to remain in your chamber? Did I tell you at least a dozen times in the past two days *not to leave your chamber*?"

"Repeating the same question three times, in slightly different ways, does not make me more inclined to answer you. Don't talk to me as if I'm a child. And don't even think you're going to blame this one on me." Lisa sniffed and averted her face. "I certainly would never have told anyone I was marrying you. Leaving my chamber didn't get us betrothed. *You* did that all by yourself."

Circenn studied her through narrowed eyes, then lowered his head menacingly near hers. "Perhaps I will wed you, lass. Do you know that a wife must obey her husband in all things?" he purred against her ear. He stopped scowling abruptly. "Renaud!" He clapped another Templar on the shoulder and smiled painfully.

"We are pleased, milord," Renaud de Vichiers said formally.

"Thank you," Circenn replied. "If you will excuse me, Renaud, my betrothed is feeling a bit faint. She grows swiftly overtaxed." With a dismissive nod to Renaud, he whisked Lisa away from the crowd and pushed her into a corner of the hall, uncaring what anyone thought. For the moment, they were as alone as they could be in the crowded room.

"I do *not* grow swiftly overtaxed. I am the picture of calm, considering all I've been through. And I am *not* marrying you," she said defiantly.

His response chilled her blood: "In three months' time, lass, neither of us will have any choice. Now I will escort you to your room, and you will remain in it this time."

Glibly informing the room at large that his wife-to-be was overexcited by the commotion—a fib that Lisa resented because it made her appear fragile—Circenn guided her abovestairs, his hand a steely vise on her arm. He stopped at her door and informed her that if she left the room, he would ensure that she had extreme cause to regret it.

She opened the door and began to step in, when he suddenly spun her around into his arms.

Without a word, he closed his mouth over hers brutally.

Too shocked to resist, Lisa stood motionless, her lips parting at the insistence of his tongue. He darted it between her lips in blatant mimicry of sexual play, probing firmly, receding, only to thrust again. She tipped back her head, her body sparking to life. He was angry, she could feel it in the bruising crush of his lips, and it fed her own anger.

Then it occurred to her that kissing was quite a useful and fascinating way to express anger, so she worked diligently at putting every bit of her irritation and displeasure into her response. She bit, she nipped, she fought his tongue with hers. When his tongue withdrew, she followed it with hers and sucked it hard back into her mouth, priding herself on how nicely she won *that* battle. When he kissed her so deeply she couldn't breathe around it, she dropped her hands to his waist, then dipped lower, just to show him she was completely in control. *Tight, muscled ass;* the thought was accompanied by a surge of excitement as she imagined his powerful hips tensing in a timeless rhythm.

When his teeth nudged against hers, a moan blossomed in her throat. She brought up her hands and plunged them into his hair, sliding her fingers through black silk. Her fingers moved down the nape of his neck, then she wrapped her arms around him and kissed him back so uninhibitedly that he stiffened abruptly, stepped back, and gazed at her with a startled expression.

Briefly, he looked pleased, then his eyes narrowed swiftly. "I doona like you, and I will *not* tolerate you complicating my life."

"Ditto," she clipped through swollen lips.

"Then we understand each other," he said.

"Mm-hmm," she said. "Perfectly."

"Good."

They stared at each other. She noticed that his lips were slightly fuller. *She* had done that. Her own lips felt tingly, warm, and most assuredly not finished expressing her anger.

"Doona forget who's in control in this castle, lass," he snarled before stalking off down the hallway.

If that was how he asserted his control, she might just have to challenge his authority more often.

RISING . . .

What is your substance, whereof are you made,
That millions of strange shadows on you tend?

—Shakespeare, *Sonnet 53*

CHAPTER 13

THE JOURNEY FROM DUNNOTTAR TO INVERNESS AND from there to Castle Brodie would live long in Lisa's memory. With dismay she tallied each day of their journey that ticked by, knowing it was one more day she was losing in the future, and the thought made her miserable. She feared that the farther they rode from Dunnottar, the slimmer her chances became of returning home. She knew it probably wasn't true, because if anything had the power to return her, it was the flask, and she suspected Circenn wouldn't permit it out of his care. Still, each step she took deeper into his lush, wild land made her feel she was moving a step farther away from her own life, farther into a realm in which she had no control and might lose herself entirely.

Shortly after Circenn had deposited her in her room—or more accurately left her reeling in the hallway—he'd sent Duncan and Galan to whisk her out of the keep, and the three of them had ridden off ahead. Circenn and the rest of his entourage had joined them hours later. She was acutely aware that the knights studied her far too intently for her comfort. They were not men she wished to slip up around, so she spoke as little as possible, choosing her words with great caution.

The first night they journeyed across Scotland, a nearly full moon hung above the shadowy ridges and valleys, and the thunder of more than a hundred horses carrying packs and heavily muscled men was deafening. The ground trembled as they galloped the hills. Cold despite the thick plaid covering her gown, she was awed by the miles of untouched, open country. Although her body ached after riding only a few hours, she would have ridden all night to savor the untamed vista.

She was of a far different mind the next morning, though, and wouldn't have ridden at all had it been left to her discretion. She'd arrogantly thought she was in good condition, but riding a horse was quite different from rappelling or tumbling, and she quickly realized that her athletic skills had better trained her for falling off the horse properly than for staying on it with any degree of finesse.

The second thing that lingered in her mind was Circenn Brodie, who rode beside her the entire way, not speaking, but watching every move she made, every expression. She hid her discomfort well, determined not to reveal any weakness to the indefatigable warrior. Since leaving Dunnottar the man had scarcely uttered two words to her, had not so much as touched her to help her dismount; she could tell he was seething. He moved away from her side occasionally to talk with his men in low voices.

In every village they passed through, she noted the people heralded Circenn as befitted royalty, and he comported himself with regal reserve. If he appeared a bit detached, none of the villagers seemed to mind. Children gazed at him with awe; old men clapped him on the shoulder and smiled proudly; the gazes of young warriors followed him admiringly. It was clear that the man was a legend in his own time. With each admiring, flirtatious glance flashed by a woman beneath lowered lids, Lisa felt a surge of irritation. In more than one village, women found a reason to approach him and try to lure him off "to discuss a most private matter, milord." She was relieved to see that none of them succeeded. However, she wasn't certain if it was because he genuinely wasn't interested or because they were riding so hard. They rarely slept more than a few hours each evening, but she was used to inadequate sleep from working two jobs.

The third thing that weighed upon her mind was the flask, which she now knew that Circenn had with him, because she'd caught a glimpse of it one night as he rummaged in his satchel. Unfortunately he was such a light sleeper that trying to get the flask while he was asleep would be a fool's venture. Better to bide her time, waiting for the right moment.

It was the last night of their ride, however, that would live longest in her memory—the night they approached the perimeter of Castle Brodie. Throughout the physically punishing journey, Lisa had worried about Catherine, wondering who was taking care of her, weeping silently under cover of darkness. All the while Scotland was subtly invading her veins, and despite her fear and feelings of helplessness, she knew she was falling in love.

With a country.

It was too early for spring in the Highlands, but she could sense the dormant earth waiting to burst into bloom. Although she knew she must find a way home, part of her ached to remain in the past long enough to glimpse the valleys filled with heather, to watch the golden eagles fly above the mountains, to see the carpet of bracken and brush turn lush and bud with spring.

The final night of their journey, the weather warmed slightly. Due to exhaustion, her emotions bubbled dangerously near the surface, and in the past few hours she'd gone from euphoria over the beauty of the Highland night to utter terror at what her future might hold. Lisa wasn't certain what she had expected of Castle Brodie but it wasn't the elegant stone structure she'd caught glimpses of from the tops of distant hills, as she'd strained in her saddle to see as much as possible.

They descended into a valley, and the castle was again hidden from sight. The silence was broken only by the beat of hooves against the sod and the occasional sighs of men glad to be returning home. The sky was deep royal blue, minutes from becoming black—it was "gloaming," their word for twilight. The path they were traveling climbed a ridge that stretched across the horizon, and beyond it lay Circenn's home. As they topped the crest, her gaze swept up and she sighed at the sight that greeted her.

Castle Brodie was as magnificent as the man who owned the palatial structure. Brilliantly lit by torches, it seemed something from a dream. Beyond an arched gate that gleamed palely in the moonlight rose a structure of square towers and turrets, high spires, and low walkways connecting the various wings. A great wall encircled the estate, and with the gate shut, it would be an insurmountable fortress. Guards stalked the parapets and paced the perimeter. She could just imagine the dozens of servants and their families inside, scurrying to and fro, their children's laughter filling the air. Safe. Warm and surrounded by clan, governed by a warlord who committed his life to protecting them.

Lisa felt a twinge of impossible longing. What a life this was. Someday he would wed in truth and carry his wife home to this magical place. This was his world—this magnificent castle shining pale gray in the moonlight, these men surrounding him who fought on his command and would lay down their lives for him. *What an incredible world to be part of,* she thought.

She felt torn. Her need to get back home battled an overwhelming desire to belong in a place like this, to be surrounded by family.

Exhausted beyond the ability to deceive herself any longer, Lisa confronted a truth she'd been trying desperately to avoid.

She knew she had no real future to look forward to in either place or time.

*　*　*

Circenn cornered Duncan and Galan in the stables of Castle Brodie. He backed them against a wall with the sheer force of his glare.

"I heard you laughing, Duncan," he accused, a muscle twitching in his jaw. Circenn had been simmering for the past week, seeing the amused light in Duncan's eyes, hearing his laughter, and unable to reprimand him in front of the Templars. Already his Templars had directed curious glances his way, puzzled by his sullen temper on the journey.

Duncan was the portrait of innocence. "If you mean on the trip here, Galan and I were merely reciting bawdy poems, nothing more."

"Galan?" Circenn snorted disbelievingly. "Galan could not recite a bawdy poem if the outcome of a battle depended upon it."

"I could," Galan protested. "I am not quite as bad as you make me out to be."

"Do you realize that I am utterly compromised? Do you realize that I made a pledge to Adam to kill her and to Robert to marry her?" Circenn demanded irritably.

Duncan's amusement didn't diminish one whit. "Considering that Adam isn't allowed to visit you without invitation—that was part of your deal, if you recall—it sounds to me as if you'd better wed the lass. She could be long dead by the time Adam comes to bother you again. You said sometimes fifty years pass without him troubling you."

Circenn stiffened. *She could be dead. . . .* He didn't like the thought of her dead, either by his hand or by natural causes. Even if he never fulfilled his oath, she would die long before he would. As everything else, passing away before his eyes. As he would one day bury Duncan, whose hair would gray, bones would brittle, and eyes would fog by time. He would weep over the loss of such irreverence and enthusiasm for life, a heart so full of joy. And he would bury Galan, and Robert and his servants and maids. And his horses, and any pets he might be foolish enough to love.

For that reason, it had been centuries since he'd permitted himself to sleep with a favored wolfhound lying across the foot of his bed.

Unlike the mortal span most men lived, Circenn would encounter death not a dozen times, but a thousand, making him the greater fool if he cared about anything. Perhaps that was why Adam Black was so detached; after a thousand deaths he'd simply quit caring.

Circenn turned without another word, leaving his trusted advisers gaping after him.

* * *

Lisa stood in the middle of the courtyard, drinking in the sights. After a growled "Doona move," Circenn had gone tearing off after Duncan and Galan the moment they'd come through the gate. She'd been perfectly content not to move, because it meant she could direct all her awed attention to the castle. Knights surged around her in waves, tending to their horses and unpacking gear, while she scanned the elegant lines of the medieval castle.

The rectangular estate was enclosed by a mighty stone wall. In the northeast corner, a chapel was situated amid a small grove of trees. In the northwest corner, near the main wall, in which the gate was located, was a series of low outbuildings she assumed garrisoned the soldiers. She couldn't see past the castle, as it sprawled nearly the width of the walled estate. The perimeter wall tumbled up slopes and valleys, extending as far as she could see, intermittently set with guard towers every fifty yards or so.

When Circenn took her by the elbow, a few moments later, she started.

"Come," he said quietly.

She looked at him sharply. Instead of looking angry as he had during the week-long ride, now he looked sad. And it *bothered* her that he looked sad. Anger she could deal with, but sadness brought out her nurturing instincts and tempted her to draw him aside, cradle his face gently, and ask what was wrong. Get to know him. Soothe him.

She shook her head at her own idiocy. This was one man who clearly did not need her tenderness and nurturing.

They entered the main door of the castle and he moved

away from her again, into the midst of servants, quietly giving orders. Lisa stood in the Greathall, pivoting slowly, her mouth open. *Wow.* Over the past week, she'd begun assimilating some of their archaic expressions, but under some circumstances, only a thoroughly modern "wow" would do. Dunnottar had been a ruin; Castle Brodie was a medieval castle at its finest. The Greathall was vast, with a high ceiling and five hearths—two each on the east and west walls of the room, and a central hearth that looked as if it had long been inactive. The walls were hung with enormous tapestries, and a long, ornately carved table with dozens of chairs was positioned near one of the hearths.

She looked down, eager to see a rush-covered floor firsthand, but was disappointed to discover that the floor was of scrubbed pale-gray stone. There was an abundance of light in the room, and she recognized the "rushlights"— candles of wax and tallow impaled on vertical spikes in an iron candlestick with a tripod base. In the Cincinnati Museum, they'd had two authentic rushlights. Here, many were supported on wall brackets, while others sat on the tables scattered through the hall. Still others were set in iron loops, carried over the arms of servants.

"Your mouth is ajar," Circenn said beside her ear.

She blinked. "Yours would be too, if you suddenly found yourself in my home." He would certainly gawk over television, the radio, the Internet.

"Is it to your liking?" he asked stiffly.

"It's lovely," she breathed.

He permitted himself a small smile. "Come, they've prepared a chamber for you."

"During the past two minutes?" How efficient was his staff?

"I sent a scouting troop ahead, lass, and since they expect you to be my wife"—he grimaced—"they may have made quite a fuss. Doona mistake that for my doing. I could hardly deny my servants their . . . enthusiasm. They are likely beside themselves with pleasure that I am hand-fasted," he muttered dryly.

Without thinking, she laid a hand on his forearm, plagued by curiosity, her animosity temporarily forgotten. "Why haven't you wed before now?"

He glanced down at her hand on his arm. His gaze lingered overlong on her fingers. "What? Have you suddenly become interested in me?" he asked, with a mocking lift of a dark brow.

"I suppose when I saw you at Dunnottar, I saw you merely as a warrior, but here I see you—"

"As a man?" he finished for her, in a dangerous tone. "How intriguing," he murmured. "Foolish, but intriguing."

"Why is that foolish? You *are* a man. This is your home," she said. "Your men give you their trust and loyalty, your servants are pleased to see you return. This is a spacious castle, and you must be at least thirty or thirty-five. How old are you?" Her brow furrowed as she realized that she knew very little about this man.

Circenn regarded her impassively.

Impatiently she barreled on. "Have you never been married? Surely you intend to be someday, don't you? Don't you want children? Do you have brothers and sisters, or are you as solitary as you make yourself out to be?"

His eyes narrowed. "Lass, I am weary from the journey. Fabricate your own answers as they may please you. For the now, let me see you to your chamber, so I might get on with my other duties. If you would like to turn your mind to a puzzle, puzzle a way out of a formal wedding in less than three moons."

"I guess that means you can't kill me, doesn't it?" she said, half jesting.

He scowled. "Correct." Then, close to her ear so no one could overhear, he said, "How could I kill a royal cousin? How could I dispose of you when the Bruce has given you to me in marriage? We're handfasted now. We're nearly as good as wed. Killing you now would cause more problems for me than failing to fulfill my vow ever would have."

"So your oath—"

"Is well and truly broken," he finished bitterly.

"Is that why you've been looking so angry?"

"*Stop* asking questions!" he thundered.

"Sorry," Lisa said defensively.

He propelled her up the staircase by her elbow and deposited her at the entrance to her chamber, in the east wing.

"I'll have hot water sent up so you may refresh yourself. Stay in your room for the duration of the night, lass, or I may have to kill you anyway."

Lisa shook her head and began to turn toward the door.

"Give me your hands, lass."

She turned back toward him. "What?"

He extended his hands. "Place your hands in mine." It was not a request.

Lisa held out her hands warily.

Circenn closed them in his and locked his gaze with hers. He used his body, as was his way—a subtle leaning, a slight shifting, an unspoken dominance—to press her back against the stone wall beside the door, holding her gaze. Fascinated, she couldn't tear her eyes away him.

When he stretched her hands above her head, she sucked in a worried breath.

He moved so slowly that, lulled by a false sense of

security, she didn't utter a word. Gently, he brushed his lips against hers. It was incredibly intimate, being kissed so slowly and tenderly. Had he kissed her heatedly, it wouldn't have been nearly as devastating.

With excruciating leisure, he kissed her so slowly that she could hear a dozen of her own heartbeats between each slight alteration in the caress of his lips. She dropped her head back against the wall and closed her eyes, lost in the butterfly-light friction of his lips brushing hers as if he had all the time in the world. The castle suddenly seemed unnaturally silent, her breath uncommonly loud. If it was five minutes or fifteen that he kissed her in such a fashion, she had no way of knowing. She would have held still forever.

He captured her wrists with one hand and, with the other, he traced the contour of her cheekbone. Her heart sank as she realized how close she was to being utterly seduced by his tantalizingly slow and delicious touches.

His fingers pressed at the corner of her mouth and her lips parted on a sigh of pleasure. He continued kissing her, but did not offer his tongue, and it was driving her mad. Slowly. Gently. With intimacy so prolonged that it made her aware of every nuance of what he was doing. He drew back, his gaze dark, and ran his finger across her lower lip. Instinctively, she touched his finger with her tongue.

With a husky groan, he cradled her head in his hands, closed his mouth over hers, and slipped a long velvety stroke of his tongue against hers. The moment she melted against him, he drew back sharply, spun on his heel, and stalked away.

Her lips tingled, and she touched the tips of her fingers to her mouth as he walked down the corridor. At the end of the hallway, he glanced back over his shoulder, and when he saw her standing there with her fingers pressed to her mouth, he flashed her a smile of masculine satisfaction. He *knew* the effect he had on her.

She stepped into her chamber and slammed the door shut.

*　*　*

Something had changed between them, she realized, during the ride from Dunnottar to Brodie. Or perhaps shortly after they'd arrived, when he'd left her side looking so angry and come back looking sad. He seemed more . . . human, less the ruthless savage. Or was she beginning to trust him, driven by the dawning realization that she had no one else to turn to?

Yawning and eager to stretch out on something besides the hard ground, she looked around the chamber. It was beautiful, the walls hung with palls of silk and tapestries that looked as if they'd been stolen from England. The thought amused her greatly, that Circenn decorated his castle with stolen English goods. Her bed, canopied with curtains of sheer ivory and covered with dozens of pillows, was so wide she could lie across it without her legs sticking off the edge. The headboard was a wonder of drawers and cubbyholes, and the maids had sprinkled the nooks and crannies with herbs and dried flowers.

Of course, they'd gone to such pains to make her chamber welcoming and bright because they thought she was going to be mistress of this castle, but she knew better. There was no way she would still be in the fourteenth century three months from now. It was simply not an option. Come tomorrow, she resolved sleepily, lulled by the wine she'd drunk and the gently burning fire, she would track down the flask and get back to her own time. She drifted off to sleep.

✶ ✶ ✶

Lisa was running as fast as she could, chasing her mother through the halls of the hospital. She'd be able to catch up with her if the doctors would just quit pushing her bed so fast! Didn't they understand that Catherine needed her?

But if they did, they didn't care. They wound down one hallway and up the next, turned right and circled around, almost as if they were purposefully trying to elude her. The entire time she chased them, her mother was struggling to sit up, holding her hand out, reaching imploringly for her. Several times Lisa came within inches of grasping that fragile hand, only to lose it when the doctors picked up a sudden burst of speed.

Finally she closed in on them near the reception desk. The desk was situated in a corner, with an aisle all around it, but there was only one hallway open to the left. There was no way they could escape her. She would cut them off, by circling around to the left, and gather Catherine up— she weighed so little now!—and take her home, where she wanted to be.

But as she raced around and blocked the hallway, an elevator appeared in the previously solid wall, and the doctors rushed her mother in, glancing at Lisa reprovingly.

"Lisa!" Catherine cried, as the doors began to close.

Lisa pushed forward, straining against the suddenly thickened air that prevented her from moving. She watched in horror as the elevator door closed and her mother was lost to her forever.

CHAPTER 14

ARMAND RODE SWIFTLY THROUGH THE FOREST AS DAWN broke over the high country, glancing frequently over his shoulder to ascertain that he wasn't being followed. Renaud had been far too curious about his urge to go for a solitary ride beyond the walls, but Armand had told him he needed to meditate, that his faith was often renewed by the breaking day and he found his prayers more easily recited in God's natural splendor.

Armand had rolled his eyes and cursed. God's natural temple was not, nor would ever be, enough for him. Certainly not now, living in the abject poverty and humiliation he'd endured since the overthrow of their Order. He longed for a fine roof over his head, luxurious surroundings, wealth, and respect. He'd lost all of those things when they'd been driven out of France, ousted by King Philippe the Fair, who had desired the Templars' wealth.

Many had coveted that wealth, and feared the Templars' growing power, but only Philippe had been clever and avaricious enough—and had been owed enough political favors—to bring the mighty Order crashing to its knees. Being forced to his knees was not a position Armand could accept. His life had been precisely as he'd wanted it, and each day he'd come closer to the true secrets of the Order, becoming more trusted and taken into greater confidences. As Commander of Knights, he'd nearly been able to taste the privilege and power of the enticing inner circle he'd been laboring to penetrate. Then the false arrests had been made and the knights had been driven from their homeland. Only a barbaric, excommunicated king had been willing to grant them clemency. When the Order of Templars had been dissolved by papal decree in 1307, no order of suppression was issued in Scotland; and under Robert the Bruce, the Templars had sought haven and become the *Militi Templi Scotia*.

Ha, he thought morosely, more like the *Minutiae Puppets Scotia*, for they danced to a new king's tune now, a king who, while he did not seek to take from them, had no wealth to confer upon them, no respect and no lands. They were fugitives, hunted and reviled.

But Armand Berard would not be so for long. The recent years of running and hiding, of pretending to keep the faith when the Order was so utterly destroyed, had firmed his resolve. His brother knights might cling to the absurd hope that they would be able to rebuild their Order in Scotland and eventually regain their prominence, but Armand knew better. The shining hour of the Knights Templar had passed.

He pitied his pious brothers, who believed that power was never to be used for personal gain. For what other reason would one ever use it?

He cursed and spat furiously. He'd been so close—so near the forbidden knowledge of the Templars' true power.

Armand reined in his mount, ducking under a low-hanging limb and slowing to a trot as he entered the clearing. He nodded a greeting to the cloaked rider awaiting him there.

"What have you for us, Berard?"

Armand smiled. It had been impossible to get word to his co-conspirator, James Comyn, while stationed at Dunnottar, but he hadn't had anything to tell him at the time. In the past week, however, he had come upon powerful information and knew it was a portent of good things to come. Armand Berard would sell his services for wealth and titles in England, and set about making up for lost time with wine, women, and weaving his way into the inner circles of Edward's court, by whatever means were necessary. He was a muscular, attractive man, and word was that Edward had a special fondness for personal services from well-favored men. Armand smiled, pondering how he would bend the English king to his will.

"Have you been able to find out any more about Brodie?" the Comyn pressed impatiently.

Armand regarded the thin, sadistic face of his companion. Grizzled white brows arched over pale blue eyes that were far colder than the iciest loch. "Little. He is a private man and those closest to him do not speak of him freely." Armand tightened his hold on the reins, soothing his mount to a standstill.

"Edward is advocating laying siege to his castle. He wants the hallows, Berard, and he grows impatient. Have you been able to confirm they are there?"

"As yet it is still rumor. But now that I am finally in his keep, I will be able to search thoroughly. That's what Edward wanted, wasn't it—a spy within his walls? Bid him be content that someone has finally managed to penetrate Brodie, and grant me time to search. It would be better that I find the spear and the sword than you storm his walls and try to take them," Armand warned.

Find them he would, and then sell them to the highest

bidder. The four hallows had been under the protection of the Templars until the Order fell. If he could now lay his hands on the Spear that Roars for Blood—the lance that had allegedly wounded Christ's side—there would be no limit to the wealth and power he might obtain. If he also found the Sword of Light, rumored to blaze with holy fire when wielded, his future would be assured. Allegedly, the cauldron and the Stone of Destiny were also somewhere in Brodie's keep. Now that he was being housed in the middle of that keep, Armand would not fail to exploit the opportunity.

To dissuade Edward's men from attacking Castle Brodie before he located the hallows, he warned, "Brodie has fifty Templars in residence, in addition to his troops, and if he indeed possesses the sacred objects, he possesses the ability to crush you before you so much as breach his gate."

The Comyn shifted irritably. "We know that. It has thus far restrained Edward's hand."

"Besides," Armand added thoughtfully, "I wonder if he truly has them. If he did, one would think he would have turned them to Scotland's aid long ago."

"Perhaps he is as self-serving as you and keeps them for the power they give him. Or perhaps he is devout, and believes they may only be used for God's will."

"It scarce matters, for I now have the means to lure him forth," Armand replied.

The Comyn straightened abruptly and snapped his fingers. "Information. Now."

"It will cost you," Armand said coldly. "Dearly."

"Edward will pay dearly if you deliver Castle Brodie and its notorious master to us. I assume you have a price in mind?"

"No less than my weight in purest gold."

"And what do you offer us for such an extravagance?"

"Circenn recently became betrothed, to one Lisa Mac-Robertson, who happens to be Robert the Bruce's cousin by blood," Armand said. "I will deliver her into your hands. How you destroy Brodie from there is your doing."

James Comyn's excitement was palpable, and it translated to his mount, who nickered and paced in skittish circles. Calming him with a thin white hand, Comyn kneed the horse close to Armand's. "Is she fair?" he demanded, his eyes glittering.

"Extraordinarily," Armand assured him, knowing the woman would beg for death at this man's hands, long before it was granted. "She is well curved and lush. A fiery woman, too proud for her own good."

The Comyn rubbed his hands. "Once we have her, Brodie will follow. Edward will delight in caging and quartering another of the Bruce's kin."

"I will bring her to you for the gold *and* a title and lands in England."

"Greedy, are we not?" James mocked.

"If I bring the sword and spear, I may ask for the crown," Armand said, with a chilly smile.

"For the sword and the spear, I might try to help you get it," his companion purred.

Armand raised his hand in a mock salute. "To England."

The Comyn smiled. "To England."

Armand rode back to Castle Brodie well pleased. He need only entice the woman outside the walls of the castle, and his new life would begin.

* * *

Lisa sighed as she rummaged through the chest. Four days had passed since they'd arrived at Castle Brodie, and her quest to find the flask had not been successful. She was beginning to despair. The man could have a thousand hiding places in a castle so large. For all she knew, he might have buried it in the dungeon—which was one place she wasn't in a hurry to see. She now understood the expression "looking for a needle in a haystack." Castle Brodie had two floors, with dozens of other floors in the turrets and towers that popped up at unexpected intervals, and the wings circled around not one but four enclosed courtyards. Quite simply, the castle was so large it could take her a year to search every room thoroughly. She'd tried to think like Circenn, to put herself inside his mind, but that had proved impossible; the man was an enigma to her.

He'd carefully avoided her since their arrival and had meals sent up to her room. She had seen him stomping about the outer bailey with his men. Once, he'd glanced up as she'd watched him through a window, as if he'd felt her gaze. The smile he'd given her had bared teeth and not much more. His eyes had been distant, troubled. Defiantly, she'd blown him a kiss to agitate him. It had worked. He'd pivoted in a whirl of cloak and stalked away.

Lisa rubbed her temples and returned her attention to the chest she'd been digging through. She was better off not thinking about him.

"Here ye be, lassie. I was wondering where ye'd gotten off to in this drafty old castle."

Lisa abruptly stopped poking through the chest and turned around. Her eyes felt gritty and heavy; she'd woken to a pillow wet from tears again this morning. She dimly recalled her dream—she'd been having horrible ones for days now, and she felt bruised from them. But her nightmares had galvanized her into action. She *had* to find the flask.

Her hands fell to her sides. Eirren stood a few paces away, leaning against a chair and watching her, his eyes bright with amusement.

"Have ye found what yer searching for?" he asked.

"I wasn't searching for anything," Lisa lied hastily. "I was merely admiring the room and wondering what treasures this chest might hold. I can't help myself, I'm a curious girl," she added breezily.

"Me mam used to tell me curiosity was one of the eight deadly sins."

"There are only seven sins," Lisa said defensively, "and curiosity can be a good thing. It encourages one to learn."

"Me, I've ne'er wanted to learn much of anything," Eirren said with a shrug. "Doin' is much more fun than learnin'."

"Spoken like a true male," Lisa said dryly. "You are in dire need of a mam. Speaking of which, you and I have a date with warm water and soap later this afternoon."

Eirren laughed and tossed himself into the chair. His thin legs protruded from beneath his dirty plaid and he dangled them over the side, bare feet swinging. "It's not a bad castle, is it, lassie? Have ye seen the buttery? The laird stocks a fine larder and hosts a grander feast—that is, when he's not planning wars and battling. There havna been many feasts in this castle for years now. Sad," he added dejectedly. "A lad could starve for want of spiced plums and sugared hams."

Lisa had a feeling that Eirren didn't want for much of anything his clever little mind could deduce a method to obtain. "How did you get to Castle Brodie, Eirren? I don't recall seeing you with the men when we were riding from Dunnottar."

"Me and me da dinna leave till later that night. We doona travel with the troops. Me da is of the serving folk; it doesna sit well to mix with warriors."

"Who is your da?" she asked.

"No one ye would ken," he replied, leaping from the chair. "I hear the laird told his men ye were cousin to the Bruce," Eirren said, changing the subject swiftly. "Is that the way of things?"

"No," Lisa said, wondering why she trusted him enough to share confidences. Possibly because she had no one else to trust, and if she couldn't trust a child, whom could she trust? "I told you I'm not from this time."

"Did the fae folk muck about wi' ye?"

"What?" Lisa asked blankly.

"The fairies—you ken we have 'em in Scotland. Oft they are wily little folk, mussing about with time and whatnot better left alone."

"Actually, it was the laird himself who's responsible for my being here. He cursed something and it brought me to him when I touched it."

Eirren shook his head disparagingly. "That man has ne'er cursed a thing well. Ye'd think he'd stop trying."

"He's cursed things before?" Lisa asked.

Eirren shook his head. "Doona be asking me, lassie. Ask him these questions. I only ken the few things I hear, and it's not always the truth of the matter. I hear tell yer handfasted to the laird."

"I'm not really. What does that mean anyway?"

"Means yer as good as wed, and if within a year an' a day yer carrying his bairn, 'tis a weddin' without a weddin' being needed. Are ye carryin' his bairn?"

"No!" Lisa was certain she looked as appalled as she

felt. Then she briefly considered what a child of his would be like, and how she would have to go about getting one. She drop-kicked the intriguing thought from her mind.

Eirren smiled gamely. "Ye can forgive curiosity, canna ye? Yer guilty of it as well. Would ye like to explore? I can give ye a wee tour before me da is needing me."

"Thank you, Eirren, but I'm happy here." She had to get back to her search and needed privacy to do it. "I thought I'd look through some of these manuscripts and pass the rainy afternoon in the . . . er . . . study." What did one call a room like this? It was a medieval version of a modern den. A circular piece of wood served as a desk, for lack of a better word. It looked as if it had been hewn from a massive tree trunk and was nearly five feet in diameter. Centered before the hearth, it had smoothly rounded drawers that had surely been a woodcarver's nightmare to create.

On either side of the hearth were recessed bookcases in which manuscripts bound in leather and rolled scrolls were neatly arranged on the shelves. Carved chairs with pillowed arms and cushions—someone in the keep was a clever seamstress—were strewn in cozy arrangements. Colorful tapestries adorned the walls, and the floor was dotted with woven rugs. It was obviously the room where Circenn tallied accounts, went through correspondence, and drew up maps and battle plans. The east wall was lined with tall windows, paned with a greenish glazed glass through which the green lawn was visible. Circenn Brodie was wealthy, that was a certainty, for in some of the rooms in the castle she'd seen clear windows.

"Suit yerself, lassie. I'll be seeing ye before anon, I'm fair certain." Eirren flashed her a grin and left as quickly and silently as he'd arrived.

"Wait—Eirren!" she called after him, hoping to set a time to meet with him later. The lad needed a bath, and she had a dozen questions to ask. She suspected his cheerful demeanor was much as hers—a façade shielding a lonely heart—and she believed he would welcome her mothering once he grew accustomed to it.

She would track him down in a few hours, she decided, but for now it was back to the business at hand: Where would Circenn hide the flask? She had no doubt he'd secreted it away as soon as they'd arrived. She had tried to watch what he did with his pack when they'd entered the castle, and had last seen it lying beside the door, but it had been gone the next morning when she'd sneaked down to begin her search. Whatever was in the silvery container must be extraordinarily valuable for him to be so careful with it. Was it indeed a potion to manipulate time? Was he blatantly lying to her about whether he could return her? She might consider drinking whatever it contained once she found it; perhaps the contents were magic.

She rummaged through the chest, sorting past ledgers. A few lumpy cushions, throws, and balls of thick thread had been casually tossed in with the mix. Nearing the bottom, she uncovered a sheaf of papers filled with slanted scrawl. The words looked angry, as had the words carved on top of the chest in the museum.

"Have you found what you seek, Lisa?" Circenn Brodie asked quietly.

Lisa dropped the papers back into the chest, closed her eyes, and sighed. With a gazillion rooms in this castle, everyone seemed hell-bent on joining her in this one. "I was getting a blanket out of the chest"—she snatched up a plaid that had been folded near the top—"when one of my earring backs came off," she lied splendidly.

"You are not wearing ear rings, lass," he said, breaking it into two distinct words, eyeing her ears. "On either ear," he said impassively.

Lisa clutched at her ears, then nearly assaulted the chest in a frenzied search. "Oh heavens, they *both* fell off," she cried. "Can you believe that?"

She flinched when his strong hands settled upon her waist as she bent over the chest. "No," he said quietly. "I cannot. Why doona you simply tell me what you are looking for, lass? Perhaps I can help you. I know the castle well. It is mine, after all."

Lisa straightened slowly; she hadn't fooled him for a moment. She was excruciatingly aware of his presence behind her, could feel the brush of his chest against her back. His hands were hot through the fabric of her gown. She glanced down, and the sight of his elegant fingers curving around her waist quickened her breath. "You don't need to touch me to talk to me," she said softly. She wasn't in full command of her mental faculties when Circenn touched her, and she needed every ounce of her wits to deal with him.

He removed his hands, and she exhaled a sigh of relief that served also to calm her erratic heartbeat, but then he gripped her by the shoulders and turned her about to face him. She tilted back her head to look at him. He regarded her in silence until she was too nervous to hold her tongue any longer.

"I was merely snooping. I'm curious about this place. It's my history—"

"Had you been strolling about the castle studying portraits, examining the weapons, or looking at furniture, you might have convinced me, but rummaging through my chest strikes me as somewhat odd. My servants tell me they've seen you in every wing of my castle."

Lisa swallowed, daunted by the cool expression on his face. A muscle jumped in his jaw and she realized she had upset him more than he was letting on. *Danger,* her mind cautioned. *This man is a warrior, Lisa.*

"Were you looking for battle plans, lass?" he asked tightly.

"No!" she assured him hastily. "I'm not interested in that."

Circenn stepped past her, bent over the chest, and poked through it. Apparently he found little to warrant concern, but he removed the sheaf of papers she'd discovered, folded them, and placed them in his sporran. He pivoted behind her and angled his body so that his chest brushed her shoulder.

She could smell him—that faint spicy scent that lured, befuddled, and seduced her. He was much too close for comfort. Lisa stolidly refused to budge an inch; she would not turn to meet his gaze again. *Let him talk to my cheek,* she thought defiantly. She was not going to let him use his body to intimidate her, although she had no doubt he'd used it effectively to that purpose for most of his life.

His breath fanning her ear, he said, "I came to tell you Duncan awaits you in the oriel—that is the room above the Greathall. He will give you a tour and has more to teach you before you mingle with my people. I expect you for dinner this evening—"

"We've not dined together before. I see no reason to start now," she interrupted hastily.

He continued as if she'd not spoken. "And I've had some gowns sent to your room. I suggest you spend the early evening with Gillendria, who will arrange for a bath and dress your hair—"

"I don't need to fuss," she protested quickly, her eyes fixed on the wall.

"My future wife would fuss with her appearance to befit her station."

Circenn dropped his hand from where it was suspended above her nape and clenched it so he wouldn't give in to the temptation to caress her hair, perhaps place a finger beneath her chin, and turn her face to his. Over the past few days, knowing she lay in his bed, slept in his castle, he'd grown deeply intrigued with the thought of being handfasted to her. His desire for her had in no way responded to his efforts at discipline; rather, it seemed to be growing defiantly, in inverse proportion to his attempts to contain it. Handfasting seemed to be acquiring the elements of a nicely bent rule, to the new and decidedly not improved Circenn Brodie.

If she turned to look at him, she would clearly see his hunger for her, and he *wanted* her to see it; it was like a volcano inside him—hot, far from dormant, and bordering on dangerous. He wanted to see how she would react, if her eyes would widen, her pupils dilate, her lips part. He gazed at her for a moment, willing her to turn and face him, but she was stalwart in her stance.

* * *

Circenn entered his chambers, gliding soundlessly across the floor. He drew a deep breath and let himself feel the raw power surging in his veins. *Why fight it now?* he thought sardonically. The past four days had been hellish. Since they'd returned to his castle, he'd tried to keep himself busy training, attempting to exhaust himself physically so he might sleep at night, but to no avail. At every moment he was exquisitely conscious of the woman in his keep.

And exquisitely tempted.

He'd broken every damned rule on his list but two, and now he'd come to this chamber to bend yet another one. He'd come to scry his future.

He paused before the brightly burning fire. Perhaps, if he had peered into his future the moment she had appeared, he might have glimpsed the disasters coming and been able to avert them. Perhaps he should have broken that rule first. Or perhaps he should have practiced scrying years ago and foreseen her arrival, but he hadn't for two reasons: He disliked using magic, and scrying was not an exact art. Sometimes he could see clearly, and at other times his visions were impossible to decipher, more confusing than helpful.

Circenn stared into the flames for a long moment, arguing with himself over such things as fate and free choice. He'd never been able to reach a solid conclusion about predestination. When Adam had first shown him the art of scrying his future days, Circenn had scoffed, arguing that to believe one could see one's future meant that it was unchangeable, which annihilated the concept of personal control, something he couldn't accept. Adam had merely laughed and goaded Circenn that if he refused to learn all the arts, he couldn't expect to understand the few he did know. *A bird's eye views the entire terrain over which it flies, a mouse sees only dirt. Be ye free or be ye mouse?* Adam had asked, his mouth curved in that perpetually mocking smile.

Sighing, Circenn knelt by the fireplace and ran his hand beneath the crack where the hearth met the floor. A portion of the wall containing the hearth silently revolved ninety degrees, revealing a pitch-black chamber behind it. He picked up a candle and stepped into the hidden chamber. With a slight movement of his foot, he depressed the lever that spun the wall closed. It took a few moments for his eyes to adjust to the room with no windows. It was an uncomfortable place for him, a place he sought only in his darkest hours.

He passed the small tables, toying idly with the various "gifts" the blackest elf had brought him. Some he understood, some he never wanted to understand. Adam had given them strange names: batteries, automatic rifles, lighters, tampons. Circenn had explored a few of them, and one he'd found himself drawn to many times over the centuries. Adam called it a "portable CD player." His usual favorite was Mozart's *Requiem*, but today, however, he was more in the mood for a piece called *Ride of the Valkyries* by Richard Wagner. Slipping the device over his ears, he thumbed the gauge to full volume and sank into a chair in the corner, staring at the candle flame. Papers crackled in his sporran and he removed them with a wry smile. He'd long ago forgotten stuffing those sheaves in the chest in his study, but he had narrowly escaped a disastrous situation by retrieving them. The last thing she needed to stumble upon was his scribbled and maudlin introspections. She would truly think him deranged.

He knew the first sheaf by heart:

~4 Dec. 858~
I have lived forty-one years, and today I have discovered that I will live forever, courtesy of Adam Black. I can scarcely dip my quill in ink; my hand trembles with rage. He gave me no choice—but what matter the wishes of

*mere mortals to an immortal race that has lost the
ability to feel?*

*He didn't tell me until after my wedding today, and even
then he would not tell me all, he merely acknowledged
that he had slipped the potion in my wine sometime in
the past ten years. Now I shall watch my wife grow old
and lose her to death, while I continue on, solitary.
Shall I become a monster like Adam? Will time dim my
ability to feel? Will a thousand years make me weary
beyond enduring and tinge my mind with that puckish
madness that delights in mischievous manipulation?
Will two thousand years make me become like them—
enamored of mortal struggles they can no longer feel?
'Tis no curse I would wish upon my love; better she
should live and die as nature intended.*

*Ah . . . was it only this summer past I dreamed of my
children, playing around the reflecting pool? Now I
pause and think—what, give the fool more fodder?
What atrocities might he commit upon my sons and
daughters? Och, Naya, forgive me, love. You shall find
me seedless as the grape in wine.*

And the second, the one that had laid the course of his
life:

*~31 Dec. 858~
My mind is consumed with this immortality. I have
pondered naught but these questions during the waxing
and waning of the moon, and now on this eve before
the new year dawns—the first of forevermore—I have*

*at long last achieved resolution. I will not permit the
immortal madness to take me, and I shall conquer it
thus: I have devised a set of rules.*

*I, Circenn Brodie, Laird and Thane of Brodie, do vow
to adhere faithfully to these tenets, never to break
them, for if I should, I may tumble headlong into
Adam's destructive irreverence and become a creature
who holds nothing sacred.*

I shall not lie.
I shall not spill innocent blood.
I shall not break an oath sworn.
I shall not use magic for personal gain or glory.
I shall never betray my honor.

And the third, when brutal understanding had finally
dawned and he'd tasted the bitter dregs hidden in the cup
of immortal life, camouflaged by the sweet nectar of perfect health and longevity:

~1, April 947~
*I buried my foster son Jamie today, knowing it was
only one of an eternal succession of burials. The hour
grows late and my mind turns, as it oft is wont, to
Naya. It has been a score of years since I lay with a
woman. Dare I love again? How many people will I
lower into their graves, and is it with such grim doings
that madness begins? Ah, fie. 'Tis a lonely life.*

A lonely life, indeed.

The savage music thundering in his ears, he gazed deep
into the flame and deliberately opened that part of his mind

he usually kept tightly shut. Unlike Druidism, which was a ritualistic art that included binding curses and spells, true magic required neither ceremonies nor rhymes. Adam's kind of magic was a process of opening one's mind and using a focus for the power once summoned. Circenn had found that the glassy surface of the reflecting pool in the rear gardens, or a polished metal disk, was often the best focus.

He retreated into his mind, staring intently at the shield propped against the wall. He'd fashioned it himself hundreds of years past, and although it was far too battered to carry into battle, it served him well as a focal point. The last time he'd tried to scry his life, he'd been trying to see himself five hundred years in the future, to determine what he might become. The vision that had flickered within this same shield had been bitter indeed. His vision had told him that by the seventeenth century, he would be possessed by a depraved madness.

Fate? Predestination?

His visions had told him truly when and how Naya would die; still, he'd been unable to save her. Natural causes, old age—a thing against which he possessed no weapon. Impotent in all his power, he'd lost her. And she'd raged against him as she'd died, cursing him a demon, for his hair had never grayed, his face had never lined.

He shook off the memory and intensified his focus. Images blurred and slowly coalesced. At first he could define only blobs of color: pink, bronze, dusky rose, and a backdrop of ivory. He narrowed the span of control, focusing on what the next few months would bring him.

When the pictures became clear, his hands closed like claws upon the arms of his chair.

He stared, first in shock, then with fascination, and finally with acquiescence, a faint smile playing about his lips.

Who was he to argue with fate? If that was what his time held, who was he to be so arrogant to think he could change it? He had sworn this would not happen, yet all events had consistently carved the path to it, from the first day she'd arrived.

He would be the worst kind of liar if he tried to convince himself that he'd hoped to see anything different.

He sucked in a shallow breath as he watched the nude woman reflected in the shield roll astride his naked body. His abdomen tightened and his cock hardened painfully as she straddled him and lowered her hot, wet sheath onto him inch by inch. In the shield, he had a clear view of her, as if he were lying on his back, looking up at her as she rode him. Her full breasts bobbed tantalizingly above him, her nipples tight. His hands swept up to palm them roughly, to tease the puckered crests. She arched her back, tossing her head and baring the column of her neck. The muscles in her neck were taut with passion as she strained for her pleasure, and it aroused him immeasurably. His hot gaze swept down over her breasts, followed the hollows and planes of her stomach, to the soft curls between her thighs, and he stared, fascinated, as she impaled herself upon his shaft, watched as the thick column of his cock was revealed, then buried again in her mound. She had a tiny dark mole on the inside of her left thigh, and in his vision, his fingers splayed over it. He ached to kiss it, to run his tongue over it.

He could nearly feel her body clench around him: tight, hot, and slick with that woman's wetness that made a man feel invincible—the measure of which bespoke his prowess: the wetter the woman, the more desired the man.

When the shield finally went dark, he came to himself

with his hand on his cock. It was swollen and aching for release.

"So, that is what is to be," he mused aloud. "Fate."

He couldn't deny that he'd wanted it since the day he first saw her; he'd had to forcibly restrain himself from taking her on several occasions. The vision had just confirmed that he would indeed have her, and that she would indeed be willing.

Why do you fight it? Adam had asked him angrily on more than one occasion. *Why can you not glory in what you are and enjoy the power of being Circenn Brodie? You possess the ability to give and take more pleasure than most mortals ever know. Soar, Circenn. Drink of the life of my kind. I offer you it, freely.*

Not freely, Circenn scoffed. *There was a price.* He squeezed his eyes shut as the music thundered in his ears.

It was his fate that she would ride like a mighty, demanding Valkyrie upon his body.

She already sang like a siren to his heart, this woman of defiance and fear, of curiosity and contradiction. Naya had been soft and passive toward her lot in life, until the end when she'd turned bitter. Never before had he met a woman like Lisa, a woman with needs and desires and a mind of her own. Deep emotions roiled in her breast, cunning intelligence glowed in her eyes, and a fierceness that vied with the legendary Valkyries' breathed in her veins.

Rules be damned. How could he argue with the future? It was written. He could only take it, enjoy it, and make the most of it, praying he would survive it when he lost his heart to her, then inevitably lost her in a short span of years. If he was going to be mad in the future, he may as well savor the present.

Circenn Brodie rose from his chair, ripped the machine from the future off his head, and did what he'd never dared do before:

He eased his control a tiny bit and encouraged the magic to throb inside him.

Dark angel, Adam had inveigled him, *soar into my world and fear nothing.*

He tossed back his head and tasted the power running through his formidable body.

It was a very different creature who left the dark, hidden room to find his woman.

* * *

Adam Black smiled as he removed the tampon from the barrel of the rifle. Although Circenn had refused to use any of the weapons Adam had brought him, the warrior within him could not permit time to tarnish them. He snorted, dangling the tampon from its string. Only his fastidious Circenn Brodie would decide that the soft white swabs were to be used for cleaning.

Eyeing the rifle, Adam grinned. They *were* the perfect size to slip inside the barrel—it nearly seemed sensible. But he hadn't brought tampons back to medieval Scotland for Circenn to play with; he'd brought them—and every gift he'd chosen—for another reason. Although if he had his way, there would be many nine-month intervals during which she would have no use for them.

CHAPTER 15

"YER A BEAUTY, LASS," GILLENDRIA SAID, CLAPPING her hands. "I thought I could refashion it well, but 'tis the woman who makes this gown."

Lisa stood before the mirror, gazing at herself with no small measure of shock.

Gillendria had refitted a dress that she said had belonged to Circenn's mother, Morganna. Now she slipped it over her shoulders, atop a shift of softest linen. Midnight-blue silk clung to her breasts, and the scooped neck slipped off her shoulders, accentuating her translucent skin and fine collarbones. It hugged her hips and fell to the floor in a rustle of blue embroidered with gold. At her waist, Gillendria had fastened a gold girdle that knotted low and from which hundreds of tiny gold moons and stars dangled. Matching slippers encased her feet, and a lovely gold torque that predated medieval times encircled her throat. An embroidered surcoat was tied below her breasts. Gillendria had curled her hair, carefully picking out the gold highlights and curling them a bit tighter so that they lay atop the wavy mass, then mussed it gently. A dab of some combination of root, herb, and flower colored her lips ruby.

Who was this woman in the mirror who looked like sin?
she wondered. *Like Sin's,* she amended fancifully, for even
she had to admit that the woman in the mirror now looked
a suitable companion for the laird of the castle. For once
she didn't curse herself for being tall, because in this gown
her height added an unmistakable touch of elegance.

"You're incredible, Gillendria," Lisa breathed.

"I am, aren't I?" Gillendria replied without a trace of
arrogance. "Although I have not had a woman with yer
perfect figure to clothe for some time, I have not forgotten
how. The laird will be well pleased."

Lisa was well pleased. She'd never known she could
look like this. At seventeen, she'd hoped one day to look
like Catherine—a golden, striking beauty—but work had
become all-consuming as she'd struggled to provide for
her mother, and Lisa hadn't spared another thought for her
own appearance in five long years. Her mother would
love— *Oh! Mom!*

She shivered. How could she have forgotten even for an
instant?

"Are ye cold, milady?" Gillendria asked. "I can fetch a
wrap."

"Nay," Lisa said softly. "Just a momentary chill, nothing more. Go on with you now, Gillendria. I'll find my way
to the Greathall."

After Gillendria left, Lisa sank down on the bed. Castle
Brodie was the loveliest place she'd ever been, and there
she sat in a dress made for a princess, about to have dinner
with a man who was the stuff of her every romantic dream.
For a few minutes she'd forgotten all about Catherine.
She'd been too busy experiencing all the anticipation and
excitement of a woman preparing for a special date.

But this was no date, and there would be no happily ever after. Her mother needed her desperately, and Lisa was doing something she had never before permitted herself to do: She was failing to carry out her responsibilities to Catherine. Failure was not a thing to which she was accustomed. She'd always been able to work harder, or for longer hours, to ensure, if not success, at least safety, food, and a roof over their heads. She had no right to feel even a brief moment of happiness, she admonished herself, until she found the flask and established her way home.

And then will you feel happy, Lisa? her heart asked gently. *When you leave him and go home to sit at your mother's bedside? When she's gone and you are left alone in the twenty-first century? Will you be happy then?*

* * *

Her resolve to feel no pleasure lasted all of an hour. Lisa finished her dessert and sighed contentedly. If she'd learned nothing else, she'd learned to appreciate the good things that were interspersed with the bad, and dinner had been the best. The formal dining hall was beautiful, lit by dozens of candles. She was warm, clean, and full. For the first time since she'd been in the fourteenth century she'd eaten a splendid meal. Admittedly, her meals back in her century had never been seven courses of heaven, but even White Castle hamburgers fared well against the bland, tough meat and hard bread to which she'd been subjected. During the past few weeks, she'd despaired of ever eating a decent meal again.

Twenty feet of table separated them—like in the old movies, she thought. She *needed* twenty feet between her and the lord of Brodie Castle. They'd dined mostly in silence, and he'd been the epitome of a gracious host. He hadn't scowled at her even once. In fact, several times she'd caught him regarding her with an admiring gaze. His previous bad temper seemed to have melted away without a trace, and he appeared as close to relaxed as she'd ever seen him. She wondered what had changed his mood; perhaps he was going to war soon, she decided, which would suit them both fine. He'd get to throw his weight around being the brash overbearing male, and she'd be free to tear the castle apart from top to bottom in search of the flask, without fear of his watchful gaze. He certainly wouldn't carry such a valuable relic into battle. He'd have to leave it here somewhere. The idea made her feel positively magnanimous.

She glanced at him, feeling secure in the distance between them, and smiled. "Thank you," she murmured.

"For what, lass?" He idly licked a swirl of fluffy topping from his spoon.

"For feeding me," she replied, assuring herself that the mere glimpse of his tongue flicking over a spoon was not sufficient cause for her blood pressure to rise.

"I've fed you every day since you've been here and you've not thanked me before," he observed mockingly.

"That's because you never fed me anything worth eating before." She watched as he licked a dab of cream from the tip of his spoon. "I think you got it all," she said uneasily. Suddenly the cavernous room seemed to shrink and she felt as if she were sitting mere inches away from him, not twenty feet. And who had poked up the dratted fire? She fanned at her face with a hand that betrayed not the slightest tremor she was feeling.

"Got what all?" he asked absently, filling his spoon with a mound of berries and cream.

"How is this topping made?" she asked, changing the subject swiftly.

"Much like butter. You churn it with paddles or shake it in a jug. It is merely cream skimmed from the top of milk, mixed with sugar and a touch of cinnamon. It thickens as you paddle it and add the sweetening. I used to watch them make it when I was a lad, flattering cook and anyone else in the kitchen to get my hands on it."

Whipped cream in the fourteenth century, she marveled. She wondered how many things these "barbarians" had that modern scholars never discussed. But why wouldn't they have such condiments? In the few days she'd been in Castle Brodie, she'd noted many things that surprised her. It all just seemed too civilized.

She fixed her gaze on her plate trying to prevent herself from rising from her chair, taking his spoon away, and giving him something else to lick. Her finger. Her lower lip. The hollow of her spine.

Although she'd had little experience with men, she was innately sensual and she'd fantasized often. Perhaps more than most, because she'd tasted so little of sexuality. Tonight, with this magnificent warrior dining regally at the end of the table, her imagination took flight.

In her fantasy he walked to her end of the table, capturing and holding her gaze with that subtle magnetism he had. His eyes were heavy lidded, banking a challenge: *Become a woman, Lisa?* He took her hand, pulled her to her feet, and kissed her, a soft brush of his lips, a quick velvety stroke of his tongue, promising so much more, slipping deep into her mouth when her lips parted on a sigh. Her fantasy picked up speed, fast-forwarded abruptly to his pressing her back onto the table, slipping the gown from her body, dropping whipped cream on her breasts, and licking it from her moist, warm skin with the same careful deliberation he'd given his spoon. Perhaps a dab of warm, rich cream would inadvertently fall where she'd touched herself before, and with his lips he would . . .

Swallowing hard, she looked at him.

He raised his eyes from the frothy concoction on his spoon at the precise moment she looked up, and their gazes locked over the length of the polished wood table. *Where would you drip whipped cream on him, Lisa?* The answer came with frightening swiftness and conviction: *Everywhere.* She wanted to explore his body, the hard ripples, the smooth skin. The candlelight bathed his olive skin with a golden hue, and his dark good looks were set off perfectly by his linen shirt and the splash of black and crimson draped across his chest. He was mesmerizing.

"Are you hungry, lass?" He licked his spoon languidly.

She couldn't tear her gaze away. "No. I've eaten quite enough," she managed.

"You seem to be watching my dessert most intently. Are you certain there isn't something else you wish to sate your appetite?"

Besides you to remove your clothing, lie on the table, and let me finger paint you with whipped cream, you mean? "Nope," she said casually. "Not a thing." She watched him for a moment; he still had a great deal of dessert left. How was she going to get through this? "Actually," she said, leaping to her feet, "I'm exhausted and would like to retire."

He dropped his spoon and moved swiftly to her side. "I will escort you to your chambers," he murmured, taking her arm and tucking it into his. Lisa shivered. The man was throwing off the heat of a small forge. His scent enveloped her, faint but spicy. It was a fragrance she couldn't quite put her finger on. She was certain she'd smelled it before but couldn't figure out where. It was definitely a unique scent, one that modern-day perfumers would have killed to get their hands on.

"I can walk by myself perfectly well," she said, removing her arm from his.

"As you wish, Lisa," he replied easily.

Her eyes narrowed. "Why are you suddenly being so nice to me? I thought you were angry with me. I thought you didn't want to marry me. I thought you thought I was a spy."

He shrugged innocently "First, I've always been reasonably pleasant to you. Second, I doona have any choice but to marry you, and third, marrying you renders distrusting you obsolete. I am a logical man, lass. When a warrior realizes he has only one course of action, he makes the best of it. Anything else would be foolish. That doesn't mean that I doona still have many questions. I plan to learn everything about you, lass," he said meaningfully. "But I am no longer going to fight my situation." *Not one bit of it,* he added silently. *Not my magic, not my dark side, not my adherence to rules. I am a new man, Lisa Stone,* he told her inside his head. And it felt good. Never before had he accepted any portion of what he considered his dark side, but never before had he been so tempted by a woman to do so. He had a feeling that a man might need a little magic to woo and win Lisa Stone.

They ascended the stairs in silence. He smiled, thinking he'd finally managed to still her acerbic tongue merely by being as nice to her as he'd wanted to be, but, constrained by his oath and his rules, had resisted. She would encounter no further resistance from him.

At the door to her chambers, she stopped and looked up at him. He was pleased by her action, for it told him clearly that she desired his kiss.

And he planned to give her much more than a kiss before the night was through.

CHAPTER 16

LISA WAITED, CURSING HERSELF SILENTLY. DURING THE walk to her chambers she'd thought of a dozen excuses to escape him and flee to her room alone, but one thing had prevented her: She wanted a good-night kiss. Dinner had been perfect, and she wanted to end it like a real date. With a real kiss.

So she faced him and turned her face up expectantly.

But he neither kissed her nor left her there. Rather, he reached around her to the door, pushed it open, and smoothly backed her into the room.

"What are you doing?" she asked uneasily.

"I thought merely to visit with you awhile, lass."

"I don't think that's a good idea," she said. "You may bid me good night now." Her fantasy was too fresh in her mind. She wanted a simple kiss to dream on, not the whole man. She couldn't handle the entire man.

"Why? Do I make you uncomfortable, lass?" He stepped farther into the room and closed the door behind him.

"Of course not," she lied, moving away from him quickly. "Infuriate me? Frequently." She suddenly realized she was pacing and forced her feet to still. "I just don't see any reason for you to be in my chambers. Go." She waved her hand at him.

He laughed, a husky rumble. "I think you find being in a room with me and a bed disturbing."

Lisa moved swiftly to the plump mattresses and plunked herself upon them defiantly. "No, I don't. It doesn't bother me in the slightest. It's simply that I'm tired and would like to sleep." She yawned hugely.

"Quite a yawn. Lovely pink tongue, by the way. Do you recall how it feels when yours jousts with mine? I haven't forgotten. I want more."

Despite her resolve not to, she looked at him, fascinated.

"I want your tongue in my mouth."

She averted her gaze with effort.

"I want mine all over your body."

Lisa swallowed. "I am not interested," she said faintly.

"Doona lie to yourself, Lisa. Doona lie to me. You want me. I can feel it in the air between us. I can smell it."

Lisa didn't dare breathe. She harbored an absurd hope that he would just leave after declaring that truth and not force her to confront the enormity of it. She *did* want him. Desperately. Fantasies collided in her mind, daring her to relinquish her innocence and embrace womanhood.

He moved slowly toward her and sat on the edge of her bed. She scooted back hastily, her back flush to the head-board, and hugged a pillow to her chest.

"You enjoy looking at me, doona you, Lisa?"

She enjoyed doing more than looking at him. She liked fighting him with her kisses. Tasting the salt and honey of his skin.

With deft fingers, he untied the laces of his linen shirt and shrugged it off over his head. The muscles in his abdomen rippled, the curves of his biceps flexed. "Then look," he said, his voice rough. "Look your fill. Think you I doona recall how you gazed at me in my bath?" When his wide shoulders were revealed, she shook her head and sucked in a breath.

"St-stop that! What are you doing?" Lisa exclaimed. Lounging at the foot of her bed was six feet seven inches of dark, seductive man, with rippling muscles beneath bronzed skin; a warrior in every sense of the word. Fine black hair dusted his powerful chest and thick forearms. A finer trail of hair skittered down his abdomen and crept beneath the brilliant red and black tartan knotted at his waist. All in all, Circenn Brodie was the most desirable man Lisa had ever seen.

"Use me, Lisa," he encouraged softly. "Take whatever you want." When she made no reply, he said, "You have never been with a man, have you?"

Lisa smoothed the coverlet, her mouth dry. She had no intention of discussing this with him. She wet her traitorous lips and was appalled when they parted and said, "Is it so apparent?"

"To me. Perhaps not to other men. Why? You are old enough to have been with many men. You are beautiful enough that many must have tried. Did you find none to your liking?"

Lisa hugged the pillow tighter. In high school, she'd had several boyfriends, but they'd always seemed so immature to her. Catherine said it was because she was an only child, that she was more accustomed to being around adults. She'd suspected her mom was right.

"Did I take you from someone? A lover perhaps?" A muscle twitched in his jaw.

"No. There's been no one."

"I find that difficult—nay, impossible to believe."

"Trust me," Lisa said with a self-deprecating laugh. "Men were not exactly beating down my door." If they had been, they would have fled shortly after gaining entrance and discovering her financial straits and her caretaker role.

"Ah, perhaps they were afraid of you, because you are so much woman?"

"I am *not* fat," Lisa bristled. "I'm . . . healthy," she supplied defensively.

Circenn smiled. "That you are, but that is not what I meant."

"Well, I'm not too tall. A giantess wouldn't be too tall for you." At five feet ten, she had towered over many of the boys in her class until the last two years of high school.

"Not what I meant either."

"Then what did you mean?" she asked, feeling wounded.

"You are smart—"

"No, I'm not," she said. *Anything but smart.*

"Yes, you are. You were smart enough to realize it would be foolish to escape me at Dunnottar, and clever enough to deduce a way out of my chambers. Aye, even fearless enough to dare it. Tell me, do you read and write?"

"Yes." Inwardly, Lisa glowed. She *was* smart in the fourteenth century.

"You are persistent. Tenacious. Determined. Strong. You doona need anyone, do you?"

"I haven't had the *opportunity* to need anyone. Everyone's always been too busy needing me," she muttered, then felt guilty for voicing her most secret resentment.

"Need *me*, Lisa."

She searched his face. What had changed him? Why was he acting this way? It was as if he genuinely cared and sincerely desired her.

"Need me," he repeated firmly. "Use me to explore the woman who has never been given the opportunity to live. Take from me, need from me, and satisfy all that curiosity I feel burning in you. And by Dagda, let go of that maidenhead. Do you wish to live and die, never having known passion? Never having tasted what I offer you? Be bold. Take." He uttered the last word in a low, masculine tone.

Take. The word lingered in her mind. It was almost as if it had rolled from his tongue imbued with some kind of sorcery. What would it be like to *take*, as he said it—to utterly consume without guilt or fear? *Take* because her blood demanded it, because her body needed it. Lisa's lips parted as she contemplated his words. His upper torso was a vast expanse of olive skin that would be velvety to the touch. Her fingers ached to trail over the hard ridges of his chest, to linger over his shoulders, to curve around his powerful neck and drag him into a kiss that would make her forget where he began and she ended. "I thought you medieval men prized virginity. Don't you think it's wrong for a woman to have her own desires and act on them?"

"Your virginity is a piece of skin, a membrane, Lisa. My first love was long ago and it has not changed who I am in any fashion. Mind you, I am not saying you should give the gift of lovemaking to just anyone. But an obsession with virginity is absurd and serves no purpose but to make a woman turn away from a fine part of her nature. Women and men have the same desires—at least they do until the priests have their go at the women and convince them it is shameful. What the priests should be saying is 'choose well.' "

"How many—" she broke off quickly. *What a stupid question to ask.* She would sound like a childish, possessive adolescent. But she wanted to know. It said something about the man. A man who'd been with hundreds of women had a real problem, as far as she was concerned.

"Seven." His teeth flashed white against his face.

"That's not very many. I mean for a man, you know," she added hastily.

What would she think if she knew it was only seven in five hundred years? Thousands of times with those seven, enough to know well how to please any woman, but only seven all the same. "Each woman was a country, rich and lush as Scotland, and I loved them with the same dedication and thorough attention I give my homeland. I confess, the first few were naught but the man in me celebrating life when I was less than a score of years. But the last two were wonderful women, both friends and lovers."

"Then why did you leave them?"

A shadow crossed his beautiful face. "They left me," he said softly. *Died. Too young, in a land too harsh.*

"Why?"

"Lisa, touch me." He moved closer, close enough that she could smell the spice of his skin. Close enough that she could feel the heat radiating from his body, mingling with the heat from hers. Close enough that his lips were a breath and a "yes" away from hers. Tempting, more compelling than her need for basic survival. Fingers extended, she reached for him, but at the last moment she dropped her hand, forming a fist in her lap.

He was silent for a long moment. "You aren't ready yet. Very well. I can wait." He rose in a fluid motion. As he stood, the knot on his tartan slipped and the fabric dropped lower on his hips, giving her a sinful glimpse of what she was denying herself. Her gaze fixed on the black trail of hair that fanned below his belly button, then dropped lower to the thicker hair that peeked above the tartan. The sight of it gave her a heavy feeling in the pit of her stomach, an awful empty pressure. Whether he moved or the plaid slid, she didn't know, but suddenly it dipped lower, revealing the thick base of his shaft amid silky dark hair. She couldn't see the length of it, but that wasn't what made her heart pound. It was the thickness of him. She would never be able to wrap her hand around it. What would it feel like to have him push that inside her? Her mouth went dry.

His eyes lit appreciatively as her gaze snagged there. "I could pick you up and wrap those lovely long legs of yours around my waist. Slip deep inside you, rock you against me and love you till you lay in my arms and slept like a babe. I will spend each night stretched beside you, teaching you what you want me to teach you. I can feel that you want it from me. Yet it will be at your pace, when you choose. I will wait as long as I must.

"But know this, Lisa—when you are across the dinner table from me on the morrow, in my mind I am pushing you back on a bed. In my fantasy"—he laughed, as if at his own brashness—"you are discovering yourself with my willing body. Who knows, perhaps even laying siege to the heart that beats within this chest." He thumped his chest with a fist and silently admitted she'd already begun to do that, otherwise he wouldn't have offered himself. But she didn't need to know that. He knotted the tartan slowly, never taking his eyes from hers.

"Good night, Lisa. Sleep with the angels."

Her eyes stung from quick tears. It had been her mother's

nightly benediction: *Sleep with the angels.* But then he added words her mother never had:

"Then come back to earth and sleep with your devil, who would burn in hell for one night in your arms."

Wow! was all her reeling mind could come up with as he slipped from the room.

CHAPTER 17

THREE DAYS HAD PASSED SINCE THEIR FIRST DINNER IN the formal dining room. That was seventy-two hours. Four thousand three hundred and twenty minutes, and Lisa had felt each one of them whiz past her—gone forever.

Nine shifts of nurses had changed at home. Nine meals had been taken by her mother—bland food, she was certain. No ripe plums and apricots carefully selected from the market on her lunch hour. Illness had changed Catherine's appetite, and she'd developed a craving for fruits.

Lisa had spent the days snooping as furtively as possible, but she had begun to suspect it was futile. She didn't have the first idea where to look for the flask. She'd tried his chambers several times during the day, but the door was always locked. She'd even gone to the turret to the left of his chambers to see if there was a way she could manage to scale the outside wall to get there, but it was hopeless. His chambers were on the second floor of the east wing, and there were guards on the battlements above it at all times.

She'd passed the evenings indulging herself in offensively sumptuous meals. Last night, the first course had been a mixture of plums, quince, apples, and pears with

rosemary, basil, and rue in a pastry tart. The second course
had been a chopped meat pastry, the third an omelet with
almonds, currants, honey, and saffron, the fourth roasted
salmon in onion and wine sauce, the fifth artichokes stuffed
with rice. By the honey-glazed chicken rolled in mustard,
rosemary, and pine nuts, she'd been wallowing in guilt. By
the berry pastries with whipped cream, she'd despised herself.

And each night, he'd savored his dessert with the same
lazy sensuality that made her long to be a berry or a fluff
of topping. She couldn't fault his demeanor, he'd been an
impeccable dinner companion and host. They'd made cautious small talk; he'd told her of the Templars and their
plight, spoke of their training and extolled the strengths
of his Highland fortress. She'd asked about his villagers,
whom he seemed to know surprisingly little about. He'd
asked about her century and she'd made him talk about his
instead. When she'd asked about his family, he'd turned
the tables and asked about hers. After a few moments of
strained evasions, they'd mutually conceded to leave each
other alone on that topic.

He seemed to be going out of his way to be gracious,
patient, and accommodating. In turn, she'd been carefully
reserved, finding an excuse each night to dash from the table after the final course and hole up in her room.

He permitted her escape, for the price of a tantalizing
kiss each night at her door. He had not tried again to enter
her chambers; she knew he was waiting for her invitation.
She also knew she was perilously close to extending it.
Each night it was more difficult to find a reason not to take
what she so desperately desired. After all, it wasn't as if
letting him spend one night in her bed would have the
same effect as Persephone eating six seeds in Hades.

Her problem was twofold: Not only was she losing precious time and getting no closer to finding the flask, but she was beginning to adapt in insidious little ways. The immediacy of her presence in fourteenth-century Scotland seemed to be sapping her resolve. She'd never had a time in her life that was so peaceful, so filled with idle time, so safe. No one was relying on her, no one's life would fall apart if she caught a bad cold and was unable to work for a few days. No bills were pressing, no deep blanket of gloom encompassed her.

She felt like such a traitor.

Bills *were* pressing; someone *was* relying on her. And she was helpless to do a damn thing about it until she found that flask.

She sighed, wishing fervently that she had something to do. Work would be cathartic; immersing herself in physical duties was the only way she'd ever managed to keep her demons at bay. Perhaps she could help a few of the maids, insinuate herself into their confidence and learn more about the laird and his customs, like which were his favorite rooms, where he stored his treasures.

Leaping from her perch in the window seat in the study, she went off, determined to track down a job for herself.

* * *

"Gillendria, wait!" Lisa called as the maid hurried down the corridor.

"Milady?" Gillendria paused and turned, her arms heaped with bed linens.

"Where are you going?" Lisa asked, catching up. She extended her hands to relieve a portion of Gillendria's burden. "Here, let me help you carry some of those."

The maid's face was half hidden behind the mountain

of linens, but what Lisa could see of it was quickly transformed by an expression of horror: her blue eyes widened, her dark brows flew up, and her mouth parted in a gasp. "Milady! These are soiled," Gillendria exclaimed.

"That's all right. You're doing wash today. I can help," she said cheerfully.

Gillendria skittered back. "Nay! The laird would banish me!" She turned and scurried down the hall as quickly as she could beneath the towering pile of linens.

Heavens, Lisa thought, *I was only trying to help.*

* * *

After searching for half an hour, Lisa found the kitchen. It was as splendid as the rest of the castle, spotless, efficiently designed, and currently occupied by a dozen servants preparing the afternoon meal. Buzzing with conversation, warmed by melodic laughter, the kitchen was made even cozier by a brightly leaping fire over which sauces simmered and meats roasted. The flames hissed and flickered as basting juices drizzled onto the logs.

She smiled and called a cheery hello.

All hands stilled: knives stopped dicing in midslice, brushes stopped basting, fingers stopped kneading dough, even the dog curled on the floor near the hearth dropped his head on his paws and whimpered. As one, the servants sank low in deference to her station. "Milady," they murmured nervously.

Lisa studied the frozen tableau for a moment, struck by the absurdity of the situation. Why hadn't she anticipated this? She knew her history. No one in the castle would permit her to labor: not the kitchen staff, not the laundress, not even the maids dusting the tapestries. She was a lady— and a lady was to be kept, not to keep.

But she didn't know how to be kept. Depressed, she mumbled a courteous good-bye and fled the kitchen.

* * *

Lisa sank into a chair by the hearth in the Greathall and indulged herself in a serious brood. She had two things with which to occupy her mind: her mother and Circenn— both were dangerous, although for vastly different reasons. She was considering cleaning out the hearth and scrubbing the stones when Circenn entered.

He glanced at her. "Lass," he greeted her. "Have you had breakfast?"

"Yes," she replied with a dejected sigh.

"What's amiss?" he asked. "I mean other than the usual—that which is always amiss with you. Perhaps I shall preface each conversation we have by assuring you that I still cannot return you. Now, what has you looking glum so early on a fine Highland morn?"

"Sarcasm does not become you," Lisa muttered.

He bared his teeth in a smile, and although she kept her face inscrutable, inwardly she sighed with pleasure. Tall, powerful, and utterly gorgeous, he was a vision a woman could get used to seeing first thing in the morning. He was wearing his tartan and a white linen shirt. His sporran was buckled around him, accentuating his trim waist and long muscled legs. He'd just shaved, and a bit of water glistened on his jaw. And he was huge—she liked that, a mountain of masculinity.

"What do you expect me to do with myself, Circenn Brodie?" she asked irritably.

He was very still. "What did you call me?"

Lisa hesitated, wondering if the arrogant man could really expect her to call him "milord," even after he'd offered himself to her a few nights ago. Fine. It would keep things impersonal. She rose and bowed sweepingly. "My lord," she purred.

"Sarcasm does not become you. That is the first time I've heard my name on your lips. As we are to be wed, you must use it henceforth. You may call me Cin."

Lisa blinked at him from her servile position. *Sin.* That he was. And that was the bulk of her problem. If he were not so irresistible, she wouldn't feel so alive around him, ergo she wouldn't constantly feel so guilty about her mom. Had he been an unattractive, spineless, stupid man, she would have felt miserable every minute of the day—and that would have been acceptable. She *should* be miserable. She had abandoned her own mother, for heaven's sake. Her back stiffened and she stood up straight. "Perhaps I should preface each of our conversations as well, by reminding you that I won't be marrying you. *My lord.*"

A corner of his mouth quirked. "You are truly possessed of a streak of defiance, aren't you? What did the men in your time make of it?"

Before she could answer, Duncan came bounding into the hall, followed by Galan. "Morning all, and a fine day it is, eh?" Duncan said brightly.

Lisa snorted. Couldn't the handsome Highlander be pessimistic just once?

"Circenn, Galan was down in the village early this morning, hearing some of the disputes that have backed up in the manor courts—"

"Isn't the lord supposed to decide those?" Lisa asked acerbically.

Circenn's gaze shot to her. "How would you know that? And what business of yours is it?"

Lisa blinked innocently. "I must have overheard it somewhere. And I was merely curious."

"One would think you might learn to tame that curiosity, seeing where it has led you."

"And while Galan was in the village," Duncan forged on, "he realized the villagers are expecting to have a celebration."

"I don't understand why you don't hear the cases. Aren't you the laird?" Lisa pushed. "Or are you just too busy mucking up everyone else's life and brooding all the time?" she added sweetly. Her inactivity was getting on her nerves, and if she didn't start being mean to him, she'd end up being entirely too nice. Her resolve might not withstand another dessert with him.

Duncan's laughter rang to the rafters.

"It's none of your business why I doona hear them," Circenn growled.

"Fine. Nothing's any of my business, is it? What do you expect me to do? Just sit around, ask no questions, have no desires, and be a lump of spineless femininity?"

"You could not be spineless if you tried," Circenn said with a long-suffering sigh.

"A celebration," Duncan said loudly. "The villagers are planning for the feast—"

"*What* are you blathering about?" Circenn grudgingly rerouted his attention to Duncan.

"If you would permit me to complete an entire sentence, you might know," Duncan said evenly.

"Well?" Circenn encouraged. "You have my full attention."

"The villagers wish to celebrate your return and the upcoming wedding."

"No celebration," Lisa said immediately.

"The idea is appealing," Circenn countered.

Lisa glared at him as if he'd lost his mind. "I am not marrying you, remember? I'm not going to be here."

The three warriors turned to regard her as if she'd just informed them she would sprout wings and fly back to her time.

"I will not be party to this," she snapped.

"A celebration might be just the thing for you, lass," Duncan said. "And you will have the opportunity to meet your people."

"They are not my people, nor will they ever be," Lisa said stiffly. "I won't be here." With that she turned and fled up the stairs.

*　*　*

But she found she couldn't stay away for long. Stealthily, she crept back to the top of the stairs, fascinated by the events ongoing below.

They were planning her wedding, and it was enough to boggle the mind.

There they were, sprawled around the table in the Greathall, and the overbearing but irresistibly sexy hunk of a Highland laird had his hands buried in fabric.

"Nay. It is not soft enough. Gillendria, go fetch the silks stored in the tapestry room. Adam gave me something that should suit well. Bring me the bolt of gold silk."

Duncan leaned back in his chair, his arms folded behind his head and his boots propped on the table. The front legs of his chair hovered precariously a few inches above the floor, then hit the floor with a thump when Galan kicked the back of the chair.

"What is wrong with you, Galan?" Duncan complained.

"Keep your feet off the table," Galan reprimanded. "They're dirty."

"Leave him be, Galan. The table can be wiped," Circenn said absently, fingering a pale blue wool and discarding it with a shake of his head.

Duncan and Galan looked at Circenn as if he'd lost his mind. "What have we come to? Mud on the table? You—sorting through fabric? Does this mean tupping in the kitchen is acceptable now, too?" Duncan asked, disbelievingly.

"Far be it from me to regulate tupping," Circenn said mildly, lifting a fold of crimson velvet.

Galan snapped Duncan's mouth shut with a finger beneath his chin. "I thought you hated the gifts Adam brought you, Circenn," Galan reminded the laird.

Circenn tossed aside a pale rose linen. "Only bold colors for the lass," he told the maids. "Except perhaps lavender." He glanced at the seamstress standing near his chair. "Have you any lavender?"

At the top of the stairs, Lisa blushed. He was obviously recalling her bra and panties. The thought sent a flush of heat through her. But then her brow furrowed: Who was Adam and why did he bring gifts and why did Circenn hate them? She shook her head, watching him pick through the bolts spread across the table. A half-dozen women were gathered around Circenn, picking up the fabrics he had approved.

"A cloak from the velvet," he said, "with black fur at the rim of the hood and cuffs. My colors," he added smugly.

Lisa froze, thrown off balance by the possessive note in

his voice. *My colors,* he'd said, but she'd clearly heard him say, *my woman*.

And it had thrilled her.

She stepped back quickly and ducked into a corner, leaning against the wall, her heart pounding.

What was she doing?

She'd been standing at the top of the stairs in the fourteenth century, watching him select fabric for her wedding gown!

Dear God, she was completely *losing* herself. The immediacy of the present was so compelling, so rich and exciting, that it was eroding her ties to her real life, undermining her determination to return to her mother.

She sank to the floor and closed her eyes, forcing herself to think of Catherine, to imagine what she was doing, how sick with worry she was, how alone. Lisa remained crouched on the floor, brutally forcing herself back to reality until she felt tears sting her eyes.

And then she rose, determined to take control of things for once and for all.

CHAPTER 18

LISA PRESSED BACK INTO THE DEEP STONE ARCH OF THE doorway, scarcely daring to breathe. Her feet were numb and cramped from huddling on the chilly floor. She tightened her fingers around the hilt of the knife she'd filched from the kitchen. It was a lethal blade, razor sharp, as wide as her palm and at least twelve inches long. It would serve nicely to demonstrate her point. She was through biding her time and trying patiently to find the flask. She was going to get back to the future—now.

Watching him plan her wedding gown had been the final straw: Circenn had accepted that she was going to be here forever—worse, she had started to accept it as well. Concealing the knife in the folds of her gown, she'd slipped up to the second floor and hidden in the shadows of a doorway diagonal to Circenn's chambers, waiting for him to come up to change for dinner, as he did every night. She conceded that if she hadn't had an ill mother, she might well have embraced this experience. In her century, there were no men who could begin to compare to the masculine splendor of Circenn Brodie. But Catherine needed her and would always come first.

The staircase creaked faintly and she tensed. Peeking

around the corner of the doorway she glimpsed Circenn gliding silently down the hallway. For such a large man he certainly moved quietly. In a moment, his back was to her. He inserted the key in the lock and she realized the time was upon her. She would obtain the flask, no matter whom she had to go through to get it. No more passive, bewildered, susceptible-to-seduction Lisa.

She surged from her hiding place, pressed the tip of the blade to his back, directly in line with his heart, and commanded, "Move. In the door. *Now*." Placing her other hand at the small of his back, she pushed him forward.

His spine went rigid beneath her palm.

"Now, I said. Get in the room."

Circenn kicked the door open and entered the chamber.

"Stop," she ordered. "Do not turn around."

"I saw you spying in the Greathall, lass," he said easily. "If you doona like the gold silk, you needn't get so fussy about it. You may select your own gown. It was not my intention to offend you with my choice."

"Don't be obtuse. You know that's not what I'm upset about," she hissed. "The flask, Brodie. Now. Get it." She pressed the tip of the blade harder against his back to illustrate her resolve, and bit her lip when a drop of blood blossomed below his shoulder blade, spreading on the white linen of his shirt. She wished desperately that she could see his face. Was it dark with fury? Was he amused at her tenacity, or foolishly underestimating her resolve?

He sighed heavily. "For what purpose do you wish my flask? Are you in truth the traitor we feared?"

"No! I want to go home. I have no desire for your flask, I only need it to take me back."

"You still believe the flask will return you?"

"It brought me here—"

"I have explained to you—"

"All you've said is that it isn't the flask's power, but you won't tell me what it *can* do. Do you expect me to trust your word? Why should I?"

"I would not lie to you, lass. But I see that you will not believe me. Had I known you still harbored this foolish hope, I would have obliged you sooner." He pivoted so swiftly that she fumbled, but recovered and jabbed the tip of the knife into his chest. More blood blossomed as the lethally sharpened blade slipped through his shirt as if it were butter.

"Careful with that thing, lass. Unless it pleases you to ruin my shirts."

"Don't move and I won't have to cut you," she snapped.

He dropped his hands to his side. "I must move to collect the flask."

"I'll follow you."

"Nay, you will not. I will not take you to my lair."

"I am the one with the knife," she reminded him. "And it currently rests above your heart."

If he moved, she didn't see it. All she knew was that one moment she had the knife at his chest, and the next it was gone.

She blinked, trying to bring the room back into focus.

The blade was flush against her throat.

Her eyes flared wide and she gasped. "How did you do that?"

"You cannot control me, lass. No one can," he said wearily. "If I give to you, it is because I choose to give to you. And, Lisa, I would choose to give you everything, if you would but permit."

"Then give me the flask," she demanded, ignoring the cold metal at her neck.

"Why do you seek it? To what do you wish to return? I have told you I will wed you and care for you. I am offering you my home."

A groan of frustration escaped her. Nothing was working out as she'd planned. He had so easily disarmed her, stripped away her control. *I am offering you my home,* he had said, and a treacherous part of her was deeply intrigued by that offer. She was doing it again—vacillating. She glared at him, a sheen of tears clouding her vision.

At the sight of her tears, he flung the knife to the bed, where it landed with a soft thud. Pulling her into his arms, he caressed her hair tenderly. "Tell me, lass, what is it? What causes you to weep?"

Lisa pulled from his embrace. Thrumming with frustration, she began pacing between him and the door. "Where is my baseball cap, anyway? Did you have to take that away from me, too?"

He cocked his head. "Your base ball cap?" he repeated awkwardly.

"My"—what had he called it?—"bonnet."

He moved to a chest beneath a window, lifted the lid, and retrieved her clothing. Her jeans and T-shirt had been neatly folded, and atop them was her cap.

She leaped toward him and snatched it greedily from his hand, clutching it to her breast. It seemed a lifetime ago that she and her father had sat in the third row, in the blue seats, directly behind home base. They'd laughed and yelled at the baseball players, drunk sodas and eaten hot dogs drenched with mustard and relish. She'd decided that very day that she would one day marry a man just like her daddy. Charming, smart, with a fabulous sense of humor, tender, and always willing to take time for his family.

Then she'd met this capable, mighty warrior, and in his

shadow the real Jack Stone had come into sharper focus. As had her real feelings about him.

She was angry at her father. Angry at his irresponsibility: his failure to have cars serviced, to take out life insurance, to carry adequate auto coverage, to plan for a future that might stretch beyond his present. In so many ways her father had been an overgrown child, no matter how charming he was. But Circenn Brodie would always plan for his family's future. If he wed, he would keep his wife and children safe, no matter the cost to himself. Circenn Brodie took precautions, controlled his environment, and built an impenetrable fortress for those he called his own.

"Talk to me, lass."

Lisa dragged herself from her bitter thoughts.

"If you tell me why you seek so desperately to return, I will bring you the flask. Is it a man?" he asked warily. "I thought you told me there had been no one."

The tension that had quickened in her veins while she'd sat in the doorway, clutching the knife and waiting for him, dissipated suddenly. She chided herself for her foolishness: She should have foreseen that force wouldn't work with this man.

The primary reason she'd refused to discuss Catherine with him was that she hadn't wanted to make a fool of herself, to start talking and end up weeping openly before the impassive warrior. But her emotions were no longer under her control, and the need to talk consumed her, the need to have someone to trust, to confide in. Her defenses slipped further, leaving her raw and exposed. She sank to the floor. "No. It's nothing like that. It's my mother," she whispered.

"Your mother what?" he pushed gently, sinking down beside her.

"She's d-dying," she said. She dropped her head forward, creating a curtain with her hair.

"Dying?"

"Yes." She drew a deep breath. "I'm all she has left, Circenn. She's ill and won't live much longer. I was taking care of her, feeding her, working to support us. Now she is completely alone." Once the words had started coming, they tumbled forth more easily. Maybe he *did* care enough to help her. Maybe if she told him all of it, he would find a way to return her.

"She was in a car wreck five years ago. We all were. My daddy died in it." She stroked the baseball cap lovingly. "He bought me this a week before the wreck." A bittersweet smile crossed her face at the memory. "The Reds won that day, and we went to dinner afterward with Mom, and that's the last time I remember us all being together except for the day of the wreck. It's my last good memory. After that, all I see are the crushed, jagged pieces of a blue Mercedes covered with blood and . . ."

Circenn winced. Placing a finger beneath her chin, he forced her to look at him. "Och, lass," he whispered. He traced her tears with his thumb, his eyes mirroring her grief.

Lisa was soothed by his compassion. She'd never spoken aloud of this, even to Ruby, although her best friend had tried many times to get her to talk about it. She was discovering that it wasn't as hard to confide in him as she'd feared. "Mom was crippled in the car wreck—"

"Car wreck?" he asked softly.

She struggled to explain. "Machines. The Mercedes was a car. In my time we don't ride horses, we have metal"—she searched for a word to which he might relate—"carriages that carry us. Fast, sometimes too fast. The tire . . . er, wheel of the carriage came apart and we crashed into other machines. Daddy was crushed behind the steering wheel and died instantly." Lisa blew out a breath and paused for a moment. "When they released me from the hospital, I found a job as quickly as I could, and a second one to take care of me and Mom and pay the bills. We lost everything," she whispered. "It was horrible. We couldn't pay the lawsuits, so they took our home and everything we had. And I'd accepted it—I *had*—I'd accepted that was how my life would be, until you took me away in the middle of something that I have to finish. My mother has cancer and only a short time to live. No one is there to feed her, pay the bills, or hold her hand."

Circenn swallowed. He could not interpret much of what Lisa had said, but he understood that her mother was dying and she had been trying to take care of everything for quite some time. "She is entirely alone? There is no other of your clan left alive?"

Lisa shook her head. "Families aren't like yours in my time. My father's parents died long ago, and my mother was adopted. Now there's only Mom, and I'm stuck here."

"Och, lass." He drew her into his arms.

"Don't try to comfort me," she cried, pushing against his chest. "It's my fault. I'm the one who had to work in a museum. I'm the one who had to touch that damned flask. I'm the selfish one."

Circenn dropped his hands and expelled a frustrated breath. There was not one selfish bone in her body, yet she was lambasting herself, carrying the blame for everything. He watched helplessly as she rocked back and forth, her arms wrapped around herself—a posture of deep grieving he'd seen far too many times in his life. "No one has ever been there to comfort you, have they?" he asked grimly.

"You carried the weight of it all alone. This is untenable. This is what a husband is for," he muttered.

"I don't have one."

"Well, you do now," he said. "Let me be strong enough for both of us. I can, you know."

She wiped angrily at her tears with the back of her hand. "I can't. Now do you see why I must return? For God's sake, will you *please* give me the flask? You promised when we were at Dunnottar that if there was a way for me to return, you would help me. Was that something you said merely to placate me? Must I beg? Is that what you want?"

"Nay, lass," he said violently. "I never want that from you. I will give you the flask, but I must collect it. It is in a safe place. Will you trust me? Will you go to your chambers and await me there?"

Lisa searched his face frantically. "Will you really bring it?" she whispered.

"Aye. Lisa, I'd bring you the stars if it would cease your tears. I did not know. I knew none of this. You did not tell me."

"You never asked."

Circenn scowled as he mentally kicked himself. She was right. He hadn't. Not once had he said, *Excuse me, lass, but were you doing something when I snatched you out of time with my curse? Were you wed? Did you have children? A dying mother who relied upon you, perhaps?* He helped her to her feet, but the moment she had her balance she tugged her arm from his hand.

"How long will it take you to retrieve it?"

"A short time, a quarter hour, no more."

"If you don't come to me, I will return with a bigger knife."

"You won't need a knife, lass," he assured her. "I will bring it."

She left silently, carrying part of his heart out the door with her.

* * *

Circenn opened his secret chamber and grimly retrieved the flask from the hidden compartment in the stone floor. It had never occurred to him that she'd had a full life in her time; he'd been so selfish that he'd never once asked her what he'd taken her away from. He had seen her only as proud, tenacious, sensual Lisa, as if she'd lived nowhere before she had come to him, but now he understood clearly. She had sacrificed most of her adult years caring for her mother, carrying burdens a laird would stagger beneath, nurturing the only clan she had left. It explained much: her resistance to adaptation, her continued attempts to search his castle, her illogical unwillingness to give up on the flask as a way to return home. He knew Lisa was an intelligent woman, and he suspected that deep down she realized that the flask wouldn't return her, but if she formally gave up on the flask, she would have no hope. People often clung to irrational hopes to avoid despair.

His heart wept for her, because he knew that the only man who could return her would see her dead first. For the first time in his life he was furious with himself for refusing to learn the things Adam had so often offered to teach him.

Come train with my kind, Adam had coaxed on numerous occasions. *Let me teach you the fae arts. Let me show you the worlds you might explore.*

Never, Circenn had replied scornfully. *I will never become like you.*

But the magic is inside you—
I will never accept it.

Yet now he would have given anything for the art of sifting time. Anything Adam wanted at all. He straightened his
shoulders, closed the hidden chamber, and moved to the
door. How could he have been so blind as not to realize that
she'd had a life and lost it? How could he have ever thought
she was duplicitous? The image of her huge green eyes,
shimmering with tears as she'd gazed up at him, refusing
his solace because she'd obviously never been given comfort and didn't know how to accept it, would burn forever
in his mind.

He had a difficult path to walk with her now. He
squeezed his eyes shut for a moment, bracing himself for
her discovery that she was truly trapped. With a deep sigh,
he left his chambers.

*   *   *

"Lass," he said softly.

Lisa glanced up as he entered the room. She was huddled in the center of her bed, her pale face stained with
tears. He fished about in his sporran and moved slowly to
her side, making a journey he was reluctant to complete.

"Stand up, lass," he said quietly.

Lisa rose swiftly.

He held out the flask.

"You brought it," she whispered.

"I told you I would. I should have done so before now. I
knew you wanted it. I saw the look on your face when we
were riding from Dunnottar and you glimpsed it in my
pack."

"You can read me so easily?"

"Not always. Sometimes I can't read you at all, but that night I could. You'd been crying—"

"I was not. I almost never cry. I only cried now because I'm so frustrated."

"My apologies—it had been raining," he corrected swiftly, protecting her pride. His heart was touched: She was embarrassed by her tears. There was no shame in weeping. He'd seen her cheeks wet with tears several nights on their journey, but they'd been quiet tears, and he'd assumed it was part of her acceptance of her transition, never suspecting she was grieving over her mother. He was amazed that she hadn't wept openly before now. But she was resilient and tough, and that gave him hope that she would recover in time.

"That night it was raining," she agreed. "Go on."

"You glimpsed the flask as I removed an extra plaid. To protect you from the rain," he teased, hoping to lighten her grim mood.

She arched a brow, but her eyes were sad, filled with unshed tears.

He sighed and continued. "And I saw the hope in your eyes—a hope that centered upon my flask. I knew it couldn't return you, so I dismissed the thought, but I should have realized that you would need to prove to yourself that it wouldn't work," he said gently.

"Give it to me," she demanded.

He dreaded this, dreaded the moment when he would see in her lovely green eyes stark certainty that she could never return. He proffered the shimmering silver flask in silence.

She reached for it. "How does it work?" she whispered.

"It doesn't," he whispered back. "You only think it does."

Her fingers closed on the flask. He watched as she wrapped her hand reverently around it. Wrapped both hands around it, did something funny with her feet, and closed her eyes. She muttered softly.

"What are you saying?"

"There's no place like home." The words were half mumbled but painfully clear to his ears. He winced. Aye, there was no place like home, he agreed silently, and he would do his best to make this feel like home to her, since he was the one who'd uprooted her with his thoughtless curse. "I am verra sorry, lass," he said softly, his brogue thickened by emotion.

She didn't open her eyes, refused to move. Finally she crossed to the bed and lowered herself on it, tightly holding the flask. She looked as if she was mentally reciting every prayer or rhyme she'd ever learned. After a long time, she rose and stood by the fire.

She stood like that, frozen, clutching the flask, for so long he finally sank into a chair beside her. How much time passed, he had no idea, but he would not move an inch until she accepted it, and then he would be there to wrap her in the shelter of his body.

Full night had descended when she finally stirred, the dinner hour long past. Her hair shimmered in the firelight, her face was ashen, and her lashes were dark fans against her pale skin. He cursed when a tear slipped down her cheek.

When she finally opened her eyes he saw pain in the brilliant green depths. Denial and acceptance warred on her expressive features—acceptance the brutal victor. She had held the flask, she had performed whatever ritual she believed in, and she had experienced incontestable defeat.

"It didn't work," she said in a small voice.

"Och, lass," he said with a sigh, helpless to alleviate her suffering.

She began to fiddle with the stopper on the flask.

"What are you doing?" he thundered, half rising from the chair, ready to rip the flask from her hand.

"Perhaps if I drink this?" she said hesitantly.

"Never, lass," he said, his olive complexion paling. "Trust me, you *doona* wish to do something so foolish."

"What's in it?" she gasped, clearly stricken by his reaction.

"Lisa, what is in that flask would not only fail to return you to your home, it would be the purest glimpse of hell for you. I would not lie to you. It is a poison of the vilest origin."

He didn't need to say more to convince her. He could see her acceptance that not only wouldn't it take her home, it might kill her—or make her wish she were dead. He understood that Lisa, as sensible as she was, had now acknowledged that she'd been clinging to an impossible hope and would not do so again. If he said it wouldn't work, that was enough. By trusting her, he had gained her trust.

She sniffed and, to her apparent chagrin, another tear slipped out. She dropped her head forward to hide behind her hair in the way he'd noticed she did when she was uncomfortable or embarrassed.

Circenn moved swiftly, intending to catch the tear upon his finger, kiss it away, then kiss away all her pain and fear, and assure her that he would permit no harm to touch her and would spend his life making things up to her; but she dropped the flask onto the table and turned swiftly.

"Please, leave me alone," she said and turned away from him.

"Let me comfort you, Lisa," he entreated.

"Leave me alone."

For the first time in his life, Circenn felt utterly help-less. *Let her grieve,* his heart instructed. She would need to grieve, for discovering that the flask didn't work was tantamount to lowering her mother into a solitary grave. She would grieve her mother as if she'd in truth died that very day. *May God forgive me,* he prayed. *I did not know what I was doing when I cursed that flask.* He snatched the flask from the table, tucked it into his sporran, and left the room.

* * *

And that was that, Lisa admitted, curling up on the bed and pulling the curtains tight. In her cozy nest all she lacked was her stuffed Tigger and her mother's shoulder to cry on, but such comforts would never again be hers. As long as she hadn't tried the flask, she'd been able to pin all her hopes on it. She'd been astonished by Circenn's reaction to her confession—she'd glimpsed a kindred moisture in his eyes.

You're falling, Lisa, her heart said softly, *for more than a country.*

Good thing, she told her heart acerbically, *because it looks like he's all I've got, for now and forever.*

She glanced around the curtained bed and snuggled deeper into the covers. The fire made her chamber toasty, and there was a flask of cider wine in a cubbyhole in the headboard. As she took a deep swallow, savoring the spicy, fruity taste, she gave in to her grief. Her mother would die alone and there was nothing Lisa could do to prevent it. She drank and cried until she was too exhausted to do more than roll onto her side and slip into the gentle, wine-induced oblivion of sleep.

All I wanted was to hold her hand when she died was her last thought before dreaming.

* * *

Circenn Brodie stood beside the bed and watched Lisa sleep. He parted the filmy bed curtains and stepped close, dropping his hand to lightly touch her hair. Curled on her side, she'd folded both hands beneath one cheek, like a child. The faded red bill of her bonnet—base ball cap, he reminded himself—was crushed between her hands and a plaid she'd bunched up into a pillow of sorts. She had clearly cried herself to sleep, and it looked as if she had fought a losing battle with her covers. Gently, he eased the plaid away from her neck so she wouldn't strangle herself with it, then straightened the fabric twisted about her legs. She sighed and snuggled deeper into the soft mattress. Removing the wineskin from where it was nestled close to her side, he winced when he discovered it was empty, although he understood what had driven her to drink it.

She had been seeking oblivion, a quest he'd embarked upon a time or two himself.

She was lost. Torn from her home. Stranded in the middle of a century she couldn't possibly understand.

And it was his fault.

He would marry her, help her adjust, protect her from discovery—and most of all, protect her from Adam Black. One way or another, he promised himself firmly, he would make her smile again and win her heart. She was everything Brude and more. His mother would have loved this woman.

"Sleep with the angels, my Brude queen," he said softly. *But come back. This devil needs you like he's never needed anything before.*

As he turned to leave he spared a last glance over his shoulder. A faint smile curved his lips as he recalled her fascination with whipped cream. He hoped one day she would trust him, desire him enough to allow him to take his spoonful of whipped cream, trail it across her lovely body, and remove the sweet confection with his tongue.

He would heal her. With his love.

And he would never die on her—that he could promise.

*   *   *

"What's wrong?" Galan asked, taking one look at Circenn's grim expression as he entered the Greathall.

The laird dropped himself heavily into a chair and picked up a flask of cider wine, absently turning it in his hands.

"Is it Lisa?" Duncan asked swiftly. "What happened? I thought the two of you were . . . growing closer."

"I gave her the flask," Circenn grunted, barely intelligible.

"You *what?*" Galan roared, leaping from the chair. "You made her like you?"

"Nay." Circenn waved an impatient hand. "I would never do that. I merely gave it to her so she could see for herself it would not return her to her home." He paused, then raised his eyes from the floor. "I found out why she wants to return so badly," he said. Then, haltingly, he told him what Lisa had confided.

"Och, Christ," Duncan said when he was finished. "This is a fankle. Can you not return her? It *is* her mother." Galan murmured his agreement.

Circenn shrugged and spread his hands in a helpless gesture. "I doona know how. The only creature who knows how is Adam—"

"And Adam would kill her," Duncan finished bitterly.

"Aye."

Duncan shook his head. "I never knew. She told me that a woman was depending on her, but she wouldn't tell me more."

"She told you that?" Circenn snapped.

"Aye."

Circenn's lips twitched bitterly. "Well, here I have been offering to be her husband and she didn't tell me that much."

"Did you ever ask?" Galan asked softly.

Circenn muttered a curse, uncapped the wine, and started to drink.

CHAPTER 19

ARMAND GRITTED HIS TEETH AND PERMITTED JAMES Comyn to vent his anger, assuring himself that soon the tables would be turned, and then he would revel in crushing the traitorous Scot. He understood the Comyn's motivations well. Ten years ago, when Robert the Bruce had slain Red John Comyn in Greyfriars Kirk at Dumfries, thereby eliminating the only other real contender for the Scottish crown, the remainder of the Comyn clan had eagerly allied themselves with the English. They were avid to murder any relative of the Bruce they could get their hands on.

"It has been weeks, Berard! And you bring me nothing. No woman, no sacred hallows."

Armand shrugged. "I have done all I can. The woman has not left her chambers in weeks. She stays holed up there, although I cannot fathom why."

"Then go in and get her," Comyn spat. "The war grows fiercer, and the Bruce's brother Edward has made a foolish wager."

"What say you?" Armand had heard nothing of this.

"Only last night he made a wager that may win or lose this war. King Edward is most displeased."

"What wager?" Armand pressed.

"It is not my place to speak of it. Even the Bruce hasn't received word of it yet, and he will be furious when he hears what his brother has done. It is imperative that we capture the woman. At least then we will have something to appease his temper. You must get her," Comyn ordered.

"There are guards outside her chambers day and night, James. I must wait until she comes out." He raised a hand as the Comyn started to argue. "She will have to come out soon." And while he waited, he would continue to search the castle for the sacred hallows. Thus far he'd managed to search only the north wing; somehow, he had to get into both the laird's and the lady's chambers.

"A fortnight, Berard. Any longer and I cannot assure you I will be able to prevent King Edward from ordering his men to attack."

"It will be done before a fortnight is up."

* * *

Lisa rolled over, stretching gingerly. She knew that she would have to leave her bed eventually but hadn't been able to face it. She sat up slowly, surprised to discover that the painful knot in her chest seemed to have loosened. She glanced around her room as if seeing it for the first time.

She'd been sleeping more than sixteen hours a day and wondered if perhaps the past five years had finally claimed their price. She'd slept and grieved for everything—not just her mother, but the car accident, her father's death, and the loss of her childhood. She hadn't let herself feel any of that for five years, and when she'd finally permitted a tiny sliver of pain, all of it had come crashing in and she'd lost herself for a time. She hadn't realized how much buried anger she held. She suspected that only a bit of it had been released.

But now she had to face the facts: The flask would not return her, Circenn could not curse her back, and this was going to be her life—for the rest of her life.

She rose from the bed, rubbing her neck to ease the kinks. She had no idea how long it had been since she'd bathed. Disgusted with her protracted inertia, she moved to the door. While closeted in her room, she'd been dimly aware that men were posted outside in the corridor. She'd never spoken to them, had merely accepted the food they handed in through the door and picked at it listlessly.

She fumbled with the handle and pulled the door open.

Circenn crashed in and hit the floor. He rolled smoothly onto his back and sprang to his feet, hand on his sword, looking dazed. She realized he must have been sitting on the floor, leaning back against it, and when she'd opened it she'd taken him by surprise. He blinked several times, as if he'd fallen asleep in that position and been awakened abruptly. She was startled and touched: Had he been outside her room all this time?

He gazed down at her and they regarded each other silently. There were dark circles under his dark eyes, his face was lined with fatigue and worry, and the look he gave her was so tender and self-effacing that it made her catch her breath.

"A bath," she said softly. "Might I have a bath?"

His smile was slow to form, but dazzling when it did. "Absolutely, lass. Wait right here. Doona move. I'll see to the preparation myself." He rushed out to fulfill her request.

*　*　*

"She wants a bath," Circenn bellowed, barreling into the Greathall. He'd been waiting weeks for some spark of life. That she was aware of her body again meant she was slowly retreating from the dark place within, where she'd languished so long. He roared for the maids, who came at a run.

"Have hot water drawn immediately. And a meal. Send her all the tempting food you can find. And wine. Clothing! She must have clean clothing as well. See to my lady. She wants a bath!"

He smiled. By Dagda, the day was looking brighter already.

* * *

The last person Lisa would have imagined might slip into her chambers while she was bathing was Eirren. She'd indulged in a two-second fantasy that Circenn might come in uninvited, with seduction on his mind, but had quickly squashed that thought, obviously a leftover from the historical romances she'd devoured in lieu of a social life. Things like that didn't really happen. What really happened was that small, mischievous children invaded. "What are you doing in here, Eirren?" She swished her hands in the water, trying to whisk up more bubbles to cover her breasts. When that failed, she placed her wash cloth atop them.

The rascal grinned broadly, waggling his brows in a comically lecherous expression.

"I didn't even hear you open the door." She sank lower in the tub.

"Ye were too engrossed in yer bath, lassie. I even knocked," he lied. He moved swiftly to the hearth near Lisa.

"I hardly think this is appropriate," she said. Then she regarded him thoughtfully. "On second thought, it's perfectly appropriate. You may use my bath when I'm done, and we'll finally get you clean."

Eirren grinned puckishly. "In order to do that, ye'll have to be gettin' out. For my first look at a naked lass, I'd even consent to washin' meself. For a look at ye, I'd wash twice. Behind me ears, even."

His grin faded as he took a seat on the stone base of the hearth. "Are ye feelin' better, lassie? Ye've been in here a long time. I couldna help but hear grim gossip."

Lisa was touched. "You were worried about me, weren't you? That's why you came today."

"Aye, I was," Eirren muttered. "And I dinna like it a bit. I overheard the men sayin' ye really are from another time and ye discovered ye can never return." He looked at her questioningly.

"That is so," Lisa said sadly.

"Will ye be givin' up on life, lassie?"

Lisa glanced at him sharply. "Sometimes you seem far older than thirteen, Eirren."

He shrugged his bony shoulders. " 'Tis the way of this world. Children doona stay children long. We see too much."

Lisa felt a flash of longing to shield his eyes, to ensure he never again glimpsed anything a child shouldn't see. Then she caught him trying to peek beneath the water line. "Stop that!" She splashed water at him.

He laughed and wiped his face gamely. " 'Tis natural. I'm a lad. But I'll be lookin' out yon window if it makes ye feel better."

She smiled, watching him lift his chin and turn his face toward the window, making quite a production of it. He was such a melodramatic boy.

"Will ye be wedding the laird?" he asked after a moment.

Lisa's brows lifted as she pondered that. A shiver skittered up her spine. She could not return home. *This* was her life. What would Catherine want her to make of it? Lisa knew the answer to that. Catherine would have fussed and cosseted and dressed Lisa in the finest wedding gown, pushed her into bed with the brawny Highlander, and hovered outside the door to ascertain that Lisa made appropriately satisfied honeymoon sounds.

"I do believe I will," she said slowly, trying to accustom herself to the thought.

Eirren clapped his hands and beamed at her. "Ye willna regret it."

Lisa's eyes narrowed astutely. "Do you have a special interest in this, Eirren?"

"I merely wish to be seein' a lassie happy."

"That's not all of it," Lisa said. "Confess. You like the laird, don't you? You admire him and you think he needs to get married, don't you?"

Eirren nodded, his eyes bright. "I suppose I have a fondness for him."

Probably because his own father didn't have much time for him, she thought. Circenn Brodie would be easy for a lad to worship. "Hand me my towel, Eirren," Lisa ordered. She would get the filthy boy in the bath if she had to parade around nude to do it. Someone needed to take responsibility for him, treat him to tender arms and loving discipline.

With an arch glance, he picked up her towel and, with an exaggerated swing of his arm, flung it far across the room to land on the bed. "Get it yerself."

She gave him her most forbidding you-will-obey-me-little-boy-or-die glance. They waged a battle with their glares—his challenging, hers promising divine retribution—until with a gamin grin he leaped to his feet, slipped behind her, and was gone. She didn't even hear the door open and close.

She sighed and leaned her head back against the tub, admitting that she hadn't really wanted to leave the warm, soapy water anyway. "I'll get you for this, Eirren," she vowed. "You will have a bath before the week is out."

She wasn't certain but she thought she heard a soft tinkle of laughter outside the door.

* * *

The sun was shining, Lisa observed with pleasure. After bathing, she had slipped on a clean gown but forgone slippers. While the maids had removed her bath water, she'd flung open the window and realized that spring had graced the countryside while she'd grieved. She'd felt a fierce need to venture outside, to feel the sun, to savor the birdsong, to connect with what was to be her world. God, she needed to get out of her room. It was suffocating after so long.

She strolled the courtyard at a leisurely pace, curling her bare toes in the lush green grass. Following the perimeter wall of the castle, she was acutely aware of the curious gazes of the guards in the high towers. They watched her intently, and she suspected that Circenn had instructed them not to let her slip from their sight. Rather than feeling guarded or trapped, she found it comforting. While finishing her bath she'd realized that she'd been lucky; things could have been much worse. She might have been dumped through time into the keep of a true barbarian, who would have abused her, turned her out, or simply killed her.

She skirted a small grove of trees and paused, captivated by a clear reflecting pool encircled by smooth white rocks and cornered by four massive standing stones with Pict inscriptions. Lured by history, she trailed her fingertips over

•

the engravings. A lovely stone bench squatted in a small copse before an unusual mound of earth that was about twenty feet long and a dozen feet wide. It was nearly as tall as she was, and the grass on it was a brilliant green, thicker and lusher than the rest of the lawn. Her toes ached to touch it. She stood regarding it, wondering what it was. A medieval burial mound?

"It is a fairy mound. A *shian*," Circenn said, moving behind her. He placed his hand on her waist and inhaled the clean fragrance of her freshly washed hair.

Lisa tipped back her head and smiled.

"It is said that if you circle the mound seven times and spill your blood upon the peak, the Queen of the Fairies may appear and grant you a wish. I cannot guess how many young lads and lasses have pricked their fingers here. Old, tall tales—this land is full of them. Most likely some prior kin once emptied the chamber pots here. It would explain how thick and green the grass is." He dropped a kiss on her hair, wrapping his arms around her from behind. "I glimpsed you from the window and thought I might seek a word with you. How are you, lass?" he asked gently.

"Better," she said quietly. "I'm sorry. I didn't plan to stay in there for so long. I just needed time to think. Until you'd given me the flask I still believed I might return. I needed time to come to terms with the reality of my situation."

"You need offer me no apology. It is I who should offer you one." He turned her to face him. "Lisa, I am sorry you were ensnared by my curse. I would like to say that I'm sorry you came here, but I must confess that I . . ."

Lisa glanced up at him searchingly.

He took a deep breath. "That I will devote my life to

making it up to you. That I wish to wed you and will see you well cared for."

Lisa averted her gaze, mortified to feel tears threatening.

He stepped back, sensing that she was fighting for control. "That was all I wished to say, lass. I will leave you to your walk now. I merely wished to be certain you knew how I felt."

"Thank you," she said. As she watched him retreat, a part of her longed to summon him back, to make small, idle talk and while away the sunny afternoon, but tears still came too easily.

After he'd gone she continued strolling, drawn to explore her new home. She soaked up the warm rays, stopping periodically to examine small buds and unusual foliage. It occurred to her that since she was to stay there, she could finally do something she'd longed to do for years—she could have a puppy. She'd always wanted a dog but their apartment had been too small. When she returned to the castle, she would ask Circenn if he knew of any recent litters in the village.

As she approached the bothy, she realized she was going to survive. Her normal feelings were returning, her customary optimism, her desire to be involved in the world and to explore it. She wondered what a bothy actually was. A storehouse? A workshop? Turning the handle, she opened the door open and quietly stepped inside.

Duncan Douglas stood there, nude, his back to her. *My God,* she thought. Not Circenn, but certainly remarkable. Overwhelmingly curious about all things sensual, she was unable to look away. An equally unclothed maid was pressed between his body and the wall. The maid's cheek was flush to the wooden wall and her palms were flattened against it above her head, with Duncan's strong hands covering them. His hips bucked against her, pushing into her from behind.

Lisa wet her lips and breathed softly. She knew she should slip out quietly before they realized they'd been observed.

In just a minute, she told herself, cheeks flaming. Her gaze dropped from his wide shoulders to his waist, over a muscled, tight ass that flexed as he pounded into her. Lisa couldn't move, assaulted by erotic images of Circenn doing the same to her.

"Oh, my heavens." She was so fascinated, the words escaped her before she could spare thought to prevent them.

They both turned to look at her at the same moment. The maid shrieked. The outrageous Duncan merely grinned. "Oops," he said nonchalantly.

Lisa fled the bothy.

At least now she knew what the ancients had used the outbuilding for.

Privacy.

✳ ✳ ✳

The days passed quickly, in a haze of warm sunny mornings and afternoons spent with Duncan, who took her on tours of the castle and estate, and quiet evenings spent with Circenn over scrumptious dinners.

Circenn had been noticeably absent during the afternoons, neither training with his men nor present around the castle, and as they finished dessert that night she inquired about it.

"Come." He rose from the table and motioned for her to follow. "I have something for you, Lisa. I hope it pleases you."

She let him tuck her arm through his and guide her

down a corridor she hadn't yet explored. It led to the end
of the east wing, down winding and narrow stone hall-
ways, through high arched doors, and up a circular stone
staircase. He paused outside the door to a tower and removed a key from his sporran.

"I hope you doona think I have . . ." He blew out a
sigh, looking uncomfortable. "Lass, this seemed an excel-
lent idea when I struck upon it, but now I have some con-
cerns. . . ."

"What?" she asked, perplexed.

"Have you ever come up with an idea that you think
will make someone happy, then when it is time to give it to
them you worry if perhaps you were wrong?"

"Did you make something for me?" she asked, recalling the flecks of wood dust she'd glimpsed him brushing
off his tartan the day before.

"Aye," he muttered, running a hand through his hair.
"But it suddenly occurred to me that if I doona know you
as well as I think I do, it may make you sad."

"Well, I'll just have to see it," she said, slipping the key
from his hand.

Whatever he'd done, he'd pleased her simply by caring,
and thinking about her, not to mention investing his time
in labor with the intent to please her. Aside from her parents and Ruby, she'd received few impulsive gifts in her
lifetime, and never one someone had fashioned by hand.

Curious, she inserted the key in the door, opened it, and
stepped inside. Dozens of candles flickered, filling the
room with a warm glow. The ceiling rose and met in a high
wooden arch, and there were small benches strewn about.
At the front of the room, before four beautifully colored
windows, was a flat slab mounted on a thick base of

stone—an altar. She realized he'd brought her to his private place of worship.

"Look down, lass," he said quietly.

Her gaze dropped to the floor. "Heavens, did you do this?" She glanced at Circenn, bewildered.

"I had a lot of idle time a few years past," he said with a shrug. *About thirty years,* he didn't add. Years during which he had thought he might go insane from loneliness, and so he'd buried his anguish in creating.

Her gaze flew back to the floor. It was an exquisite mosaic hand fashioned of wood, ranging out like a star from the center of the chapel. Light pine, dark walnut, and deep cherry interwove to create the patterns. Some of the pieces of wood were no more than an inch in diameter. *It must have taken him years,* she thought, amazed. One man, designing this floor, carefully carving and sanding the pieces and laying them in a fabulous geometric pattern that would have made M. C. Escher wild with envy.

"Go up near the altar," he encouraged. "That is where I changed it."

Lisa walked gently across the floor, reluctant to mar it with her footsteps. In front of the altar, he'd torn up the old pattern and laid a new one. The area in front of the slab had been divided into two sections: to the right, painstakingly inlaid into the pattern in deep ebony was MORGANNA, BELOVED MOTHER OF CIRCENN. To her left, in the same black wood, was CATHERINE, BELOVED MOTHER OF LISA. There were no dates, an omission she understood, because they certainly wouldn't want anyone to see twenty-first-century dates in a medieval chapel. She could just imagine the heyday modern scholars would have had with that. The names were encircled by elaborate inlaid Celtic knot work.

Dropping to her knees, she ran her fingers over the freshly laid wood, her heart swelling with emotion. He'd placed her mother right next to his, clearly showing her she was half of his life. Now she could go there when she was missing her mother and feel as if she had a place to be near her.

It startled her, his keen insight. When Catherine had been diagnosed with cancer, Lisa had devoured "how to" books on dealing with the loss of a loved one, hoping to find some magic way of handling the impending loss of her mother. One of the things each book had addressed was that closure was a critical part of the healing process. In making this marker for her mother, Circenn had created a tangible and, by ancient social custom, innately comforting symbol of her absence, so that her absence became a soothing presence.

Lisa swallowed a lump in her throat and looked up. He was regarding her as if she were the most infinitely precious thing to him in the world.

"Was I a fool?" he worried.

"No. Circenn, I don't think you could ever be a fool," she said quietly. "Thank you. We do this in my time, too. And I will come here often to . . . to . . ." She trailed off, shaken by the depth of her emotion.

When he said, "Come," she moved easily into his arms.

CHAPTER 20

CIRCENN STALKED TO THE MIRROR AND STUDIED HIM-self for the fifth time in as many minutes. He turned his face to the side and eyed his profile. He ran his hand over his shadow beard thoughtfully. Lisa's skin was very sensi-tive; perhaps he should shave more frequently.

But that wasn't the problem, he mused. Although she'd opened up considerably in the past few days, she retained a distance between them. She was healing, and it was time to complete the process. He needed to woo her into a closer intimacy, to help her fully accept her position as his soon-to-be wife.

Whom was he trying to deceive? He needed to bed her before he turned into a ravening beast. Not for a moment had he forgotten the vision he'd spied in his shield. And he wanted it, was eager to embrace his future. He'd been going excruciatingly slowly with her, allowing her time to heal. But she was changing again, becoming stronger.

He snorted, reflecting that she was not the only one who had undergone changes since her arrival. A few months ago he'd been a man of rigid discipline who despised many things about himself. Now he was a man of deep passion who welcomed what he might become—with her. A few months ago he'd eschewed physical intimacy, compiling dozens of reasons why it was logical to forswear it. Now he longed for physical intimacy, armed with dozens of reason why it was logical, arguably even necessary that he embrace it.

After he'd given her the chapel, he'd escorted her to her room, hoping to sweep her past a good-night kiss, but she'd been reticent. Her kiss had been stormy, and he'd plainly scented the desire in her body, but she'd been the one to stop the kiss, bidding him good sleep before leaving him at the door. He suspected that while she would allow herself to be somewhat happy, she was still not quite ready to believe that she shouldn't continue to suffer for sins she hadn't committed.

For her sake, he needed to be ruthless. He needed to penetrate her shell and ease her fully into his life. He wanted her, this fascinating woman with her deep emotions, her passionate heart, her witty and curious mind. He wanted her droll sense of humor, which had been noticeably absent of late. He needed her to accept the deepest physical bond with him because he knew that once she did, she would bar no quarter of her heart from him. And he wanted to explore every private nook and cranny of her soul.

Ruthlessly seductive, that was what he would be.

He gathered his hair back into a thong and considered shaving, but was too impatient for her. They had retired from dinner a half-hour past, and with any luck she would be curled up in bed.

And he would join her. It was time.

Tonight he would make her his.

* * *

Lisa sipped her cider wine and watched the fire, feeling remarkably dissatisfied after finishing a delicious meal with a delicious companion and being given the lovely gift of the chapel. Her body was thrumming with frustration and she'd been having a perfectly vicious argument with herself.

Since she'd emerged from her chambers after her bout of grieving, Circenn had repeatedly given her every indication that he desired to enter a sexual relationship with her, but something was holding her back and she didn't have the faintest idea what it was. She'd studied it from every angle but still was no closer to understanding why she pulled away each time he tried to do more than kiss her. She hovered on the verge of asking him if *he* knew why she did, but couldn't bring herself to be quite so brutally honest.

A part of her wished he would try to storm her walls, so she could figure out what the damned walls were. She thought she'd decided to be happy here, but then why resist his seduction?

A knock at the door set her heart to pounding.

"Come in," she called softly, desperately hoping it would not be Gillendria who entered, carrying yet another restitched gown or surcoat.

"Lass," Circenn murmured, as he closed the door behind him.

Lisa sat up straight and placed her wine goblet on the table. *Don't say anything—just kiss me,* she thought. *Kiss me hard and fast and don't give me time to think.*

"There was something I wanted to discuss with you, lass," he said. He crossed the room and pulled her up from the chair.

"Yes?"

He stopped and gazed down at her for a long moment. "Och, sometimes I make a fankle of things with words," he finally said. "I've been a warrior all my life, not a blethering bard." Cradling her head in his hands, he seized her mouth with his.

He buried his fingers in her hair, slipped his tongue between her lips with a smooth velvety stroke, kissing her slowly and thoroughly. He gave her a long, deliciously romantic kiss that left her clinging to him breathlessly. He nibbled her lower lip, sucking and tugging, then swept inside again, possessing her mouth. His hands slid down her back and over her bottom, and he groaned. He needed her desperately, but he also needed her to seek his affection. His tongue retreated and he paused, waiting for her to seek its return.

She didn't.

He sighed and moved back an inch to look at her. "At least fight me, lass, like you did when the Bruce declared us handfasted. Think you I've forgotten that? When I took my tongue from you then, you would have none of it."

Lisa averted her gaze.

Ruthless, Circenn reminded himself, *or she will slip away from you. You cannot leave her trapped in grief and guilt.*

When she moved to sit on the bed, he exhaled a small sigh of relief. The fact that she felt comfortable perching on the target of his seduction told him she wasn't entirely adverse to it.

"What are you waiting for, Lisa?" He sank next to her onto the bed. He was heartened that she didn't pull away but merely sat together, shoulder brushing shoulder. "Do you remember what you said to me the night that you arrived here, when you feared I might take your life?"

She glanced warily at him, indicating that she was listening.

"*I have not even* lived *yet*. Those are the words you said to me, and I heard many things in that statement. I heard frustration and regret. I heard curiosity and hunger for experiences, and a terrible fear that you would never get to have them. *I cannot die. I have not even lived yet!* you said to me. I thought you meant it. That given the chance you would live boldly."

Lisa flinched. She could feel the echo welling up inside her. It was true, she thought defiantly, she *hadn't* even lived yet. She felt a sudden flash of fury. She'd spent years denying herself the luxury of feelings, and with a few simple sentences, Circenn stripped them bare in front of her. She resented his psychoanalyzing her. It made her angry that he dared be so intimate with her feelings. Her eyes narrowed.

His lips curving in a faint, understanding smile, he said, "Go on, be angry with me, lass, for giving voice to the things you try not to feel. Be angry with me for saying aloud what you scarcely permit yourself to think—that a part of you resents your mother being ill because you cannot give yourself permission to live while she is dying. Be angry with me for saying that it tears you into little pieces, and that you feel you should suffer, because how could you not when your own mother lies dying? Be angry with me for demanding that you live now. Live with me. Fully."

Her hands clenched around wads of blanket. She couldn't deny anything he'd said. She *did* feel that she should suffer, since her mother was suffering. She *did* feel that every small smile she permitted herself was somehow a betrayal of Catherine. How dare Lisa smile when her mother was dying? What kind of monster could be happy for even an instant? Yet, she'd smiled occasionally, and even laughed, and then had hated herself for it. He was right on—this was what had been holding her back. An insidious little belief that she still had no right to be happy.

"Will you continue to punish yourself for sins not of your making? How much must you suffer before you feel you have paid in full? Would your lifetime be enough?"

Her lashes swept down, shielding her eyes.

"Would it be so wrong to plunge headlong into the love I offer you? Take—draw of life, suck it into your body, taste it with a vengeance."

"Damn you," she whispered.

"For saying what you think? Lass, I am the one you may say anything to. I assure you, I will understand. I doona care how ignoble you think your thoughts or feelings are. Feelings, emotions—they are neither right nor wrong. They cannot be assigned a value. Feelings *are*. By labeling a feeling wrong, you force yourself to ignore that feeling. And what you most need is to feel it, let it burn through you, then get on with life. You are not responsible for any of what happened to your parents. But to punish yourself for a having a feeling—och, lass, that is wrong. You felt some resentment—there is no shame in that. You are young and full of life—there is no shame in that."

Lisa looked as if she desperately wished to believe him.

"It wasn't your fault—not the wreck, not your mother getting ill, not your being brought here to me. Let go of it. Stand up, Lisa. Take what you want from me. Live now."

"Damn you," she repeated, shaking her head. Feelings long denied now flooded her.

She sat still, his words echoing in her mind. Then another voice startled her, because it sounded so like Catherine's, resounding in her head: *No more punishment. He's right, you know. Do you think I didn't see what you were doing to yourself? Live, Lisa.*

Her hands were trembling. Could she? Did she know how? After years of refusing to believe that anything good might happen to her, could she reclaim the dreams she'd had of being a woman unafraid to love?

Her gaze swept over him. Magnificent Highlander, half savage, yet more civilized than most modern men. Tender, caring enough to penetrate her shell in a valiant effort to wrench her from it. She would never find a better man.

Live, she agreed.

Without a word, she rose to her feet, suffering the sensation that she was splitting into two different people. As if in the act of rising she slipped from her twenty-first-century body, leaving the old Lisa huddling on the bed, her arms wrapped around a pillow, vehemently denying her own needs. This new Lisa stood tall and composed, waiting for—inviting—his next demand. Ready to make demands of her own.

"Remove your gown, Lisa."

Her breath clawed its way from her lungs.

"I said remove your gown."

"What about you?"

"This is not about me. This is about you. Let me love you, lass. I promise you will not regret it."

Lisa drew a shallow breath. He saw her heart as it really was, full of complicated and less-than-noble emotions, yet he wanted her. And in removing her gown she was dropping her barriers and extending her arms to welcome him. Welcoming what they could be together.

Her fingers felt stiff and clumsy as they moved over her clothing, but grew more nimble the more honest she was with herself.

"I want you. I am here for you. I adore you."

I adore you . . . His words lingered. And she acknowledged that she wanted it to be just like this. To disrobe for this man, to offer him her body, to find the approval and desire she knew he felt for her. To reach out and taste what he offered, to turn her willing body over to him to be taught, initiated, savored.

To live.

Her gown rustled to the floor.

"Stop!" He sat motionless, gazing at her as she stood, pale in the candlelight, in her lavender bra and panties. He made a sound low in his throat. Lisa had never heard a man make such a sound before, but she realized that she wanted to hear him make that sound many times, looking at her in just the same way.

"Proceed," he said finally, "verra slowly, lass. Kill me with it. You know I want you; use it. It is one of your many powers."

Lisa blinked, thrilled to realize that she had such power as a woman. His plaid was lifting, his chest was falling and rising rapidly, and his eyes were dark with desire. He was inviting her to wield her feminine strength, and she wanted to. In her fantasies she'd dreamed of just this: being with a man whose attraction to her was something she was so certain of that she could tease him, revel in her femininity, provoke and invite the consequences.

Slowly she began to strip away her lingerie, sliding the straps of her bra off her shoulders, tugging playfully, provocatively at the bow between her breasts. When his eyes flared, she slipped off her soft slippers and tossed one at him. The motion made her breasts sway gently. When the slipper hit him lightly in the chest, he swallowed hard and tensed to rise from the bed.

"No. I find I like this. You encouraged me. Let me discover who I am."

Circenn sank back to the bed, but looked ready to launch himself at her at any moment. A scrap of lace fluttered to the floor, then another, and Lisa stood before him holding her breath. She saw herself reflected in the polished mirror behind him and moved a bit to the right. *Perfect,* she thought: She could now see him fully clothed, his wide shoulders and muscled back, the bed, and herself standing nude before him. It was fiercely arousing, erotic, her desire strangely heightened by the fact that he was still completely dressed.

"Turn around."

"What?" she gasped, nearly losing her composure.

His laugh was a low purr. "You are perfection, lass. But turn around and show me all of your lovely body. I've been dreaming about you for weeks."

Lisa swallowed, uncertain that she could do it. She wouldn't be able to see him. What if he thought her behind was fat? *Men never think a behind is fat,* Ruby had told her once. *They're so happy just to be seeing it.*

"Come, lass. Show me if your back arches as I think it does—a cool sweep of ivory, with your hair tumbling down it. Show me that beautiful bottom. Show me those long lovely legs. Show me every inch of what I am going to kiss and taste."

His words were more than adequately persuasive; what woman could refuse such a promise? Lisa drew a deep breath and turned. After a few moments of excruciating silence, she glanced nervously over her shoulder, seeking their reflection in the mirror. He had dropped to his knees by the bed and was crouched behind her, looking up and down, and up and down again.

Black eyes lifted to meet her gaze. The expression on his face was wild, possessive, and made her feel she was the most beautiful woman ever to stroll through his fourteenth-century world. He lunged to his feet and hauled her back against him, hard. The rough fabric of his plaid was arousing against her sensitive skin and she melted against his body. With a firm tug, he pulled her bare bottom against his hips, and she lost herself in the sensation of the fabric and the hard length of maleness that lay just beneath it. She pushed back, feeling the ridge of him pressing in the cleft of her behind. It jerked against her and she gasped with anticipation.

His hands slid up her waist, over her ribs, and he held her breasts reverently at first, then with rough excitement. Her nipples were already hard and aching from the cool air in the room, and when his fingers brushed them she nearly screamed. Her hips bucked back, and a flash of pleasure darted from her nipples to where she would take him into her body. He pinched them, and she felt her world spinning, narrowing down to nothing but her and him, and a desire to do everything with him that was possible between a man and a woman.

"That's it. Push back against me. Show me how you want me." He rocked against her, imitating the thrust and draw of lovemaking, and she felt the wetness between her thighs. Her movements became strained as wordlessly she begged for his body.

He wrapped an arm around her waist, bit the nape of her neck, catching the tendon between his teeth. It felt so . . . dominating. His other hand sought her lips, and he slipped his finger between them. She stroked it with her tongue, closing her lips over it and sucking it into her mouth.

Gently, he inched her toward the chest at the foot of the bed.

"Sit."

She sat breathlessly, so aroused that even the chest felt good to her aching bottom. Hard, that was what she wanted, something hard, and solid, and . . . *him*.

He stood before her, legs splayed, eyes dark. He brushed her nipples with his palms, his calluses deliciously abrasive against her sensitive peaks. She watched them tighten, fascinated by her body's responses to him. With his knee he nudged her legs apart slightly, seemingly transfixed by the small dark mole on the inside of her left thigh. He wet his lips, and she knew he would kiss her there many times.

Holding her gaze, he undressed for her, with excruciating leisure, never taking his eyes off her. No modern-day stripper could have competed with the performance he gave her. It had a funny effect on her emotions, that even though she was naked, even though he could have taken her quickly, he was making it as he'd promised: all about her. He was progressing slowly, feeding her every fantasy. He was still trying to woo her, despite the fact that he'd clearly already won her.

When he stood nude before her she closed her eyes, overwhelmed by him. She took a deep breath and opened them again, only to discover him bobbing before her. *It's beautiful,* she thought. She'd never realized that a man could be so beautiful. The hard bulges in his abdomen tapered into lean muscles that rippled down to his thighs, creating a vee of taut ridges that commanded attention to the raw masculinity that hung heavily between his legs. The mere sight of him made her stomach feel tight and empty. It was thick and long and raising itself eagerly. Olive-pink, smooth, velvety-looking, hooded, with a strong vein running the length of it. It would be warm—no, it would feel hot and silky beneath her hand.

Leaning closer for a better look, she was startled when it bobbed again and brushed her cheek. Laughing, she looked up at him, and lost her breath.

He stared down at her transfixed, his expression so possessive that she gasped. She would never be the same after this night. *Be bold,* she told herself. *Be brave and wanton and everything you always fantasized about being. Take from life, Lisa.*

She wrapped her hand around him, and, as she'd suspected, her fingers couldn't close. A shiver shot through her, imagining her body yielding to take so much of him. He bucked within her grip. A smile curved her lips. She could do that to him, make him jerk hungrily in response to her touch. She squeezed, sliding her hand up and down.

This part of him was such a contradiction: so hard, yet the skin so very soft and sensitive, so strong, yet so weak before a woman, so easily wielded by a man as a weapon, yet so easily used as a weapon against him. Lisa licked her lips, wondering how he tasted. Salty? Sweet? Where was her whipped cream? She dropped her head and brushed her lips over the tip of him. Just once, a tight suction with her lips, the quick flick of a tongue, just enough to taste him and assuage her curiosity.

A bit salty, and a scent of spicy man, she thought, pondering the flavor on her tongue, her hand momentarily still. His spicy scent that numbed her brain was more prevalent here, near the center of his manhood. It did alarming things to her—both relaxed and stimulated her. She glanced up, wondering why he'd gone motionless, and was stunned by the startled, savage look on his face.

He drew her up into his arms, swept her back onto the

bed, and stretched himself on top of her. "Lass, I am going to love you until you cannot walk from my bed," he whispered, before kissing her.

She responded eagerly, fiercely, molding her mouth to his.

"Slowly first." He drew back slightly. With excruciating gentleness he brushed his lips against her, once, twice, a dozen times. She parted her lips against his gentle friction, signifying her desire for more. He laughed softly and ran the tip of his tongue in a playful circle over her lips. He teased until she was moving frantically, trying to catch his tongue with hers.

"Place your hands above your head, lass, and if you have a problem keeping them there I will be happy to use fabric to secure them," he murmured.

"What? Do you want to tie me up?" she exclaimed, mildly shocked. She felt his lips curve in a smile against hers; he was amused by her reaction.

"I would not be adverse to the idea." His laughter was husky, darkly erotic. "But for now, I merely wish you to restrain your hands from my body. You need give nothing, do nothing; I assure you, I'll be taking my pleasure in the giving."

Lie back and let me pleasure you, he was saying. *Have I died and gone to heaven?* she wondered. *And he prefers to do this?* Her fantasy lovers had always been dominant and demanding illusions who exhausted themselves in bed, giving their woman pleasure. Obediently, she raised her hands above her head. The movement lifted her breasts, and he caught one roughly with his mouth.

Then she was burning, her nipples were on fire. He nipped and tongued, licked and tugged until her breasts felt swollen and hot. He raised them together and dragged his tongue down the soft crevice, then he separated them and kissed each nipple. He nipped her stomach and kissed her hips—the very sensitive part where her leg met her upper body, only inches from the soft hair between her thighs. The skin was thinner there, more delicate. He pressed hot kisses to the tiny mole inside her thigh, dragged his velvety tongue over it, and she arched against him, instinctively guiding him closer to her center.

His tongue flicked out to taste her and her hands flew down to cradle his head between her legs as she arched against him. He tasted her with long, smooth strokes against the sensitive nub, alternately fast, then languid, then fast again. "Oh, God!" She embraced the pleasure. She soared, spiraled, shuddered, and when she fell he was there to catch her, with promise in his eyes.

He slipped a finger inside her and she contracted helplessly around it. She realized that there was an entirely different sensation she'd not yet experienced. She'd heard that orgasms could be very different when a man was inside a woman, as opposed to an orgasm from external sensation. She could feel just the hint, the promise of the fullness it would offer.

"Tight. Too tight, lass. You need to be more relaxed, and I know of only one way to accomplish that." His lips burned against her skin as he kissed her mole, tongued it, then stroked his velvety kisses down to her ankles, her toes, and back up with delicious slowness. And when he returned, he lowered his head and ensured that she was completely relaxed by sending her over the edge again.

Two fingers.

The fullness!

Three. "Relax, lass. I doona wish to hurt you overmuch. I am—"

"I know," she panted. "You are. I saw you." She was awed and a little afraid.

His hands were magic, her body eased open, only to contract swiftly when he removed his fingers. *The ache, oh, the unbearable ache.*

"Please," she groaned.

He raised himself above her and positioned himself between her legs. But he didn't enter—nay, he took her lips with his and kissed her: light and teasing, kissed her deeply, kissed her so hard that his teeth bumped against hers, which she'd always thought might seem clumsy but it wasn't, it made her nearly wild beneath him. She arched her lower body, pressing against that hot male part of him, and he pressed back against her, hard.

"In me," she cried.

He laughed against her lips. "Impatient lass."

"Yes I am. In me."

"Aye aye, mistress," he whispered.

He gave it to her slowly. The first inch was a most unusual sensation and she doubted she could take him. The second inch promised pain. The third and fourth *were* painful, but the seventh and eighth promised heaven. Lisa closed her eyes and devoted her full attention to the hard man inside her. She had never felt such a pressure, such a completing sensation in her life. She could have stayed like that forever.

And then he rocked slowly within her. "Squeeze me," he whispered.

"What?"

"With your muscles." When she stared at him blankly, he tickled her suddenly, causing her to laugh. The muscles inside her contracted and she understood.

"Squeeze like that, you mean?"

He went completely still inside her. "Squeeze."

It was the most incredible sensation. She could use her woman's muscles to contract on him and release, and every time she contracted around him it sent her perilously close to the edge. He lay motionless atop her, letting her feel him, grow used to him, develop an insatiable hunger for the pleasure of him buried within her.

"Does it arouse you?" he asked.

"Oh, yes," she murmured.

He withdrew slowly, savoring every sweet contraction of her muscles, then filled her to the mouth of her womb.

The night was young, and over the course of it he made a wee bit of progress down his endless list of things he wanted to do with her. Her insatiable curiosity extended into the bedchamber, as he had hoped it would. She was a most willing conspirator throughout the long night of passion-slicked bodies and yielding hearts.

When he rose, bracing his hands wide on the bed to either side of her, threw back his head and lost a part of himself deep within her, he nearly doubled over in agony. His muscles wrenched tightly in his abdomen, his heart pounded alarmingly, and his head felt it might split. In all his life, he had never permitted himself to spill inside a woman, refusing to have children. First because he'd not been ready, then because of what Adam had done to him.

But he'd laid his fears aside, and this time he let go. And at the precise moment he filled her, he felt a bond flare into life between the two of them, as if a channel had been cut between their souls, allowing a bit of her to seep into him, and a bit of him into her. It burned through his body, tunneling to the part of his mind that held magic. It was like a blinding white heat that roared inside him and exploded in a flash of heightened awareness.

It was the most incredible sensation he had ever experienced.

Suddenly he could feel *her* pleasure, could even sense that she felt grateful to him for helping her forget her pain and making her first time such an incredible experience.

Hmm, he thought, liking this new bond. *He had exceeded her expectations for lovemaking.* His gaze flew to hers and he saw that it had been the same for her. But she didn't know, because this was her first and only time of physical intimacy, that such an awareness of each other was *not* a normal result of lovemaking. Her eyes were huge and filled with wonder.

He didn't understand what had transpired in the creation of their strange bond, and he wondered what lasting effects it might have on her. He wondered if perhaps the immortality potion had changed him, so that if he spilled seed into a woman's body they became linked. There was much he did not understand about himself.

And then he wondered no more, but cradled her in his arms and felt at peace for the first time in centuries.

* * *

Afterward, Lisa lay with her cheek pressed to Circenn's chest, one of his strong arms curled around her waist, wondering at the God who had seen fit to take so much from her, yet give her this incredible man. She'd never known that lovemaking would make her so much more aware of his feelings. It was as if someone had flipped a switch inside her: A dazzling white heat filled her, and suddenly she was able to sense his emotions; even now he was worrying for her, wondering if he'd pleased her. It was a strange awareness, a pressure that he was near, surrounding her;

she'd never before felt so linked to anyone, not even her mother, who'd carried her inside her body.

She vowed to plunge headlong into all the pleasure she could find with Circenn, because one never knew how long anything might last. He could be crushed under a rock while building an addition on his castle; he could be injured in many ways; he might be wounded in battle— oh! It was June, she realized, and the mighty battle at Bannockburn was just weeks away.

He couldn't go; that was all there was to it. She could not let him go to war. The way her luck ran, she would get a few blissful weeks with him, then he would be killed in battle and there she'd be in the fourteenth century all by herself. Her fingers clenched around his hand.

"I will not die, lass," he whispered against her hair.

"Can you read minds too, in addition to cursing things?" she asked, startled.

"Nay. But you were feeling it rather loudly. I know what you fear. You fear being abandoned. When your hand tensed on mine I surmised where your fears had gone. That I might die too young, as your father did." He acted as if their new bond was nothing out of the ordinary. It was easier for her to accept because, being untried, she didn't know it wasn't the customary result of tupping.

"But you could die," she said. "There's a war going on—"

"Shh." He drew her close and rolled from his back to his side, so they lay facing each other, their heads sharing a pillow, their noses touching. "I swear to you that I will not die. Do you trust me, lass?"

"Yes. But I don't understand. How could anyone possibly swear that they won't die? Even you can't control that."

"Trust me. Have no fear for me, Lisa. It would be wasted

fear. Let's just say my unique abilities include the knowledge of when I will die, and it will not be for a very long
time."

She was silent, and he felt a shiver run through her.

He knew she was hearing more than his words, was
feeling his intent behind them. They had a new awareness
of each other that transcended words, as if their souls had
become entangled. Via that bond, she was comforted, sensing truth in his words, although she didn't understand the
how or why of it. He held her, reveling in their strange tie.
He sensed the moment at which she relinquished her fears
and relaxed, not merely because she wet her lip and glanced
at him provocatively.

And what he felt next needed no words.

CHAPTER 21

ADAM SIFTED THE GRAINS OF TIME AND DARTED through them to the isle of Morar. He would relax there for a day or so, ponder the developments, study the potentials, and determine where his gentle nudging might be required. Things were progressing well, and he had no intention of losing what he'd thus far gained. He'd experienced a bit of concern during the time she'd remained in her chambers, grieving, but she had indeed been as strong as he'd suspected, emerging ready for love.

And how lovely she'd been in her bath, he reflected with a smile.

As his feet hit the beach, he willed his clothing gone, then he strolled languidly, burying his toes deep in the wet, silky-warm sand. Once, he'd walked on a California beach, nude in the full glory of his true form. Thousands of Californians had been stricken by high fevers that had erupted in public displays of eroticism.

He loved being Adam.

The sun beat down upon his muscled chest, a tropical breeze licked his dark hair. He was a pagan god, savoring his world—there was no better place to be.

Most of the time.

In the bay, a ship sailed past. Adam grinned and waved. The pitiful occupants of the ship could no more see the island than they could fly to the stars. The exotic isle simply didn't exist, in the usual sense of the word. But fairy isles were like that—in the mortal world, but not of the mortal world. Occasionally, a mortal was born who could see both worlds, but those creatures were rare, and usually stolen quickly after birth by the *Tuatha de Danaan*, to minimize the risk. Ever since Manannán had given his people the drink of immortality and the Compact had been negotiated, the *Tuatha de Danaan* had been exceedingly cautious when treading in the world of man.

Still, Adam thought, there were times when even a demigod such as himself couldn't resist. There was something about the world of man that fascinated him, made him think he had perhaps once been more similar to them than he could clearly recall, his memories dimmed by time's passage.

"In what merriment have you been indulging?" Aoibheal, Queen of the Fairies, purred behind him.

She joined him, her long, beautiful legs keeping pace with his, and guided him toward a crimson chaise that conveniently appeared before them. She sank into it and patted the cushions, indicating that he should join her. She glistened, sprinkled in gold dust as was her custom. Were he to run his finger down her, it would come away glittering with fine gold powder. He had long suspected the dust contained an aphrodisiac that penetrated the skin of those who touched her, rendering them powerless to refuse her.

When she beckoned him intimately near, he masked his astonishment. It had been an eternity since his queen had invited him to share her pillowed haven. What was she up to? As he sank down beside her, she molded her body

against his. He exhaled a low rush of breath, the equivalent of a human shiver. She was the Queen of the *Tuatha
de Danaan* for a reason: Her power was enormous, her al-
lure immense. She was erotic, and many found her frightening; a mere mortal could lose his life in her arms,
drained by her appetites. Even among Adam's kind, males
had walked away from her boudoir changed.

"Naught to worry, my Queen, I have been but passing
idle time with Circenn." Unable to resist, he kissed a golden
nipple, dragging his tongue across the peak.

Aoibheal watched him, her unusual eyes bright, her head
propped upon a delicate fist. She fisted her other hand in his
hair and lifted his head from her breast. Her exotically
slanted eyes were ancient in her ageless face. "Think you I
know not of the woman?" she said. "You've done it again.
How far do you think you may push our limits?"

"I did not bring her through time. It was not my doing.
Circenn cursed something, and, as a result, the woman was
brought back to his century."

"I see." She stretched her long, slim body languidly,
sweeping the curve of her breasts against him. "Please remind me, I seem to be forgetting—who was it that taught
Circenn Brodie how to curse things in the first place?"

Adam acknowledged his guilt with silence.

"Assure me, fool mine, that you had nothing to do with
precisely when and where that cursed object was found.
You did not perhaps nudge it a bit in one direction?"

"I no more nudged the object than arranged the battle
in which it was lost."

She laughed softly. "Ah, another Adam-ism—that which
confesses nothing while arrogantly concealing nothing. I
have seen her. I went to Brodie and inspected her. I find her
quite . . . interesting."

"Leave her alone," Adam snapped.

"So you do have an interest in this, although you conveniently blame it on that Scot laird." She cocked her head and regarded him coolly. "You will not interfere again. I know you've been visiting her in another guise. Eirren will pay her court no more. No." She raised a hand when he would have protested. "Amadan Dubh, I compel you thusly: You will leave neither my side nor the isle of Morar unless I grant you permission."

Adam hissed. "How dare you!"

"I dare anything. I am your Queen, though you seem to forget it from time to time. You pay clever tithes to my supremacy with your lips, but you defy me over and again. You have gone too far. You broke one of our most serious covenants with Circenn Brodie, and now you dare to compound it. I will not tolerate it."

"You are jealous," Adam said cruelly. "You resent my attachment—"

"It is unnatural!" Aoibheal hissed. "You should have no such attachment! It is not our way!"

"It was done long ago and cannot be undone. Do not think to constrain me. I will only find a way around it."

Aoibheal arched a gilded brow. "I think not, Amadan, for you are at my side until I release you. My command was clear. Ponder it. There is no weak spot for you to exploit."

In his mind, Adam sorted through her words. Her command had been simple, direct, and flawless. His eyes widened as he comprehended how completely she had snared him with so few words. Most who tried to command him composed lengthy written canons, like that boorish Sidheach Douglas at Dalkeith-Upon-the-Sea, who'd written a veritable book. But sometimes, less was truly more, and she had chosen her words well. He could leave neither her nor the island unless and until she said so. "But they will sully my creation."

"I care not. From this moment on, you are powerless in their lives. Amadan Dubh: I take from you the gift of sifting time."

"Stop!"

"Obey me and cease your tiresome protests."

"You *bitch*."

"For that I take from you your ability to weave worlds."

Adam fell silent, his face ashen. The Queen could strip everything from him, if she so desired.

"Are you quite finished?" she asked silkily.

Adam nodded, not trusting himself to speak.

"Good. When it is done, I will release you. When they have played out their choices. Now come, lovely fool: Show me you still know how to please a Queen, and make it your finest effort, for you have offended me most egregiously and I shall require much in the way of . . . *mmm*."

✳   ✳   ✳

Robert the Bruce was fuming. The travel-stained, weary messenger who stood before him shuffled miserably, awaiting the fatal blow. He eyed the Bruce's sword, knowing that the moment his king pulled it from its scabbard, he would likely lose his courage and dignity and beg or, worse, run.

"What was my brother *thinking*?"

"I doona know that he was," the messenger replied dejectedly. "They were well besotted with whisky."

"Had he been drinking with the English again?" Robert's lips curled in a sneer.

The messenger nodded, afraid to speak.

"How dare he be the one to determine the time and place for my battles?" Robert thundered. He couldn't believe what the messenger had imparted: His brother Edward, who was in charge of the siege against Stirling Castle, which was being held by the English, had made a "wager" with the Englishman holding it. A wager! A drink-induced challenge, and booty far more valuable than Stirling itself was the prize.

An admission of defeat was the prize, a full retreat from the battle for the crown. Robert could nearly feel his kingdom slipping from his tenuous grasp. His men weren't yet ready for this battle. He needed more time.

"You may be underestimating your men," Niall McIllioch said. "I know it often seems the present is not the right time, but perhaps it is."

Robert shot him a furious glance. "Exactly what were the words exchanged?" he demanded of the ashen messenger.

The messenger winced and glanced around the dim interior of the Bruce's tent, seeking help. No one came to his aid. Two blue-eyed Berserkers watched his every move from the shadows—as if that wasn't enough to make a man collapse in a puddle of fear! He sighed, resigned to further infuriating his king.

"Sir Philip de Mowbray, the current commander of the English forces at Stirling, wagered with your brother thusly: If a relieving English army does not approach to within three miles of Stirling Castle by Midsummer's Day, he will surrender the castle to you and your brother and leave Scotland, never to return. If the relieving army successfully attains Stirling, you will give up your fight for Scotland's independence."

"And my dim-witted brother Edward accepted this?" Robert roared.

"Aye."

Robert shook his head. "Does he not realize what this means? Does he not realize that King Edward will gather every troop he has—English, Welsh, Irish, French, supported by every mercenary he can hire—and drive them into my land in less than two weeks' time?"

No one breathed in the tent.

"Does my idiot brother not realize that England has triple our mounted men, quadruple our spearmen and archers?"

"But they're *our* hills and valleys," Niall reminded softly. "We know this land. We know what advantages to exploit, and doona forget, we have Brodie and his Templars. We have the gentle mists and bogs. We can do this, Robert. We've been fighting for years for our freedom and we have yet attained no decisive victory. It is time now. Doona underestimate the men who follow you. We have two weeks to rally the forces. Believe in us as we have believed in you."

Robert drew a deep breath and pondered Niall's words. *Had* he been too cautious? Had he been willing to fight only small battles because it wouldn't be such a terrible loss if they failed? Had he unwisely restrained his men from a major war because he feared the possibility of defeat? Circenn had been impatient to war. His Berserkers were impatient to war, aye—and his own impatient brother had wagered their future. Perhaps they were all impatient because it was time.

"Let us summon Brodie. This is what you've been waiting for," Niall said firmly.

"Aye, milord," said Lulach, Niall's brother. "If we prevent Edward's army from reaching Stirling, we will have turned the tides. We will be unstoppable, and if ever the time was now, the time is now. Plantagenet grows weaker in his own country; many of his own lords will not follow him into our land. I say we face this wager boldly, as a gift of fate."

Robert nodded finally. To the messenger, he said, "Get you to Castle Brodie with all haste. Command Circenn to bring his men to join us at St. Ninian's Church by the Roman road. Tell him time is of the essence and to bring every weapon he possesses."

The messenger expelled a relieved breath and fled the tent for Inverness.

* * *

Lisa and Circenn explored each other with uninhibited joy, withdrawing completely into a world of their own making. Circenn laughed more than he had in centuries. Lisa talked more, voicing thoughts and feelings she hadn't even suspected lay dormant within her. In this way they rediscovered themselves, opening up closed compartments that needed the light of day.

The two of them roamed the estate, picnicking in the fresh spring air, dashing off to the bothy for a private moment. It was there that Lisa confided to Circenn what she'd seen Duncan doing with Alesone.

"Did you look?" He scowled possessively. "Did you see him entirely in the blush?"

"Yes." Lisa's cheeks heated.

"I doona care for that thought. You will not look upon another man unclothed for the rest of your life."

Lisa laughed. He sounded so thoroughly medieval. "He didn't look as good as you."

"I still doona care. It makes me angry with Duncan merely for being a man."

Then he erased her memory of the young, virile Douglas, against the wall in the bothy.

Twice.

They spent long nights in his bed, in her bed, on the stairs late one night when the Greathall was deserted. She told him about her life, and slowly, haltingly, he began to tell her of his. But there she sensed he was holding something back. Because of their odd connection, she could feel a darkness in him that waxed and waned without explanation. Sometimes, when he watched the children playing outside in the courtyard, he grew silent, and she could feel that peculiar mixture of anguish and anger that she simply didn't understand.

The castle staff was delighted with the laird's newfound laughter, and Duncan and Galan beamed when they dined together. Gone were the private seduction dinners—Circenn saved that for later in the privacy of their chambers. Meals were now taken not in the formal dining hall but in the Greathall, with an assortment of knights and the occasional Templar.

Lisa was slowly and irresistibly becoming fourteenth-century. She learned to love the flowing gowns and tartans, even sitting with some of the women, watching them dye the fibers and fashion the Brodie weave.

She loved the fact that people sat about the hearth and talked in the evening, rather than retreating to their individual electronic worlds of television, phones, and computer games. They possessed richly detailed oral histories and were eager to share them. Duncan and Galan knew their clan history centuries back and wove grand tales of the many Douglas heroes. Lisa listened and sorted through her own genealogy, looking for a Stone to speak of, but who cared if one's uncle was a lawyer? Could he chop wood and carry water?

Blissfully the days and nights unfurled, and Lisa realized

that she now understood why her mother had lost the will to live when Jack died. If her mom had felt a tenth of what Lisa felt for Circenn, it would have been devastating for Catherine to lose her husband. And her mother had lost so much in one day—her love, her ability to walk, her entire way of life. Lisa attained a new respect for her mother's strength, only now understanding the extent of her mother's loss and the pain it must have caused her to continue living without Jack.

Circenn's strength and love were always curled around her like a protective cloak. She couldn't imagine how she'd lived before without it. The link between them kept her constantly aware of him, no matter where he was. It was never invasive, but she'd discovered—feeling a need for complete privacy while using the chamber pot—that it could be dimmed if she wished. She would never be lonely again. Sometimes, when he was far away, riding with his men, something would amuse him and she would sense his rich laughter rolling inside her, although she would have no idea what had made him laugh.

At other times she would feel his frustration while he was off with his knights, and without even knowing what he was angry about, she would be flooded by his raw masculinity that roared to wield a battle-ax and actively protect his homeland. Via their bond, she experienced masculine emotions and drives she'd never understood before, and was fascinated by the knowledge that he was feeling her more tender, womanly ones.

It wasn't until she asked him if he knew of a puppy she might adopt that she choked on a deep, bitter swallow of the blackness inside him.

They were sitting on the stone bench by the reflecting pool—it had become a favorite spot of theirs—watching

some children tossing a bladder ball in the courtyard.
A small mutt had plunged into the melee and grabbed
the ball between his sharp teeth, and when it had burst
against his whiskers, he'd shot straight up into the air,
yipping frantically, comically trying to scrape the remains
of the skin off his nose. While the children had giggled
helplessly, Lisa had laughed until tears sparkled in her
eyes.

"I want a puppy," she said, when her amusement sub-
sided. "I've always wanted one, but our apartment was too
small and—"

"No."

Perplexed, her smile faded. A wave of sorrow engulfed
her, radiating from him. It cloaked her in a deep sense of
futility. "Why?"

He brooded, staring at the yapping mutt. "Why would
you want a puppy? They doona live long, you know."

"Yes, they do. They can live ten to fifteen years, depending on the breed."

"Ten to fifteen years. Then they die."

"Yes," Lisa agreed, unable to fathom his resistance. Another wave of darkness and anger surged around her. "Did
you have a puppy once?"

"No. Come. Let us walk." He rose and extended his
hand. Guiding her away from the playing children, he led
her into a thick copse.

"But, Circenn, I don't mind that a puppy will die. At
least I get to love it for the time I have with it."

He pushed her back against a tree and covered her
mouth with his, savagely.

Her breath came out in a soft *humph*, as he crushed her
between his body and the tree. She was smothered in his
emotions: pain, hopelessness, and hunger tinged by a savage

need to possess her completely, to brand her with his body. And something more, something that danced tantalizingly out of her reach.

"Mine," he whispered against her lips.

"What a totally barbaric"—she drew a deep breath beneath the onslaught of his lips—"medieval, arrogant, warlord thing to say."

"And true. You are mine." He dragged his tongue across her lower lip, tasting, suckling. His fingers dug into the soft flesh of her hips. He crowded her against the tree, pressing her into it. His blackness charged the air between them and infiltrated her, drenching her with his tension. He raised her skirts and slipped his hand up her thigh, abruptly burying his finger inside her. "You are wet, lass," he said roughly. "Dripping for me yet I've scarce kissed you. I like knowing you walk around ready for me."

He turned her around to face the tree. He shoved his tartan aside and pushed the folds of her gown out of his way, trapping the fabric between her body and the bark. He cupped her exposed curves, spreading and opening her for him. His breathing was harsh, and she gasped when she felt him heavy and swollen between her buttocks. Then suddenly he thrust into her.

He was too big from behind. Lisa tried to push him away with her hips, but he pushed back relentlessly.

She grabbed the tree with her hands, confused by the intensity of his emotions, doubly confused because she was caught up in the maelstrom of his fury. It imbued her with an unidentifiable rage that had no object she could discern, translating into a fierce need to possess, to dominate, to take even that which would, under other circumstances, be willingly given. The only release for the anger was in the taking.

His rage consumed her, and she bucked back against him and turned, forcing him from her body. She rammed the heels of her palms against his chest.

"I don't understand you," she snapped, her eyes flashing. Still, his intense darkness seeped inside her, driving her, goading her to release it somehow.

His eyes were dark, unfathomable pools, and danger radiated from him. He shoved her back against the tree.

She knocked his hands from her shoulders with a swift outward thrust of both arms. "Oh no. You said I get to be in control, too. Don't think I've forgotten. You do what *I* want this time."

"And what do you want, Lisa?" he asked, his voice dangerously soft.

She grabbed his plaid and ripped it from his body. She dropped it to the ground, spreading it with the toe of her slipper. "Lie down," she demanded, his strange darkness fueling her.

He complied, his eyes glittering. Although he'd honored her demand, he was by no means subdued. He was dangerous and deadly, but she didn't care one bit, because his emotions made her feel every bit as lethal.

She dropped on top of him and kissed him with all his frustrated rage. She became a wild thing, uncaring that she filled the air with sounds of passion. Her hands cupped his face and she kissed him deeply, tonguing his mouth, nibbling his lips, shifting her hips so she was astride him. The movement with which she claimed him inside her body was not a gentle one. Their eyes met and locked, and she imagined sparks flying from the sheer heat of it.

She felt like a Valkyrie, demanding satisfaction from her mate. His hands swept up and closed over her breasts, his gaze fixed on the mole inside her left thigh. She rocked herself on him, raising and lowering her hips again and again, her palms flush to his chest, bracing herself, watching the area where their bodies were joined by his thick shaft. He reared up hungrily, suckling her nipples as her breasts swayed above him, his hips thrusting urgently. When he exploded inside her, savage satisfaction flooded her and she nearly swooned from the intensity of both their emotions. It was overwhelming, and pushed her swiftly past the edge. She arched her neck and cried out.

Afterward, she lay on his chest, wondering what had just happened. Had she taken him with his desire, or had he taken her with hers? It was so confusing, so mind paralyzing, their strange bond. When their passions were high and their bodies sweat-slicked against each other, she truly couldn't see where he began and she ended, because she felt it all. It heightened her pleasure a hundredfold.

"What just happened?" she whispered.

"I think we demonstrated the true extent of our need for each other, lass," he said softly, stroking her hair. "Sometimes need can be a violent thing."

"But what was all the darkness I was getting from you?" she pressed.

"What did it feel like, lass?" he asked carefully.

"Like you were furious with something or someone, and almost like you thought I wouldn't be here tomorrow."

He sighed against her hair. His arms tightened around her and she felt his throat work as he swallowed. "Time is too short, love. That's all you felt. That no matter how long I might have with you, it would never be enough."

"We have a whole lifetime, Circenn," she reassured him, kissing him. "You have all of my life."

"I know," he said sadly. "I know. All of yours."

"There's something you're not saying, Circenn."

"It's still not enough," he replied. "I begin to fear that only forever will satisfy me."

"Then I'm yours forever," she said easily.

"Be careful what you promise, lass." His eyes were dark. "I may hold you to it."

Lisa pressed her cheek against his chest, weary from the outburst of emotion and confused by his strange words. She sensed some dark threat there that she wasn't certain she wished to understand.

* * *

"Tell me everything about your life, lass," he demanded later, as they lay in his bed. He shifted inside her and rocked.

"Everything?" Her breathing was rapid and shallow. *God, but he knew how to touch her.* She had never understood being touched, until this Highlander had placed his hands on her body.

"Everything. Did you ever know a woman's pleasure before I made you mine?"

"Do you mean did I ever have an orgasm? That's what we call them in my time. A climax or an orgasm."

"Aye. Did you?"

Lisa blushed. "Yes," she said softly. His fingers tensed on her hips, and he buried his face in her thighs, lapping gently.

"When?" he growled. The vibration was exquisite.

"This is really rather personal," she protested weakly, arching against him.

"Yes, 'this is really rather personal,' " he mocked. "And you think to withhold mere words when I'm doing this to you?"

"I was curious. I . . . touched myself a time or two."

"And?"

"And I found a most unusual sensation. So I bought a book that explained it all."

"And?"

"And what?" she said, feeling embarrassed.

"Did it feel like this?" He slipped a finger inside her.

"Nothing feels like you," she whispered, arching against his hand.

"Did you touch yourself like this?" He drew back so she could see him. One hand palmed her mound, the heel of it exerting gentle friction; the other he wrapped around himself.

She lost her breath, mesmerized by the sight of his hand holding his heavy shaft. Jealous of his hand being where hers longed to be. She reached out and knocked his hand away and he laughed.

"Mine," she said roughly.

"Ah, yes."

* * *

Later he began again. "Tell me everything about your life. Tell me about the wreck and what's wrong with your mother and what you missed and what you longed for." He quickly tried to mask his feelings, ashamed of what he was thinking. He must have been successful at hiding his emotions, for she confided readily, teaching him many new words as they went along.

A dangerous thought had formed in the back of his mind, and he pressed against it, trying to force it into submission.

But he knew well the danger of seeds once sown.

CHAPTER 22

"GALAN, WE'VE DONE IT," DUNCAN SAID SMUGLY. THE two brothers were leaning against a stone column near the entrance of the Greathall, observing the revelry. Circenn was teaching Lisa one of their less complicated Highland dances. Engrossed in watching her feet, every few moments she tossed back her head and laughed at him. She was adorable, Duncan decided.

The villagers had finally gotten their feast, thanks to Galan, Duncan, and the enthusiastic castle staff who had planned it without awaiting further input or permission. While Circenn and Lisa had wandered about, oblivious and infatuated, the residents of Castle Brodie had finalized the plans, simply informing the couple when the celebration would be. The laird's blossoming romance with his lady had infused the estate with good humor.

Duncan conceded that they'd done an astonishing job; the staff had devoted loving care to transforming Castle Brodie for the festivities. Brilliantly lit by hundreds of rushlights, the hall was warm, the atmosphere most conducive to romance. Rippling banners of crimson and black Brodie tartan decked the walls. Thirty long tables formed a rectangle around the room, each laden with a sumptuous feast. The musicians gathered behind the laird's table at the head of the hall, while in the center of the rectangle, on the floor cleared for dancing, couples, children, even an occasional wolfhound indulged the fierce Scot penchant for celebrating. In such a war-torn land, any cause was reason to feast as if there was no tomorrow, because there might not be. The musicians were playing a sprightly, edgy tune and the dancers faced the challenge with relish. As feet flew, the tempo increased, and ripples of laughter broke out as they kept pace with the frenetic beat.

"Look at them," Galan said softly.

Duncan didn't have to ask whom he meant; Galan's eyes were fixed on Lisa and Circenn, as were many other eyes in the room. The laird and his lady were clearly in their own universe, absorbed in each other.

Duncan had heard the strange note in Galan's voice and now gazed at him sharply, seeing his older brother in a new light.

"They are so in love." Galan sounded weary, and longing infused his voice.

Duncan frowned, confounded by a new and uncomfortable sensation—as if he were the older brother and should take care of Galan. It occurred to him that Galan was thirty years old and had single-mindedly devoted the past ten years of his life to warring for Scotland's independence. That didn't leave much time for a disciplined warrior to taste the comforts of family and home life. How had he failed to see that Galan, in the midst of all the warriors and the fighting and the splendid wenching to be had, was lonely?

"Wasn't there a lass in Edinburgh you visited when last we were there?" Duncan asked.

Galan glowered. "Doona try to finagle a match for me, little brother. I'm fine."

Duncan lifted a brow. How often had Galan assured him that he was fine, and Duncan had gone about his merry way, leaving him alone? Bewildered by his new insight, he uneasily filed the subject away for future consideration. His brother needed a woman, but not in the way Duncan needed a woman; Galan needed a wife.

"Think you they will have children?" Duncan changed the subject, noting Galan relax visibly when he did so.

"Bah! If they haven't already conceived one. I hear they have taken over one of your favored tupping spots."

"My bothy?" Duncan exclaimed indignantly. "A man can't have any privacy."

Neither brother spoke for a time, each absorbed in his own thoughts. The musicians commenced a slow, haunting ballad and the dancers moved into more intimate embraces.

Suddenly Galan said, "Och, by Dagda—look yonder, Duncan. Who is that stunning lass?" He pointed across the hall. "Too lovely for me, that's for certain."

Duncan glanced swiftly where Galan pointed, his body tightening with anticipation. *Too lovely for me* was the slap of an irresistible gauntlet to Duncan. He adored such words, his innate maleness rose to them aggressively; he'd long been restless and ready for something different.

"Where? I see no one of note." Duncan craned his neck to peer through the crowd. When the dancers parted for a moment, he glimpsed a mane of shimmering red hair. He sucked in a breath. "The redhead. Is she the one you meant? You know what they say—fire on top, fiery tup."

Galan punched him in the arm. "Is that *all* you ever think about? There she is again." The dancers moved apart again, and this time the woman was turned slightly toward them.

Duncan's brows lifted as heat lanced through his groin. She was exquisite. Masses of red hair, streaked with blond and honey, spilled over her shoulders. Her face was delicate, pointed at the chin with high cheekbones and dark eyes. Her lips were full. Ridiculously full. Erotically full. *Come suck me full,* he thought irritably. No woman should have lips so lush and plump. Her skin was flawlessly translucent, her lips a perfect rose. And full.

Composed and graceful, she exuded confidence that he would soon shatter with his seductive charm. "Untouchable" might have been branded on her forehead, and been more subtle than the way she carried herself. But he was man enough for such a dare; he would penetrate her reserve, gain entrance where he suspected few men had ever gone, and be satisfied only when she became a wanton she-animal in his bed. His gaze swept the length of her. Clad in a simple white gown beneath a green surcoat, her body in it was the only adornment necessary.

"Well?" Galan demanded. "What are you waiting for? Doona you need to tup to conquer?"

"Och, and aye," Duncan said, melting into the crowd.

Galan shook his head, and if his smile was a bit melancholy, he'd learned not to feel it.

* * *

Duncan surfaced behind her. He held his breath as his gaze played admiringly over her sensual mane. Soft, silky, and of a dozen flame hues, he longed to wrap his fists in it. He harbored a special passion for redheads. He longed to tug her head back and take her throat with his lips. He ached to spread her hair across his pillow. She, he would claim in a bed. Her fine body would require the soft mattresses beneath her, to handle his intensity.

"Shall we dance?" he murmured in her ear.

She pivoted so quickly it startled him, and he fell back a step. Her lips were even more luscious up close, and when she moistened them with her tongue, he nearly groaned aloud.

Her eyes narrowed, and her lips parted around a knowing laugh. "Oh. It's *you*."

"Pardon?" He was taken aback. "Do we know each other, lass?" He was quite certain they didn't; he could never have forgotten this woman. The enticing manner in which her lips were currently pursed would have been seared into his memory.

"The answer is no. *I* don't know you. But every other woman in this room does. Duncan Douglas, isn't it?" she said dryly.

Duncan studied her face. Although she was young—perhaps no more than twenty—she had a regal bearing beyond her years. "I do have some reputation with the lasses," he conceded, downplaying his prowess, confident of her impending maidenly swoon.

The look she gave him was far from admiring.

He did a double take when he realized her gaze was downright disparaging.

"Not something I care for in a man," she said coolly. "Thank you for your offer, but I'd sooner dance with last week's rushes. They would be less used. Who wants what everyone else has already had?" The words were delivered in a cool, modulated tone, shaped by an odd accent he couldn't place. Quite finished with him, she presented her back and resumed talking to her companion.

Duncan was immobilized by shock.

Who wants what everyone else has already had? She made it sound as if he were all used up. Indeed! He certainly had much more to spare, and she would soon learn it. His hand closed upon the fine bones of her shoulder, and he spun her around. "That means I have all the more experience with which to pleasure you. And pleasure you I will," he promised. He waited for her to melt. The women he'd seduced in the past had shivered at his possessive promises. He'd learned to offer them with a husky note in his voice, learned precisely what to say to affect a lass most.

"It *means*," she corrected with a mocking smile, "that you are a lothario. It *means* that you can't keep your tartan about your knees. It *means* that I am no different than anyone else, and that you hold no special regard for a cherished act of intimacy. I am not intrigued. I care naught for leftovers."

The infuriating woman gave him her back again.

He eyed the supple arch of her back, the lovely hips, the longs legs moving in restless tempo to the music beneath her soft white gown. She tossed her head and laughed at something her companion said.

Abashed, he studied her companion. A foot taller than she, the man was lean and well muscled. They obviously shared a close relationship, leaning their heads close and laughing. Duncan's hands fisted at his sides.

What did a man say to that? *Yes, but now that I've seen you, I doona wish anyone else? All that was merely practice, preparing me for you?* He doubted that would be effective with this woman. She'd only laugh at him again.

Seething, he tapped her companion on the shoulder. "Pardon me, but are you her lover?"

"Who the hell are *you*?"

The redhead placed a soothing hand on her companion's arm, ignoring the look of fury Duncan directed at her fingers. "This is Duncan Douglas, Tally."

"Ah." Her companion smirked. "And as any blackguard worth his salt, confronted with the insurmountable challenge of your beauty, he must conquer you, eh, Beth?"

They shared an intimate glance. "I'm afraid so."

"Who *are* the two of you?" Duncan demanded. Never had he been so mocked, never had he felt so . . . so . . . insignificant. Unimportant.

"We are friends of Renaud de Vichiers, one of your Templars," she replied easily. "We were on our way to Edinburgh when we heard Renaud was at Castle Brodie. I am Elizabeth . . . MacBreide." She gestured with an elegant, slim hand. "And this is my brother, Tally."

"MacBreide of Shallotan?"

"Near there," Tally replied evasively.

"Your brother," Duncan observed aloud, as the significance of their relationship sunk in. He was not her lover. He wouldn't have to kill him.

"And protector," Tally added dryly. "Do not think to attempt to seduce my sister, Duncan Douglas. We heard of your exploits shortly after arriving, and Beth said she saw you dallying with one of the maids."

Duncan cringed inwardly. He had indeed tupped less than privately early this morn. So, she had noticed him—and how long had she watched?

"Chasing her about in the bailey, then up onto the parapet," Elizabeth added, without the slightest blush. "The maids here cannot say enough about you. Even as far as the taverns in Inverness we'd heard of the wild and irreverent Douglas brother. They say there isn't a fair maid you haven't tumbled."

Words that would have made him preen with masculine pleasure on any other tongue made him wince, coming from her absurdly full lips. It was all too obvious what she thought of him. There was nothing he could say in his own defense; she plainly did not care for casual tupping, and he'd never concealed the fact that he relished it. There were certain rooms he'd entered in his life that had held a dozen different women he'd tupped. Never before had that fact bothered him.

Retreat and reform into a fresh attack, he advised himself, *then charge again when she least expects it.* By God, this was battle, and if the front line couldn't be breached, he would find a way to circumvent her outlying guards and penetrate her flank. That he'd blown the first attack didn't mean he'd lost the war.

He raised her hand and kissed the air above it. "Elizabeth, Tally, welcome to Brodie," he said coolly before turning away.

As he moved off into the crowd, he walked tall, concealing the uncomfortable sensation of slinking away from a resounding set-down. As he wove through the dancers, Duncan muttered darkly to himself. How dare she criticize him for being a good lover, an enthusiastic man? He was considerate with his wenches, he was patient, always ensuring their pleasure. How dare she belittle him for his . . . frequency. *Leftovers,* indeed!

Scowling, he headed for the courtyard, the glorious night now fractured by her disdain.

* * *

Armand watched the lord and lady with growing frustration. He'd been impatiently following her for days now, and not once had he been able to catch her alone. The laird was at her side constantly.

He must capture her tonight, or he would never make it to the arranged meeting place with James Comyn on time. He'd completed searching the castle, all but the laird's chambers, into which there was no entrance without the key. He'd even climbed to the roof, only to encounter a dozen forbidding guards, at which point he'd pretended to have sought the gloaming to meditate closer to God. There would be no scaling the wall to the laird's room, for the castle was too carefully observed. But surely she had a key, and once he snared her, he would spare time to search their private bedchambers before leaving. He needed those weapons.

He gritted his teeth, watching Circenn toss back more wine. The man had consumed such quantities that any other man would have sought the garderobe long before now. His eyes narrowed as he watched Lisa whisper something in Circenn's ear. He noted that she briefly pressed her hand to her abdomen.

Ah, although he might hold his drink well, she did not. Armand slipped through the crowd, maintaining an innocuous distance, ready to sprint to her side the moment she left the protective arms of the forbidding laird of Brodie.

*　*　*

Lisa was dazzled by her first medieval feast. She'd never forgotten the night she'd first arrived at Castle Brodie and gazed up at the towering structure, thinking how incredible it would be to belong within its walls, to be part of a laughing, warm group of clansmen. To belong.

And now she did.

Circenn had proudly introduced her to his people, and although she'd noticed he stumbled over many of their names, that didn't worry her overmuch. She could change that. She would help him get reacquainted with his clan and draw him into the joy of their lives.

"Why do you smile, lass?"

Lisa tipped back her head. Happiness radiated from him, increasing hers tenfold. Clad in full clan regalia, he looked like a savage Scot warlord, but she knew what kind of man he really was. Intense and deeply emotional. Mercilessly sexual. Gentle. A dizzying wave of feeling grew and spread inside her. "So this is what it feels like," she whispered. She gazed up at him, her eyes wide with discovery.

"What what feels like?"

"Circenn." A wealth of emotion infused his name.

He watched her, unblinking.

"I love you."

Circenn drew a sudden, deep breath. There it was. There was no coyness about her, no games, no attempt to hide the truth or manipulate him into making such a declaration first. Boldly she gave her heart. Why would he have expected anything less?

He swept her into his arms and closed his eyes, absorbing the feelings ebbing and flowing between them.

"Does this mean you are not adverse to the fact that I've lost my heart to you?" she teased.

"Could a man be adverse to the sunshine warming his skin? A spring rain quenching his thirst or a night such as this one, when any wonder seems possible? Thank you." His smile was devastating. "I'd begun to fear you might never give me those words."

"And?" she encouraged. He said nothing, but suddenly a shiver of pleasure danced beneath her skin. It penetrated her thoroughly, leaving her breathless. "What was *that*?"

"I've been practicing trying to say it without words. Did it work?"

She blew out a calming breath. "Oh yes," she said. "I want you to do that tonight when we're . . . you know."

"Aye, aye, mistress," he teased. "And how about this one?"

Lisa's nipples stiffened as a wave of dark eroticism washed over her. "Oh, God. That was truly amazing."

"This bond can be wonderful, can it not?"

Smiling her agreement, Lisa stood on tiptoe and kissed him. When he moved to deepen the kiss, she pulled back. He looked startled, so she hastened to reassure him. "I've drunk too much wine, Circenn. I'm afraid I must find one of those dratted chamber pots." She sighed morosely. "There are some things I really miss about my century."

"A chamber pot? Why not use the garderobe?"

"The *what*?"

"The garderobe."

"You have garderobes here?" she said stiffly.

He looked at her as if she'd lost her mind. "Not that I wish to pry, lass, but where have you been going?"

"Chamber pots," she muttered.

"And what have you been doing . . . er . . ."

"Dumping them out the window," she said, prickly as a porcupine. So much for demure privacy. If there was a garderobe, why on earth had Eirren told her to use the chamber pot? Then she realized how mischievous the lad could be. It was just like Eirren to be prankish. "Was there a garderobe at Dunnottar, too?"

"It is *you* who has been dumping them out the windows? I have been blaming it on my men, making them wash down the stones. Aye, there was one at Dunnottar. I had garderobes put in every keep I own or visit."

"You never told me."

"You never asked. How was I to know? When you first arrived here, I wasn't about to address such private issues. I assumed you had found our garderobe on your own."

Lisa snorted. Eirren had truly bamboozled her, and her pride had kept her tidily trapped in his jest. "I can't believe all this time I've . . . Oh! Where *is* the blasted garderobe?"

He told her, biting his lip to keep from smiling. He watched her hips sway gently in her emerald gown as she climbed the stairs. She'd said she loved him. That was promising.

Perhaps it was nearly time to talk to her about loving him forever.

CHAPTER 23

LISA SHOOK HER HEAD AS SHE EXITED THE GARDEROBE. Very civilized. Now that she knew where it was, she couldn't believe she'd bypassed it while she'd searched the castle for the flask, but the entrance gave the impression of a servant's door, so she'd not given it a second thought. The garderobe was not what she had expected; it was larger than most modern bathrooms, and spotless. It was obvious that the laird of Brodie prided himself on tidy garderobes. Fresh herbs and dried petals were scattered amid the hay piled inside the chamber—medieval toilet paper.

She resolved not only to bathe Eirren the next time she saw him but to dunk him a time or two as well for all those miserable chamber-pot moments.

Slipping from the small room, she was surprised to encounter Armand Berard loitering in the corridor.

"Milady, are you enjoying the festivities?"

"Yes, I am." Her feet were still tapping from the cheery music and she was eager to return and perfect her steps. But she hadn't seen Armand for over a month and had rather missed the opportunity to get to know a real live Knight Templar. She frowned, eyeing his somber attire.

Circenn had told her the Templars would stay in their garrison and not join the revelry. "I thought your Order did not hold with feasting such as this."

He shrugged. "Some of my brothers are more rigid than others. A few of us have accepted that the Order is destroyed, bitter though it is to admit that you have pledged your life to something that no longer exists."

"I'm sorry," Lisa said, feeling awkward. Before her stood one of the legendary Knights Templars and she couldn't think of one thing to say to make him feel better. "Are your men hunted, even here in Scotland?" she rushed on. She was intensely curious about the Templars, their legendary powers and myths.

"It depends on who encounters us. If it's an Englishman, he might try to take us across the border. A Scot is far less inclined to do so. Most of your people care little for the edicts of France, England, or even the Pope." He uttered a harsh laugh. "Your own king was excommunicated by the Pope for the murder of the Red Comyn in the church at Dumfries. Your land is a wild one. When a country is fighting merely for the right to survive, they are less inclined to be judgmental. Come."

He offered his arm, and she looped hers through it. Within moments, she was so engrossed in their conversation that she paid no heed to where he was leading her.

She listened, fascinated, while he spoke of the Order, of their residence outside Paris, of their lifelong commitment to their vows. His expression grew bitter as he recounted how the papal bull *Pastoralis praeeminentiae*, issued on November 22, 1307, had ordered all monarchs of Christendom to arrest the Templars and sequester their lands in the name of the papacy. He skimmed over the persecution, the interrogations, and the torture, unwilling to give such detail to a woman, for which she was grateful. There were some limits to even her curiosity.

He explained how, in 1310, six hundred of their brothers had agreed to mount a defense against the unjust persecution, and Pope Clement had finally agreed to postpone the Council of Vienne for a year while they prepared. Then, Philippe the Fair, desperate to crush the Order and line his coffers before it was too late, circumvented the Pope, reopened his episcopal inquiry, and had fifty-four Templars burned at the stake outside Paris, silencing the remaining Templars' protests. In 1312, the papal bull *Vox in excelso* was issued, forever suppressing the Order.

There were many questions she wanted to ask him, and this was a rare opportunity to explore history from a Templar's perspective, but her first question was patently twenty-first century, brushed by a bit of romanticism.

"What *is* the secret of the Templars, Armand?" So many rumors abounded: that they had protected the Holy Grail, that the Grail was really the genetic bloodline of Christ, that the Templars had uncovered a personal alchemy for the transformation of the soul, that such alchemy could manipulate time and space. She didn't really expect him to answer, but since she had her arm through the arm of a Templar, there was no harm in asking.

Armand's smile made her shiver. "Do you mean what could we possibly possess that would make a king and a Pope fear us so greatly they would use every weapon they had to destroy us? Are you a religious woman, Lisa MacRobertson?"

"A bit," she conceded.

"What might the Pope and king want from us?"

"Gold?" she guessed. "Religious artifacts?"

His laughter sent a chill up her spine. "Consider this:

What if the Templars had discovered something that would tear asunder beliefs that had been held for centuries by nearly every land in the world?"

Now he really had her curiosity going. "You *must* tell me," she breathed.

"I didn't say that we had," he prevaricated. "I merely postulated the possibility."

"So, is it true then?" she asked, fascinated. "Does your Order possess such knowledge?"

He didn't answer. His face was averted, so she didn't see it contort with rage, hence she was completely unprepared when he grabbed her arm and twisted it behind her back, arcing it up between her shoulder blades, forcing her to double over in an effort to escape the pain.

He shoved her against the wall and pressed a knife to her side.

Lisa was so stunned that she made no sound. One moment she was strolling with a perfectly sociable Templar, indulging her incessant curiosity, teetering on the brink of stunning revelations, and the next her life was being threatened. It had happened too swiftly for her to grasp, and, in shock, she had wasted precious seconds during which she might have fought back.

"Give me the key," Armand growled into her ear. "And if you so much as whimper, I will kill you."

"The key to what?"

"Circenn's chambers."

"I don't have one!"

"You lying little—" Hooking a thick forearm around her throat, he patted her body, searching for a key ring. "Then it is in your room," he accused.

"He has never given me one!"

Armand tightened his arm around her throat, cutting

into her windpipe. His arm was an unrelenting band of steel, and Lisa felt her air supply being cut off. Her cheek smashed against the stone wall, and she grew dangerously light-headed.

"We can play as rough as you like, lass," Armand murmured into her hair. "Where is the key?"

Lisa closed her eyes and reached for Circenn.

* * *

Circenn crushed his metal goblet in his hand, spraying half a dozen villagers with wine. He glanced about, his eyes wild.

Lisa.

Danger. Frightened. Can't breathe.

But where?

He raced up the stairs to the garderobe, feeling for her with his heart, reassuring her he was coming.

Pain.

He cursed the emotional bond by which he could share her feelings but not obtain words or a hint of her location. Where would she have gone? How could she be in danger? Who could possibly wish her ill?

He ranged the corridors like a maddened beast, fighting an urge to bellow for her, aware that that would only alert whoever was threatening her. He paced up the south corridor, then back. Every ounce of his intellect was absorbing her fear, sponging it up, and it was rendering him senseless. He plunged down a hall, then stopped abruptly.

Brash fury would not serve. He must be logical. He should check his room and hers, then other areas she had been inclined to attend. Perhaps the chapel. He pivoted sharply and raced back down the hall. He flew through the castle and into the east wing.

As he neared his chambers he slowed, alerted by a soft murmur and a strangled sound. Drawing to a halt, he slipped stealthily around the corner.

Armand had Lisa pressed up against the wall outside his chambers, his thick forearm choking her to unconsciousness. Circenn labored to draw slow, silent breaths when his lips begged to roar. She was going limp in the Templar's arms, giving up the fight as she lost her precious breath.

A flicker of silver flashed in the dim glow from the rushlights mounted on the walls. The Templar had a blade. Circenn didn't wait to see more. He drew on his unnatural abilities and moved like the wind, stopping behind the Templar, who had no warning that Circenn stood a breath behind his heart.

"The key, you stupid bitch," Armand muttered. "Don't pass out on me." He shook her. "Where does he keep the hallows?"

Circenn's mouth twisted. So that was what this was about. A rogue Templar, turned on his Order. Armand wasn't the only knight who'd lost his faith. Circenn had heard of others who, believing that God had abandoned them, had turned mercenary and faithless.

In an instant of blurred space, Circenn disarmed the knight and flung him across the corridor, where he struck the stone wall with a sharp crack of his head. He slumped to the floor. Circenn spared no regret that the attack had been unfair. When in the past he'd suffered guilt over using his enhanced abilities, he now felt grim satisfaction. He towered over the fallen knight and raised his sword for the fatal blow.

"Stop!" Lisa cried.

Circenn's jaw locked, his face contorted with fury. His arm suspended at eye level, the point angled down, ready for one swift thrust into Armand's heart. When he plunged down, it would be with such anger that the force would likely shatter his blade against the stone beneath the knight's back. He spared her a glance, and from her horrified expression he realized that she was feeling his internal landscape: barren, bleak, and murderous. Hot. Hellishly hot. He would never understand—not even should he live to be five thousand—why women consistently protected villains. It was simple in a man's mind: *Kill the man who tries to harm your own.* But women made it much more complex. They held out hope that evil could be redeemed. A foolish hope, to his way of thinking.

"Don't kill him, Circenn. He didn't harm me." She touched her throat with gentle fingertips. "I will be fine. A few bruises, nothing more. You found us in time."

"He touched you," Circenn snarled. "He planned to harm you."

"But he didn't succeed." She appealed to his logic: "Question him, determine what he is after, then banish him, but please . . ."

She trailed off and he stared helplessly at her. *Damn her,* he thought. She was deliberately flooding him with mercy, forgiveness, and the cool wind of logic. All those feminine things, they tumbled like snowflakes upon his masculine heat.

Dousing it.

Loath though he was to admit it, she was right. By killing Armand swiftly, he would never know his motives. He needed to uncover the Templar's purpose, determine with whom he was in collusion and if there were other corrupt knights in his employ. He needed information first. Then he would kill him. He lowered the sword with a low growl of unsatisfied rage.

* * *

Lisa crept down the stairs. She'd tried to wait in bed for Circenn to come up, but had been unable to stand it any longer. It had been hours since Armand's attack, and although Circenn had promised not to kill the Templar, vowing angrily that he would turn him over to his own brothers, Lisa still felt his murderous fury. Their bond was frazzling her nerves. She had no idea why the knight had turned on her. Perhaps she shouldn't have questioned him. Perhaps it was simply too upsetting for him to speak of the atrocities he'd endured.

The feast was still under way in the Greathall, the villagers oblivious to the bitter events of the evening. Circenn would keep the problem quiet, resolve it, and no one would suffer for it. She admired his methods. He was a laird who would not trouble his clan with dissension that he could resolve alone.

Moving stealthily, she slipped down the corridor to the study. The door was ajar and she peered in cautiously. He was there, as she'd suspected, with Duncan and Galan.

A dozen grim-faced Templars filed before him, and from the light misting of rain on their robes, she deduced that she'd missed their entrance by mere minutes.

"It is done, milord. We have finished our interrogation," Renaud de Vichiers said wearily.

"And?" Circenn growled.

"It was worse than we feared. He was doubly a traitor, both to his own brothers and to Scotland. His plan was to abduct your lady and sell her to the English king for his weight in gold, plus titles and lands in England." Renaud shook his head. "I do not know what to say. It grieves me. Armand was a Commander of Knights in our Order, and highly regarded. We had no idea. I swear to you upon our Order that he acted entirely alone." Renaud directed his gaze to the floor. "We await your decision regarding the rest of us. We understand if you decide you must send us away from here."

Circenn shook his head. "I will not hold the rest of you responsible for his actions. You have been loyal to me for years."

The Templars rustled with murmurs of gratitude and repeated vows of loyalty. "You have been good to us, milord," Renaud said. He took a deep breath, and when he spoke again, it was with such fervency that his words sounded stilted. "We do not wish to jeopardize your goodwill in any way. We look forward to a future in Scotland. What can we do to restore your faith in us?"

"It was never lost," Circenn said, rubbing his jaw. "If Armand hadn't been acting alone, you likely would have succeeded in taking her. I do not underestimate the powers of your Order, Renaud. I know what you can do when you pit multiple Templar wills against a problem. An attack from multiple brethren would have peacefully lured her where you wished her to go. You do not use violence. You use . . . powerful persuasion."

Renaud looked abashed. "I hadn't considered that, but it's true. We could have taken her as a group. I forget you know so much about us." He bowed, a posture of abject apology. "Milord, we would never harm your lady. We shall protect her as our own."

Circenn inclined his head. "What of Armand?"

"As a show of our allegiance, we resolved that matter. He will trouble you no more."

Lisa leaned a bit closer to the door. What had they done

to him? Banished him? Would they drive him across the border for the English to catch?

"Explain," Circenn ordered.

"We determined his crime and dispensed fitting punishment."

"He is dead?" Circenn asked wearily.

"He died by receiving the price he himself had named for his corruption. We gave him his weight in gold."

Lisa made a strangled sound that was fortunately masked by Circenn's own. Her eyes flew to his, but he hadn't yet noticed her. He looked shocked.

"Do not fear we acted wastefully," Renaud hastened to assure him. "We know we will require the gold to rebuild both our Order and Scotland once the warring is over. We will reclaim it when we quarter Armand."

Lisa retched instinctively, unable to contain it. A dozen eyes flew to the door, where she stood clutching her stomach.

"Lisa," Circenn exclaimed, half rising. His eyes were wide and apologetic. "I asked you to wait in your room."

"You know I never do," she said irritably. "Why would you expect me to this time?" She looked directly into Renaud's eyes. "What do you mean you gave him his weight in gold and will retrieve it?" She knew she shouldn't ask, but her suspicions were so awful that she couldn't help herself. If they didn't tell her, she would just imagine atrocities. She'd long ago found it was easier to deal with reality than imagined fears.

Renaud did not respond, clearly reluctant to discuss the matter with a woman.

"Tell me," she repeated, through clenched teeth. She glanced at Circenn, who was watching her with sorrow and understanding. She appreciated that he did not try to shield her; he understood that she needed her own answers in things.

Renaud cleared his throat uneasily. "Molten. Poured down his throat. It will cool and be removed without difficulty."

"Lisa!" Circenn rose from the desk, but it was too late. She was already running down the hall.

CHAPTER 24

It was several days before Lisa returned to her normal self. Circenn spent the time busying himself on the estate, waiting patiently as she worked through her feelings. He was never alone, always accompanied by the pressure of her heart. One day, he'd almost sworn that he'd heard her voice right next to his ear, muttering *pig-headed, bloodthirsty primates*, but the phrase had not made any sense to him. Whatever it meant, she must have been feeling it very strongly for him to pick it up. He wondered if their bond would continue to grow stronger over time, affording them deeper communication.

He respected her mild retreat, accepting that it was a necessary part of her adjustment to their way of life. His time must seem strange to her, and the ways of the Templars would likely seem extreme in any century. He was deeply grieved that she had found out about Armand, but if he had learned nothing else about Lisa Stone, he had learned how great her curiosity was. She wished to be shielded from nothing; she wished to be accorded respect and given all the knowledge available so she could make her own choices from a well-informed position.

He would not have wished Armand's gruesome death

upon any man, yet the Templars had their own justice and dispensed it with the same unyielding discipline with which they performed all their duties. In his heart he acknowledged that he was not sorry the man was dead. Armand had nearly killed his woman, nearly snuffed her fragile, tiny, delicate life.

And that terrified him.

Armand's brutality had elevated Lisa's mortality to an obsession with him. He loathed it, resented it—her mortality had become his archenemy.

Was he becoming like Adam? Was it in this fashion that such a monster had been fabricated? Did one broken rule permit the next and the next, until finally he would be able to justify taking anything he wanted? Where was the line that he must not traverse before it was too late?

You could make her immortal. You know you want to. You wouldn't even have to tell her.

Aye, he wanted to. And it confounded him. He'd been married twice and never once considered trying to make his wife immortal.

But no other woman was Lisa.

Besides, up until now, he'd viewed what Adam had done to him as a curse, a vile corruption of the natural order of things. But now that he'd found Lisa, things were no longer so clear. Since she'd arrived in his life, he'd been reevaluating his beliefs, his objections, and his prejudices. He longed to storm into his castle, unearth the flask from its compartment in the stone, and force it between her lips, but he could never justify taking her choice away from her. Somehow, he had to bring himself to tell her.

Argh! he thought, closing his eyes. *How?*

Though he grudgingly accepted his immortality, after five hundred years there was much about himself he still despised. By Dagda, he'd been born in the ninth century! There was a part of him that was hopelessly old-fashioned. Although time's passage had carried him out of the ninth century, nothing could remove the ninth-century sensibilities from his heart. Part of him was a simple warrior and superstitious man who believed that magic sprang from evil; hence, he was an abomination teetering on the brink of corruption.

He suspected that holding on to his birth-century's mores made him a bit of a barbarian, but that was preferable to what he might have become.

Still, he had to reach a decision, and soon. He needed to tell Lisa what he was and offer her the same, before her mortality completely undid him.

Helplessly, he'd begun to obsess about her environment. She suddenly seemed incredibly vulnerable. He'd begun to blow out rushlights compulsively, afraid they might spark and catch the tapestries and she would die in something as senseless as a castle fire. He'd begun to study every man he encountered, seeking hints of any possible threat to her existence. Armand's attempt to abduct her had escalated his fears. She was delicate, and one slip of a knife could steal her from him forever. Once, he'd thought forever was bitter indeed, but now, having loved her, if he lost her, forever would be a cold, bleak hell.

Perhaps, via their special bond, she would understand and accept. Perhaps the thought of living forever would appeal to her. He would never know until he tried. The worst that could happen was that she would be horrified, reject him, and try to escape. If that occurred, he worried, he might truly revert to his ninth-century self, and lock her up until she agreed to drink from the flask. Or worse—do to her what Adam had done to him.

* * *

Lisa was curled in a chair before the fire when he entered the study. She smiled warmly at him. They shared a wordless greeting with their eyes, then she patted the chair beside her. He moved to her side and rested a portion of his weight on the arm of the chair, and bent to kiss her thoroughly. God, he couldn't bear the thought of ever losing her.

When he finally forced himself to break the kiss—it was either that or tup her right there in the chair with the study door open—she glanced at him curiously and said, "You were frustrated today. Many times. What is worrying you, Circenn?"

He sighed. Sometimes their bond was a troublesome thing; there wasn't much he could hide from her, and the effort of withholding his emotions was exhausting. "You were stricken by ennui," he countered, not yet ready to broach the difficult conversation. Better to savor a few moments of peace and intimacy. "But then you seem to be that way often when you are not in my bed," he teased. In bed was precisely where he wanted her now. Perhaps lulled by sensual satisfaction she would be more receptive. A mercenary tactic, but deployed with love. He caressed her hair, savoring the silky feel between his fingers.

Lisa laughed, a low, inviting sound. "Circenn, I need something to do with myself. I need to feel . . . *involved*."

He'd been thinking that very thing, as her frustration had attended him for quite some time now, ever since their bond had blossomed into existence. He knew that in her century Lisa had worked constantly, and she was a woman who needed to feel she had accomplished something worthwhile at the end of the day.

"I will have Duncan bring you the list of the pending disputes to be heard in the manor court in Ballyhock.

Would you like that? Galan has been hearing the cases for the past few years and would be pleased to get quit of the position."

"Really?" Lisa was delighted. She would love to immerse herself in the villagers' lives, perhaps make friends among the young women. Someday, she would have children with Circenn, and she missed having a girlfriend. She would want her children to have playmates. She didn't understand why Circenn had kept himself so distant from his people in the past, but she planned to bring him close again. Hearing the cases and mingling with the clansmen would be the perfect way to set her plans in motion.

"Certainly. They will be most pleased."

"Are you certain they will accept a mere lass deciding disputes?" she asked worriedly.

"You are *not* a mere lass. And they adored you when they met you at the feast. Besides, I am Brude, Lisa."

"I must have missed that part of history in school. Who were the Brude?"

"Ah, merely the most valiant warriors who ever lived," he said, arching an arrogant brow. "We are the original Picts; many of our kings were named Brude, until we assumed that as our name. Brodie is merely another form." *Is now the time to tell her more of my history? That my half-brother Drust the Fourth was slain by Kenneth McAlpin in 838?* "Being Brude, the descent of royalty in my line was matrilineal for centuries, handed down through the queens, not our kings. The crown transferred to brothers or nephews or cousins as traced by a complicated series of intermarriages by seven royal houses. My people will readily accept the decisions of the Lady of Brodie."

"Sounds like the Picts were more civilized than the Scots," Lisa said dryly.

" 'This legion which curbs the savage Scots' is how Emperor Claudius referred to my people, and for a time we did. Until Kenneth McAlpin murdered most of the members of our royal house in an attempt to erase us from Scotland forever."

"But you still live, so apparently he wasn't too successful."

Ah, yes. I do still live.

"So why were you frustrated today?" she asked, circling back to her initial observation. "I can feel you all the time, you know. I could feel impatience and anger."

Circenn stood and scooped her from the chair. He dropped into it and reseated her across his lap. "That's better. I like being beneath you."

"I like you *being* beneath me. But don't try to distract me. Why?"

Circenn sighed, gathering her close. He was afraid. He, the fearless warrior, feared her reaction to what he was about to tell her.

As he drew a breath to begin, he heard the door to the Greathall crash open, as guards all over the castle sent up a resounding cry.

They both tensed instantly.

"Is someone attacking?" Lisa worried.

Circenn rose swiftly, depositing her on the floor with a kiss. "I doona know," he said, taking off for the Greathall at a run. Lisa raced after him, as the noise outside grew to an immense roar.

As she entered the Greathall, she saw dozens of knights clamoring excitedly, gathered around a lone stranger.

Duncan glanced up as they entered, and his smile was blinding. "To Stirling, Circenn! The Bruce's messenger has arrived. We finally go to war!"

CHAPTER 25

"WHAT SAY YOU?" CIRCENN DEMANDED, HIS EYES GLIT-
tering with anticipation.

The messenger spoke quickly. "The Bruce's brother has
made a wager, and we must prevent the English from
reaching Stirling Castle by Midsummer's Day. The Bruce
has ordered you to present your troops with all weapons at
St. Ninian's by the Roman road—"

Circenn cut him off with a deafening bellow of joy that
was echoed by all the men in the hall. Lisa moved closer to
his side and he caught her in his arms, swinging her high
in the air. "We go to war!" he shouted, elated.

Men, she thought, amazed. *I will never understand
them.* Then a worse thought followed: *What if I lose him?*

"But you must hurry," the messenger yelled into the
din. "If we ride without pause we will scarce arrive in
time. Every moment is critical."

Circenn hugged her close. "I will not die. I promise,"
he said fervently. He kissed her deeply, then slipped from
her arms. There was no time to tell her more. He would go
to war, and upon his return they would have their long-
overdue talk. In the meantime, he would send constant reassurance to her via their bond.

War! It's about damned time! he thought, elated.

"I must gather my weapons," he muttered, racing from the hall.

* * *

Drawn to spend every possible moment with him before he left, Lisa left the hall shortly after he had. The estate was a riot of activity as the men prepared to ride out immediately. She should have remembered that Circenn would have to leave soon. She'd known that the battle at Bannockburn occurred on June 24; history records had placed the thane of Brodie and his Templars in the midst of the legendary battle. But in the pleasure of their newfound love, and then in the fright of Armand's abduction attempt, she'd given little thought to the date or the impending war.

She headed for Circenn's chambers and slipped quietly into his room, wondering if there was enough time to steal a moment of passion. She doubted it; she sensed that his mind was already far away. He was all masculine warrior right now, consumed with the looming battle. As she moved deeper into his room, she was shocked to see a great gaping maw in the wall where the hearth normally was.

A hidden room. *How fantastic,* she thought, *and how appropriate for a medieval castle.* Curious to see what he kept in there, she slipped past the hearth and entered. The fabric of her gown caught on the rough stones of the rotated hearth and ripped audibly. Busy trying to disengage the fabric from the sharp edge of the stone, she didn't see Circenn look up. Nor did she see his expression.

"Get out, lass," he thundered, leaping to his feet.

As Lisa glanced up, Circenn froze in mid-leap, his plan to thrust her from the room aborted. He watched with dawning horror as her gaze skimmed the interior of his hidden room. He stood motionless, surrounded by incriminating evidence. Standing amid items from her time, he knew that she would never believe him, and worse, that he must leave immediately if they were to prevent the English troops from reaching Stirling by Midsummer's Day.

Lisa was motionless but for her gaze, which roamed disbelievingly over the items in the room. Her eyes widened, narrowed, and widened again as she realized what she was seeing. Weapons, yes. Arms and shields, yes.

Inexplicably, items from her own century?

Yes.

The first wave of emotion that buffeted her was hers: a suffocating feeling of pain, bewilderment, and humiliation that she'd bequeathed her heart so wrongly. The second wave was his: an enveloping cloak of fear.

How could he possess such things? How could he have items from her time, yet not be able to send her home?

Simple. He'd lied. That was the only possible explanation.

"You lied," she whispered. She could have gone home to Catherine, but he'd lied. What else had he lied about?

Her hands closed on a CD player. *A CD player!* She raised it with shaking hands, peering closely at it, as if she couldn't quite believe what she was seeing. SONY was emblazoned on the chrome-colored case. Eyes narrowed, she flung it across the room, where it shattered into bits of plastic, narrowly missing his head. Unappeased, she reached for another missile, closing her fingers around an oddly familiar cardboard box. She spared it a glance, and her lip curled in disbelief.

"Tampons?" she cried. "You had *tampons*? All this time? How *dare* you!"

Circenn gestured helplessly. "I didn't know you had anything to clean."

She growled, a feral sound of pain and anger, as she flung the box of Playtex easy-glide applicators at him. It missed, too, hitting the wall behind him, showering the room with small white missiles. "No!" She raised a shaking hand when he moved to approach her. "Stay there. How much have you lied to me about? How many other women have you brought back here—that you needed tampons for? Did I not rate tampons? Was I won so easily that you didn't have to bribe me with conveniences? Was it all a lie? Is this some sick game I can't fathom? Didn't the fact that my mother is dying touch your heart at all? What are you made of? Stone? Ice? Are you even human? All this time you could have returned me, but you wouldn't?"

"Nay." He moved forward again, but stopped when she cringed back from him. His pained expression deepened.

"Don't even *think* of touching me. How you must have been amusing yourself with me. Me and my pathetic tears, me and my weeping for my mom, and all this time you could have returned me at anytime. You—"

He let loose a bellow of pain and frustration. It had the desired effect of terminating her accusations, silencing her with its sheer volume.

As she stood there gaping, he said, "Listen to me because I doona have much time!"

"I'm listening," she hissed. "Like a fool, I'm waiting for you to give me one decent explanation for all of this. Go ahead—tell me more lies."

He ran a hand over his face and shook his head. "Lass, I have never lied to you. I adore you and there have never been any other women from the future here. And these"— he flung a tampon in the air—"cleaning swabs, I cannot fathom why they upset you so greatly, but I assure you I have never let the maids use them."

Lisa's brow furrowed. No man could be so stupid. "Cleaning swabs?"

He snatched up a gun and jerked the barrel in her direction, and an unwrapped tampon shot out. It was coated with black from the slow corrosion of the steel. She eyed it for a moment, bent, and plucked it from the floor. "You clean your guns with these?"

He lowered the gun. "Is that not the purpose for which they were designed? I vow I could not conceive of another."

"Didn't you read the box?"

"There were too many words I didn't understand!"

Lisa's eyes widened and she reached for him internally, wondering why she hadn't done that first. There, where they joined, he could hide nothing from her. But she'd been so stunned that she hadn't been thinking clearly. She reached and felt . . .

Fear that she wouldn't believe him.

Pain.

And honesty. He genuinely didn't know what the tampons were. But there was something else, something he was willfully concealing. A monstrous dark thing, cloaked in despair. It made her shiver.

He raised his hands in a gesture of supplication. "Lisa, I never lied to you about the fact that I cannot return you. These are gifts a man named Adam brought me. I have never been to your time, nor can I get there, nor send anyone else."

She pondered his words, weighing them for truth. She recalled watching him pick through the fabrics and overhearing mention of this Adam person: Adam whose gifts

Circenn had disdained, except for the gold fabric he'd chosen for her wedding gown.

One floor beneath them, men roared for Circenn.

Ignoring the summons, he said, "I would not have had it come out like this—not now, when I have no choice but to race off to battle. You must believe that I have never lied to you, Lisa. Believe in me and await my return. I promise we will speak of it all then. I will answer any questions you have, explain everything." He sighed, rubbing his jaw. His eyes were dark with emotion. "I love you, lass."

"I know. I can feel it." She inclined her head stiffly. "You do love me. If I hadn't blown up so quickly, I would have sensed your feelings and realized that all this aside, you harbored no intent to harm me."

He heaved a sigh of relief. "Thank Dagda for our bond."

"Go on," she said, encouraging him to reveal the dark secret that was yet untold. As Circenn moved toward the entrance she realized he'd misunderstood her words.

He looked askance when she didn't step aside. "I must reseal the chamber, lass, before I can ride out. I promise to let you examine it to your fill upon my return." He moved toward her, edging her back into his chamber.

"No," Lisa said quickly. "I meant go on and tell me the rest."

He stopped moving reluctantly. "I thought you meant that I should join my men and we would speak of this upon my return." He noted her tense jaw, her unyielding gaze. "What else do you sense?" he evaded.

"Something that terrifies me, because it scares you, and I suspect that anything that causes you fear would crush me. There is something you aren't telling me that your fear cloaks. You must tell me, Circenn. Now. The quicker you tell me, the more quickly you may go. What are you hiding from me?"

He drew a deep breath. "Adam, who gave me these oddities"—he gestured sweepingly—"could return you to your time. I did not tell you that because it was pointless. Recall that I swore an oath to kill the bearer of the flask?"

She nodded.

"Adam is the one I swore the oath to."

Lisa closed her eyes. "In other words, the only person who could return me would kill me first. All right. What is the other thing?"

He looked at her with an expression of innocence she didn't buy for a moment. "I can still feel it, Circenn. You haven't told me the biggest thing."

"Lisa, I will tell you all, but now I must get to Stirling."

Conveniently—*it must be part of a male timing conspiracy,* Lisa thought—Duncan bellowed Circenn's name with obvious frustration.

"You see?" Circenn said. "The men await me. It will be a near race, Lisa. I must go."

"Tell me," she repeated evenly.

"Doona make me do this now."

"Circenn, do you really think I could bear sitting here for weeks wondering what other fantastic fact you've been concealing? It would be torture for me."

Circenn's hands clenched around the gun.

"I will follow you on horse, if I must, right into battle."

A pregnant, tense silence filled the space between them. The continued bellows of the men below heightened her tension. Whom would he heed? His men or her? Lisa felt her heart pounding. He licked his lips and started to speak several times, then stopped, averting his gaze. When he finally spoke, his voice was tight and weary.

"My mother was a Brude queen who was born five hundred and seventy-odd years ago. I am immortal."

Lisa went as still as the stone walls around her. She blinked rapidly, deciding she must have misunderstood. "Say that again."

He knew which word she needed repeated. "Immortal. I am immortal."

Lisa stepped back. "As in live forever, like Duncan McLeod—the Highlander?"

"I doona know this Duncan McLeod, lass. I was unaware there was another like me. The McLeod have never spoken of such a man."

Lisa could not speak for a moment. "Im-immortal?" she managed in a dry whisper.

He nodded. He thumped the stock of the gun on the floor in response to a particularly furious summons.

Rejecting the absurd possibility, Lisa reached for him emotionally. Her incredulity was squashed with one firm draw on their bond.

He was telling the truth. He was immortal.

Or at least he believed he was.

Could he be deluded? After a moment of reflection, she discarded that possibility. A person would know if he had lived five hundred years—it wasn't exactly something one could overlook.

Not looking at her, he continued, "I discovered I was immortal when I was forty-one."

"But you don't look forty-one," she protested, eager to object to any small part of such madness.

"I wasn't when Adam changed me. I was, as near as I can calculate, nearer thirty than forty. He never would admit exactly when he slipped me the potion. But when I confronted him, he confessed that he had indeed poisoned my wine."

"Why? And who is this man that possesses the power to make you live forever? Who is this Adam who could send me home? *What* is he?"

Circenn sighed. There was no point in trying to rush away now. He would give her a few answers to consider while he was gone. When he returned, he would tell her all, and offer her the flask again—to drink, this time. "He is of the old race called the *Tuatha de Danaan*. He is what some call the fairy."

"Fairy?" Lisa was incredulous. "You expect me to believe in fairies?"

Circenn smiled bitterly. "You accept that you have traveled seven hundred years across time, yet dispute the existence of creatures who predate us by millennia and possess unusual powers? You cannot pick and choose your madnesses, lass."

"The fairy," Lisa repeated, sagging against the edge of the rotated hearth. "No wonder my traveling through time didn't seem so strange to you. I thought you'd accepted it unusually well."

"Think not of the fairies as wispy, ethereal creatures, flitting about on wings—they are not. They are an advanced civilization that inhabited some faraway world before they came to ours in a cloud of mist, thousands of years ago. No one knows whence they came. No one knows who or what they really are, but they are powerful beyond compare. They are immortal, and they are capable of sifting time."

"But *why* did he make you immortal?"

Circenn exhaled a bitter sigh. "He said he did it because

his race had selected me as guardian of their treasures, of which the damned flask is one. That is why he made me swear to kill whoever found it. He said his race had long been looking for someone who could keep their hallows safe; they needed someone who would never die and could not be bested in battle."

"So you will truly live . . . forever?"

Circenn said nothing, his eyes dark with emotion. He nodded.

Lisa shook her head, beyond coherent thought. Her gaze swept over him, disbelievingly.

"Lisa—"

"No." She raised her hands as if to protect herself. "No more. That's it. I've heard enough for today. That's all I can hear. My ears are full."

"Is it so terrible a thing to accept? I accepted that you were from my future," he said. *"Haud yer wheesht!"* he roared, thumping on the floor again.

"Just let me have time to think. Please? Go. Go off to your war," she said, pointing to the door. Then a small, half-hysterical laugh escaped her.

"Lisa, I am not leaving you like this."

"Oh yes you are," she said firmly, "because according to my recollection of events, you and your Templars are necessary at Bannockburn." She needed desperately to be alone, to think. It was not hard for her to push him out to war, now that she knew he could not die. "But you bled when I poked you with the knife," she added, as an afterthought.

"Beneath my shirt the wound closed instantly, lass. I can bleed, briefly."

Footsteps thundered down the corridor; his men had exceeded their patience.

Circenn nudged her back a step and swiftly sealed the

chamber. "You said my Templars were necessary at Bannockburn. You know of this battle?" he said, his gaze brooding.

"Yes."

"So it seems perhaps we've both been withholding information from each other," he pointed out quietly. "Is there anything else I should know?"

"Is there anything else *I* should know?" she countered.

Suddenly he looked weary. "Just that I love you with all my heart, lass."

He kissed her swiftly and was gone.

CHAPTER 26

IMMORTAL. CIRCENN BRODIE WAS IMMORTAL.

How ironic, she thought. In the twenty-first century, she'd raged against her mother's mortality. Now, in the fourteenth, she was raging against his *im*mortality.

Her life couldn't be a simple one of going to college and collecting kisses from handsome and mostly harmless young men. That just wouldn't do for Lisa Stone. She suddenly understood how bewildered and put-upon Buffy must have felt upon discovering it was her plight in life to slay vampires.

She hurt.

He rode miles away from her, but their bond did not diminish. She was battered by his feelings, buffeted by his anger and sorrow and guilt. She found herself pushing it away, relegating it to the background. She could not afford to feel what *he* was feeling right now. She needed to feel only her own emotions, to sort through them undistracted by his pulsing intensity.

The man was downright overwhelming sometimes, and it was no wonder. He had over five hundred years of living, and loving and losing his loved ones, and being invincible. She felt a surge of concern emanating from him because she was trying to shut him out. Too exhausted to do more, she sent a burst of reassurance, then firmly corralled his emotions in a corner of her mind.

That was better.

Perhaps a walk would clear her thoughts, she decided, rising from his bed, where she'd been sitting since he'd left.

She strolled through the silent castle and ventured into the night. It was strangely quiet: there were no knights jousting in the courtyard, no children playing—war was grim business indeed. She didn't have to worry about Circenn dying, but most families at Brodie had a loved one who might be mortally wounded in battle. An air of sobriety draped the estate.

Absorbed in her thoughts, she wandered to the reflecting pool and sank down on the stone bench. Tilting her head, she gazed up at the velvety black sky. Why couldn't she have fallen in love with a normal, mortal man? She'd been so happy with Circenn, but she was a realist, if nothing else.

She had some idea of what it would be like to age. She knew how she would feel when she was forty and he was thirty still. She could only imagine with horror how she would feel when she was fifty, yet he still appeared thirty. She could taste the fear of being sixty—when she would be old enough that most would think she was his mother, or worse—in this land where women had children at fourteen—his grandmother.

Oh, God. Her body would age and wrinkle, but his never would.

Lisa didn't think she was a shallow person, but there was only so much a woman's vanity could willingly embrace. Would he still make love to her? Would she be able to permit him to gaze upon her when her body was so aged? It wasn't merely a question of vanity; the physical contrast between them would be a daily reminder that she was dying but he was not.

Take the years and don't think too far ahead, a part of her offered hopefully.

But she knew herself too well. She wouldn't be able to. She would be living in fear, watching her mirror, waiting for the inevitable.

And there was an even bigger picture to be considered.

Not only would she age while he didn't, she would ultimately die, while he continued to live. He would be left without her, and she knew she would have to encourage him to love again when she was gone—and, God forgive her, she didn't think she possessed such a noble soul.

Encourage Circenn to share such a precious, intimate bond again with some other woman? She was seized by hatred for her faceless, nameless successor.

But she would have to, because she knew him well enough to know that he shared her tendency for self-inflicted atonement. He would deny himself. He could spend thousands of years alone, refusing intimacy, and such stark solitude would drive any person mad. He *must* love again after she was gone, for the sake of his own soul.

Then, too, there was her intimate knowledge of what her death would do to him; because of their bond, he would feel every less-than-noble emotion she endured, and every bit of the pain. She knew what it felt like to watch a loved one die. It went beyond hell.

What if she had actually been able to feel her mother's physical pain over the last few months? Her despair and her fear?

Circenn would feel every bit of hers, unless she could somehow hide it.

I can't! I'm not strong enough!

Frantic, she lunged to her feet, driven to movement.

She walked swiftly, skirting the pool, gazing up at the heavens as if they might hear her and grant a prayer. Focused on the sky, she tripped and fell to the ground.

It was the final straw. Crying, she huddled with her arms about her knees and began to rock. After a few moments she realized that she had fallen on the side of the mound and was weeping in probable chamber-pot remains.

She went very still.

It is said that if you circle the mound seven times and spill your blood upon the peak, the Queen of the Fairies may appear and grant you a wish.

Recalling Circenn's words, she slowly opened her eyes.

But what would she wish?

I cannot guess how many young lads and lasses have pricked their fingers here. Old, tall tales—this land is full of them. Most likely some prior kin once emptied the chamber pots here. It would explain how thick and green the grass is.

But she didn't know what might happen next in her life. Why not try it? She could decide upon a wish later, if it worked.

Numbly, she stood and began circling the *shian*. Slowly at first, then picking up speed and determination as she progressed around the mound.

One time, three times, five, then seven.

She stopped. She realized she didn't have anything to cut herself with. With a peculiar detachment, she pierced the heel of her palm with her teeth, drawing blood. She ascended to the peak of the *shian* and, applying pressure with her fingers, forced the droplets to fall on the center of the mound.

She waited.

She had no idea what she expected, if anything. But considering how strange her life had been for the past few months, it would not surprise her overmuch if a fairy sprang from the earth, waving a magic wand.

She held her breath. The night was eerily still, even the night creatures strangely mute.

Nothing happened.

Oh, Lisa—no Fairy Queen will spring from this mound, and you will simply have to deal with the fact that you are in love with an immortal man.

She closed her eyes and shook her head, amused by her foolish fancy. After a moment more, she descended the unusually symmetric pile of sod.

This land had definitely done something to her blood. She'd nearly believed that a mythical creature would appear. Magic pervaded Scotland's air as thick and frequent as the mist, and she'd discovered little that seemed beyond the realm of possibility. Circenn was immortal. She had traveled through time. Making a wish seemed very reasonable in comparison.

She turned her back on the mound, tilted her head, and gazed at the moon, admitting that despite her hurt and fear, she was more than a little relieved. Too many choices could be overwhelming. Now she had none; she had no choice but to stay there and love Circenn Brodie.

Perhaps she would learn to view aging, while he remained ageless, as a small price for the kind of love they shared. She felt for him with her inner senses, slowly removing her earlier barricades. From their bond, she knew he was hurt, angry, and deeply worried. He was also consumed with fear that she would somehow try to leave him.

Well, he needn't worry about that. She couldn't.

"What shall you wish, human?" A voice that held a thousand cool shades of snow shattered her reverie, chilling her blood.

Lisa froze.

CHAPTER 27

THE VOICE HAD COME FROM BEHIND HER, WHERE THE fairy mound lay.

"You were watching the moon, as one entranced. Do you wish to fly to it? To count the stars as you touch them? Or something more . . . earthy?"

Lisa drew a deep breath as the voice shivered through her. Not a mortal voice. She could never mistake such a sound for a mortal voice. It resonated with time and with passionless observation. It frightened her. She turned slowly on her heel. The sight that greeted her was frightening only in the magnitude of its beauty. The air caught in her windpipe, forcing her to draw rapid, shallow breaths.

"Lovely," she whispered. "Oh, God." She suddenly understood the lure of fairy tales, of creatures who were so blindingly beautiful that it nearly hurt to look at them. This creature overwhelmed her senses.

The vision inclined her head regally. "We are. Lovely, that is. But not gods. Most call us children of the Goddess Danu."

Lisa stared, lips parted on a sigh, mesmerized. The woman had silver hair—moonbeams had brushed her delicate head, loath to depart. The night air shimmered around her, as if lit by a thousand tiny suns. Her brows arched above exotic almond-shaped eyes in a pale face. And her eyes—they were of no color known to man, but conjured images of the iridescent hues of a mermaid's wet tail gleaming in the sun.

Her cheekbones were so high that they lent her face a feline cant, and her lips were full, blood-red, and uptilted at the corners as if caught in a perpetual smile. Her skin was dusted with gold; a sheer gown of white clothed her without covering a thing, and the body that was clearly visible beneath the shimmering fabric sparkled gilded pearl and rose, and made Lisa feel like she was twelve years old.

Perfection.

"What shall you wish, human?" Remote eyes held hers, widened by the barest hint of curiosity. "You made this door with your own blood, now wish before I weary of you."

Lisa swallowed. Here was her chance. All she had to say was, *I want to go home to my mother.* But could she leave Circenn? And how could she know whether her mother was still alive?

"Yes," the Fairy Queen said, tucking a strand of moon-beam behind her ear.

"What?" Lisa gasped.

"Your mother lives. If you call that living." Her lips shaped a moue of distaste. "A mortal bane, the body. She is dying."

"How did you know what I was thinking?" Lisa whispered.

The fairy laughed and the sound slithered around Lisa. For a moment, she lost herself in it: forgot who she was, that she had a mother, that she loved a man, that she was human.

For an instant she wanted nothing more than to linger as close to this creature as she would permit. To kiss the hem of her fairy skein, to breathe her exhales, to dance barefoot upon a mound of green. She recognized it for an enchanted madness, when the compulsion eased as the laughter faded.

"I am of the *Tuatha de Danaan*. We see all. So what shall it be, human? Shall I send you home to die with your mother? Is she so important? Shall you leave this lord who loves you?"

"I need time to think," Lisa protested faintly.

"You summoned me *now*."

"I didn't really think it would work. I have not prepared my wish—"

"If thou needed time to think, thou should not have disturbed me." The Fairy Queen's face grew thunderous. A breeze kicked up around the *shian*, tossing leaves into the air. Lisa was startled, turning around, absorbing the suddenly charged night. Charged by the Fairy Queen's displeasure.

"We are Scotland," the Queen stated, observing the disturbance. "The land once wept when we wept, and spring came when we danced. Now the seasons roll consistently, and aside from the fool's pranks, this soil is mostly tame."

"Because you are consistently detached, remote," Lisa said, before thinking. "Has time done that to you?"

The Fairy Queen blinked. Just a blink, but it said, *Tread not here, mortal,* in a forbidding glance that promised wrath Lisa never wanted to experience.

Lisa recovered quickly from her fumble. "I meant, will my mother be alive if I return?"

"For a time."

Lisa squeezed her eyes shut. She hadn't really believed that the Fairy Queen would appear and grant her wish. But now here stood a being that could, and apparently was offering to return her to her mother.

How could she choose? To stay in Scotland and watch her body grow old and fall apart while her beloved never aged, or to return to her time and watch her mother die?

Neither choice was unanimously appealing.

"I don't suppose you could bring my mother here? Maybe make her well?" Lisa suggested hopefully. "Perhaps you could make me immortal?"

"Two choices, human. Stay or go. I am not feeling generous, nor am I inclined to rearrange on a grand scale. It requires much will. A wish is a stone, and my granting is the toss into a loch. There are ripples. Shall I read your heart and find your true choice? You mortals think living is a war: Heart or mind? Silly child, guilt is not mind. Duty is not heart. Hear with that which your race claims we no longer possess. Shall I read your desire?"

Lisa's hand flew instinctively to her breast as if she could shield her heart from this creature. "No, I will choose, if you'll just give me a few moments."

"I weary of waiting. Would you like to see her?" The fairy unfurled a slim white hand toward the reflecting pool, and it grew glassy and still. Within the water, like a silvery portal, her mother's bedroom took shape. It was dawn in the twenty-first century and Catherine was awake, a rosary clasped between her gnarled hands. Lisa cried out when she saw her, for illness had taken so much of her life that it was hard to believe she still breathed. She was praying aloud. *She was alive!*

During the past few weeks—convinced she would never see her again—Lisa had nearly laid her to rest in her heart, but her mother still lived and breathed and was missing her desperately, worried sick.

Lisa shook her head bitterly, confounded by her choices. The vision of her mother was a fatal blow. Catherine was alive in the twenty-first century, and after all these months she must certainly have given up Lisa for dead. But Lisa had the chance to go back and hold her hand, and reassure her that her only child was well. To hold her hand while she died. To comfort and love, and keep her from dying alone.

Emotions overwhelmed her, and dimly she felt Circenn panicking somewhere out in the night—reading her feelings. Firmly, she shut him out.

Lisa glanced again at the pool and suffered a killing vision of herself in Catherine; weakened by life, faded, a brittle wisp of desire to live, gazing up at Circenn, who would be untouched by time.

Circenn had given her love. Catherine had given her love. Circenn would live forever. Lisa knew how Catherine's death was destroying her, breaking her heart. When she died, Circenn would be subjected to such pain. If she stayed what would she have? To grow old while Circenn never aged, to die while the magnificent warrior stood by her bed, holding her hand, his heart breaking. He, who had lost so many loved ones over five hundred years. Wouldn't it be kinder to go now than to make him suffer her death in ten or thirty or fifty years? She knew intimately the pain of losing someone so deeply loved.

Her head hurt and the back of her throat burned with the effort of suppressing tears.

Lisa turned in a slow circle, taking a long look at Castle Brodie, the enchanted night, the beauty that was the Scottish Highlands. *I love you with all my heart, Circenn,* she willed into the night. *But I fear I am a coward and have little stamina. The years would destroy me.*

"Well?" the Fairy Queen demanded.

"Oh," she gasped around a swift intake of air, jarred from her thoughts.

"Now," the Queen pushed.

"I . . . oh . . . h-home," she said so softly that the wind snatched it from her lips and it was nearly lost. But the Fairy Queen heard.

"What of the lord? Do you not wish to say farewell?"

"He is gone," she said, tears slipping down her cheeks. "He's on his way to Bannockburn—"

"Bannockburn!" The fairy stiffened, and looked nearly alarmed, although it was difficult to tell in such a face. She clapped her hands, spoke in a language Lisa couldn't understand, and suddenly the night went mad around her.

The *shian* glowed, light rushed from within it, and Lisa was treated to a sight few humans ever glimpsed, or lived to tell of.

Fairies by the dozens poured from the *shian*, bursting into the night, mounted on mighty horses. A tempest blew up around her, tossing leaves and limbs, and the very earth seemed to strain as it loosed its strange cargo—the wild hunt.

"To Bannockburn," they cried.

She had no idea how long it lasted, the mad surge of exotic creatures rushing by. The ground trembled, the moon hid nervously behind a cloud, even the trees seemed to draw back from the *shian*. Lisa couldn't help it—near the end she had to close her eyes.

At last the night was silent and she cautiously peeped at the *shian*. A man stood there, tall, powerful, with silky dark hair, regarding her.

"They forget the time," he said dryly. "Edward has more than triple the Scots' troops, and my people have a vested interest in this battle. Circenn and his men will arrive in time to save the day. My people love to observe mortal triumphs and casualties."

"Who are you?" Lisa gasped, praying he wouldn't laugh. Sensuality dripped from the man, a sensuality that nearly competed with the effect Circenn had upon her. If he laughed as the Fairy Queen had, she feared she might lose herself in his seductive madness.

Send her, came the Fairy Queen's bodiless command. *And then you are free to leave my side.*

What of my sifting time and weaving worlds? he demanded.

I withhold them still. You are restrained until I otherwise decree, Adam.

Adam made a furious gesture, then returned his attention to Lisa. "It seems your wish has been granted." The corner of his mouth curved into a mocking expression of displeasure. "And they call *me* a fool."

What right do you have to gaze at me with such disappointment? she thought, bewildered. Almost as if he cared. As if he felt she'd made a terrible decision. Then the Fairy Queen's words sank in: *Adam.* "But wait—" Lisa began.

She never got to finish her sentence.

"Are you *the* Adam Black?" she yelled, flooded with murderous rage.

But it was too late. She was . . .

Falling . . .

Again . . .

* * *

Near the Ferh Bog, Circenn doubled over in his saddle and clutched his stomach. Deep rasping breaths exploded from his lungs and he stared into the night with dawning horror.

Galan and Duncan jerked to an immediate stop at his side.

"What is it? What is it, Circenn? Talk to me!" Duncan yelled. He'd never seen Circenn Brodie's face so anguished.

"She is gone," he whispered. "I cannot feel Lisa anymore."

"What does this mean?" Duncan asked swiftly. "Has she somehow returned to her time?"

Circenn's gaze was savage. "Either that—or Adam found her."

"Why didn't you give her the flask?" Duncan demanded. "Then this *couldn't* have happened!"

Circenn nearly lunged from his mount at Duncan. "You argued *against* it when last we spoke."

"But that was *before* Armand—"

"I didn't have *time!*" Circenn roared.

"You must go back."

"She's *gone,*" Circenn said through tightly clenched teeth. "If she has left this century, it is too late for me to seek her. If Adam found her, it is too late for me to seek her. Doona you understand—it is one or the other, and either way it is already too late because she is *gone.*"

He raised his hand and slapped Duncan's mount on the rump. "Now ride!" he commanded his troops. "Ride and avenge," he swore softly, knowing that every Englishman who fell beneath his ax or his sword would bear Adam's face.

CHAPTER 28

THE BATTLE NEAR THE STREAM FROM WHICH IT TOOK ITS
name—the Bannock Burn—lasted only two days, but they
were two glorious days that resonated throughout the
country, from end to end.

Edward Plantagenet's troops assembled near the burn.
They were boisterous, they outnumbered the Scots by five
to one, and they were arrogantly certain that victory was
scant hours away. They were mere miles from Stirling,
they had a supreme advantage in numbers, and they still
had two days to defeat the barbaric Scots.

Edward scoffed, joking with his men. It would take no
more than two hours, he gloated.

The opposing troops engaged, and much to Edward's dismay, over the course of the next two hours a large number of
the English fell prey to the Bruce's cleverly concealed pits
and caltrops—spiked pieces of iron treacherously hidden in
the brush.

Their confidence shaken by the concealed traps, they
regrouped, having belatedly discovered that the Scottish
front was virtually impenetrable.

Circling around to attack from the side would necessitate

skirting the swampy Carse, while Scottish spearmen sat the high ground, waiting to pick them off.

Edward was chagrined by how well the Bruce had chosen his battle site, and how foolishly his troops had discounted the Scots' abilities. The end of the first day saw Edward's heavy horsemen repulsed twice, and large numbers of Englishmen slain.

The Bruce's camp retired to the fringes of the forest of the New Park that night, elated by their success in repelling the English troops.

The English camp made their second deadly mistake by taking refuge in the soggy ground between the burn and the River Forth, a tactical error that would call its due in the morning.

When Sir Alexander Seton, a Scottish knight in Edward's English army, defected late the first night, advising all who would listen that the Scots would win on the morrow, and if they didn't he would willingly forfeit his own head, the English troops were further demoralized.

On the second day the English swiftly realized the error they'd made in choosing their campsite. The Scots descended upon them, trapping the English army immediately after their first charge, cornering them between the Bannock Burn and the River Forth, in a space too constricted for them to maneuver into formation for another charge.

The Scots had cunningly chosen their position, forcing the English to wage war on foot—a tactic for which they were grossly unprepared.

The Scots were far superior to the English on the ground, well accustomed to fighting in the swampy bogs and marshes, and free to move easily without the binding weight of armor.

The English began to break into unorganized formations,

and it was at that weakened moment that the laird of Brodie arrived with his Templars. Into the fray they galloped as one, the holy knights ripping off their plaids, revealing the stark white robes and blood-red crosses of their Order.

Across the field of mud and broken bodies, the wave of brilliant white knights cut like a scythe of death. Many of the battle-weary, discouraged Englishmen simply turned and fled upon glimpsing the robes. The Templars were legendary for their invincibility in battle. Few encountered a warrior Templar and lived to tell of it. The Englishmen who were astute enough to notice that they rode into battle under the banner of the notorious laird of Brodie reared their mounts about and raced away from certain death.

Along the Bannock Burn, Circenn Brodie was an animal, merciless and swift. Later the men would claim he vied with the Berserkers in his deadly rage, and epics would be composed in his honor. He was cold and sharp and hard, and good for nothing but slaughter. He lost himself in a blackness so complete that he cared naught if he slew legions, he simply raged, hoping to exhaust himself and gain the respite of unconsciousness, a temporary kind of death.

When at last one of his lieutenants took the English king's mount by the bridle and rushed Edward from the battlefield in a blatant admission of defeat, a bellow of triumph echoed across the bogs.

The English swiftly decamped and fled upon seeing Edward's standard leave the field, while the Scots roared their joy.

In the midst of the celebration, Circenn felt only a savage sorrow—it was finished too swiftly. One measly day of battle, and he had no choice but to face both his pain and his ancient enemy. A month-long war would have made him far happier.

While the men celebrated and paraded through the country proclaiming the English defeat, Circenn Brodie turned his mount and, without stopping to eat or rest, rode back to Castle Brodie to destroy his nemesis.

*　*　*

Circenn sensed Adam the moment he entered Castle Brodie.

While riding, he'd conceded the possibility that a natural disaster or an accident had befallen his beloved. But Adam's presence could mean only one thing: The fairy had found Lisa and discovered she'd brought the flask.

Either you do it, or I will, the blackest elf had insisted.

The blood roared in his ears, howling for recompense. He would be satisfied with nothing less than the immortal's death. Circenn belatedly understood that he should never have left her alone, even for a moment, no matter how safe he'd thought she was at Brodie. Although Adam had sworn never to come there without an invitation, apparently he thought as little of breaking vows as Circenn did.

Perhaps they truly *were* two of a kind, he thought bitterly. He berated himself endlessly on the ride back to Brodie. He should have stayed to comfort her, then this never would have happened. He should have slipped the immortality potion into her wine months ago, then this never would have happened. He should have explained to her that he could make her immortal. He should never have left her side, not even for a moment. Fighting in a battle now seemed as trivial as it truly was, measured against the loss of his love. He should have sent his Templars ahead without him—they would have won anyway.

He slammed his packs to the floor and stalked into the Greathall. He would die inside later, after he'd taken action to ensure that the *sin siriche du* would never again manipulate another mortal.

Now he understood why his vision had shown him that he would soon be mad, for once he finished with Adam, his rage would dissipate and he would be consumed by bottomless grief. He would unravel and embrace insanity.

As Adam turned to greet him, Circenn raised a hand. "Stay right there. Doona move. Doona even speak to me," he gritted through clenched teeth, and loped up the stairs.

He snorted as he traversed the corridor. Adam was so arrogant that he failed to foresee what Circenn was about to do. Throwing back the door to his chambers, he kicked open the hidden room and swiftly unearthed the Sword of Light.

When he stalked back down to the Greathall, the sword swinging in his grip, Adam flinched.

"What do you plan to do with that, Circenn Brodie?" the fairy asked stiffly.

Circenn's gaze held no mercy. "Do you recall the vow I took over five hundred years ago?"

"Of course I do," Adam said irritably. "Now put that thing down."

Circenn continued as if Adam hadn't spoken. "I said: 'I will protect the hallows. I will never permit them to be used for mortal gain. I will never use them for my or Scotland's gain.' But most important to *you*, I swore that I would never permit the hallowed weapons to be used to destroy an immortal *Tuatha de Danaan*. He hefted the shimmering sword in one swift stroke. "I no longer believe in oaths, Adam.

And I hold the means of your destruction. An oathless man could destroy your entire race, one by one."

"And then what would you have?" Adam countered. "You would be left alone. Besides, you don't know how to find the rest of my kind."

"I will find them. And once I have slain them all, I will impale myself upon your damned sword."

"It won't work. An immortal cannot kill himself, not even with the sacred hallows."

"How do you know? Has one ever tried?"

"She is *not* dead," Adam snapped. "Quit being so melodramatic."

Circenn went very still. "I cannot feel her. She is dead to me."

"I assure you she is alive. I give you my word upon *myself*, since you think that is all I hold sacred. She is safe. She wished upon the mound, and it amused Aoibheal to appear and confer a boon upon her."

"Where is she?" he demanded. *She was alive.* Relief coursed through his body so strongly that he shuddered with the intensity of it. "And what did she wish?"

"She wished to go home," Adam said, more gently. "But she didn't really mean it, I was there. I've been stuck to Aoibheal's side for quite some time now, ever since she took my powers."

"Why did she take your powers?" Circenn was so stunned that Adam had been so harshly punished, that he was briefly sidetracked.

Adam looked abashed. "For interfering with you."

"Ah, there is some small justice in your world, after all," Circenn said dryly. "So, Lisa has returned to the twenty-first century?" He could endure seven hundred years of solitude to be with her again.

"No."

"What do you mean *no*? You said she wished to go back."

"She did. Sort of. She was very unresolved on that point. I could feel her indecision. So I neither complied nor failed to comply. Aoibheal gave me the order to 'send her.' I obeyed the gist of her command by sending her to a safe place, out of time, until you returned. That's why you cannot feel her. She is not . . . quite in this world."

"Where is she?" Circenn said through gritted teeth.

Adam cast him a mocking glance. "I knew better than to send her home. Had I returned her to the future, you would have patiently sat on your disciplined warrior's ass and waited seven hundred years to see her again. So passive, so damned human. And then I wouldn't have gotten what I wanted."

"Where is she?" Circenn roared, swinging the sword.

Adam grinned.

* * *

Lisa kicked at the sand in disbelief.

She was on a tropical island.

"Un-bee-*lee*vable," she muttered.

But it wasn't really, she amended. It was perfectly in keeping with the sorry state of her existence. Somewhere, God was convulsing with laughter, each time she zoomed around another blind curve along the mad course he'd mapped out for her life.

She gazed out over the ocean, breathing deeply. Despite her irritation, she adored the beach, had never gotten to spend much time at it, and couldn't help but greedily inhale the salt air.

Waves swept the sand gently. The sea was so beautiful

that it was difficult to regard it for any protracted length of time. The water was unusual—a breathtaking, exotic aqua one glimpsed only inside the pages of misleading, photo-shop-enhanced travel brochures. It lapped at the perfect white beach with foamy tendrils.

Sparkling white froth, glittering white sand, endless expanse of aqua crystalline water.

She narrowed her eyes.

It was *too* perfect. Something was askew here. Even the air felt strange. It smelled . . . She sniffed cautiously.

Like Circenn.

How could an island smell like Circenn?

She felt a pain deep inside at the thought of him. First she'd had her mother, but no life. Then she'd had Circenn, but no mother. Now she had neither, and missed them both with the whole of her heart.

"What did I do to deserve this?" she demanded of the cloudless sky.

"As if there is anyone up there who cares," she heard someone say dryly. "Why do they always look *up* when they wax rhetoric? Better the creature should tithe to us."

She pivoted on the sand. Two utterly beautiful men stood on the beach, dressed in simple white robes. One was as dark as the other was fair, and both were regarding her with disdain.

The blond Adonis gestured to his companion. "How strange, for a moment I almost thought it heard me. It appears to be looking at us."

"Not possible. It can neither see nor hear us unless we permit it."

"I hate to burst your smug bubble, but I *do* see you and I *am* mortal. Are you more of those pernicious fairy-things?" she asked irritably. The hell with them. They were not going to manipulate her. Besides, how much worse could her life get?

"Fairy-things?" The blond one's eyes widened. "It called us a fairy-thing," he informed his companion. "It *sees* us. Do you think it may be one of those meddling mortals who see both worlds—the ones our Queen and King kidnap at birth?"

The dark one arched a brow. "Then where has it been since then? For it appears fully grown to me."

"I am not an 'it' and I *am* fully grown and I was *not* kidnapped at birth and I would appreciate it if you did not speak of me as if I didn't exist."

"Then how did you come to be here?"

"Where is here?" Lisa asked swiftly. She was going to assume control of events from moment one in this strange place.

"Morar. It is where the *Tuatha de Danaan* repaired after the Compact," the Adonis said.

"Take me to your Queen," Lisa commanded imperiously.

They exchanged glances, then simply vanished.

Lisa's shoulders slumped. So much for imperial demeanor. She'd thought she'd sounded pretty regal.

She blew out a breath and started walking down the beach, determined to greet with aplomb whatever new phenomenon fate chose to spew from the ocean's teeth. A whale-sized piranha biking down the beach wouldn't have surprised her right now.

*　*　*

"Morar," Circenn repeated, his jaw tightening. "And why did you send her to the isle of your people?"

"To keep her out of time for a bit, while I awaited your return. To buy you time to make up your mind."

"Make up my mind about what?" Circenn asked icily.

"About what you wish to do with her."

"I doona need time to decide that: I want to marry her, I want her here, and I want her immortal. But I doona understand your motives. I thought you wanted her dead, Adam. Did you not force an oath from me—"

"Never take anything I say or do at face value, Circenn. It was never about that. You needed to break some of your ridiculous rules. I merely put you in a position where you would be forced to question them. Had you truly killed her, I would have been vastly disappointed. You never understood what I was really after."

Circenn shook his head, muttering beneath his breath. All his angst about breaking the vow had been for naught, because Adam had never wished it fulfilled to begin with. "And I doona understand now, so why not explain it to me?"

Adam circled around him, studying him. "Why don't you put down that sword?" He shuddered. "We gave it to you so we wouldn't be tempted to fight among our own kind. We trusted you."

"You coerced me into the guardianship and well you know it," he said bitterly. Still, he let the tip dip toward the floor, although he kept his hand firmly on the hilt.

Adam relaxed. "The way I see it, you have several choices. You can go join her where she is. In my world," he added smugly. "Or you may bring her back here. Or you may go fix her future and then send her back. She is safely out of time while you decide."

"Why do you mock me, Adam? You know I doona

know how to accomplish any of those things. Are you offering to perform such magic for me?"

Adam looked pained. "I cannot. Aoibheal has clipped my wings, so to speak."

"Then exactly how do you expect me to dart about through time? Morar is not accessible by mortal means. You have trapped my woman on a fairy isle to which I have no means of traveling," he said, growing angry again.

Adam eyed Circenn challengingly. "Yes, you do."

Circenn flung a hand up in the air. "I cannot sift time— if I could, I would have offered to return her when I discovered what she'd lost and how much it pained her."

"You *can* sift time. You know that. You know also that there was a time recently when you would have given anything to have long ago accepted my lessons. You refused to let me teach you, but you know you have the power—it seethes within you. It begs to be freed. You would learn quickly. It would take me mere days to teach you how to sift time. We can practice with short jaunts."

Circenn regarded him, saying nothing. A muscle in his jaw twitched.

"Circenn, I have been telling you for five hundred years that I can teach you how to move through time and place. You have always sneered and walked away. Now I offer again: I can teach you how to sift time, weave worlds, how to change her future so her parents don't die. I can teach you enough that you can prevent the car wreck, perhaps even prevent the cancer, and return her to her future with her memory of you intact. When it is done you may join her there, or bring her back. Or split your lives between the two places. You can do *anything* you want, Circenn Brodie. I've always told you this."

"And what price for such knowledge, Adam? What price for my woman back?"

"Oh, it's so simple," Adam said gently. "It's all I have ever wanted, all along." He nodded encouragingly. "You know what I want. I offer you a trade. Let me teach you. Let me take you where you belong. Let me show you my world. It is *not* evil."

Circenn grunted and rubbed his eyes. Five hundred years ago he'd sworn to avoid this moment at all costs. Throughout the centuries Adam had tempted him repeatedly with anything he could think of, and failed each time. Apparently Adam had realized that the trap would have to be more cunningly laid, and this one had succeeded brilliantly. That which Circenn had refused for five centuries had now become inevitable. The ninth-century man within him shrugged, stepped down, and ceded defeat. Was it evil? Were Adam and his race evil? Or had Circenn simply never forgiven Adam for slights inflicted long ago?

His choices were painfully simple: Be with Lisa, or not be with Lisa.

The latter was unacceptable, and Adam knew that. Circenn felt bitterly manipulated by Adam, and anger burned within him. This situation had been designed and orchestrated by Adam Black from the onset.

But then he thought of Lisa. What existed between them had nothing to do with Adam. Adam may have cleverly manipulated events, but Circenn alone had fallen in love with Lisa. He would have loved her no matter where he'd found her. His anger melted away.

If he accepted what Adam was offering, he could change her life: He could slip to the future and save her parents and return to her everything she'd ever wanted, and be with her again. And hadn't he been toying with that idea for some time now? When he'd asked her to tell him everything about her life, when he'd listened and taken mental notes—aye, even then he'd been analyzing possibilities in the back of his mind. His bitterness over Adam's making him immortal five hundred years past had caused him to violently reject everything about the *Tuatha de Danaan*. But perhaps it wouldn't be so bad after all.

He knew she loved him. Since he had to accept Adam's lessons, if only to rescue her from the fairy isle, why not go all the way? Why not perfect her world and give her *all* her heart's desires? What a gift, to be so powerful that he could ensure her wildest dreams. What else might he be able to give her?

Everything, Adam said wordlessly.

Circenn glanced at Adam.

Dare he brave her time? Dare he go forward and love her there?

He would love her anywhere.

Dare he give Adam what he wanted?

Circenn Brodie drew a deep breath and regarded the blackest elf. He saw before him the potential for corruption, unlimited power, terrifying freedom.

Perhaps he saw a bit of himself in those dark eyes.

"It's so easy," Adam assured him. "It won't hurt a bit, once you've said it for the first time. You'll find it feels quite natural after a while."

Circenn nodded. "Then teach me. Teach me everything you know . . . Father."

SOARING . . .

So sweet a kiss yestreen frae thee I reft,
In bowing doun thy body on the bed,
That even my life within thy lips I left.
Sensyne (since then) from thee my spirits
wald never shed.

—*To His Mistress*/Alexander Montgomerie

CHAPTER 29

"DOONA THINK THIS MEANS I FORGIVE YOU FOR SEDUC-ing my mother," Circenn said later.

"I didn't ask you to," Adam said with a chiding, paternal expression that made Circenn uncomfortable. "She was irresistible, you know. Rarely has one of our kind successfully bred with a mortal, and had the child survive to maturity. But you Brudes have such life force that it was possible, as I'd suspected when I seduced her."

"You destroyed my father."

"His own jealousy destroyed him. I did not raise a hand against him. And that man had nothing to do with siring you. You are my son, and mine only. No seed of his made you. When Morganna died, I refused to lose you, too."

"So you made me immortal. I hated you for that."

"I know that."

The two men were silent for a time.

"Is it truly possible to alter her future and return her to a better one?" Circenn asked.

"Yes. We will go to her future and change it, twice. Actually," he amended, "we will likely need many trips to her time to get it right. Then we will go to Morar, and we will send her on to the new future."

"But won't she have lived portions of it twice?"

"She will have the equivalent of five years of dual memory."

"Will it damage her mind?"

"Lisa? Need you ask that? The woman is nearly Brude."

Circenn felt a flash of pride. "Aye, that she is." He was silent for a moment. "But I doona understand how to do it."

"Patience. You've been a quick study on your own, you know. I've watched you. I know you use heightened speed, I know you scry, I know you've altered space around you without even being aware of it. We will proceed slowly."

"Slowly is good," Circenn said. "My head pounds with too many strange concepts."

"We will move at a snail's pace," Adam assured him. "There is much to be learned about our kind, Circenn, but you must learn it in stages. The madness doesn't result from immortality. It is an annoying and temporary side effect of our far-vision. We see how everything interconnects, and if you seek that knowledge too quickly, it can make you lose perspective, even cause madness."

"Someday I will be able to see those things too?"

"Yes. I learned too quickly, arrogantly certain that nothing could ever harm me. When the understanding came, it overwhelmed me just as Aoibheal had warned it would. But I will bring you to the knowledge of our race slowly enough that you can absorb it while learning it."

"Adam—the spear," Circenn said hesitantly.

"What of it?" Adam replied, a hint of amusement curving his lip.

"The spear and the sword are the only weapons that can kill immortals. The spear was used to wound Christ."

"You're beginning to see connections. Keep looking."

"But what—"

"You will find your own way. These are the things that must come slowly. You cannot expect to overthrow too quickly everything you've thought was true. You are still a ninth-century man in many ways. There will be plenty of time to talk of these things later. For now, let us concentrate on Lisa, and you discovering who and what you are. This is all I ever wanted from the beginning, Circenn—for you to accept that I am your father and be willing to learn about your heritage. I am the only *Tuatha de Danaan* who has a full-grown son," he added smugly. "Some of them resent me for it."

Circenn rolled his eyes, and Adam, caught up in adoring himself, ignored it.

"I can teach you to sift time, but a fuller understanding of your abilities will not come for many years. Are you certain you wish to proceed? I will not have you later cry foul and be angry with me again. Five hundred years of your bad temper is all I can stand."

"I am certain. Teach me."

"Come." Adam extended his hand. "Let us begin and regain your mate. Welcome to my world, son."

* * *

Circenn's instruction at Adam's hands commenced the next morning, and the laird of Brodie began slowly to understand what he'd always sensed within him, and feared: the potential for unlimited power. He began to see why it had frightened him, he—a warrior who feared nothing. Such power was terrifying because the ability to use it carried immense responsibilities. What had once seemed a vast unexplored wilderness—his country, Scotland—was now put into astonishing perspective.

There were other worlds, far beyond the one they inhabited. He realized why the *Tuatha de Danaan* seemed detached to mortals. The tiny bit of land called Scotland and their tiny war for independence was one of millions in the universe.

Over the next few days of learning just a tiny bit about himself, he began to develop (loath though he was to admit it) some respect for the man who had sired him. Adam was indeed given to strange amusements, prone to meddle and to be prankish. However, considering the extent of what his "blackest elf " could actually do, Circenn realized that Adam generally exercised admirable restraint. He also began to realize how mortals, who had no such magic, could so gravely misunderstand those who wielded it.

He eyed his father, who was bent over an ancient tome from which he'd been reading aloud, giving Circenn more background on his race. It was difficult to conceive of the exotic man as his father, for Adam wore his customary glamour that made him seem even younger than Circenn.

"Adam, what of this bond I have with her? What happened that night when she and I . . ."

"Made love? Ah, tupped as Duncan would say." Adam raised his head from the book. "What did Morganna tell you when you were a lad?"

"About what? She told me many things." Circenn shrugged.

"What did she tell you about spilling your seed in a woman?" Adam asked, trying not to laugh.

"Oh, *that*. She told me it would fall off," Circenn muttered darkly.

Adam tossed back his head, shaking with mirth. "That is exactly something Morganna would have said. She knew better than to reason with the stubborn boy you were. And did you ever spill in a woman?"

"Nay. At first I believed her and feared it would indeed fall off. Then, when I was old enough to realize she'd been jesting with me, I didn't because I didn't wish to scatter my bastards across the land. Finally, when I wed Naya and was ready to have a family, I discovered what you had done—"

"I told you the same day, didn't I? I knew you would plan children."

"You told me to prevent me?" Circenn said, startled.

"Of course. I knew what would happen if you did. You would have been bound to a woman you did not love, and that is the purest hell for us."

"So spilling my seed in a woman links us?"

"It seems to be a side effect of our immortality. Our life force is so strong, so potent, that when we find our release inside a mortal woman the union that is forged connects us. And that link will soon include your child."

"Lisa's not pregnant," Circenn said quickly.

Adam glanced at him mockingly. "Of course she is. You—half-fae and half-mortal—are much more virile than we are. You might be our hope for the future."

"Lisa is carrying my child?" Circenn roared.

"Yes, from the moment you spent your seed, the first time you made love to her."

Circenn was stuck silent.

"The first seven months are splendid. It's amazing when the child's force starts to mingle with yours and hers. You feel the babe's awakening, its excitement, and burgeoning life. You marvel at what you have created, you hunger to see it arrive. Then the last two months become hellish. You, Circenn, were a pain in the ass. You wanted out, you kicked and brooded and argued, and suddenly I developed cravings for ridiculous foods I'd never wanted before, and ah—the birth, sweet Dagda! I suffered her labor. I felt the pain, and I felt the creation, the wonder. By the time you birth your first child, you and Lisa will be so deeply bound you won't be able to imagine breathing without her."

Circenn was silent, awed by the thought of Lisa's pregnancy and what was to come. Then the enormity of what Adam had just admitted struck him. "You had such a bond with my mother?"

"I am not without emotion, Circenn," Adam replied stiffly. "I endeavor to keep it still."

"But she died."

"Yes," Adam said. "And I ran to the farthest ends of the earth trying not to feel her death. But I couldn't escape it. Even on Morar, even on other worlds, I felt her dying."

"Why did you *let* her?"

Adam gave him a black look. "At least now that you understand that what I had with Morganna is what you have with Lisa, imagine what I endured permitting her to die. Perhaps you can find it within you to be less harsh in your judgment of me."

"But why did you let her?" Circenn repeated.

Adam shook his head. "My life with Morganna is another story and we have no time for it now."

Circenn studied the exotic man, who would no longer meet his gaze. Permit Lisa to die? Never. "But you *could* have made her immortal?" he pressed, with a sense of desperation.

Adam's jaw was rigid. He shot Circenn a furious gaze. "She wouldn't accept it. Now leave it."

Circenn closed his eyes. Why had his mother refused the potion if Adam had offered it? Would Lisa refuse?

He would not allow her to do so, he resolved. Never would he permit her to die. Gone were the vague feelings of guilt for his thoughts of making her immortal. After what Adam had just told him, he knew he could never endure losing the union they shared. A child! She carried his babe, and the bond would swell to include their son or daughter.

Live through Lisa's death? No. But in recompense for taking her mortality he would give her the perfect future with her family. It would be his way of making amends.

* * *

Circenn materialized at dawn on the day of her graduation. Swiftly he scaled the wall surrounding the Stone estate. Swiftly he punctured the wheels on the small machine to prevent it from moving. Then he regarded the bigger machine irritably. *Which one is a Mercedes?* he wondered with a scowl. Moving quickly, he punctured those wheels, too. But what if they changed the wheels? What if they had new wheels somewhere in their keep?

He glared at the keep, then he glowered at the machines for a long moment, holding them personally responsible for hurting his woman. He struggled against an intense desire to creep into the home and peer down at the sleeping eighteen-year-old Lisa he hadn't yet met.

"Stay away from her. You are so dense sometimes, Circenn," Adam's bodiless voice mocked. "You still don't understand the power you have. Why are you trying to harm the machines, when you can simply make them go away? For that matter, why did you appear outside the gate

and climb the wall, when you might have appeared within
the gates?"

Circenn frowned. "I am unaccustomed to this power.
And where would I send them?"

"Send them to Morar. That should be interesting."
Adam laughed.

Circenn shrugged and focused his newfound center of
power. He closed his eyes and visualized the silica sands
of Morar. With a small nudge, the machines disappeared.

If they landed on the isle of Morar with a soft *woosh* of
white silica sand, only one mortal was there to see it, and
she hadn't been surprised by anything in quite some time.

* * *

"Our cars have been stolen!" Catherine exclaimed.

Jack peered over his newspaper. "Did you look for
them?" he asked absently, as if a Mercedes and a Jeep
could be overlooked.

"Of course I did, Jack," Catherine said. "How are we
going to get to Lisa's graduation? We can't miss her big
day!"

* * *

Circenn tugged the cap low on Adam's forehead,
stepped back, and grinned. "Perfect."

"I don't see why *I* have to do this."

"I doona wish to risk being seen, nor dare I trust myself
to see her. I doona know that I could restrain myself, so
you must do it."

"This uniform is ridiculous." Adam tugged at the crotch.
"It's too small."

"Then make it bigger, O powerful one," Circenn said

dryly. "Quit procrastinating and call their number. Tell them the cab is on the way."

"But they didn't call for one."

"I'm counting on whoever answers to think someone else must have."

Adam arched a brow. "You're good at this."

"Call."

Sure enough, Catherine assumed that Jack had called and ordered a cab to arrive at precisely 9:00 A.M. When it appeared, Jack assumed that Catherine had called. In the fuss over filing stolen-car reports with the police and the insurance company, neither thought to ask the other.

* * *

"What's next?" Adam asked, rubbing his hands.

Circenn shot him a dark look. "You seem to be enjoying this."

Adam shrugged. "I have never before manipulated in such fine detail. It's quite fascinating."

"Cancer. She said her mother was dying of cancer," Circenn said. "We doona even know what kind. I suspect this is not going to be as simple as making two machines disappear. We must find a way to prevent her from catching this disease, and from what I've read, they doona seem to know what causes it. I've been flipping through these books all night." He gestured to the medical books scattered across his desk in the study at Castle Brodie.

Adam picked up several and scanned them. THE CINCINNATI PUBLIC LIBRARY was stamped on the spine. "You pilfered from the library?" Adam said with mock dismay.

"I had to. I tried to borrow them but they wanted papers I didn't have. So I went back when they were closed, and a security guard—they protect their books even in the future—nearly attacked me before I'd finished finding what I wanted." He sighed. "But I'm no closer to discovering how to prevent the disease. I must know what type of cancer she had."

Adam thought for a moment. "Are you up to some more nocturnal raiding? I believe there are no more than a half-dozen hospitals in her city."

"Hospitals?" Circenn's brow furrowed.

"You really are a medieval brute. Hospitals are where they treat the ill. We will go to her time and steal her records. Come. Sift time, and I will be your faithful guide."

✻ ✻ ✻

"She has cervical cancer," Circenn said softly, glancing over his shoulder at Adam, who was reclining on the desk in a private office at Good Samaritan Hospital. "Listen to this: The diagnosis was severe dysplasia. Over time it became advanced invasive cancer. They refer to something called *cervical intraepithelial neoplasia*." His tongue felt thick over the strange words, and he pronounced them very slowly. "The notes indicate Catherine might have been diagnosed in time to prevent the cancer had she had something called a Pap test. The notes indicate that Catherine told the doctor her last Pap test was eight years before they diagnosed the cancer. It seems cervical cancer is caused by a type of virus that is easily treated in the early stages."

Adam fanned rapidly through the textbook he had plucked off the desk. Locating an applicable entry, he read aloud: " 'Pap screening test: a cancer screening test developed in 1943 by Dr. George Papanicolaou. The Pap test examines cells from the cervix, or the mouth of the womb, located at the top of the vagina.' " Adam was silent for a long moment. "It says a woman should have a Pap test annually. Why didn't she?"

Circenn shrugged. "I doona know. But it sounds as if we go back a few years, we should be able to prevent it."

Adam arched a brow. "How can we fix this? Just how do you intend to get a woman who obviously hates to go to the doctor to go see the doctor?"

Circenn grinned. "A little gentle persuasion."

* * *

Catherine thumbed through the mail, hunting for a letter from her friend Sarah, who was in England for the summer. She tossed aside two fliers, snorting indelicately. Recently she'd been receiving a rash of junk mail dealing with one thing—gynecologists and cervical cancer.

Have you had your Pap smear this year? one banner screamed.

Cervical Cancer is preventable! a bright pink flier exclaimed.

They were all from a nonprofit organization she'd never heard of. Apparently some do-gooder who had money to burn. She tossed them in the wastebasket and resumed flipping through the mail.

But something nagged at her, so she retrieved the last flier. She must have received fifty of those things over the past month, and each time she threw one away, she felt a peculiar sense of déjà vu. She'd even received a call from a doctor's office this week, offering a free exam. She had never heard of any doctor offering free Pap tests before.

When was my last checkup? she wondered, fingering the flier. At nearly sixteen, Lisa was ready to start having annual checkups. It might be a bit difficult to persuade her daughter to have her first visit when Catherine wasn't faithful about making and keeping her own appointments. She regarded the pamphlet thoughtfully. It said that cancer of the cervix was preventable—that a routine Pap smear could detect many abnormalities. And that women in all age groups were at risk.

Decisively, she plunked down the pamphlet and called her gynecologist to schedule appointments for herself and Lisa. Sometimes she and Jack tended to be irresponsible about things like checkups and life insurance and servicing the cars. She'd not seen her gynecologist because she felt perfectly fine. But that was like saying the car didn't need service because it was running perfectly fine. Maintenance was different from repairs. *Preventive medicine can save your life,* the pamphlet said.

Life was good, and Catherine certainly didn't want to miss one moment of Lisa's growing up. She had grandchildren to look forward to one day.

Perhaps she should have Jack look into some life insurance, while she was at it.

CHAPTER 30

"You are certain this will work?" Circenn
worried.

"Yes. We will remove her from Morar while she sleeps
and return her to her new future. I've done this before;
however, this is the only time I have allowed the person to
retain dual memories. Are you certain you wish her to recall the other reality? The one where her father died and
her mother is ill?"

"Yes. If we take it from her she will not know me. She
will have no memory of our time together. Without those
memories she would be a different person, and I love her
precisely the way she is."

"Then let's do it," Adam said. "She will be very confused at first. You will need to get to her quickly, to help
her understand. Once she has been returned, race to her
side. She'll need you."

* * *

Lisa was drifting when she heard the voices.

"You must do it *now*, Circenn."

Circenn, my love, her dreaming mind purred.

I'm coming, Lisa.

* * *

Lisa woke from a sleep that felt drugged. Her pillow smelled funny. She sniffed it: jasmine and sandalwood. The scent brought tears to her eyes; it reminded her of Circenn, the way the faint smell had always seemed part of his skin. Another scent overpowered it swiftly: frying bacon. She kept her eyes closed and puzzled over that thought. Where was she? Had she stumbled down the beach and in her delirium found a house and a bed?

She opened her eyes cautiously.

She looked about the room, seeking traces of the fourteenth century—her first thought was that she'd blessedly traveled back to Circenn. But as her gaze skimmed again over the pale blue walls, her heart thudded painfully—she *recognized* this room, and had thought to never see it again.

She dropped her disbelieving gaze to the bed in which she lay. A four-poster of blond wood with a frothy white canopy, she'd adored this bed in their home in Indian Hill, a lifetime ago.

She shot straight up in bed, trembling violently.

Had she finally, irrevocably lost her mind?

"M-Mom?" she called, knowing full well no one was going to answer her. And because no one would answer her she felt safe tossing her head back and wailing it.

"Mom!"

She heard the rush of feet on the stairs, and held her breath as the door opened. It seemed to inch inward in slow motion, as if she were watching a movie and the door opened frame by frame. Her heart tightened painfully when Catherine stepped in, a spatula in her hand, her brows drawn together in an expression of concern.

"What is it, Lisa? Did you have a bad dream, darling?"

Lisa swallowed, unable to speak. Her mother looked precisely as she would have looked had the car accident never happened, had the cancer never taken her. Eyes wide, she feasted on the impossible vision.

"Mom," she croaked.

Catherine looked at her expectantly.

"Is, um . . . D-Daddy here?" Lisa asked faintly, struggling to comprehend this new "reality."

"Of course not, sleepy-head. You know he leaves for work at seven. Are you hungry?"

Lisa stared. *Of course not, sleepy-head.* So normal, so routine, as if Catherine and Lisa had never been separated. As if Daddy had always been alive and the tragic past that had torn their family apart had never happened.

"What year is it?" she managed.

Her mother laughed. "Lisa!" She reached out a hand and tousled her hair. "It must have been quite a dream."

Lisa narrowed her eyes, thinking hard.

Downstairs, the doorbell chimed, and Catherine turned toward the sound. "Who could that be this early?" She glanced back at Lisa. "Come down for breakfast, darling. I made your favorite. Poached eggs, bacon, and toast."

Lisa watched her mom leave the room, stunned. She fought the urge to leap from her bed, wrap her arms around her mother's departing knees, and hang on for dear life. Her mother's knees were unscarred and strong. Joy flooded her. She must have died, she decided, on that strange beach in the stranger land. Was this heaven?

She'd take it—whatever it was.

Snatches of conversation floated up from the foyer. She tuned them out, studying her room. She'd kept a calendar on her desk and was itching to know "when" she was now, but before she could move, her mother called up.

"Lisa, darling, come down. You have a guest. He says he's a friend of yours from the university." Her mother's voice sounded excited and oh-so-approving.

University? She was in college? Oh, this *was* heaven. Now all she needed was Circenn to make it complete.

Lisa leaped from the bed, tugged on her favorite white fluffy robe (astonishing that it was hanging right on her bedpost where she'd always hung it!) and hurried down the stairs, wondering who could possibly be calling for her. As she rounded the curved staircase, her heart thumped hard in her chest.

Circenn Brodie arched a brow and smiled. Simultaneously, a wave of love hit her, sent along their special bond.

Lisa nearly whimpered, overwhelmed with pleasure, disbelief, and confusion. He was wearing charcoal trousers and a black silk polo shirt that rippled across his muscular chest, from which he was dusting a light misting of rain. His hair had been trimmed and was pulled back in a leather thong. Expensive Italian boots made her blink and shake her head. She'd never seen him in such fitted clothing and could only imagine the stir he must have caused strolling around in the twenty-first century. Clothing didn't make this man, *he* made the clothing, molding it with his powerful body; six feet seven inches of rippling brawn. She briefly envisioned him in a pair of faded jeans and nearly swooned.

"Mrs. Stone, would you mind terribly if I took your daughter out to breakfast? We have some catching up to do."

Catherine eyed the magnificent man standing in the

doorway. "No, not at all. Why don't just come in and have some coffee while Lisa gets dressed," she invited graciously.

"Wear jeans, lass." Circenn said, his gaze intense. "And your 'you-knows,' " he added in a voice roughened by desire.

Catherine glanced back and forth between them, taking in the tender, passionate look from the tall, elegant man in the doorway and the startled yet dreamy expression on Lisa's face. She wondered why Lisa had hidden the fact that she was in love, and from her own mother, at that. Not once had Lisa mentioned a boyfriend, but Catherine decided that perhaps she hadn't spoken of it because it was the "real thing." When Catherine had first met Jack, she'd told no one about him; she'd felt that talking about it might somehow debase the private sanctity of their bond.

Lisa still hadn't moved from the base of the steps. She couldn't breathe; she was riveted by him. How had this come to pass? How was Circenn Brodie standing in the doorway of her Indian Hill home, talking to her living, healthy mother, while her living, healthy father was at work, when she'd left him seven hundred years in the past?

The dream flooded back over her: *We must do it now.*

"*What* did you do?" she asked weakly.

"What did he do about what, Lisa?" Catherine asked curiously.

"We have much to discuss, lass," he said tenderly.

"Is that a brogue I detect?" Catherine exclaimed. "I've always thought Scotland was such a romantic country. Jack and I have been discussing going for summer vacation this year."

Circenn moved to Catherine, raised her hand to his lips,

and brushed her knuckles with a kiss. "Perhaps you could visit my home when you come," he said. "I would be pleased to welcome Lisa's parents into my keep."

Lisa had never seen Catherine so flustered. "Keep?" she exclaimed. "Don't tell me you have a castle. Oh! I'll just get that coffee," she said with a breathless laugh. As she turned toward the kitchen, she glanced back at her daughter, who was still standing frozen at the foot of the stairs.

"Lisa, did you hear him? He wants to take you to breakfast, although the way he's dressed, I'm not certain jeans would be appropriate, darling. Perhaps the beige dress with those strappy sandals I like so much."

Lisa nodded stupidly, just to get her mother out of the room. Then she realized that she was encouraging her healthy mother to leave the room. She flung a startled look at Circenn and mouthed, *Just a minute,* don't *move,* then flew across the foyer, catching up with her mother as she entered the hall.

"Wait!" she cried.

Catherine turned around and looked at her quizzically. "You're acting very odd today, Lisa." She smiled, leaned near to Lisa's ear, and whispered. "I like him. Oh my! Why didn't you *tell* me about him?"

Lisa threw her arms around Catherine. "I love you, Mom," she said fiercely.

Catherine gave a startled and pleased little laugh—just the kind of half-breathless sound of joy Lisa remembered from before Jack had died, in the other reality.

"I don't know what this is all about, Lisa, but I love you too, darling. Only tell me your next words aren't going to be 'and I'm sorry but I'm pregnant and running off to get married,' " she teased. "I'm not ready for an empty nest."

Lisa's hand flew to her abdomen and her eyes widened. "Uh . . . Oh! I should get dressed." Leaving her mother with raised brows and a very intrigued expression on her face, Lisa fled the hallway before she could think much harder about the possibility her mother had raised.

CHAPTER 31

LISA GLANCED AROUND THE SUITE, BEWILDERED. AFTER she had slipped on lacy you-knows, jeans, and a blouse, Circenn had efficiently navigated traffic and driven them downtown to The Cincinnatian, where he'd reserved a suite. She was stunned by how capable he was, how quickly he'd adapted to and taken control of her modern-day world. But then she remembered that the man was a born conqueror and warrior, and the twenty-first century, while overwhelming, was just one more challenge for him, and he would master it with the same aplomb as he'd mastered his own century.

He'd explained a bit on the ride there, and gravely informed her that he forgave her for leaving him, although his lower lip had been set at such an angle that she'd known his feelings had been hurt.

He'd also explained that they'd kept her on the isle of Morar while he and Adam had changed her future, and filled her in on how they'd prevented the car wreck and the cancer.

"But I thought you hated Adam."

Circenn sighed as he popped open a bottle of champagne and poured two glasses. Dropping onto the bed, he gave her a guilty look and patted the bed beside him.

He opened his arms. "Come. I need you, lass," he whispered before closing his mouth over hers. Then he proceeded to show her how very much he needed her.

Clothing fell swiftly away as they undressed each other urgently. When she was clad in nothing but a lacy pale pink bra and panties, he lifted her high in his arms above him and fell back onto the bed. Lisa sat astride him and ran her hands over his muscled chest, following the trail of silky dark hair with a feather-light finger.

Slipping the strap of her bra down, he groaned softly. "I love these lacy things."

Lisa laughed and dropped her head forward so that her hair curtained his face. "I love *you*."

"I know," her said smugly. And for a few moments she was lost in a wave of passion and tenderness and love that surged silently along their unique bond.

Never leave me, lass, you are the one and only, forever.

"What?" she exclaimed.

"Did you hear me?" With lazy sensuality, he dragged his tongue over the peak of her nipple through the thin silk of her bra. It crested eagerly.

"Words! I heard you in words!"

"Mmm," he murmured, nipping gently at the buds he'd teased beneath the silk. With a quick snap her bra was off, and he cupped her breasts in his hands, brushing the pads of his thumbs over her nipples. *Will you love me forever?* He caught a nipple between his thumb and forefinger, tugging gently.

Lisa shook her head, trying to clear it. Even after all the times she'd made love with him, she still couldn't think clearly when he was touching her. "What are you saying?"

That I need you forever, Lisa Brodie. Wed me and have babies with me and give me forever.

"Lisa Brodie?" she squeaked.

You doona think I'd leave you in shame, do you? Be my wife. I promise you will want for naught. He slipped his hands inside her panties and cupped her bottom. His gaze was fixed on her abdomen, as if he were trying to see inside her. Her hand flew to her stomach.

"Do you know something I don't know?" she asked suspiciously.

Just that you've already done one of the three things I am asking you to do.

"I'm pregnant? I'm going to have your baby?" she exclaimed, a shiver of delight racing up her spine.

Our *baby. Yes, lass, he already grows within you and he will be very . . . special. Marry me, love.*

"Yes," she said. "Oh yes yes yes, Circenn!"

I am the luckiest man in the world.

"Yes," Lisa agreed, then thought no more for a long time.

* * *

Afterward, they showered together, slipping and sliding in the huge marble shower that had six spouts, three on each wall. Circenn indulged with the unfettered pleasure of a fourteenth-century barbarian who'd never seen a shower before, standing in the streams of the water, shaking his head and spraying it everywhere. They made love on the marble floor, in the corner against the wall, and in the Jacuzzi. Lisa, wrapped in a fluffy white robe, was toweling her hair dry when she heard Circenn yelling in the bedroom.

Startled, she slipped from the bathroom only to discover Circenn standing nude in front of the TV, roaring at it.

"William Wallace did *not* look like that!" He gestured irritably at the TV.

Lisa laughed, as she realized he was pointing at a blue-faced Mel Gibson, storming into battle in *Braveheart*.

"And Robert doona look like that!" he complained.

"Perhaps you should try writing a script yourself," she teased.

"They'd never believe it. It is obvious your time has no idea what my time was really like."

"Speaking of your time and my time, where—or should I say when—will we live, Circenn?"

Circenn pressed the Off button on the remote control like a pro, and turned to her. "Any place you wish, Lisa. We can spend six months in my time and six months here, or go week to week. I know you wish to be near your family. We could take them back too."

Lisa's eyes grew wide. "We could? We could take my mom and dad to your time?"

"How would you like to be married in a fourteenth-century ceremony with your mother and father in attendance? Your father may bequeath you to me, and I in turn will grant him a handsome manor, should your parents choose to retire there. Of course Robert, Duncan, and Galan will insist upon being present as well—I'm afraid it may turn into quite a spectacle."

Lisa couldn't stop smiling. "I would love that! A fairy-tale wedding."

"Provided we are cautious not to change too many things, I see no problem arranging it. I'm beginning to understand what Adam meant when he said if one looks down the timeline, one can discern which things are ir-revocable and should not be manipulated, and which things will make little difference."

"Adam," Lisa said hesitantly. She hadn't forgotten for a moment that Circenn hadn't answered her earlier question.

"Yes," a voice said behind her, as Adam materialized in their suite. He grinned at Circenn. "So you finally got around to asking her to marry you. I was beginning to despair. Every time I tried to pop in, the two of you were . . ."

She spun around. "You!"

Adam grinned puckishly, turned into Eirren, then turned back into Adam. Lisa was speechless. But only for a moment.

She advanced on him. "You saw me in my bath!"

"What?" Circenn thundered.

"He visited me the whole time I was in your century," she clarified.

Circenn glared at his father. "Did you?"

Adam shrugged, the cameo of innocence. "I was concerned you might not be treating her well enough and checked in from time to time. You should be grateful that I decided upon full disclosure—I had considered just telling her that Eirren had run off, when she got around to asking about him. But I've decided to try to be a new person henceforth, at least around you and Lisa."

"Why do you put up with him?" Lisa said, shaking her head.

"Lisa, it's all right," Circenn said, moving swiftly to her side. "It's not what you think." He scowled at Adam. "Doona think I've forgotten you saw her in her bath. We will speak of it later, the three of us, and have the whole story out. But how did you come here by yourself? Has Aoibheal forgiven you?"

Adam preened, casting his silky dark hair over his shoulder. "Of course. I am once again all-powerful."

"Why are you being nice to him?" Lisa snapped.

"Lass, he helped me do all that I've done."

"He made you immortal!"

"And if he hadn't, I never would have met you, but would have died over a thousand years before you were born. He helped save your mother and father. And . . . Adam is . . . my father."

"Your *father*!" She gaped for a moment, as the information sunk in. Heavens, but there was obviously a great deal she still didn't know about Circenn Brodie. But she was more than willing to learn.

Circenn guided her to a chair and sat her down, then the two men took turns filling in her gaps of knowledge regarding the man who would be her husband. And once she knew, it made perfect sense, and explained everything: his unusual powers, his resentment toward Adam, Adam's unwillingness to let his son die.

A few moments of silence passed while she pondered all they'd told her, then she realized they were both watching her intently, and it seemed that they were waiting for something.

Adam moved to her side and reached in his pocket, and Lisa watched curiously, wondering what new thing they were going to spring on her next.

"You know now that I am half-fairy, Lisa," Circenn said gently. "Can you accept that?"

Lisa stood on her tiptoes and kissed him full on the lips. *Yes,* she assured him.

No regrets?

No regrets.

When Adam withdrew a shimmering flask and a pair of goblets, and poured three drops of glowing liquid into one of the glasses, Lisa scarcely breathed.

She watched in silence as Adam passed the glasses of

champagne to Circenn, who—with great deliberation—
offered Lisa the glass with the potion in it.

He regarded her gravely, then gave her a tender smile.

Love me forever, lass.

Lisa looked deep into his eyes.

*Live with me forever. Cease my endless solitude. I will
cherish you. I will show you worlds you've only dreamed
of. I will walk beside you, hand in hand, until the end of
days.*

Lisa reached for the goblet.

Champagne had never tasted sweeter.

AUTHOR'S NOTE

Catherine Stone's cervical cancer was indeed preventable. While doing research for *The Highlander's Touch*, I was distressed to discover the number of women who die from this disease each year. Cervical cancer is killing some 200,000 women annually, and at least 370,000 new cases are identified each year. It has been estimated that only 5 percent of women in developing countries have been screened for cervical dysplasia in the past five years, and only 40 to 50 percent in developed countries.

A simple Pap screening test performed by a gynecologist can detect cervical dysplasia in its precancerous stages. The earlier it is detected, the less invasive the treatment. An annual Pap screening test changed Catherine's life and could change the lives of many others. We women need to take care of ourselves!

If you'd like to learn more about the Knights Templar, I suggest *The History of the Knights Templar* by Charles G. Addison (Adventures Unlimited Press); or *The Trial of the Templars* by Malcolm Barber (Cambridge University Press). For an interesting look at the mythology surrounding the Order, I recommend *The Holy Grail* by Norma Lorre Goodrich (HarperCollins). I tried to detail the history of the Order as accurately as possible in the face of myriad conflicting sources. My research uncovered as many references to the Templar's involvement in the battle at Bannock Burn as sources that deny their involvement. However, the Scottish Order of the Knights Templar, associated with the area around Roslyn Chapel, is still in existence today.

The last I heard from Lisa, she had just graduated from a local university and was preparing to go on to medical school. She was adamant I mention that she *finally* got to go to college.

And Circenn? After having lived for so many centuries, he is not quite as driven by a thirst for knowledge as Lisa, and instead devotes his days and nights to pleasing his woman.

Oh, and I nearly forgot—Adam insists I mention him. If you'd like to know more about him (I keep reminding him he is *not* the hero, so nobody cares), you may find him in my novel *Beyond the Highland Mist*, irritating Laird Hawk Douglas.

Better him than me.

Best wishes,

Karen

ABOUT THE AUTHOR

KAREN MARIE MONING graduated from Purdue University with a bachelor's degree in Society & Law. Her novels have appeared on the *New York Times*, *USA Today*, and *Publishers Weekly* bestseller lists and have won numcrous awards, including the prestigious RITA Award. She can be reached at www.karenmoning.com.

Feel the heat and catch the fever of
Karen Marie Moning's thrilling
New York Times bestselling Fever series.

DARKFEVER

by

KAREN MARIE MONING

Read on for a seductive preview of
the first book. . .

KAREN MARIE
MONING

DARKFEVER

A MACKAYLA LANE NOVEL

DARKFEVER
On sale now

Prologue

My philosophy is pretty simple—any day no-body's trying to kill me is a good day in my book.

I haven't had many good days lately.

Not since the walls between Man and Faery came down.

But then, there's not a *sidhe*-seer alive who's had a good day since then.

Before The Compact was struck between Man and Fae (around 4000 B.C. for those of you who aren't up on your Fae history), the Unseelie Hunters hunted us down like animals and killed us. But The Compact forbade the Fae to spill human blood, so for the next six thousand years, give or take a few centuries, those with True Vision—people like me who can't be fooled by Fae glamour or magic—were taken captive and imprisoned in Faery until they died. Real big difference there: dying or being stuck in Faery until you die. Unlike some people I know, I'm not fascinated by them. Dealing with the Fae is like dealing with any addiction—you give in, they'll own you; you resist, they never will.

Now that the walls are down, the Hunters are back to killing us again. Stamping us out like we're the plague on this planet.

Aoibheal, the Seelie Queen of the Light, is no longer in charge. In fact, nobody seems to know where she is anymore, and some people are beginning to wonder *if* she is anymore. The Seelie and Unseelie have been smearing their bloody war all over our world since her disappearance, and although some might say I'm being broody and pessimistic, I think the Unseelie are gaining the distinct upper hand over their fairer brethren.

Which is a really, *really* bad thing.

Not that I like the Seelie any better. I don't. The only good Fae is a dead Fae in my book. It's just that the Seelie aren't quite as lethal as the Unseelie. They don't kill us on sight. They have a use for us.

Sex.

Though they barely credit us with sentience, they have a taste for us in bed.

When they're done with a woman, she's a mess. It gets in her blood. Unprotected Fae-sex awakens a frenzy of sexual hunger inside a woman for something she should never have had to begin with, and will never be able to forget. It takes a long time for her to recover—but at least she's alive.

Which means a chance to fight another day. To help try to find a way to return our world to what it once was.

To send those Fae bastards back to whatever hell they came from.

But I'm getting ahead of myself, ahead of the story.

It began as most things begin. Not on a dark and stormy night. Not foreshadowed by ominous here-comes-the-villain music, dire warnings at the bottom of a teacup, or dread portents in the sky.

It began small and innocuously, as most catastrophes do. A butterfly flaps its wings somewhere and the wind changes, and a warm front hits a cold front off the coast of western Africa and before you know it you've got a hurricane closing in. By the time anyone figured out the storm was coming, it was too late to do anything but batten down the hatches and exercise damage control.

My name is MacKayla. Mac for short. I'm a *sidhe*-seer, a fact I accepted only recently and very reluctantly.

There were more of us out there than anyone knew. And it's a damn good thing, too.

We're damage control.

ONE

A year earlier . . .

July 9. Ashford, Georgia.

Ninety-four degrees. Ninety-seven percent humidity.

It gets crazy hot in the South in the summer, but it's worth it to have such short, mild winters. I like most all seasons and climes. I can get into an overcast drizzly autumn day—great for curling up with a good book—every bit as much as a cloudless blue summer sky, but I've never cared much for snow and ice. I don't know how northerners put up with it. Or why. But I guess it's a good thing they do, otherwise they'd all be down here crowding us out.

Native to the sultry southern heat, I was lounging by the pool in the backyard of my parents' house, wearing my favorite pink polka-dotted bikini which went perfectly with my new I'm-Not-Really-a-Waitress-Pink manicure and pedicure. I was sprawled in a cushion-topped chaise soaking up the sun, my long blond hair twisted up in a spiky knot on top of my head in one of those hairdos you really hope nobody ever catches you wearing. Mom and Dad were away on vacation, celebrating their thirtieth wedding anniversary with a twenty-one-day island-hopping cruise through the tropics, which had begun two weeks ago in Maui and ended next weekend in Miami.

I'd been working devotedly on my tan in their absence, taking quick dips in the cool sparkling blue, then stretching out to let the sun toast drops of water from my skin, wishing my sister Alina was around to hang out with, and maybe invite a few friends over.

My iPod was tucked into my dad's Bose SoundDock on the patio table next to me, bopping cheerily through a playlist I'd put together specifically for poolside sunning, composed of the top one hundred one-hit wonders from the past few decades, plus a few others that make me smile— happy mindless music to pass happy mindless time. It was currently playing an old Louis Armstrong song—"What a Wonderful World." Born in a generation that thinks cynical and disenchanted is cool, sometimes I'm a little off the beaten track. Oh well.

A tall glass of chilled sweet tea was at hand, and the phone was nearby in case Mom and Dad made ground sooner than expected. They weren't due ashore the next island until tomorrow, but twice now they'd landed sooner than scheduled. Since I'd accidentally dropped my cell phone in the pool a few days ago, I'd been toting the cordless around so I wouldn't miss a call.

Fact was, I missed my parents like crazy.

At first, when they left, I'd been elated by the prospect of time alone. I live at home and when my parents are there the house sometimes feels annoyingly like Grand Central Station, with Mom's friends, Dad's golf buddies, and ladies from the church popping in, punctuated by neighborhood kids stopping over with one excuse or another, conveniently clad in their swim trunks—gee, could they be angling for an invitation?

But after two weeks of much-longed-for solitude, I'd begun choking on it. The rambling house seemed achingly quiet, especially in the evenings. Around supper time I'd been feeling downright lost. Hungry, too. Mom's an amazing cook and I'd burned out fast on pizza, potato chips, and mac-'n'-cheese. I couldn't wait for one of her fried chicken, mashed potatoes, fresh turnip greens, and peach pie with homemade whipped-cream dinners. I'd even done the grocery shopping in anticipation, stocking up on everything she needed.

I love to eat. Fortunately, it doesn't show. I'm healthy through the bust and bottom, but slim through the waist and thighs. I have good metabolism, though Mom says, *Ha, wait until you're thirty. Then forty, then fifty.* Dad says, *More to love, Rainey* and gives Mom a look that makes me concentrate really hard on something else. Anything else. I adore my parents, but there's such a thing as TMI. *Too much information.*

All in all, I have a great life, short of missing my parents and counting the days until Alina gets home from Ireland, but both of those are temporary, soon to be rectified. My life will go back to being perfect again before much longer.

Is there such a thing as tempting the Fates to slice one of the most important threads that holds your life together simply by being too happy?

When the phone rang, I thought it was my parents.

It wasn't.

It's funny how such a tiny, insignificant, dozen-times-a-day action can become a line of demarcation.

The picking up of a phone. The pressing of an on button.

Before I pressed it—as far as I knew—my sister Alina was alive. At the moment of pressing, my life split into two distinct epochs: Before the call and After.

Before the call, I had no use for a word like "demarcation," one of those fifty-cent words I knew only because I was an avid reader. Before, I floated through life from one happy moment to the next. Before, I thought I knew everything. I thought I knew who I was, where I fit, and exactly what my future would bring.

Before, I thought I knew I *had* a future.

After, I began to discover that I'd never really known anything at all.

I waited two weeks from the day that I learned my sister had been murdered for somebody to do something—anything— besides plant her in the ground after a closed-casket funeral, cover her with roses, and grieve.

Grieving wasn't going to bring her back, and it sure wasn't going to make me feel better about whoever'd killed her walking around alive out there somewhere, happy in their sick little psychotic way, while my sister lay icy and white beneath six feet of dirt.

Those weeks will remain forever foggy to me. I wept the entire time, vision and memory blurred by tears. My tears were involuntary. My soul was leaking. Alina wasn't just my sister; she was my best friend. Though she'd been away studying at Trinity College in Dublin for the past eight months, we'd e-mailed incessantly and spoken weekly, sharing everything, keeping no secrets.

Or so I thought. Boy was I ever wrong.

We'd been planning to get an apartment together when she came home. We'd been planning to move to the city, where I was finally going to get serious about college, and Alina was going to work on her Ph.D. at the same Atlanta university. It was no secret that my sister had gotten all the ambition in the family. Since graduating high school, I'd been perfectly content bartending at The Brickyard four or five nights a week, living at home, saving most of my money, and taking just enough college courses at the local Podunk university (one or two a semester, and classes like How to Use the Internet and Travel Etiquette didn't cut it with my folks) to keep Mom and Dad reasonably hopeful that I might one day graduate and get a *Real Job* in the *Real World*. Still, ambition or no, I'd been planning to really buckle down and make some big changes in my life when Alina returned.

When I'd said good-bye to her months ago at the airport, the thought that I wouldn't see her alive again had never crossed my mind. Alina was as certain as the sun rising and setting. She was charmed. She was twenty-four and I was twenty-two. We were going to live forever. Thirty was a million light-years away. Forty wasn't even in the same galaxy. Death? Ha. Death happened to really old people.

Not.

After two weeks, my teary fog started to lift a little. I didn't stop hurting. I think I just finally expelled the last drop of moisture from my body that wasn't absolutely necessary to keep me alive. And rage watered my parched soul. I wanted answers. I wanted justice.

I wanted revenge.

I seemed to be the only one.

I'd taken a psych course a few years back that said people dealt with death by working their way through stages of grief. I hadn't gotten to wallow in the numbness of denial that's supposed to be the first phase. I'd flashed straight from numb to pain in the space of a heartbeat. With Mom and Dad away, I was the one who'd had to identify her body. It hadn't been pretty and there'd been no way to deny Alina was dead.

After two weeks, I was thick into the anger phase. Depression was supposed to be next. Then, if one was healthy, acceptance. Already I could see the beginning signs of acceptance in those around me, as if they'd moved directly from numbness to defeat. They talked of "random acts of violence." They spoke about "getting on with life." They said they were "sure things were in good hands with the police."

I was *so* not healthy. Nor was I remotely sure about the police in Ireland.

Accept Alina's death?

Never.

"You're *not* going, Mac, and that's final." Mom stood at the kitchen counter, a towel draped over her shoulder, a cheery red, yellow, and white magnolia-printed apron tied at her waist, her hands dusted with flour.

She'd been baking. And cooking. And cleaning. And baking some more. She'd become a veritable Tasmanian devil of domesticity. Born and raised in the Deep South, it was Mom's way of trying to deal. Down here, women nest like mother hens when people die. It's just what they do.

We'd been arguing for the past hour. Last night the Dublin police had called to tell us that they were terribly sorry, but due to a lack of evidence, in light of the fact that they didn't have a single lead or witness, there was nothing left to pursue. They were giving us official notice that they'd had no choice but to turn Alina's case over to the unsolved division, which anyone with half a brain knew wasn't a division at all but a filing cabinet in a dimly lit and largely forgotten basement storeroom somewhere. Despite assurances they would periodically reexamine the case for new evidence, that they would exercise utmost due diligence, the message was clear: Alina was dead, shipped back to her own country, and no longer their concern.

They'd given up.

Was that record time or what? Three weeks. A measly twenty-one days. It was inconceivable!

"You can bet your butt if we lived over there, they'd never have given up so quickly," I said bitterly.

"You don't know that, Mac." Mom pushed ash-blond bangs back from blue eyes that were red-rimmed from weeping, leaving a smudge of flour on her brow.

"Give me the chance to find out."

Her lips compressed into a thin white-edged line. "Absolutely not. I've already lost one daughter to that country. I will not lose another."

Impasse. And here we'd been ever since breakfast, when I'd announced my decision to take time off so I could go to Dublin and find out what the police had really been doing to solve Alina's murder.

I would demand a copy of the file, and do all in my power to motivate them to continue their investigation. I would give a face and a voice—a loud and hopefully highly persuasive one—to the victim's family. I couldn't shake the belief that if only my sister had a representative in Dublin, the investigation would be taken more seriously.

I'd tried to get Dad to go, but there just wasn't any reaching him right now. He was lost in grief. Though our faces and builds were very different, I have the same color hair and eyes as Alina, and the few times he'd actually looked at me lately, he'd gotten such an awful look on his face that it had made me wish I was invisible. Or brunette with brown eyes like him, instead of sunny blond with green.

Initially, after the funeral, he'd been a dynamo of determined action, making endless phone calls, contacting anyone and everyone. The embassy had been kind, but directed him to Interpol. Interpol had kept him busy for a few days "looking into things" before diplomatically referring him back to where he'd begun—the Dublin police. The Dublin police remained unwavering. No evidence. No leads. Nothing to investigate. *If you have a problem with that, sir, contact your embassy.*

He called the Ashford police—no, they couldn't go to Ireland and look into it. He called the Dublin police again—were they sure they'd interviewed every last one of Alina's friends and fellow students and professors? I hadn't needed to hear both sides of *that* conversation to know the Dublin police were getting testy.

He'd finally placed a call to an old college friend of his that held some high-powered, hush-hush position in the government. Whatever that friend said had deflated him completely. He'd closed the door on us and not come out since.

The climate was decidedly grim in the Lane house, with Mom a tornado in the kitchen, and Dad a black hole in the study. I couldn't sit around forever waiting for them to snap out of it. Time was wasting and the trail was growing colder by the minute. If someone was going to do something, it had to be now, which meant it had to be me.

I said, "I'm going and I don't care if you like it or not."

Mom burst into tears. She slapped the dough she'd been kneading down on the counter and ran out of the room. After a moment, I heard the bedroom door slam down the hall.

That's one thing I can't handle—my mom's tears. As if she hadn't been crying enough lately, I'd just made her cry again. I slunk from the kitchen and crept upstairs, feeling like the absolute lowest of the *lowest* scum on the face of the earth.

I got out of my pajamas, showered, dried my hair and dressed, then stood at a complete loss for a while, staring blankly down the hall at Alina's closed bedroom door.

How many thousands of times had we called back and forth during the day, whispered back and forth during the night, woken each other up for comfort when we'd had bad dreams?

I was on my own with bad dreams now.

Get a grip, Mac. I shook myself and decided to head up to campus. If I stayed home, the black hole might get me, too. Even now I could feel its event horizon expanding exponentially.

On the drive uptown, I recalled that I'd dropped my cell phone in the pool—God, had it really been all those weeks ago?—and decided I'd better stop at the mall to get a new one in case my parents needed to reach me while I was out.

If they even noticed I was gone.

I stopped at the store, bought the cheapest Nokia they had, got the old one deactivated, and powered up the replacement.

I had fourteen new messages, which was probably a record for me. I'm hardly a social butterfly. I'm not one of those plugged-in people who are always hooked up to the latest greatest find-me service. The idea of being found so easily creeps me out a little. I don't have a camera phone or text-messaging capability. I don't have Internet service or satellite radio, just your basic account, thank you. The only other gadget I need is my trusty iPod—music is my great escape.

I got back in my car, turned on the engine so the air conditioner could do battle with July's relentless heat, and began listening to my messages. Most of them were weeks old, from friends at school or The Brickyard who I'd talked to since the funeral.

I guess, somewhere in the back of my mind, I'd made the connection that I'd lost cell service a few days before Alina died and was hoping I might have a message from her. Hoping she might have called, sounding happy before she died. Hoping she might have said something that would make me forget my grief, if only for a short while. I was desperate to hear her voice just one more time.

When I did, I almost dropped the phone. Her voice burst from the tiny speaker, sounding frantic, terrified.

"Mac! Oh God, Mac, where *are* you? I need to talk to you! It rolled straight into your voice mail! What are you *doing* with your cell phone turned off? You've got to call me the *minute* you get this! I mean, the very instant!"

Despite the oppressive summer heat, I was suddenly icy, my skin clammy.

"Oh, Mac, everything has gone so wrong! I thought I knew what I was doing. I thought he was helping me, but— God, I can't believe I was so stupid! I thought I was in love with him and he's one of them, Mac! He's one of *them*!"

I blinked uncomprehendingly. One of who? For that matter, who was this "he" that was one of "them" in the first place? Alina—in love? No way! Alina and I told each other everything. Aside from a few guys she'd dated casually her first months in Dublin, she'd not mentioned any other guy in her life. And certainly not one she was in love with!

Her voice caught on a sob. My hand tightened to a death grip on the phone, as if maybe I could hold on to my sister through it. Keep *this* Alina alive and safe from harm. I got a few seconds of static, then, when she spoke again she'd lowered her voice, as if fearful of being overheard.

"We've got to talk, Mac! There's so much you don't know. My God, you don't even know what you *are*! There are so many things I should have told you, but I thought I could keep you out of it until things were safer for us. I'm going to try to make it home"—she broke off and laughed bitterly, a caustic sound totally unlike Alina—"but I don't think he'll let me out of the country. I'll call you as soon—" More static. A gasp. "Oh, Mac, he's coming!" Her voice dropped to an urgent whisper. "Listen to me! We've got to find the"—her next word sounded garbled or foreign, something like *shi-sadu*, I thought. "Everything depends on it. We can't let them have it! We've *got* to get to it first! He's been lying to me all along. I know what it is now and I know where—"

Dead air.

The call had been terminated.

I sat stunned, trying to make sense of what I'd just heard. I thought I must have a split personality and there were two Macs: one that had a clue about what was going on in the world around her, and one that could barely track reality well enough to get dressed in the morning and put her shoes on the right feet. Mac-that-had-a-clue must have died when Alina did, because *this* Mac obviously didn't know the first thing about her sister.

She'd been in love and never mentioned it to me! Not once. And now it seemed that was the least of the things she'd not told me. I was flabbergasted. I was betrayed. There was a whole huge part of my sister's life that she'd been withholding from me for *months*.

What kind of danger had she been in? What had she been trying to keep me out of? Until *what* was safer for us? What did we have to find? Had it been the man she'd thought she was in love with that had killed her? Why oh *why*— hadn't she told me his name?

I checked the date and time on the call—the afternoon after I'd dropped my cell phone in the pool. I felt sick to my stomach. She'd needed me and I hadn't been there for her. At the moment Alina had been so frantically trying to reach me, I'd been sunning lazily in the backyard, listening to my top one hundred mindless happy songs, my cell phone lying short-circuited and forgotten on the dining-room table.

I carefully pressed the save key, then listened to the rest of the messages, hoping she might have called back, but there was nothing else. According to the police, she'd died approximately four hours after she'd tried reaching me, although they hadn't found her body in an alley for nearly two days.

That was a visual I always worked real hard to block.

I closed my eyes and tried not to dwell on the thought that I'd missed my last chance to talk to her, tried not to think that maybe I could have done something to save her if only I'd answered. Those thoughts could make me crazy.

I replayed the message again. What was a *shi-sadu*? And what was the deal with her cryptic *You don't even know what you are?* What could Alina possibly have meant by that?

By my third run-through, I knew the message by heart.

I also knew that there was no way I could play it for Mom and Dad. Not only would it drive them further off the deep end (if there *was* a deeper end than the one they were currently off), but they'd probably lock me in my room and throw away the key. I couldn't see them taking any chances with their remaining child.

But . . . if I went to Dublin and played it for the police, they'd have to reopen her case, wouldn't they? This was a bona fide lead. If Alina had been in love with someone, she would have been seen with him at some point, somewhere. At school, at her apartment, at work, somewhere. Somebody would know who he was.

And if the mystery man wasn't her killer, surely he was the key to discovering who was. After all, he was "one of *them.*"

I frowned.

Whoever or whatever "they" were.